HIDE AND SEEK

"Who's there?"

I saw it blunder deeper into the darkness. I still couldn't make out what it was, but it could be heard to crush leaves underfoot.

When it didn't respond to my query, I ran after it. I plunged into the bushes, sure it was just ahead of me, though I couldn't see a thing in the darkness.

I think I touched it. My fingers trailed across something warm and giving: bare flesh, I'd swear. The blood suddenly heavy in my limbs, I stared through impenetrable shadows, trying to make out what I'd touched. I saw a flicker of reflected light, as though something stared back at me, and for one fatal moment I was paralyzed with gibbering, primal fear.

Was this my introduction to the Trouble?

SISTER
TO THE
RAIN

—

Melisa
Michaels

A ROC BOOK

ROC
Published by the Penguin Group
Penguin Putnam Inc., 375 Hudson Street,
New York, New York 10014, U.S.A.
Penguin Books Ltd, 27 Wrights Lane,
London W8 5TZ, England
Penguin Books Australia Ltd, Ringwood,
Victoria, Australia
Penguin Books Canada Ltd, 10 Alcorn Avenue,
Toronto, Ontario, Canada M4V 3B2
Penguin Books (N.Z.) Ltd, 182–190 Wairau Road,
Auckland 10, New Zealand

Penguin Books Ltd, Registered Offices:
Harmondsworth, Middlesex, England

First published by Roc, an imprint of Dutton NAL,
a member of Penguin Putnam Inc.

First Printing, October, 1998
10 9 8 7 6 5 4 3 2 1

 REGISTERED TRADEMARK—MARCA REGISTRADA

Printed in the United States of America

1

I was listening to a Cold Iron CD on the office boom box and staring out the window thinking of Killer when the elflord walked in. It was one of those glorious spring days when the sky stretches lucent blue from horizon to horizon without a hint of cloud or smog, and sunlight pours across the misty blue of the bay to pick out every pale pastel in the San Francisco skyline, turning it into an illustration out of a fairy tale. I missed Killer. And I never wanted to see another elf as long as I lived.

This one didn't walk right in and close the door behind him: he paused in the doorway, studying the lettering on the glass part of the door. It only said Arthur & Lavine, Private Investigators, just as it always did: not a difficult read. But it gave Shannon and me plenty of time to look him over.

I'd never seen an elf quite like him. They are all too pretty, and not very sturdy-looking by human standards; but this one looked positively frail. He had that over-bred, slightly foolish look common to some members of the British aristocracy and was a trifle short even for a human: very short, for an elf. Had he been human I'd have guessed he was in his early thirties, but of course with elves there's really no way to tell. They seem to live almost forever, barring accidents, and they don't show their age till they're ancient.

He had silver hair, which meant nothing about his age since most of them have it from birth. His eyes were the usual unnervingly lambent blue. His face was long and narrow, the profile regal in a way few human faces manage. His ears, of course, were pointed, overlarge, and elegant: he was, after all, an elf.

He wore a silver-gray suit that must have cost a fortune, with a pure white silk shirt ruffled at front and cuffs, a darker gray tie, and black-and-gray shoes. He carried a gold-tipped walking stick made of a burnished wood that gleamed deep in its grain, like koa. On one little finger he wore a jeweled ring that must have cost enough to feed two or three large families through a difficult winter.

Shannon and I glanced at each other, she with a look that meant I'd better not chase him away before we found out what he wanted, and I with mild amusement because I knew that was how she was going to look at me. I was curious, actually. He was too elegant to be any of the expectable elvish things except maybe an actor, and somehow I didn't think he was that. I had already asked how we could help him. Now I raised my voice and asked again.

"My good woman," he said. His voice was husky and his accent British with just the faintest burr of Faerie, every bit as dignified and refined as the suit. "I am not deaf, you know."

I didn't bother to point out that I wasn't his good woman. "No, I didn't know." I shrugged inelegantly. "You didn't answer the first time, you see. Given a choice of deaf or rude, I guessed deaf."

He favored me with the merest twitch of a superior smile. "Therein lay your mistake," he said, and closed the door. "Are you Rosalynd Lavine or Shannon Arthur?"

"The former," I said, and glanced toward Shannon, warning her to keep her mouth shut. "And this is Shannon Arthur. At your service. But we don't need any cars or insurance."

He looked at me in evident, if dignified, surprise. "Do you not, then? How fortunate for you. May I sit? Thank you. Lovely office, very tasteful."

Since it was done entirely in early thrift store, the compliment seemed odd at best. Shannon and I looked at each other again and then stared at him sitting on our secondhand couch and leaning his walking stick carefully against the Chinese blue Masonite tabletop before him. I wondered what he meant by it; but all I said was yet another repetition of my all-purpose insult-the-elf question: "How may we help you?" Elves didn't like having to ask humans for help, and I didn't like elves. I'd seen too much of them. I knew exactly what was left when the glamour came off.

"I want you to investigate something," he said.

"Why?"

Another flicker of surprise in those dauntingly blue eyes told me he was not quite as impervious as he liked to seem. He had expected me to ask about the job, not why he offered it. "I understood that to be what you do for a living. Is it not?"

"Sometimes," I said. "What do you want investigated?" Elves were sociopaths by definition: "fallen angels, not good enough to save, not bad enough to be lost," who had "every charm but conscience," according to Evans-Wentz, who had better reason to know than anyone. They had nothing even close to empathy, and their reasoning was not human. I did not want to work for him.

He studied me for a long moment before he said finally, rather awkwardly, "A manifestation."

I stared. "A manifestation? Of what?"

"We know not, I fear, but that it is something that frightens the children."

"Who's we? What children?"

"In truth, I had not expected an inquisition." His tone was mild, but his eyes were dark with warning. "At least not before you agreed to take the job."

I shrugged. "There are other private investigators. Some are less cautious than I." Shannon opened her mouth but I kicked her under the desk and she closed it again.

He studied me again before he said, "You are impervious to my glamour, are you not?" He meant that magical charm with which elves effortlessly disarm most humans. I had been as susceptible to it as the next guy, once. I got over it.

"That's none of your business," I said.

He nodded as though I'd told him something. "Few of your kind have such a talent."

He made "your kind" sound like an insult, but I ignored that. "It was a necessary survival skill," I said.

"Just so," he said.

"And I'm not half sure I want to get myself into another situation where I need it," I said.

"I mention it because it should make you able to know whether I am dealing honestly with you."

"Maybe. There are other ways than magic for people to trick each other."

He sighed, leaned back, and crossed his legs, being careful with the crease in his elegant trousers. "True. Very well: I believe you know the halfling Kyriander Stone?"

"I knew him once." I killed his father. "What about him?"

"Your firm was selected, Miss Lavine, because when a difficulty came up for which we considered employing a private investigator, Kyriander Stone recommended you."

"*Ms*. Lavine," I said; and then, "Shit." I scowled at him. He gazed back at me without expression. "All right, I'll listen," I said finally. "You want coffee while you talk?"

"I'd like that," he said with innocent pleasure, as though I'd offered something rare and precious. Perhaps I had. I was beginning to think our mystery guest was less familiar with this world than he wanted us to believe.

I went into the very large closet where we kept the coffeepot on top of the little refrigerator Shannon's boyfriend had given us. "D'you have a name?" I asked him, raising my voice to be heard through the doorway.

"Finandiel," he said in the same mild, husky tone he'd used when I was next to me. It carried surprisingly well:

the voice of a man accustomed to being heard. "Finandiel Dyrimar."

There was a small silence while he waited for us to recognize the name and we didn't. All I recognized was that he must be somebody important since only the most aristocratic Trueblood elves had two names.

Fortunately the spare cup was clean, so I didn't have to make a trip down the hall to the bathroom to wash it. "You take cream and sugar?"

Another small silence, while he absorbed the fact that I wasn't going to comment on the name. "No, thank you," he said.

That was lucky, since we hadn't any cream and only fake sugar. I poured three cups full of coffee and brought them back into the main room without spilling. "So talk, Finandiel," I said, handing him his. "Or is it Lord Dyrimar?" I handed Shannon her cup and sat down with mine.

Finandiel accepted the chipped ceramic mug I gave him without the smallest hint that he was accustomed to finer things, though I'd have bet he never before drank from so mundane a vessel. "Lord Finandiel, actually," he said. "I am the younger brother of Lord Dyrimar. This smells quite good." He sounded surprised.

"You're surprised I make good coffee?"

He lifted one eyebrow at me. It made him look even more aristocratic, somehow. "I know not," he said. "Is it a difficult skill?"

"Good God," I said. "You're way FOOF, aren't you?"

"Never have I encountered this term," he said doubtfully. "Foof?"

"Fresh out of Faerie," I said. "You are, aren't you?"

"Oh," he said. "I see." He examined his coffee for a long moment, took a careful sip, made a face, and put the cup on the table before him. "The flavor is unlike the aroma." He sat back, watching me. "I am recently come from Faerie, yes. Does that present a problem?"

"It could. Did you come here on purpose?"

Amusement made his eyes twinkle. In a human it

would have been disarming. "Did I come where on purpose? To your office?"

"Out of Faerie."

"Oh yes, certainly," he said. "And to your office as well, actually."

"That's something, anyway." I should have known: he hadn't been afraid to taste the coffee. Elves thrown out of Faerie by accident arrived with the oddest notions. "Okay, tell me about the job Kyri recommended us for."

"You will take it?"

"We might. I'm sorry, but we don't take any job, even from a lord high muckymuck FOOF, without knowing more than you've told us about this one."

His expression remained amiable and slightly befuddled, which I thought was quite a good act since his eyes were very alert indeed. "I see," he said, though I rather thought he didn't. "Very well, I expect there is no harm in the telling."

He paused as though collecting his thoughts. Since I doubted he had ever misplaced a thought in his life, I figured that was entirely for show, maybe to cover the use of some elven talent or magic. That made me more suspicious than I was already; but I couldn't detect any results to speak of. After a long moment he lifted his coffee again, wrapped long fingers around the thick, stained ceramic, and inhaled the aroma with deep appreciation.

"The problem is this," he said. "I have settled in what is called a commune or a colony. An artists' colony. There is a valley in the hills called"—here he glanced up and loosed that glittering twitch of a smile again— "Fey Valley. I take this to be an artifact of the ineffable mortal sense of humor."

"Or lack of imagination," said Shannon.

He looked at her as though a wall had spoken. "Ah." He nodded slowly. "Yes." Spring sunlight from the window caught the movement and burnished the silver of his hair. "Fey Valley is owned collectively by the residents: one purchases, not a house, but a share of all the houses. It is a most odd arrangement; but so indeed is all this sale and purchase of lands and homes one finds in this world. Most odd. It suits the artists, however."

"Are you an artist?"

"Yes." A human would have elaborated, but he didn't. "My man—my valet, I believe you would say—and I have taken a small cottage near the Community Hall." He said there were two or three dozen dwellings in Fey Valley, ranging in size from one-room shacks to a mansion as large as the Community Hall and roomy enough for a dozen artists or more, though at present only one lived there. These dwellings were widely scattered throughout the valley. "I believe none is visible from another," he said, "though perhaps some few are in hearing distance of each other. Ordinary sounds, that is. A carrying sound, as for example elven music, might be heard by all.

"The residents are of all ages, both mortal and Trueblood." He blinked. "And halflings." His tone made clear what he thought of those. Truebloods regard them with the same distaste white humans once reserved for the offspring of mixed marriages. "Some residents even have children." He seemed to have the usual elvish awe of offspring: Truebloods' birth rate is low and they tend to regard even human and halfling children as precious.

"It sounds idyllic," I said. "So what's the problem?"

"There you have it," he said. "We know not just what it is."

I don't know why people who apply to private investigators are so often reluctant to describe the problem they want solved. "Any guesses?"

He took that literally, and looked apologetic. "Some mortals believe it to be something called a Bigfoot. Others, quite naturally, think it of magical origin. The elves conclude, from signs found, that may be accurate."

"Okay," I said, "what are the symptoms?"

"It lurks," he said. "It alarms. It makes sounds in the night."

"Has it done any harm? Has anyone seen it?"

"It harms us not," he said. "One of the children believes she saw it. But understand, she is at a difficult age, and quite excitable."

"And what did she say she saw?"

"She has not been coherent on the subject," he said. "The impression given is of something large, dark, and threatening." He hesitated. "This child . . . Perhaps you know her? She is Lilie Stone, Kyriander's younger sister."

I hadn't seen any of them in nearly a year, but I could guess what Lilie might be like now. She had always been a fragile, excitable child, and she had taken her father's death hard. "Okay, so she's not a reliable witness," I said. "So. You have a thing that goes bump in the night, that may or not have been seen by one unstable child. What exactly is it that you want us to do about it?"

"Find out what it is, of course," he said in some surprise. "Stop it, if you can. It frightens the children."

2

Finandiel didn't quibble over our fees or hesitate to produce a hefty deposit. The artists had pooled their resources and agreed to trust his judgment on whether to agree to our terms. I was surprised they'd put such trust in a FOOF, but he had a lot of charisma and, more important, a title. People can be surprisingly naive about aristocratic titles.

The Fey Valley residents had a course of action all planned out, based on their three primary theories. The trouble had started shortly after a new batch of elves—Finandiel, his valet Cuthbern, a woman called Lorielle, and at least one other whose name I didn't catch—had bought in to the community, so some of the older members thought one of the new elves was playing malicious tricks.

At the same time, they had recently become aware of a giant conglomerate that wanted to buy their land, and some of them thought evil minions of the conglomerate were trying to scare them away. And last but not least, the children and a few of the more credulous adults thought it was Bigfoot.

In case it was Bigfoot or the new elves, I was to move into the community to look for clues and try to catch the perpetrator. In case it was evil minions, Shannon was to stay behind and look into the conglomerate to see whether she could find any evidence of shady dealings. It was a reasonable arrangement, so we agreed to it.

That's how I ended up moving into an artists' colony. It wasn't something I'd ever expected to find myself doing, since I'm almost completely without artistic ability of any kind; but I never expected to find myself in search of Bigfoot, either.

It was almost dark by the time we got there; I'd gone home first to pack a bag, taking Finandiel with me when we found out he hadn't brought a car of his own, and he had announced that we would stop at a grocery store afterward. "Meals are prepared at the Community Hall," he said, "but perhaps, should you know how to cook, you will want something in your own kitchen as well."

"Of course I know how to cook." I didn't say how well.

"How talented of you," he said. "Cuthbern does our cooking, and has given me a list of purchases. You will know where to find the articles he desires. I fear this is my first acquaintance with shopping."

I wondered whether they had supermarkets in Faerie. It seemed an absurd notion; but even if they had, Finandiel wouldn't have done his own shopping. "No problem," I said. Famous last words. He was as much trouble to herd through the store as a hyperactive child, though of course far more dignified about it. I was just able to see that he got everything on his list, and to get a reasonable assortment of staples for myself while I was at it.

The sun had set by the time we returned to the car. Our destination was in the hills between Oakland and Moraga: Fey Valley, shadowed by the hills around it, was purple with dusk when we started down the winding private road toward the wide, shallow stream that ran through the center of the little community I was to join.

A few lights winked through the trees from the dwellings scattered across the valley floor and up the slopes of its walls, but only the Community Hall was readily visible from the road, and even that was a mystery of spilled light in rainbow colors till we pulled up in the parking lot beside it.

"It is impossible to drive to many of the dwellings," said Finandiel. "I shall walk from here; Cuthbern awaits me in the Hall."

He had decided I would spend the night in the Hall

and wait till tomorrow to choose a dwelling. That would give me a chance to meet whatever artists and their families came down to the Hall for dinner that night. I wondered whether they would include Kyriander Stone. I would have to meet him again soon enough, but the nearer the moment came, the more I dreaded it.

"Coming?" said Finandiel. "Do not concern yourself: Cuthbern will attend to our purchases."

"I can carry my own," I said.

"You need not," said Finandiel. "Come along, do. I wish to introduce you to the others."

I had learned by now that it was no use arguing when he'd made up his mind, so I got out and followed him across the parking lot toward the Hall door. Now I could see that it was a big, barnlike structure built of redwood and a superabundance of stained glass: there were beautiful stained-glass windows in every size and shape, creating a fantastical rainbowed collage of a building.

It was too dark to notice much about Fey Valley. On the way down the hill I'd seen only the twin cones of my headlights, the shadows of deep forest crowding the road, and the distant glitter of lights from the Hall. Here in the yellow light of the Hall parking lot the surrounding redwoods loomed and eucalyptus caps crunched aromatically in the dust underfoot, but the Hall claimed all my attention with its stained light and muffled voices and the lilting strains of acoustical guitar spilling into the night.

Then the front door opened and the long shadow of a man fell across the stairs, framed in light. "Is that you, my lord?"

Finandiel relaxed visibly. I had not realized he was under a strain till I saw it go out of him. "It is I, Cuthbern," he said, and even the quality of his voice seemed lighter. "I am arriven, and with me the angel of our salvation. Sing her praises. Carry her bags."

"Very good, my lord," said Cuthbern, coming toward us. "Did you manage the shopping?"

"Yes," said Finandiel. "And such an adventure, Cuthbern. You cannot imagine. Is there dinner?" he added plaintively. "It is most hungry work, stalking the wily provisions. You never told me that."

"There is food here, my lord," said Cuthbern. "Or, an it please you, I might prepare a meal at home while you introduce your angel of salvation to the others." He paused within a few feet of us, his face clearly visible by the light of electric lanterns on the porch posts as he bowed gracefully to me and added, "Miss Lavine?" It was a pleasant face, lively and full of curiosity and ready to smile, though he tried to look as stolid and subservient as any elf could.

"Rosie," I said, certain the distinction between "miss" and "ms." would be lost on him if he was as FOOF as his master.

"Very good, miss," he said.

"No, not dinner at home tonight, I think," said Finandiel. "Just bring in our angel's bag. We shall stop here for dinner and collect our own provisions afterward."

"You bought things that need to be refrigerated," I said. "The butter and milk, at least."

Finandiel waved a negligent hand at the car and I felt the tingle of magic in the air. "That should keep them," he said. "Come along, my dear."

I glanced at Cuthbern. "You don't need to bring in my things," I said.

"It is no trouble," he said. "Only the one suitcase?" I told him yes, and that I would come back for the perishables.

"They will keep here well enough," said Finandiel. "I say, do come along."

I realized I was looking for excuses to delay going into that Hall. The night insulated us from the voices and light within. I was not ready to meet Kyriander Stone.

I don't always fall into bed with our clients, but with Kyri it had seemed as natural and necessary as breathing. I'd thought he felt the same way. But when the job ended badly, he walked away without a word. I didn't know what I would say to him now; or he to me. "Yes, okay," I said reluctantly.

We were halfway up the short flight of stairs when

Kyriander appeared in the doorway. "Rose?" He was backlighted so I couldn't see his face, but I heard the welcome in his voice.

"Kyriander," I said, disarmed. "Hello."

He plunged down the stairs to hug me. His arms were as warm and strong as I remembered. He smelled of woodlands and magic and memory. "I've missed you," he said.

"And I, you," I told his shirt collar, wondering whether it was true. Had I missed him? I'd thought of him often enough, certainly.

"Oh, yes," he said, pulling away to grin at me, the same wry, lopsided grin I remembered. I'd forgotten how handsome he was. "On tour with elfrock stars, I'm sure you missed me."

I'd been hired to protect the lead singer in the band Cold Iron. And I'd been in over my head from the moment I joined their concert tour. In a way, I still was: that was where I met Killer. Sweet, peaceful Killer, whose friendship had been all that saved me on that tour. But when I was alone with him afterward, I could not let go of the past. "I wasn't on tour with them for long," I said, avoiding the issue.

A shadow from the doorway fell across the stairs. "Kyri," said a husky woman's voice, "do you and Lord F plan to keep her to yourselves? Dinner will get cold."

Kyriander chuckled deep in his throat. "Very well," he said, gently turning me toward the stairs. "The residents are impatient to meet you and tell you all our troubles," he told me.

"Yes, do come in, dear," said the woman in the doorway, with just a hint of malicious amusement in her voice. I looked up at her silhouetted form, and for one confusing instant I thought I saw the classic Halloween witch with pointy hat, warty nose, broomstick, and all: then she smiled and the illusion shattered, leaving only an ordinary tall, slender woman in a long wool skirt and lacy shawl.

"This is our resident witch, Ariana Malloy," Kyriander said, leading me up the stairs toward her. Finandiel and Cuthbern stepped aside to let us pass, which seemed odd; but I wasn't given time to consider it. "Ariana, this is Rosie Lavine. Be gentle with her: she is precious to me."

That phrase startled me; but Ariana was already reaching to pull me into the Hall, where what seemed like dozens of curious faces were turned toward us in the doorway, and I had to file all my startled impressions away for later examination. I said, "Nice to meet you, Ms. Malloy," as though seeing the Halloween witch turn herself into a lovely, aging halfling were an everyday event.

"Ariana," she said. "We're not so formal here." Smiling, she drew me inside.

Kyriander came in right behind me, but I felt absurdly alone and vulnerable facing all those curious gazes. Not all of Fey Valley's residents had come out to meet me—some were reclusive, some busy, some perhaps being polite, and some doubtless just not interested—but there must have been at least forty or fifty people there, counting children.

They were all looking at me. Even the children stopped whatever they were doing to examine me in that curiously impersonal, appraising way that children have. For a long moment we all just looked at each other. Then the acoustical guitar started playing again—it was a slim young halfling at the far end of the room with golden curls and mocking eyes who played it—and Finandiel stepped into the room, blathering his inanities, with Cuthbern silently subservient at his heels.

"Hello, hello, all," said Finandiel. "I trust you have survived my absence in good form? And lo, I bring unto you our salvation: Rosalynd Lavine, known as Rosie, come to rescue us from the forces of evil, or at least of confusion, forsooth. Make her welcome. Bend thy knee unto her. Make obeisance to her majesty. And above all, feed her. Better still, feed me." He strode into the room, a small and silly elf wearing a foolish smile and an aristocratic arrogance that somehow made his foolishness seem dangerous. Watching him, I wondered with a sinking feeling what I'd got myself into this time.

3

"I saw it," said Lilie Stone. "It was Bigfoot." She lifted her chin to glare at me, a beautiful young woman with pointed ears and tragic eyes. She had always looked and acted young for her age. I sometimes thought she was more elf than human. Her face was elven, with a narrow chin and wide forehead, high cheekbones, and generous lips; but no elf could look so sullenly defiant. None cared enough what anyone thought of them. She was sixteen and pampered, and looked as wild and dangerous as a feral kitten. Which is to say very wild, but not as dangerous as she wanted to be.

"You never," said her brother Briande. He was three years younger than she, with a rounder and more human face. When we were introduced he'd smiled at me in easy friendship. Now he was glaring at his sister, trying to look as coldly contemptuous as she, and failing badly. "You made that up," he said.

"Kids," Kyriander said repressively, sounding far more than just ten years older than Lilie. He looked as slender and wild as she, and as mischievously sweet as Briande. It had been a long time since we'd been together, but at that moment it seemed as though very little had changed.

Briande glanced up at Kyriander and grinned.

"Did not," Lilie said childishly, and added with some dignity, to Kyriander, "Tell *him*. He started it. I'm not a kid."

"Then behave not as one," said Kyriander. I hadn't remembered him sounding so elvish before. Living among so many of them must be a strong influence.

I ate my spinach quiche in silence. Kyriander and Finandiel had introduced me to everyone present, and I'd promptly forgotten most of their names. One of the humans, a sturdy middle-aged woman with a grim face and dark, friendly eyes who reintroduced herself as Charlotte Cameron, had served us dinner: venison broth, tabouleh, and spinach quiche.

While we ate, the residents told me about their encounters with "the Trouble": the scary thing in the woods that they had at first taken for children's imagination, until small items had begun to disappear and several adults had seen the manifestation.

Tim Cameron, Charlotte's husband, a weathered old human with dust-colored eyes, told of seeing a stranger on the path behind his house one evening. When I pressed for details, he became mildly belligerent and Charlotte seemed embarrassed, so I let it go for the moment.

An elf woman called Galinda, willowy and beautiful with her hair dyed in streaks of primary colors and her eyes the color of clear summer sky, told of hearing elven music in the woods that no elves were present to play. She seemed excited to have heard it, and volunteered to show me where she'd been, if I liked.

Gary Cameron, Tim and Charlotte's teenage son, bulky and handsome in a surly adolescent way, claimed he'd seen Bigfoot tracks by the creek, but backed down when his mother spoke his name. "Well, I think they were Bigfoot tracks," he said defiantly, with a glance at Lilie that left me in no doubt as to whom he wished to impress.

"I saw something," said a little dark-eyed girl who was leaning against a slender brunette in a paint-stained dress.

"What did you see?" asked the brunette, smiling fondly.

"You know," said the girl. "That night. On my window."

"Oh," said the brunette. "I'd forgotten." She looked at me and shrugged. "I didn't see it, so I don't know what it might have been, but Dorina was sure she saw a man's—or an elf's—shadow on her windowpane one night last week." She hesitated. "We live at the top of a ravine. The path ends at our house, so there shouldn't be anybody up there but us."

"Who's us?" I asked.

"Me and Marc," said the brunette. "Um, Marc Starr: that's him over there." She gestured toward a scowling, bearded fellow whose shirt was as paint-stained as her dress. "Oh, and I'm Melanie," she said. "Melanie McGraw."

"Me," said the little girl.

"What?" said Melanie.

"I'm us too," said the little girl.

"Of course you are, sweetie," said Melanie, mildly surprised.

"Dorina McGraw," the little girl told me proudly. "I'm going to be a famous painter when I grow up."

I made a show of writing down her name with the others.

"I'm Rosetta Fulmer," announced a small, plain, gray-haired woman. "In case you've forgotten all the inductions." Someone snickered at the malapropism, but Rosetta seemed oblivious. "Which who could blame you when there are so many of us and we're all such egoists we think you'll know our names without being told. I always do, if I go to a party where there are a lot of strangers. It doesn't matter how famous they are if you never heard of them, does it?" She smiled, pleased with her reasoning.

"I remembered you," I said truthfully. She was another painter, and well-enough known that even I had heard of her. Her work was powerful, almost overwhelming. She was short and shy and unassuming, with a tendency to titter apologetically about everything.

"Why, thank you, dear," she said. "That's very kind of you. I should probably tell my manager: he'd be pleased to know our private investiture had heard of me."

"Um, that's investigator," I said.

She nodded, tittering. "Of course. Silly me. *Did* you mean you'd heard of me before?" She didn't wait for me to respond. "Or I suppose it might just be that I have such an odd name, easy to remember. I do realize that. But I don't want to get sidetracked: I was going to tell you about being chased last week, or was it the week before?"

She counted briefly on her fingers. "No, the week before, I think, by something I never did see, so I suppose it's rather like Galinda's music, isn't it? Not that I mean she makes music, because of course she doesn't, she dances to it, which is quite a different thing. Well, some dancers make music as well, I'm sure, but I've never heard that Galinda does, do you, dear?" She didn't wait for a response. "Only it was foggy. And evening, just when the light changes, so I never really got a look at what it was." Her run-on sentences were low on logical progressions; she seemed to say very much whatever came into her head.

"I'm pretty sure it was a Wednesday," she said. "I'm never at my best on Wednesdays because that's the day my manager comes out from the city and he's always nattering on and on at me about one thing and another, you know how they are. Most annoying, but they're so useful, there's nothing to do about it. So I was just taking the path down to the Hall since it's sort of a written law that Charlotte will always cook dinner, and really, what else could I do without any yellow ochre?"

"By Mab's grace, woman, can't you get to the point?" asked someone—an elf, by the curse.

"I'm so embarrassed," Rosetta said without hesitation, just a little less apologetic than before. She cast one fulminating look across the room and went on, "One of those glorious evenings when the forest seems luminous through the fog, everything perfectly detailed and the colors just fading, you know, as it got dark. I'd just had an epitome about the yellow ochre." At my confused look she explained kindly, "You know: a realization. It came to me in a blinding flash. An epitome. So when I heard it, I thought it was Tim at first, because it seemed sort of blundery, and—well, I'm sorry, Charlotte, but after all, I knew it couldn't be a bear."

"Is there some reason Tim would blunder?" I asked.

Rosetta glanced apologetically at Charlotte and said, "Well, *you* know."

"He drinks," Charlotte said bluntly.

"So I spoke, don't you see," Rosetta said quickly. "And it made this pecuniary noise." It took me a moment to realize she meant "peculiar." "I really can't describe it. A very red sort of noise, quite menacing. And it came toward me." She shuddered. "It was horrible. All of a piece, really, when you think I'd sent a list precisely because I knew it was Wednesday. Well, Monday when I sent it, of course. Which should have given him plenty of time. It might as well have been a bear, really.

"So I hurried away. Anyone would have. And the thing came after me. I have never been so frightened in all my life." She looked at me, apologizing with her eyes for having been frightened.

"Yes, I'd have been frightened too," I said involuntarily. Well, what the hell. I probably would have.

She smiled gratefully, then frowned as she took up her narrative again. "So I ran. But when I got to the Hall there wasn't anything following me after all. It was most odd. Quite as though I'd imagined the whole thing, though I know I didn't. Some of the men went out to look, just in case. Actually I think some of the women went too, because I seem to remember that Ariana was wearing that Navaho skirt she likes so well, the one that looks like a throw rug—I'd think she crafted it herself, only there are no beads on it, which I believe she inveterately puts on things she weaves, though now I think of it I haven't seen all she's done, so perhaps not—but it was no use. No tracks, no traces. Nothing."

The humans had insisted on calling in the police after that. The elves were sure the police would find nothing, since the elves had found nothing. They believed the perpetrator had concealed himself by magic; which I thought almost certainly meant it was an elf, whether resident or not. It also meant I doubted very much that the resident elves were as much at a loss as they claimed.

The police, as predicted, found no evidence of an intruder, and decided the elves must be right about the magic. That left the long-term residents suspicious of the newcomer elves. "Though you'll notice," said Ritchie Morita, glaring dramatically in my direction as though whatever we were to notice was entirely my fault, "the Trouble stopped for as long as the police were here." He paused to sneer knowingly. "In my opinion that's significant. Elves wouldn't have stopped just for the police."

Ritchie's was one of the few names I remembered from the general introduction, because he was a writer whose work I had read: earnestly depressing contemporary novels with blurbs on the jackets that talked about anger and genius and vision. His photo was usually there too, depicting a dark, serious fellow in his twenties with a pipe, a leather jacket, and dramatically shadowed eyes. In person he looked older—maybe mid-thirties—and less dramatic, but he balanced that with rudeness.

"So you think whoever's causing the Trouble was scared of the police?" I asked.

He let a cynical smile play at the corners of his mouth. "Humans might be scared of them. But elves would be, at best, respectful." He said it in the tone of one lecturing an idiot.

Ariana made a rude sound. "I've yet to meet the elf who had any real respect for anything human. It's not in their nature." She didn't seem to judge them for it: she was just stating an observed fact.

"Oh, come now," said Finandiel, surprised.

"And while they're certainly devious enough," Ritchie continued as though no one had spoken, "I doubt any of them understands us enough to think of pretending to be afraid of police."

"Sounds like you don't much like elves," I said.

He tipped his chair back and sneered at me. "Lousy detecting," he said. "As a matter of fact I think pretty well of some of them."

"More quiche?" said Charlotte, appearing at my elbow as if by magic with a pan of quiche and a broad serving knife.

"No, thank you," I said. "But it was very good. Thank you." I didn't take my gaze from Ritchie's. His expression was meant to be blandly superior, but I could see the calculations going on behind his eyes. I wondered what he had to hide. Not necessarily anything to do with the case: people with secrets become as protective of them in a P.I.'s presence as in a cop's. Still, he would bear watching.

"I have work to do," he said abruptly, rising to look down at me with shadowed eyes. It was a good effect, but he'd already overused it on his book jackets.

"Right," I said.

"Coffee, then?" said Charlotte.

"Thanks, yeah, I'd like that." I smiled at her, but she wasn't looking at me: she was watching Ritchie walk away from us, her lips compressed in disapproval.

"Isn't that just like him." She shook her head. "Usually people get their own, but I'll bring *you* some." She emphasized the pronoun, bestowing upon me a look of fierce, almost possessive approval.

"Isn't what just like him?" I said, but she had already turned away to get the coffee.

"Oh, don't worry about her," said Ariana. "She's having a running feud with Ritchie this week. Next week it'll be someone else. Charlotte just can't get over the fact that we all have ideas of our own and refuse to live our lives to please her." It was pitched just loud enough for Charlotte to hear it, and she waited for a response.

Charlotte glanced back, looking ready to take offense, and rolled her eyes when she saw Ariana's expectant smile. "*Some* people," she said meaningfully, "aren't as easygoing as you, Ariana."

Ariana laughed. "Don't I know it," she said. "Could I have some coffee too, while you're up?"

"Get your own," said Charlotte. I couldn't tell whether she meant it.

Beside me, Kyriander rose and picked up his plate.

"I'll get it." He gestured toward my empty plate, picked it up when I nodded, and looked at Ariana. "Cream, no sugar, right?"

"Right," she said, surprised. He grinned and departed after Charlotte, carrying his plate and mine. "Goodness," said Ariana, gazing pensively at his retreating back. "I wonder what that boy wants from me?" Like her remark about Charlotte, it was pitched to carry, but Kyriander made no indication he'd heard it. After a moment she shrugged and looked at me. "Well. What do you think of our infestation?"

"Infestation?"

"The Trouble," she said, investing the word with melodrama. "Oh, I'm sorry. I shouldn't make fun. It really has some people frightened." She shrugged, a gesture as unconsciously elegant as every move I'd seen her make. "Pay me no mind; I'm just exercising an old witch's odd sense of humor."

"Are you really Wicca?"

"Why do you ask?"

"Just curious."

Well, I'm not," she said. "I meant the Halloween witch. Because I look like one." She didn't: she looked like an aging halfling who had been gorgeous and had become beautiful. It wasn't the smooth, empty, youthful beauty humans admire, of course. But the elven bone structure told. The flesh might sag and wrinkle, but the elegance of line and movement remained. When I made no response, she chuckled. "You're good," she said. "Tell me, have you formulated a plan of action yet?"

"Not really," I said. "There's not enough to go on. I'll have to look around in daylight, and talk to more of the residents, first. And be shown the locations of the various sightings."

"Very wise," said Finandiel, who was seated two chairs down on Ariana's side of the table.

Cuthbern preceded Kyriander from the kitchen, bearing a tray of filled coffee cups which he distributed, giving the first one to Finandiel, while Kyriander settled back into his chair. "Wasn't my idea," Kyriander said, catching Ariana's look. "You know how FOOF servants are."

"Yes," she said, accepting a cup from Cuthbern. "Thank you, Cuthbern. But I wish you wouldn't wait on me."

"I have no wish to offend, Madam," he said. "But it is my place—"

"Bull," she said.

He accepted that with equanimity: I had the feeling they'd had this conversation before. "Yes, Madam," he said. And added, with a perfectly straight face, "Did Madam wish me to return her serving to the kitchen?"

"No, Madam didn't wish," she said, curling her long fingers protectively around the cup.

"Very well, Madam. Thank you, Madam," he said, unperturbed.

"You'll drive me mad," she said.

"Very good, Madam," said Cuthbern.

Kyriander made a mark in the air. "Point to Cuthbern," he said. Cuthbern lifted an eyebrow at him.

"I say, Cuthbern old man," said Finandiel, looking with distaste at his untouched coffee. "Mayhap we ought to toddle along, do you think?"

Cuthbern was at his side at once, one hand on the back of his chair to pull it out of his way. "Very good, my lord," he said, bowing. "I regret if the coffee is not to your liking. Your lordship mentioned a desire to try it."

"I did try it, while I was out," Finandiel said almost plaintively. "The aroma is captivating, but the flavor leaves much to be desired."

Cuthbern nodded gravely. "I observed that myself, my lord. Will your lordship require a cloak?" He looked ready to produce one from thin air. Perhaps he was: I didn't know what sort of magic he had. His lordship rejected the offer, so I didn't find out.

Finandiel took formal leave of the party, looking austere and dignified, and prattling the whole time like a silly child. Before the door was closed behind him Lilie was at Kyriander's side, whining to go home in a whispery voice with many fierce sidelong glances at me. I had to remind myself she was a teenager: she seemed more like a child. Kyriander, not noticing her glances, invited me with them.

Before I could respond, Lilie announced firmly, "No."

Kyriander stared. "What?"

"It's my home too, and I don't want her," she said.

"Kyri," I said. For a moment I thought he would argue with her, but instead he turned to me, his expression pure, arrogant elf. "We can talk tomorrow," I said.

He studied me for a long moment while Lilie tapped her foot impatiently. Finally he smiled and nodded. "Very well. Tomorrow, then," he said, and rose, one hand on Lilie's shoulder. "Let us find your brother."

"He's over there," she said.

While Kyri went to get him, she shot me such a poisonously triumphant glance that Ariana, intercepting it, lifted an eyebrow at me. "It seems you've made an enemy," she said.

"A long time ago," I said. It seemed a long time, anyway.

4

It wasn't long till all the residents except Galinda and Ritchie Morita were gone to their separate dwellings. Charlotte Cameron was the last to go, turning off the kitchen light on her way out and glaring at Ritchie as she shut the back door. He was sitting at a typewriter on a little table against the far wall of the great room and didn't notice her look.

Galinda made a very unelvish sound of amusement. "It speaks ill of a people when their servants mind them not," she said.

"I've told you before," Ritchie said without looking, "Charlotte is not a servant."

"Yes, yes, I well recall it," she said impatiently, and turned to me. "Think you this Trouble is of mortal cause?"

"And drop the dumb Faerie accent," Ritchie said, nearly snarling. "She's not impressed." The typewriter keys clicked under his fingers without pause.

"Are you writing?" I asked, impressed by his tricks if not by hers.

"No, I'm baking a goddamned cake," he said. "Jesus God." The keys clicked steadily.

Galinda smiled. "He must be working," she said. "Else he might be rude. I have known him so, when the muse failed him."

Ritchie moved his chair slightly, putting his back more toward her.

She ignored him. "Think you— Do you think you can resolve our Trouble?"

"I can't tell yet," I said. "I don't know enough about

it. It was you who heard the music, wasn't it? What sort of music was it?"

"A lullaby," she said promptly. "One I had heard, oh, full a hundred times at my foster mother's knee." She hummed a bar of melody, lilting and strange. "It was a Celtic harp, did I say? Never have I heard that played in human hands—though I understand some have the skill of it."

I nodded as though that told me something. "At least you can be pretty sure it wasn't Bigfoot."

"As to that," she said, "I fear I am unfamiliar with the term, though I hear it much of late. It is an ironworld creature, this Bigfoot?"

"Possibly," I said. "Can you tell me anything else about the music? The Celtic harp is good. What else?"

"Only that no Fey Valley residents were near when I heard it," she said. "Had they been, I would have known. Had they hidden by the arts, I would have felt it." She meant the magic arts.

"You felt no magic at all?" I wondered whether that proved it wasn't an elf. Probably not; they didn't use their magic incessantly, after all. Elves could hide by physical means as well as humans could, or better.

Galinda looked troubled. "But of course I could not tell how far away the player was," she said. "Were the music but projected from a distance, and I expecting no arts, though they be used in plenty I might notice them not."

Across the room, Ritchie muttered something and shifted in his chair. It squeaked.

"Ignore him," said Galinda. "He is but an ill-tempered journeyman at his craft."

"And you're a waste of food," he said quite clearly. The typing stopped abruptly and he turned to glare at us, his chair squeaking horribly with every movement. "Must you chatter girlishly all night? I'm trying to get some work done here."

"Your right to the Hall is no better than ours," said Galinda, lifting her chin in almost childish defiance.

"My right to *air* is better than yours," he said savagely. "And my use of it is wiser. Go away, little girls. You're not going to solve the world's problems tonight anyway. Leave me in peace."

It wasn't worth arguing. "You ought to oil that chair," I told him, and looked back at Galinda. "I think I'll choose a room and then take a walk before bed."

She rose with a dancer's sure, easy grace, ostentatiously ignoring Ritchie. "I find I weary of pests and noise," she said, and yawned. "I will see you on the morrow."

I agreed to it and she left, still ignoring Ritchie. I thought at first that was wasted effort, since he had his back to us again; but I saw the twitch of his shoulders when she closed the door softly behind her. He seemed completely indifferent to my presence. I waited a moment, wondering whether he would acknowledge me in any way, but he didn't.

Cuthbern had left my suitcase against the wall at the foot of the stairs. I carried it upstairs, where I found a wide, carpeted corridor opening onto many unoccupied rooms. After a quick reconnaissance I chose one near the front, with a balcony that had a good view of the darkened parking lot and the main paths leading away from the Hall, and tossed my suitcase on the bed.

It took only a moment to climb out of my city clothes and into soft jeans, a sweatshirt, and running shoes. I thought of tucking my handgun into my belt and decided against it. There'd been no indication that the Trouble, whatever it was, posed any real danger; true, it had chased Rosetta, but it had done her no harm, and nothing else it had done seemed even threatening. It was just a nuisance that frightened the children. I suspected I'd been hired as much to reassure them as because anyone really wanted me to do the job. In any event I didn't mean to go out of sight of the Hall tonight. I shouldn't have any need for weapons.

After sliding my suitcase onto the rack at the foot of the bed and kicking my city shoes under it, I turned out the light and stepped onto the balcony. The doors made no sound. I left them open while I stood at the rail, surveying the parking lot by moonlight. Someone had turned off all the outdoor lights. At the edge of the lot I could just make out the steep banks of the creek, though without the gentle whisper of the water I might not have guessed what that darker area was. From the main room below I could still hear Ritchie's steady typing, and the occasional creak of his chair as he shifted position.

We might have been utterly alone in the world. A cricket sang somewhere, but there were no other sounds in all that still, deep night. No hint of breeze moved the forest. Moonlight spilled between the trees in ghostly streamers, not lighting the night so much as tenanting it with shadows.

Below my balcony, at the corner of the Hall, I could just make out the broad, smooth expanse of the main path toward the residences. On the other side, nearer the creek, where the smaller path led across a narrow footbridge toward Finandiel and Cuthbern's cottage, I could see only a dark opening in the trees; nothing beyond it.

I looked up again, into the light-frosted treetops silhouetted against the moon-washed sky. How long had it been since I stood on Killer's front porch and looked out into night-shadowed forest like this? If I blocked out the sound of Ritchie's typing, I could almost imagine myself there again, with Killer sleeping somewhere in the house behind me.

But he wasn't there. He was somewhere in Europe, traveling with a new elfrock band, and I had elected to stay behind. I turned and went back into my bedroom, through it, and down the stairs. Ritchie didn't look up from his typing as I let myself out the front door, which was perhaps as well: I was in no mood to fend his sneering graciously.

The front porch was deeply shadowed, but moonlight washed across the stairs almost as bright as day. I went down them and along the wall to the broader of the two paths leading toward the valley residences. I could see my way clearly even after the forest closed around me;

the trees were well set apart here, with plenty of room for moonlight to spill between them.

The path curved gently away from the road, and it wasn't long till my city-honed sense of direction failed me. I had a mental map of the paths as they'd been described to me, but I couldn't get it to overlay the reality of bushes and trees and shadows. At first I glanced back often, trying to keep the Hall in sight, but I soon realized that was pointless. From this angle I couldn't see lights in any of the windows, so the first thicket of bushes concealed it easily.

Very soon I could no longer tell where either the Hall or the road was. Nor could I make out any other dwellings, though I knew several were fairly nearby. I watched for side paths that might lead to them, and for any sign of artificial light through the trees, but saw none.

This far from the Hall, the forest seemed to close in on the path; but there was still plenty of moonlight. What little underbrush grew there seemed to be trimmed or worn away from the path. Something white loomed out of the darkness ahead. I paused, listening to the silence of the night. Nothing happened. The white shape remained where it was, still and silent.

After a long moment I moved forward again, alert for signs of danger or even movement, but I might have been the only living thing for miles. The white shape resolved itself into a fountain statue, set in the middle of a brilliantly moon-washed forest glade.

I paused in the shadows to admire it and to listen for movement. When I was still there were none, not even of water; the fountain was dry. A delicate stone dryad bent to pour her tall stone urn onto something—I could not make out what it was, but assumed flowers or a garden—at her feet; from there, the water was meant to flow by stages down into a shallow pool that now must hold only fallen leaves. Pale silver moonlight turned it to melancholy magic, as though the artist had designed it with just that light in mind.

Benches were set at intervals around it, so the weary traveler could rest and admire both it and what looked like carefully tended flower beds at its base. Perhaps in daylight this would be a charming little nook, but in the scattered moonlight it seemed suddenly ominous. I felt very small and alone in the large, dark forest.

But I was curious, and I knew there was no real danger, so I ventured nearer the fountain. The pool held few fallen leaves; it must not have been long out of use. Perhaps it had only been shut down for cleaning.

The dryad's sweet, shy face was perfect in every detail, her eyes closed, her lips curved in some secret pleasure. Her limbs were graceful curves of marbled white flesh, the slender arms seeming far too frail to support the tipped urn even though it was carved so thin the stone was translucent. I stepped nearer, to see what it was at her feet that she was watering—and froze in disproportionate horror as I realized what I was seeing: an exquisite dryad poised on a mound of grinning human skulls.

They looked real. Even the texture was right, and the coloring, and the shape, some of them broken and some whole, with staring eye sockets and grinning teeth. A few had tumbled out of the heap and down into the edges of the pool. I don't know why I hadn't seen them before. They had been broken by the fall. I could almost hear, as though in memory, the dry, hollow sound of them rolling down to splash into the water.

At the top of the heap, the dryad's faultless, delicate toes were firmly planted across cheekbones and teeth of human skulls, seeming almost to grow from them, as though what she watered was herself: as though she, in her implacable nobility, grew out of the lost lives of all those slaughtered humans.

I looked away in revulsion. It was a long moment before I could force myself to reach, without looking, to touch that appalling heap, dreading to feel the smooth worry of ancient bones beneath my fingers.

I felt instead the cool, slick certainty of stone. Only stone. It was all stone, dryad and skulls alike, carved by some twisted genius; not a living creature growing from human death and despair.

When I looked at it again, the chilling magic was gone:

it was a sculpture only, nothing more. I wondered what it would look like in daylight, and what had driven the artist who sculpted it, and what had possessed the Fey Valley residents to install it in their forest glade. I wouldn't have had it on property of mine if I'd been paid.

Feeling somewhat less adventurous than before, I slowly retraced my path to the Hall and went to the other side of it, to the smaller trail to Finandiel and Cuthbern's house. I could just see my way between two broad redwood trunks. Beyond those, the path opened out on one side. It followed the stream, with bushes and looming tree trunks on one side and the water whispering in filigreed darkness on the other. The shadows were thicker here, so that I kept tripping on unseen roots. Just as I decided it would be wiser to turn back, the path emerged in a clearing near an arched wooden footbridge over the creek.

From the top of the bridge's arch the Hall, less than a hundred yards away, was already nearly hidden: only two lighted stained-glass windows winked between bushes and tree trunks. I wondered how much of it would be visible in daylight, and how much the residents spent on the landscaping that kept their forest paths and clearings so neatly manicured and their dwellings so artfully concealed.

Across the bridge I could see nothing at all of Finandiel and Cuthbern's dwelling, but I didn't know whether that was because it was completely hidden or only because they had all their lights out. The forest was thicker on that side of the creek. Almost no moonlight shone through the leaves. For all I knew there might be half a dozen cottages a stone's throw from me, and I wouldn't see them.

I listened for a few moments to the water in the creek whispering merrily over unseen stones before I turned back toward the Hall parking lot, ready to pack it in for the night. I hadn't gone three steps when I saw something move on the path ahead.

5

It was just a flicker of shadow that might have been a branch moving in the wind—only there was no wind. I paused, listening. There was no sound but the murmur of the creek beside me. If there were anyone else on the path I would surely hear his footsteps: nobody could walk on these brittle leaves without making some sound.

After a moment I went on, moving more cautiously now, watching for movement. Not far ahead the path curved around a big, shapeless bush that spilled black shadow across it like a blanket. Between it and me there was only open ground beside the creek, brightly moonlit. If there were anyone in the shadows, I would make a perfect target.

I reminded myself that the Trouble was only a nuisance that frightened the children. But of course I wasn't quite sure this was the Trouble. I stood still, searching the shadows. Something moved: I was sure of it this time. "Who's there?" I said, and saw something dark slide deeper into darkness.

Instinct said I should get the hell away from there while I could. Duty said it was my job to stay, to find out what this was. Reason said I should have brought my handgun with me. Duty won: I plunged after it into the shadows.

Branches tugged at my hair. A thread of spiderweb trailed across my cheeks. Leaves poked at my face. No moonlight penetrated here: I couldn't see my hand in front of my eyes. Something crashed in the distance, and I paused, listening. Did I hear footsteps running away? I couldn't be sure. Certainly I heard nothing nearby. The shadows felt tenanted, but I decided that was my nerves. Whatever it was I'd been chasing, it had evaded me and was long gone by now. Sighing as much in relief as in disappointment, I turned back toward the path, reaching blindly before me to ward off prickly branches . . . and touched something warm and giving: something like bare flesh.

I froze, staring, caught by that penetrating horror that comes when the familiar turns abruptly unfamiliar, the expected unexpected. Inches away from my face I saw a flicker of reflected light, as though something stared back at me.

A branch snapped loose, hitting me in the face, and I jerked away. Something large and solid hit me hard in the chest, knocking me off-balance. I grabbed at frail branches that broke free in my hands. The blow had propelled me backward across the path, and I felt one foot slide over the edge of the steep creek bank. I was still grabbing for support when my knees hit the edge of the bank and slid over.

And then I was sliding, feetfirst, down the damp slope, scrabbling helplessly in the loose soil for a handhold all the way. One hand closed over a root as thick as my wrist, and the other on a rock: the rock tore loose and tumbled away to splash in the water. The root held. I got both hands on it and hung there for a long moment, my feet dangling over the cheerfully burbling little stream, my knees digging into the bank, before I got my balance and found that the slope really wasn't too steep to climb.

When I reached the top again I was hot, sweaty, and smeared everywhere with mud. I had dirt in my eyes, mud under my fingernails, and a pebble in one shoe. And I had a strong sense, now, that I was completely alone on the path. Whoever had pushed me really was gone now.

Again I thought I heard footsteps in the distance, running away. This time I was pretty sure they were real. I had a strong feeling I'd frightened the Trouble as much as it had frightened me. That push hadn't been a con-

certed effort to hurt me. It had only been the desperate
shove of a trapped thing breaking free.

That didn't make the situation any better. Cursing, I
shook clumps of mud off my knees and elbows and tried
to wipe the worst of it off my shoes. "If this is somebody's idea of a joke, I'm not amused," I said savagely,
wiping the edge of my shoe on a convenient root. Soil
smeared wetly into the leather and dripped in little clots
off my shoelaces. "And if that was my introduction to
the Trouble," I muttered bitterly, "I'm not impressed.
Damn it."

Of course there was no response. The distant footsteps
had faded to silence: my voice was the only sound for
miles. I stamped my feet in vexation and yelped when
my heel came down on the stone in my shoe.

When I descended the stairs the next morning, the
table at one side of the great room was crowded with
people at various stages of breakfast. Brilliant sunlight
flooded the room, banishing last night's atmosphere of
magic and romance. Now the splinters in the rough
floorboards were obvious, and the mud on the chair legs,
and the old stains on the four carefully laundered table-
cloths it took to cover the long dining table.

But the stained-glass windows were more beautiful in
daylight, spilling vivid colors across rough wooden walls
and floor. Both doors were open, letting in a cool breeze
tangy with forest resins. A big black dog sprawled across
the doorstep with its massive head resting wearily across
one front leg. It watched me all the way down the stairs.

No one else paid much attention as I went past the
table and into the kitchen, where I found Charlotte tending pans of bacon and eggs on the big wood-burning
stove. She glanced up, said, "Good morning," and deftly
turned three eggs with one flick of a broad spatula.

"Good morning," I said. "Can I help with anything?"

She looked surprised. "That's very nice of you," she
said. "Some people think I have nothing better to do
than wait on them." She said this with a fulminating
look into the great room, her voice raised just enough

that it might be overheard. "But no, thanks, I can manage. Fix yourself a plate." She told me where to find dishes, flatware, coffee, and toast. "There's porridge if you like," she said. "Or bacon and eggs."

"Bacon and eggs, please," I said gratefully. "It smells wonderful."

She smiled in acknowledgment, served me bacon, eggs, and potatoes, said if I wanted jam for my toast it was on the table, and returned her attention to her cooking. I carried my plate and a cup of coffee to the table, where I found a seat between Ariana and a plump little halfling she introduced as Chance Winter, a well-known nature photographer. I knew his work.

"It's very nice to meet you," he said politely, offering me a limp hand to shake. I shook it dutifully. "I do hope you're able to quell our Trouble: it's so frightfully disruptive."

"I'll do my best."

"Give her back her hand, Chance," said Ariana. "Her eggs are getting cold."

"Oh!" He released me, looking startled. "So sorry. I don't know what I was thinking. Eat, eat. Don't mind me. I haven't actually seen the Trouble myself, of course, but I do hear rather a lot about it from the children. I'm teaching a class on photography on the weekends. Can I get you the jam? And the little ones are so nervous lately, it's just heart-rendering, if you'll excuse a Rosetta-ism."

"Heart-rendering!" Ariana bellowed with laughter. "That's *won*derful," she said, and added almost accusingly, "Is it real, or did you make it up?"

I glanced uncomfortably around the table to make sure Rosetta wasn't there; though very likely if they made fun of her in her presence she was accustomed to it by now. Most of the faces were unfamiliar, though I saw Melanie McGraw and Marc Starr together, and an elf I was pretty sure had been introduced as Salonian. And sure enough Rosetta was there, quietly sipping coffee and listening with a little smile of genuine amusement.

Chance was pressing his right hand melodramatically over his heart. "It's authentic, I assure you," he said. "Well outside the range of my feeble wit. It's one of her best, don't you think?"

"Oh, excellent," said Ariana, still chuckling. Neither of them so much as glanced in Rosetta's direction.

Kyriander Stone arrived and stepped over the dog in the doorway—which, doglike, chose just that moment to rise in some confusion, nearly knocking him off his feet. "Good morning, Rose." His tone was cheerful, but there was an unexpected look of reserve in his expressive almond eyes.

"Kyriander," I said, nodding.

He strode past us to the kitchen and returned a moment later with a cup of coffee. Charlotte followed him, carrying a steaming pan. While he pulled up a chair beside me, she went around the table offering the last of the bacon and eggs around. "Come sit down when you're finished," Kyriander told her.

She smiled at him. "Thank you, Kyri," she said. "But I have to do the dishes and get back to the house."

"Tim can get along without you for a few more minutes."

She shook her head seriously. "No, I have to get back," she said. "But thank you."

"She's worried he has a stash of vodka somewhere she hasn't dumped," said Ritchie Morita.

Charlotte glared at him. "Some people just think they're so damn smart," she said, and walked away, head high.

"That was unnecessary, Ritchie," said Ariana.

"Yes, Grandma," said Ritchie.

"It was true," said Chance.

"I'll fight my own battles, damn you," said Ritchie.

"My, my, aren't we fierce this morning?" said Chance.

"Boys and girls," said Kyriander, "do you realize the impression you're making here?"

"Fuck impressions," said Ritchie.

"Oooh, language," said Chance, feigning shock.

"Mortals," said Salonian. "By Mab's grace, have you no self-respect?" He was tall and gaunt, with a narrow, vulnerable face and dark, innocent eyes. The hand with which he held his coffee cup was huge and battered, making me wonder what he did for a living. This didn't seem the best moment to ask.

"Oh, right," said Melanie McGraw. "Like an elf outside Faerie is any better?"

"Elves anywhere are better," said Chance. "Just ask them. They'll be glad to tell you. And tell you, and tell you, and tell you." He glanced sideways at me and I suddenly realized what they were doing: they were like a roomful of little children insulting each other more to impress the big kids than because their hearts were in it.

That was fine with me. There was a good chance they'd forget themselves enough to let something useful slip if they kept at it. Assuming, of course, that any of them knew anything useful; but I assumed that someone in Fey Valley did. I was positive the thing that had nearly knocked me into the stream last night was no Bigfoot or any other outlandish creature, but only an ordinary human, elf, or halfling.

"We are not always like this," said Kyriander. "Really. Occasionally some of us seem quite mature."

"I doubt not you might like to see that demonstrated," said Salonian. "It grieves me to say you had best not wait upon the event, for it will be long in coming."

"Sculptors," said Ritchie, in a tone intended to give offense. He looked at me. "Go look at his fountain in the clearing west of the Hall before you decide to give credence to anything he says."

"I think I've seen it, if you mean the nymph on a mound of skulls." I looked at Salonian in shock, trying to reconcile those big, scarred hands with their fragile creation.

"It is disabled," Salonian said hastily. "Please judge it not in its present state."

"Oh, pooh," said Chance. "It's as effective without

the water as with." He looked at me with malicious interest. "What did you think of it?"

"It's horrible," I said involuntarily.

Salonian beamed at me. "Thank you very much, Miss Lavine. I see you appreciate my intent."

"I'm not just sure 'appreciate' would be the word I'd choose," I said.

His smile broadened. "Thank you," he repeated, quite as though I'd said something complimentary. It was a disarming smile, naively delighted, completely at odds with the monstrous cynicism of his work.

"I think you have her adequately horrified, Salonian," Kyriander said, and turned to me. "Have you finished eating? Will you walk with me?"

"I need to choose somewhere to stay, first," I said. "And see about getting some laundry done."

"Most of the cottages have laundry facilities," he said, and paused, taking it in. "Laundry? But how is this? You've only just arrived."

"I'm afraid I had a little accident on the path last night."

"What sort of accident?"

"Your Trouble tried to push me into the creek." I tried to watch them all as I said it, but if anyone gave evidence of anything but surprise and mild alarm, I missed it. "That was on the path to Finandiel and Cuthbern's cottage," I said when they'd calmed down. "Where have the other manifestations been?"

"On the other path," said Kyriander.

"Whatever chased me started right beside the fountain," said Rosetta, "which is partly why it frightened me, of course, because when I see it I can't help thinking of all those skulls in Taiwan, or do I mean Cambodia, you know, after that military coup or maybe it was a war, and they were trying to identify all the dead, I'm sure it was one of those Asian countries, or I suppose it might have been in South America." She looked thoughtful.

"Our cottage is across the road," said Melanie, "and Dorina saw whatever it was right at our window."

"Yet the music I heard was halfway across the valley from there," said Galinda. "Nearer Maerian's mansion."

"And Tim saw a stranger behind their house, which is across the road from here," said Kyriander.

"Things have gone missing from homes all over the valley," said Ariana. "If you're looking for a central location, you won't find it."

6

Kyriander and I stepped outside into cool, silent shadows. In daylight I could see that the valley was oddly tidy, as in a fairy story. The parking lot was filigreed with sunlight. Redwood forest surrounded it, with little deadfall and no weedy undergrowth anywhere. The bright green of bracken and sword fern made patterns against the red-brown of tree trunks and leaf-carpeted soil.

Behind the Hall, across the stream, the land rose sharply, forested slopes soaring green and tawny and golden toward numinous hilltops where ravens barked. Sunlight gilded the crest of the forest canopy above us against the lucent spring sky. Finandiel had said his cabin was visible from the Hall, but try as I might I couldn't make out even a glint of sun on a window in that direction.

On the other side, across the road, the forest was deeper and I could not see even to the place where the land tilted upward, though I knew it wasn't far. And nearer, where the path led to houses between the road and the stream, what I had mistaken for weedy underbrush the night before was pampered plantings of shade-tolerant garden flowers mixed with wild garlic, oxalis, and the ubiquitous bracken.

It looked as artlessly natural as anywhere in the Oakland hills; but aside from the occasional suspiciously tidy windfall, very little of it must have been as nature made it. "Good God," I said involuntarily. "How much do you guys spend on landscaping?"

Kyriander chuckled. "Much," he said. "But can you doubt the value?"

"It's beautiful," I said. "Where are the empty cabins?"

Kyriander led me past trailing trumpet vine onto the path. "That troubles you?" he said.

"What troubles me? Gardening?"

"Ostentatious spending."

I shrugged. "It's none of my business."

"They seek only to make it more homelike," he said.

"Who? Seek to make what more homelike?"

"The elves. They seek to make Fey Valley more like Faerie," he said. "They know they cannot succeed. But they make the effort, because they miss their home."

"If they're homesick, why do they stay?"

He looked at me. "There are as many reasons as there are elves here. You surprise me."

"I don't like elves," I said by way of explanation.

"I know," he said.

We walked on in thorny silence. The path was delineated by young aromatic fir and redwoods, bracken fern, scattered patches of oxalis and wild gloxinia, and no poison oak anywhere that I could see. Doubtless the gardeners eradicated it along with unsightly weeds and fallen branches.

Salonian's fountain, when we reached it, was as fantastic and as unnerving by day as it had been by moonlight. We paused at the edge of the sunlit clearing to look at it, and I had the feeling it made Kyriander as uncomfortable as it did me. After a long moment he shook his head slowly. "Unfortunate man," he said, more to himself than to me.

"Who? Salonian? Why?"

He seemed surprised to notice that I was still with him. "It is a long story. We will leave it for a later time. Come. There is an empty cottage just up the slope here." He led me to a narrow side path I had not noticed the night before.

We threaded our way between weedy young Scotch broom heavy with scented yellow blossoms, onto a narrow path of Corsican mint. The strong scent of it filled the air, drowning out even the pervasive oil of eucalyptus that penetrated everywhere in this valley.

"Kyri, are you angry?" I said, feeling shy.

"No," he said, not looking at me.

The forest closed in around us, bushes and vines shutting out all but a few blinding pillars of light. The ground underfoot was partly paved with great broken slabs of flagstone. The mint gave way, in the shade, to mounds of dark green moss. I could hear the stream somewhere ahead of us, the water burbling merrily over sunwarmed stones.

"Okay," I said. "If that's the way you want it."

He ignored me. The forest opened out again, letting in broad streamers of sunlight. We reached a wooden footbridge, this one flat rather than arched, its base at both ends crowded with nodding yellow oxalis basking in the sun. Kyriander stepped onto it, still ignoring me, his boots echoing hollowly on the battered wood. I looked past him at the steep slope on the other side of the creek. There were fern-shrouded stair steps there, made of railroad ties and boulders, forming a path between riotous banks of wildflowers into the live oak forest above. I thought I saw the glitter of a window among the crowding trees, but I couldn't be sure.

"Is there only one house up this way?"

"Yes." He led the way up the stairs between drooping ferns.

"Why did you want to come out with me if you don't want to talk?"

He moved silently away from me. I trudged up the uneven stairs behind him, feeling increasingly cross. On one side the ferns gave way unexpectedly to thick blackberry vines heavily dusted with blossoms: in a month or two they would be loaded with delicious black berries. They looked wild and untended, yet not a single shoot intruded on the path.

I didn't see the house we were approaching till I stepped onto the top stair, realized there were no more, and lifted my head. We were on a mossy landing at the foot of wooden stairs up to a porch that jutted out into sunlight over the ravine. Comfortable outdoor chairs with brightly patterned cushions were arranged on it at the best vantage points.

Kyriander was watching me, smiling a little. "I knew you would like it," he said.

"Have I said that?" I asked sourly.

"You need not," he said. "Go on up. I think you'll like the inside too." He gestured to let me past him, and I went.

Half the porch was roofed for foul weather, and the other half an open deck from which one could see the valley from end to end. I could even make out parts of the road snaking down the far valley wall. But most of the view was of treetops: all the paths were hidden under the forest canopy. A splash of frothy yellow caught my eye: an acacia stretching up above the live oak and manzanita, clouds of blossoms glowing against the green backdrop.

"It's beautiful," I said.

Kyriander came up the steps behind me and opened the front door. "It is one of the smaller cabins," he said, "but I thought you would have little need of more space."

I tore myself away from the view to step inside. The living room was large, bare-floored, the walls paneled in knotty pine and broken by many large clear-glass windows. The ones in front looked out over the porch or the forest, while the ones at the sides were intimately shaded by bushes and vines.

The furniture was utilitarian but attractive, covered in sturdy fabrics patterned in greens and blues. There was a little kitchenette at one end with all the modern accoutrements—no wood-burning cookstove for me—and a windowed back door dappled with shadows. Kyriander moved to open another door, exposing a big shady bedroom with a picture window overlooking the valley, and a bright, clean bathroom off that.

Even the bathroom had a big window opening onto

that sweeping view. It made sense: no one could see in from below. "It's perfect," I said.

"The laundry facilities are in a shed out back," he said, leading me toward the back door. The shed held a modern washer and dryer, side by side under a dusty window. "The electrical wiring for the valley is run underground," he said. "Once it ran through the trees, but two years ago we had it buried." He looked away from me into the trees, mildly bored, as though I were a stranger to whom he was showing a house he hoped to sell.

His mercurial moods were bewildering. I went back inside and stood at the front window. The porch was narrow at that point, so it blocked very little of the view. He had followed me, his footsteps solid on the wooden floor. I said without turning, "Thank you for showing me the house. It's very nice."

"You're welcome," he said. I could feel him standing at a little distance behind me, looking over my shoulder.

"I don't understand you," I said.

"I know," he said. "I'm sorry."

"It was you who left me, Kyriander Stone," I said. "I needed you, and you walked away from me without a word."

"The children needed me. They must come first."

"They didn't prevent you from saying good-bye."

"It is but a word. You knew how I felt."

"I didn't. That's the point."

"I could not have told you, then. A word would have told you nothing my actions had not."

"Your actions told me you had no further use for me."

He hesitated. "You use words advisedly," he said at last. "I know that of you. Do you say you felt used?"

"Yes, I say it. Of course I felt used. You walked away when the job was done."

Another hesitation, before he said slowly, stiffly, "I was . . . attracted. To you. But the children came first. What could I do?"

"Say good-bye."

"Good-bye," he said, and left without another word.

I wanted to say, "I meant *then*, not now!" but all I did was step aside to let him pass, and watch with a surprising sense of desolation as he retreated down the stairs and disappeared beneath a spreading live oak tree. A butterfly fumbling among the blackberry blossoms rose into the air at his passing and fluttered clumsily like a scrap of yellow paper caught in the wind.

There was a lock in the front door, with the key in it; I turned it and put the key in my pocket, then followed Kyriander down the stairs. He must have gone in the other direction; I didn't see him anywhere on the way to my car. I scowled at Salonian's fountain in passing, and was entirely unmoved by either it or the bright mounds of oxalis and trillium at its feet. In the distance I heard a dirt bike shattering the late-morning silence.

I got my groceries from the car and hauled them back to the cabin, put them away, and trudged back to the Hall to get my suitcase and dirty clothes. When I came back downstairs the dirt bike was on the road, approaching the Hall, its unmuffled engine so loud the big dog napping in the doorway lumbered to its feet with a grunt of distress and retreated, tail tucked, to the safety of the kitchen.

An inarticulate bellow from inside the Hall was nearly drowned by the revving engine and clash of gears as the dirt bike screamed into view, added insult to injury by beeping its horn, and zoomed out of sight again, the noise mercifully diminishing with distance. "I'll kill that little son of a bitch!" Ritchie Morita ran onto the porch to shake his fist dramatically after the dirt bike.

"Someone you know?" I asked him.

He noticed me with some surprise, paused to look me over in apparent revulsion, snapped, "Ask Charlotte," and went back inside.

Someone Charlotte knew, then. That was interesting. Considering her prim and judgmental nature, I wouldn't have thought she would be acquainted with a dirt biker.

Then I remembered Gary, her teenage son. I looked back at the empty road in sudden speculation, my own prejudices coming right to the fore: teenagers, dirt bikes, Trouble. I resolved to look into the matter of Tim and Charlotte's offspring. For starters, if that was he who just drove past, why wasn't he in school?

But I didn't go inside and ask Charlotte. I started to, but then realized Kyriander might come to the Hall at any moment, and I was overwhelmed with a sudden fierce desire to be out of this valley and away.

I took my clothes back to the cabin, shoved them inside, locked the door again, and returned to the parking lot, half-running. The urgency of my need to leave embarrassed me, but I didn't let that stop me. There would be grocery stores in Moraga, just outside the valley. I didn't need more groceries; but shopping made a good excuse to go.

7

The road out of Fey Valley was a tunnel under the forest canopy, broken occasionally by bright splashes of sunlight where the trees opened up briefly before closing in again, seemingly thicker than before. By the time I rounded the final curve that led out of the valley I wanted sunlight almost as much as I had wanted just to get away.

I was granted both: the forest dwindled on the last slopes until, immediately outside the gate between Fey Valley and the rest of the world, it gave way entirely to a broader inland valley whose acres of grasslands and orchards lay baking in the midday sun. The narrow valley road joined Orinda-Moraga Way in the pear orchards just outside Moraga. I paused at the stop sign to roll down both front windows and bask in the warm breeze that flowed through the car.

Little traffic passed on the main road, and none on the Fey Valley road. In the rearview mirror, the gate to the valley stood shrouded in gloom, mysterious and forbidding. I pulled out onto Orinda-Moraga Way with a vague sense of having escaped my doom.

Moraga was a small village, where life proceeded at a lazy, country pace. I pulled into the lot next to the combination grocery store and gas station and watched suntanned matrons maneuver shopping carts through the new automatic doors set awkwardly in the old wooden wall. Signs in the big front window advertised laundry soap, toilet paper, cuts of beef, inexpensive vegetables, and overpriced fruits; they would be imported at this time of year, and not as good as the later local-grown varieties.

I wondered suddenly whether my new cabin had laundry soap, dish soap, or even toilet paper. I hadn't looked. Maybe this shopping excursion wasn't a mere pretense after all. I'd want bath soap, and shampoo, and a dish sponge. Maybe paper towels, since I hadn't brought any cloth ones. Come to that, I hadn't brought any bath towels. Luckily this was the sort of one-stop country store that would probably offer anything I might need.

Feeling oddly encouraged by this train of thought, I rolled up the windows, locked the doors, and climbed out of the car. A ponytailed young mother in jogging shorts and a tee shirt advertising an elfrock band came out of the store pushing a double jogging stroller that held two infants she looked too young to have borne. She had fastened two heavy plastic bags of groceries to the push bar so they hung swaying behind the seat. I wondered whether, if she started jogging, they would collide with the infants' heads.

She smiled at me as I locked the car door. "Good morning," she said in a small, ridiculously cheerful voice.

"Morning," I said heartily. Ah, the country life, where everybody speaks to anybody in the hope of a little fresh gossip.

"Warm, isn't it?" she said.

"Very," I said. "But I'm glad of it: I just came out of Fey Valley. It's chilly back there in the trees."

She paused, looking very much impressed. "Fey Valley? Do you live there?"

"Just temporarily. Do you know it?"

She shook her head. "Not really. I mean I've never been there. But everybody knows about Fey Valley, you know? Are you an artist?"

"Nope. Private investigator."

Her eyes widened. "Wow, what an interesting job that must be. Are you there about the Trouble?"

I was surprised to hear an outsider call it by the valley residents' name for it, though I shouldn't have been. In a place like this, everybody would know everybody else's business. "Yeah. What have you heard about it?"

"That they're *haunted*." She said it with simple, child-like pleasure. "Are they really?"

I smiled. "Well, I doubt if it's ghosts."

"Bigfoot, maybe?"

"No, I really doubt that too."

"Elves, then," she said with satisfaction. "You'd expect it, really; it's only natural that an elf with an artistic bent would wander the woods at night, singing."

"Um," I said, trying to imagine the comfort-loving elves I knew abandoning their warm, dry lodgings to wander the damp, chilly nighttime forest. "Sure."

"That's what I told Paul. He's my husband. He thought it was kid gangs, but he blames everything on kid gangs. I don't think they'd come all the way out here into the country, do you?" She didn't leave me room to answer. "No, I figured it was the elves right along. You can't trust them, you know. Well, of course you know. Everyone knows that. They're devious. Fallen angels, Evans-Wentz called them. Have you read him?"

"Yeah," I said, leaning against the car, looking at her infants. "What pretty children." They were parboiled little monsters, but as far as I could tell that was what infants were supposed to look like. It's always risky to comment on children, since their doting parents may natter on forever about them; but I figured it would disarm her, and Fey Valley would prove a fascinating enough topic that I wouldn't have any trouble getting her back to it after the obligatory infant-worship.

She rewarded me with a blinding smile. "Oh, thank you," she said. "Little Paul and Paula. They're just three months old. And they're such good babies. And friendly. Smile for the pretty lady, children."

The infants glared balefully.

"Aren't they just the sweetest things?" said their fond parent. "Never a moment's trouble. They're very advanced for their age, you know. They're already on solid food, though of course I'm nursing them too."

There wasn't much I could say to that. "They're darling," I lied. "Twins?"

"Yes," she said. "Fraternal." This in a confiding tone, as though I might have thought them identical despite their sex-specific names. Maybe she didn't know identical twins were always the same sex. Or maybe she just thought I didn't know.

"That's very nice," I said inadequately.

"Are there many children in Fey Valley?" she asked. "I feel sorry for the little things, growing up *there*." She made it sound like a den of iniquity.

"It's actually quite a nice valley," I said noncommittally.

"I'm sure it is." She didn't sound sure at all. "But all those artists. And *elves*."

I didn't know how to respond to that. Apparently elves were all depraved monsters. Which I admit, from some points of view, is pretty nearly true. They're also people, and most of them have a strong sense of honor to balance their utter lack of conscience. It doesn't always look like honor to us, incomprehensibly alien and elvish as it is, but it's there, and it's real, and it has kept their society from chaos for thousands of years. "There's that," I said. "But of course, some of the children are elves too."

"Truebloods?" she asked in surprise, and didn't wait for my response. "Surely not. I thought there would only be halfling children. And humans, of course, poor babies. There oughta be a law."

"Against children?" I blurted inadvertently.

She laughed as though I'd made a joke. "No, of course not. I meant against raising the poor things mixed in with elves. It's a disgrace. Who knows what kind of values they'll grow up with? Paul was telling me just the other day about this study he read. You know, about raising human children with elves. How they'll all turn out to be sociopaths. And I don't doubt it," she added contentiously.

"No, I'm sure you don't." It seemed unlikely that I was going to get any useful information from her, so I pushed myself away from the car and turned toward the store. "It's been nice talking to you," I said, "but I have to get some shopping done." I smiled insincerely. "Have a nice day."

After so much time standing in the midday sun, I was grateful for the store's air-conditioning. The glass doors swished closed behind me, shutting little Paul and Paula and their bigoted mother outside in the golden light. I blinked under the store's fluorescents, waiting for my eyes to adjust.

"Did Connie tell you all about how her babies are eating solid food?" asked a laughing female voice. "I swear to God, if that woman tells me one more time how advanced those brats are for their age, I think I'll strangle her."

I realized I was standing next to the checkout counter, and that the woman behind it had a full view of the parking lot and everything that went on in it. She was a thin, middle-aged, cheerful woman with kind eyes and a ready smile.

"Was that Connie? She did mention how advanced her twins are," I said, glancing back out the door. Connie and the twins had turned and were jogging down the sidewalk toward the town. The shopping bags on the handlebar didn't quite bump the infants. Maybe if she turned a sharp corner they would.

The woman behind the counter made an indelicate sound. "Advanced, my eye," she said. "Fact is Connie couldn't make enough milk for the poor mites, what with her diets and her food fads and her exercise regimes, and that's the truth. Hi, I'm Becky. Let me know if you need any help."

"Rosie," I said. "Rose Lavine. Thanks. I just moved into one of the Fey Valley cottages, so I need to pick up a bunch of essentials."

She looked interested. "Artist?" she asked.

"No: private investigator," I said.

"Ah." She nodded. "Come about the Trouble?"

"Got it in one," I said.

"It's about time they called someone in," she said.

"It's frightening the children, and that's a fact. Now, did you look around your cottage to see what you had already, honey? Because I know they're supposed to be stocked with the basics: toilet paper, towels, soaps, that sort of thing. So unless you have strong brand preferences, you probably don't need as much as you might have been thinking."

"Oh," I said. "Thanks. But you've just done yourself out of some profits, you know."

She shrugged. "Business is business," she said, "and I'll take your money quick enough if you want to spend it. But I don't hold with trying to sell people things they don't need."

"That's a rare attitude."

"Ain't it the truth? I could wish more folks were like me in that. Though they'd do well not to be like me some other ways I could mention." She laughed easily. "But I won't. Lord knows I got my vices, but there's no call to advertise them, is what I say."

My eyes were fully adjusted now, and I was surprised I had found the store gloomy. It seemed bright, clean, and cheerful, its battered wooden floors and Formica shelves lending it a distinctly fifties air that the ancient advertising posters and hand-drawn pricing signs did nothing to dispel. I took my shopping cart up and down the aisles, comforted by the familiar ritual, and put more things into the basket than I was really likely to need. They carried my favorite brand of shampoo, and sweetly scented bath soap, and lotion in a pretty bottle that I hadn't tried before. As I had hoped, they had towels; but I took Becky's word for it and didn't buy any. I did buy paper towels, on the theory that I could use them at home if I didn't need them in Fey Valley.

There were only a few other customers, and none of them spoke beyond a friendly greeting. When I brought the cart to the front of the store, Becky shook her head over the number of my purchases. "You figuring on a long stay?" she asked.

"I don't know," I said, feeling foolish. "I guess I did get a little carried away, didn't I?"

She shrugged. "You want it, I'll sell it," she said.

"What the hell," I said. "If I don't need any of this, I can take it home with me. Or give it to Charlotte to use in the Hall."

"That poor woman," said Becky, beginning to ring up my purchases.

"Charlotte?" I asked in surprise.

"Yeah, Charlotte," she said, looking at me intently. "You met all the residents yet?"

"I don't think so."

She rang up another item. "Well, hell. Even so, Tim'd likely be on his best behavior in front of a stranger. Though he can't stick to it, and that's the truth." She shook her head. "That poor woman waits on that man hand and foot, *and* on his spoiled-brat son, and in her spare time she waits on the whole damn community with her meals and tending the cottages and doing the shopping and all, and what thanks does she get?" It seemed to be a rhetorical question; she didn't wait for me to answer. "Not that you can blame them. That woman never stands up for herself. I've seen her in here when she was like to die with a cold or even the flu, and nobody out in that damn valley even noticed. Not as long as she keeps up with her work, they don't.

"Which, seeing they're elves and artists and she ain't, prob'ly seems fitting to them." She shook her head again. "They're all right, as far as that goes: decent enough folks, and meaning no trouble to anybody. But they got no kindness for plain folk like us and Charlotte, and that's the truth." She rang up the last item, named the total, and began bagging. "You need help getting this out to your car?"

I wondered whether she would abandon the counter to help me herself if I asked. Very possibly she would have. "No, I can manage," I said, counting out the money. "Thanks, though."

She plopped the first bag onto the counter and began filling a second. "What I think, if you want to know, now that Swilhurst Associates wants to buy the place for a resort or whatever it is, the residents plain ought to sell. They'll never get a better offer, and that's the truth."

"But if they want to stay there?" I said.

She finished bagging my groceries and came around the counter to set the bags in my shopping cart. "Why would they? The money they're being offered, they could buy some other valley somewhere. Maybe farther from towns, you know what I mean? They could prob'ly get a bigger place, more secluded, *and* rebuild all their cottages with the money they're offered."

"You'd lose some business," I said.

"Oh, yes. And Scotland Yard would lose their contract, unless they wanted to follow the community to the new valley, which I happen to know they probably wouldn't, because the MacLeods have been here in Moraga for three generations now." At my look of confusion, she said, "They're Scotland Yard. They do the landscaping in Fey Valley."

"Oh. It's very nicely done."

"Yes, they do good work," she said.

"Can you tell me where to find them?"

"Sure." She did. "But they won't talk to you about their clients. Not without permission."

"When you said the Fey Valley people should move, did you mean you wish they would?"

"Oh, no, it's not that I *want* them to move; I just think if I were them, I would move." She saw what I was getting at. "I guess, having talked to Connie, you'd have to know there is some bigotry in town." She shrugged. "You know how people are about elves, and the artists don't help matters any with their airs and graces. When we see them at all. But I'm sure that's not the source of your Trouble: nobody here would do that sort of thing."

Unfortunately, the bad guys are always somebody's friends and neighbors. They're somebody's family. And we always want to believe that "nobody here would do that sort of thing."

8

I drove around Moraga a bit before heading back to Fey Valley, but all I saw was just what one would expect of a little country town with weedy streets: some individual houses, an apartment building or two, subdivisions of ranch-style homes, occasionally a fine old Victorian house, all with neatly tended lawns, and dusty vans parked in their drives.

The grade school and high school were across the street from each other at the far end of town from Fey Valley. I had asked Finandiel about schooling for Fey Valley kids: there was a one-room public school in the valley for the younger ones, which the residents had fought to keep when the state said the population was too small to support it. The older children were bused to the high school here.

Curious, I pulled into the high-school parking lot, not sure what I was looking for. The cars were what one would expect in a high-school parking lot. The teachers' were without exception cheap and battered. The students' ranged from ancient trucks to brand-new sports cars.

A section at one side was roped off for motor scooters. Half a dozen motorcycles shared the space with them. I wondered whether the one I'd heard that morning in Fey Valley was there. There was no way to tell. In the hot sun, they would all feel as warm as if they'd just been parked.

I pulled back onto the street and followed Becky's directions to the Scotland Yard office. It was in a small old wooden building with a neat little porch decorated with plant pots, flower boxes, and hanging baskets full of lush vegetation. The office itself was heavily decorated with houseplants: spider plants throwing their plantlets out from hanging baskets, philodendrons piled like little bushes in ceramic pots, and even orchids, heavy with blossom, in the windowsills. The floor was raw wood with a big Oriental carpet in the center, the walls were paneled with wood, and the furniture was beautiful antique oak.

The only desk was a big old rolltop at which an earnest-looking halfling leaned over a pile of correspondence. She looked up at me with a chilly smile and tucked her hair behind one pointed ear. "May I help you?"

"I hope so: I'm Rose Lavine, private investigator." I handed her my card. "The Fey Valley Association hired me to look into, um."

"The Trouble," she said helpfully. "Yes?"

"I'd like to interview your people who work there," I said. "They may have seen something that will help me."

"If they knew anything about the Trouble, they would have told the police," she said, and turned back to her correspondence.

"They might not know they know it," I said. "I'd like to talk to them."

"I'm sorry, they're not available just now."

"Okay, could you tell me where I might find them?"

"No."

I kept at it for a while, but I didn't get anything more out of her. She wouldn't even give me the names of the workers assigned to Fey Valley. She said they wouldn't talk about their clients, and she stuck to it. It didn't matter that I didn't want her to talk about their clients, or that their clients had hired me to get the information I was asking for. She wasn't even willing to say whether, if I returned with authorization from the Fey Valley Association, she'd be any more forthcoming. All in all it was a very frustrating waste of time.

She did unbend enough to direct me to a gas station

that had a pay phone. Shannon answered on the first ring. "Any luck with Swilhurst Associates?" I asked her.

"I have a lunch date with a Marilyn Sanford tomorrow," she said. "I'm not sure anything will come of it, though. Swilhurst Associates is fronting for somebody, and I'm not sure even this Sanford woman knows who. How 'bout you? Things okay out there?"

"Pretty much," I said. "Somebody tried to push me into the creek last night. No harm done. I'm assuming that was the Trouble, but I couldn't ID him."

"It's a he?"

"Actually I don't even know that much. I didn't get a look at him at all. It's not a ghost or a Bigfoot. I'm sure of that much."

She chuckled. "Well, it's early days yet. You're sure you weren't hurt?"

"My pride took a severe blow. I'm fine otherwise."

"Did they give you a nice cabin?"

"A beautiful cabin," I said. "The whole valley is spectacular. You should come out and see."

"I might," she said. "But I'll see what I can learn here, first."

Driving back to Fey Valley, I felt a little better, and I'd been long enough in the sun that I welcomed the shade when the forest closed in around me. Even at the edge of the valley, where the trees were mostly madrone and manzanita with plenty of room between them for weeds to grow, they didn't. The grasses were unmowed, and sprinkled with patches of mustard and poppies, but thanks to the work of Scotland Yard there was no leggy Queen Anne's lace, no coarse-blossomed salsify, no impenetrable banks of thorns.

It occurred to me that the Scotland Yard workers must know the valley better than anyone else. If they hadn't found any clues to the Trouble's origin or identity, there must be nothing to find.

Fat lot of good that did me if I couldn't get them to talk. I would ask the residents for some sort of authorization to take to Scotland Yard, but I didn't hold out much hope it would loosen that prissy halfling's tongue any. Maybe I could find out by some other means which workers were assigned out here, and interview them without going through their office. Charlotte might know. Or Kyriander.

But I didn't much want to seek out Kyriander just now. The scene this morning had been too strange. I'd thought we could just slip back into the relationship we'd had before, but I'd been wrong. Too much had happened to both of us since then.

I pulled into the Hall parking lot and turned off the engine. Stillness fell around me. After a moment I became aware of the quiet rush of the stream over stones, and the harsh cry of a crow somewhere not far away, and the steady clatter of Ritchie Morita's typewriter.

"*Damn* it," I said helplessly. My voice seemed muffled by the stillness around me, as though there were a spell of silence cast over the valley. For a fractional instant I wondered whether there was; then I laughed at my citified thinking. Forests generate their own magic. They need no one to do it for them.

I rolled up the windows, got out of the car, locked the door, and closed it. The creek whispered secrets to the rocks. Bright coins of sunlight dappled the parking lot. There was nothing among my groceries that wouldn't keep unrefrigerated for a time, so I did what I should have done that morning: I took the path toward Finandiel and Cuthbern's cottage, looking for some sign of whoever or whatever pushed me into the creek last night.

In daylight the path entrance was a leafy and inviting tunnel, bright with spring flowers. When the path opened out on the other side, the bushes and tree trunks that had loomed so mysteriously last night were quite ordinary. The stream glinted with sunlight, the rocky bottom clearly visible through the quick, shallow water.

I had not realized last night till I was pushed into it how deeply the stream had cut into the earth here in its brisk rush to the sea. The banks were heavily overhung with delicate creepers, but beneath their matted leaves I could see the crumbling steepness of the slope. I'd been lucky to fall at a place where I could climb out as easily as I did.

Nor was it at all difficult to find the place where I had fallen. The marks were clearly evident. A section of the bank had fallen away with me, nibbling at the edge of the path. Only the living roots of a redwood had prevented worse erosion. New roots were bared, with clumps of damp soil still clinging to them. In time the path would take on a broader curve to avoid the encroaching edge. The redwood itself would fall, its vast roots lifting out of the loosened soil, its broad trunk forming a house-sized bridge across the little stream. Would Scotland Yard tidy that up too? Or would they just plant the root ball with bracken and encourage the velvet moss on its rough bark?

The bushes in which I had seen and felt the Trouble hiding were actually crowded young Douglas fir. I pushed my way between their springy branches, searching the ground, but found nothing. Not even my own footprints. Neither I nor whoever had shared the darkness with me had left any useful trace that I could find. Some scuffed leaves, a clump of mud, and a broken twig or two—nothing that meant anything to me.

After ten minutes' search I gave up and returned to the path. Dauntless forest tracker that I was, I couldn't even tell that Finandiel and Cuthbern had ever been this way; there might have been no one on this path since the dawn of time.

Except, of course, that someone had to have been here, to make the path in the first place. I sat down on the edge of the bank and stared absently at the patterns of light and shadow on the water spilling from pool to pool below. There was a eucalyptus cap under my hand. I picked it up and broke it, inhaling the cough-drop scent of it mixed with damp loam and water and sun. A mourning dove grieved somewhere nearby. The water whispered dark secrets among the rocks.

"Rose?"

I looked up in surprise. Kyriander was coming toward me from the direction of the Hall, his footsteps, elflike, perfectly silent: if he hadn't spoken, I wouldn't have known he was there till he was right beside me. "Hi, Kyri." I would have scrambled to my feet to meet him, but he gestured for me to stay.

"I thought I saw you come this way." He sat beside me, long legs dangling, and stared at the water. His hair veiled his face from me, but I could see the tip of one pointed ear. I didn't know what to say to him, so I said nothing. He picked up a fallen leaf and crushed it to dust between his slender, graceful fingers. "I'm sorry," he said.

I shrugged inelegantly. "Me too."

After a long, silent moment, he said, "I read about your elfrock star, what is his name? Killer?" The last fragments of leaf fell sparkling in the light, past his knees and the edge of the bank and down toward the creek.

"How did you know . . . ?" I broke off, oddly reluctant to say it aloud.

"Lilie told me about you and him." He shook his head, long hair swinging gracefully. There were signs of old dye in it, where he'd done trendy green and blue streaks and then not bothered to renew the color. "She should have told me sooner." He dusted his fingers and clasped them on his knees, still not looking at me.

"How did she know? I didn't think it was public knowledge."

"A paragraph in a newspaper: she showed me." Unclasping his hands, he looked around helplessly as though uncertain what to do with them. "It said only that you went to Hawaii with him this last winter." He crumbled another eucalyptus leaf. "I suppose she meant to make me jealous."

"I'm sorry." I didn't really know whether I was apologizing for Lilie's behavior or for mine.

He shrugged. "No matter."

"Something's troubling you," I said, not quite asking.

He hesitated. "I fear something ails Lilie," he said. "She seems frail of health, and wild of mood—yet she will discuss it not with me."

I shifted mental gears with difficulty. "Frail in health how?"

"I cannot say, exactly. Small matters. Her appetite is not what it was. She eats no breakfast, and seldom lunch. Only dinner, and that small."

"Is she losing weight? Maybe she thinks she needs to diet? Girls her age get odd body images, and try to correct things that aren't wrong."

He gestured helplessly. "I know not. How would I know?"

"Have you taken her to a doctor?"

"She will not go. She insists her health is fine."

"Maybe it is. Maybe it's just normal hormones. Adolescence is a difficult time." I remembered suddenly what was one of the most difficult aspects of adolescence for a girl, and how awkward that might be if one's only parent substitute were an older brother. "Has she started her periods? Would she talk to you about that? Does she know what it's about, and how to cope?"

"Yes," he said. "We had the onset of her menses last year. We coped reasonably well, I think." He made a wry face. "Whether she really knows what it's about, I cannot say. I have made the information available. The more so, since she began to fancy herself in love with Gary."

"Charlotte's son? The one with the motorcycle?"

"Yes, he." He sighed. Sunlight sparkled on the water. "Is this where you were pushed?" he asked.

I accepted the change in subject without comment. He'd told me what he wanted me to know, about himself more than about Lilie. It was as close to an apology as I would get. And indeed, I wasn't sure who owed whom an apology anyway. "Yes," I said. "From those bushes. But I've searched already. There's no sign anybody's ever been this way but me."

He nodded. "It is ever so. Shall I show you where the Trouble has been sighted?"

"Thanks," I said. "That might help. At least maybe I can get a better feel for the lay of the land."

He took my hand to help me to my feet. "There is no correlation anyone can find," he said.

"No, but that reminds me: has anyone talked to the Scotland Yard people?"

"The gardeners?" He steadied me while I dusted off the seat of my pants. "Why would we?"

"Because they might have seen something," I said. "The receptionist wouldn't give me any information without an okay from the Association, but those workers must be all over this place. If there's a clue loose on the ground, I'd think they'd have found it. If no one else has talked to them, I want to. Maybe even if somebody has."

He looked at me as though I'd evidenced genius—or complete idiocy. "Now that," he said, "is precisely why we needed you. Let us investigate."

9

Nothing came of it, though: we couldn't find any of the gardeners. They were paid to stay out of sight, and they did it as well as they did the rest of their job. I would just have to ask the Association for a letter of authorization, and try the Scotland Yard office again.

Meantime Kyriander showed me where incidents had been reported. We turned off from the main path onto one that climbed up over a dreaming hillside, where live oak spread gnarled branches across grassy meadows clotted with colorful blooms. When we came even with a large thicket of broom bent under the weight of its blossoms, blocking all view of the valley below, he turned abruptly off the path and led me through a narrow gap between the trees.

A tumble of hot gray boulders had been cunningly arranged, by nature or by Scotland Yard, into a shelf of sun-washed seats, completely hidden from the path. It was a cozy, private nook, with a breathtaking view down through the valley toward Moraga, of towering redwoods with occasional splashes of broom or acacia between. A solitary hawk soared effortlessly against the brilliant sky.

"Lilie says she was seated here," said Kyriander. He dropped down onto a huge, smooth slab and pointed into the valley below us. "And that she saw the Bigfoot there, by the stream."

I sat beside him to see where he pointed. The sun-baked stone warmed the back of my legs. From this distance the creek was just an infrequent glimmer in the shadows, and I couldn't make out the banks at all through the shifting leaves. "Either Bigfoot is even bigger than I'd imagined," I said, "or she can't have had a very clear view."

"I fear she may have had no view at all," he said. "It has come to my attention that my sister may harbor what Ritchie calls romantic fantasies. I have long known her fondness for melodrama." He turned to me, looking apologetic. "She may only have wished for a share of the attention."

"Or she may have actually seen someone and mistaken it for Bigfoot," I said. "Maybe one of the gardeners. Maybe anybody." A robin landed tamely near us and cocked its head inquisitively. "Maybe we should go down and look where she claims the Bigfoot was; but I can do that later. Where's next?" I said.

The path plunged back down the hillside, and we with it, through tangled manzanita and madrone to another quaint arched bridge over the stream. "If you have a taste for hiking," he said, "we could go out to the mansion; Galinda heard music in that direction. Or—" He glanced at the sky, where the sun was already sliding behind the green western wall of the valley. "You might wish to leave that for another day. Perhaps if I just show you the nearer locations this afternoon? The school is this way; one can see it from the Hall." He gestured. "Many of the children have had interesting encounters near there. And the Camerons' house, where Tim saw the stranger, is past it, and across the road."

"Let's skip the hike," I said, "and do the others in order of convenience from here." I ticked them off on my fingers. "Tim Cameron, Dorina McGraw, the sightings near the school, Rosetta Fulmer—or was that near the fountain? I've probably seen it already, then."

"Well enough: we'll make a circle back toward my house. Will you stop for dinner with us then?"

"Thank you. I'd like that—if you think it won't make Lilie cross."

"She must learn to accommodate others' wishes," he said. "I would have you dine with us."

"Then I will, and thank you." I grinned at him.

"You've been too long among elves; your English is atrophying."

I could see him replaying what he'd said. "So it is," he said, and looked at me. "Does that bother you?"

"I think it's cute."

He made a face. "Then I need not concern myself." He took my hand to lead me on: an unthinking gesture of friendly intimacy as pleasant as it was unexpected. "The paths are so designed that we cannot avoid some backtracking. The McGraws, for example, are alone on their path, and I know of no crosspaths from there. But let us begin with the school. It is through here."

We'd been wandering enough that I'd got thoroughly turned around: where we were standing beside the bridge felt completely isolated from any valley dwellings, but when we'd gone only ten yards or so the crowding fir saplings opened up and I saw that we were almost in the playground of the valley's grade school.

It was built in the same style as the Hall, and looked so much a part of the landscape that even from here, where the trees did not obscure it, I might not have noticed it straightaway were it not for the children squealing with pleasure at being released into the playground for recess.

"Not, perhaps, the best of timing," said Kyriander. "I apologize."

I shrugged. "I can come back and look the place over later. Doubt I'll find anything, anyway. If there was any evidence, the kids will have trampled it by now."

We crossed the road, went through a gap in the fence, and onto a path that snaked its way through bracken and between redwood trunks in such a way that none of it was visible from the road. "The McGraws live at the top of this path," he said, gesturing vaguely ahead of us.

Dorina McGraw was the child who'd seen a shadow on a windowpane. Her parents, Melanie McGraw and Marc Starr, were painters. "Doesn't Marc Starr live there too?"

"Sometimes. I am uncertain whether he lives there at

present." The path widened as the redwoods thinned toward the hillside, and he dropped back to walk beside me. "It is not one of our more stable family groups."

"Will they mind us dropping by like this?"

"Only if Marc is there." He smiled, not pleasantly. "I will tend to that if need be."

But there was no need: no one was home. It was an older cottage than mine, more picturesque, with creepers obscuring the front wall and Scotch broom growing through the porch rail; and more lived-in-looking, with toys strewn on the deck and the one table covered with painting supplies. It looked larger than mine, but it was built in the same style: rough wood constructed at unexpected angles, with a huge porch hanging out over the ravine the path had followed to bring us here.

The ground was steep on the sides facing the hill, and bracken had been left in a wild state right up to the walls, but it might have been possible for someone to approach the bedroom windows. At the right phase of the moon, such an intruder's shadow might be cast on the glass for Dorina to see. But in that case I'd have expected to find some evidence of trespass: crushed ferns, broken branches, even footprints. I found nothing of the sort, though I left enough of my own in the search.

"Perhaps talk of Bigfoot gave the Dorina nightmares," said Kyriander, "and that was all she saw."

"Maybe. Did the resident elves investigate?"

"I recall not," he said.

"They're hiding something," I said, wondering whether he was too.

He looked at me in surprise. "Hiding what?"

"I don't know," I said. "But I mean to find out."

We went back down the long, shady trail almost to the road before he took a turning I hadn't noticed on the way up, and led me away from the ravine, through live oak forest whose fallen leaves crunched underfoot and had an annoying tendency to cling to shoelaces and pant legs. The path was not well beaten. Indeed, I wasn't quite sure it was a path, and not just a shortcut through sun-dappled woods.

We came out on a broad path beside another ravine, having crossed the hump of land between them. Here Kyriander turned uphill again and I followed, feeling rather like a wilderness explorer. The path followed the ravine's edge, curving as needed around trees whose gnarled roots had been exposed by years of foot traffic that wore the path down into a shelflike ribbon on the side of the ravine. Like the one the McGraw house was built over, this was doubtless only a winter runoff, dry in summer, unless there was a year-round spring somewhere above. I couldn't hear flowing water, nor catch any glimpse of sun-sparked silver through the leaves downslope.

"I know not where Tim saw the stranger," said Kyriander. "Near the house, is all he's said."

Before we reached the house, though, we came upon another of the artful nooks the Scotland Yard people created throughout the valley. The path curved past a huge, spreading live oak. As we came around the far side of it, we were facing the hillside. There one live oak drooped a wide branch toward the ground, and lifted it again in a graceful curve that formed a living bench just off the path. The gardeners had cleared away the bracken beneath it and laid down a bright carpet of Corsican mint.

Two flagstone steps led up to the shady seat. I climbed them and sat on the branch. The pungent odor of crushed mint filled the air as Kyriander followed to stand beside me. The young trees on the slope below had been carefully shaped to give a clear view into the ravine. Its walls of rock and scrub were open to the sun, and luminous with crocus, hyacinth, and narcissus blossoms tumbling down the steep slope in every shade and color.

I stared, enchanted. "How in the world do they get these things to grow here?" I asked. "I'd have sworn Corsican mint was delicate and needed, oh, I don't know, more water than you have rainfall in summer, just for starters. And those spring bulbs over there. They shouldn't survive in the wild."

"Think you this is the wild?" he said. "Scotland Yard plans every leaf and stem, here as in all the valley."

"But good heavens. How big is Scotland Yard, anyway? How many people do they devote to just this one valley? Don't they have any other jobs?"

"Many, I should think," he said.

"People?"

"Jobs."

"But this must be so much work."

"I'm sure it is," he said. "Though perhaps not as much as you imagine. They are not mortals, you know."

"Who aren't?"

"The Scotland Yard workers. At least not all of them."

"They're elves?" I said. "But the woman in the grocery store said they'd been living there for generations."

I felt his smile. "Elves have generations too." Before I could protest, he said, "Sorry. But the Scotland Yard people always have a few elves among them. And the whole family is halflings one way and another."

"I thought most halflings didn't have magic."

"That is what we would have you think."

I twisted my neck to look up at him. "What do you mean? Do you have magic?"

He met my gaze, his eyes hooded. "A little."

"You never said."

He shrugged. "It is nothing. Children's tricks."

"It's not children's tricks that tend those flowers."

"No. Most of it is hard, human labor. But there is also magic, believe me."

I looked again at the wall of brilliant blossoms across the way. "Oh, I believe you. But I've always just taken it for granted that the common wisdom about halflings was true, that most of them have no magic."

"Common wisdom is not always wise."

I turned to look at him. He looked all elf again, suddenly a stranger. "I always knew some halflings had magic," I said, "but is it really so many?"

"Most, if they but knew it," he said. "But most are raised by the mortal of their parents, since even the

Truebloods who beget us revile us." He said that without expression, quite as though he weren't speaking of his own mother. "Who is to tell us the secrets of elven ways? Magic is more than having: it is a talent that must be used, a skill that must be honed.

"And even if a halfling's elven parent stays with him, even if that parent takes the time to teach the child, it may not always work. The magic is there, but so is the iron will of mortals that gave this world its name. In most cases the will outweighs the wish, and the magic cannot manifest. Or, if it does, it is only in ways that even the iron of human will does not think to destroy: music, gardening, arts. We all have our little magics." He smiled, a wry little twist of the mouth. "Some is spectacular, some is not."

I stared at the riot of color across the ravine. "This is new. It'll take me a minute to wrap my mind around it. What was that you said about how this world got its name? You mean the human lands, right?"

"The ironworld," he said.

"That's from the old myth about elves being allergic to iron, right?"

"They are allergic to iron," he said. "The iron will of mortals against magic. Primitive peoples believed well enough, but as human civilization grew, so grew your disbelief; magic cannot be measured, quantified, proved. Your science accepts nothing that cannot be objectified. Increasing numbers of mortals believe with increasing confidence that magic is impossible: and so it is, or very nearly, in a world where the will of the people is set against it."

"Iron will. That was it." I looked at him. "I've never heard that theory before."

"It is a weakness of sorts. They do not advertise it. You understand, few halflings have any sort of magic not easily mistaken for a mortal talent. Fewer still are taught to use what they have. And yet fewer are capable of learning it. The iron of the mortal will to disbelieve, to block, to disable magic is within as well as without.

Most halflings are as practical as any mortal, and as willing to deny what cannot be explained by science.

"If magic is involved in the Trouble, and I think it is, you must know that you cannot safely rule out halflings. None of us has the power of a Trueblood, but nor are we helpless cripples, as they would have you believe." He stood abruptly. "Shall we continue?"

But there was no more to be seen at the Camerons' than at the McGraws' house. The Trouble, whatever it was, left no physical evidence anywhere that I could find.

The light was fading when we trudged up the path to Kyriander's cottage, hand in hand, and laughing at some silly thing one of us had said. It would be hours yet till dark, but the sun was long since hidden behind the western hills. The long shadows of late afternoon spread dusk like a thick blanket over all the valley but the farthest hilltops. Those were washed with a golden clarity of light that we stopped to admire whenever the turnings of the path permitted.

It was after one such enraptured pause that, drunk on beauty, turning lazily uphill again through swimming purple shadows, we first heard the jumbled cries of distress and hysteria from his cottage above.

10

"The child is hysterical," said Ariana. "You'll learn nothing useful from her today. Ask her tomorrow when she's feeling less important."

Kyriander might not have heard her. "What did you think you were doing?" he demanded of poor Lilie, whose wrists were tightly bound in clean white gauze where she had cut them.

When we first heard the commotion and ran up the hill to see what was wrong, we found her sobbing and shrieking at Ariana, who was binding her wrists. Since then she had taken a turn at everyone in the room; and since seemingly half the valley's population had got there before we did, that was quite a lot of sobbing and shrieking.

It was my turn, now. She saw me and squealed in fury. "Get her out of here!" she sobbed. "It's not fair, Kyri, it's not. You're going to have an affair with her and I hate her, I hate her!" She had been lying back in a chair, dramatically frail: now she rose up gracefully with one arm extended, finger pointing accusingly at me. "She killed my father!"

Well, that was true enough. At the helpless look Kyriander threw me, I retreated from his living room to the broad porch overlooking the valley, where Lilie couldn't see me. I could still hear her, hurling embittered accusations. Poor desperate child. The hysterics were disingenuous, but the underlying distress was not. Children who are not in pain do not even pretend to suicide.

Ariana put her hand on my shoulder. "Whatever it is," she said, "let it go. It's past. And I've no doubt that

spoiled child has it wrong anyway. You're not responsible for this, Rose."

Evening was settling over the valley. Kyriander's cottage was set high on the valley wall, with a view through
madrone and live oak to the prominent redwood forest
whose canopy was a blanket of shadow. The sky overhead was washed in fading pastels as the last light left
the western hilltops and darkness rolled in behind the
sun.

"How did so many people get here so fast?" I asked.

"Briande telephoned the Hall for help," she said. "I
suppose nearly everyone who was there at the time must
have trooped up here."

Earlier I had heard, and dismissed, the roar of a motorcycle on the road below. Someone had mentioned
Gary Cameron, and someone else had cursed the noise,
and Lilie had broken into the bout of dramatics that had
ended in my retreat to the porch. Now I heard someone
blundering up the darkened path from the road, and
knew it would be Gary.

He stopped on the top stair step onto the porch, glaring at me beneath his heavy brows. "You!" he said with
deep loathing.

"Hello, Gary," I said mildly.

He was nice-looking in a sullen, rather bulky way. He
was wearing leather pants, a leather jacket, and tall black
boots. His wide leather belt was studded with gaudy bits
of silver in prickly shapes, and his boots and jacket both
had bits of steel chain as design elements. Very motorcycle, very teenage, very pathetic. Like Lilie's wild-kitten
looks, it gave more an impression of vulnerability than
of the intended menace. With the boyishly sulky scowl
he granted me, it seemed almost disarming. But his tone
was not. "Murderer," he said. "You're not wanted here.
Why don't you go back to town where you belong?"

Before I could frame any sort of reply, Ariana stepped
between him and me. "Don't be more foolish than you
must, Gary," she said. "Rose hasn't killed anyone."

"Oh?" he said archly, perhaps meaning to sound both

sinister and superior, but achieving neither. "What about Lilie's father? The bitch killed him."

Ariana must not have heard Lilie's earlier accusation. She spared me one startled, speculative glance before she smiled at him and said sweetly, "Perhaps he deserved it. As do you."

He stared, his young face stunned. "Is that a threat?" he said finally, with awkward belligerence.

"Why, no, why would it be?" said Ariana.

He tried another tack. "This isn't your place." He stomped up the last step onto the porch and faced us, not yet able to tower over grownups but bulky enough to try. "Get out. Both of you. You're not wanted here."

"Gary." She said it in the quelling tone of a grade-school teacher. "Stop that."

He seemed to deflate; but renewed, audible sobs from Lilie brought his shoulders up again. She was saying something about me, and he took up her cause with a will. "Okay, you don't have to go," he told Ariana. "But this bitch has no right here." He glared at me so balefully I was very nearly frightened: large children can be every bit as hazardous as any other wild animals.

Ariana chuckled. "Gary, you silly twit, run along now, do," she said kindly. "You can't help Lilie, and you're in the way."

As though to prove her point, Charlotte came out the door just then, saw her son, and instantly achieved a much more baleful look than his. "Gary, get out of here," she said. "There's nothing you can do, and the last thing Lilie needs is a lovesick puppy hovering over her right now."

Gary blushed but stood his ground. "Mom," he said, making a full three syllables of it.

"I mean it," she said, pushing him ahead of her down the stairs. "Go home. Go. You'll do more harm than good if she sees you." She nudged him with knuckle blows to the shoulder till he stumbled reluctantly down the path before her, she holding her flashlight so it lit the way ahead of him. "Honestly," she said. "Some people."

Moments later Kyriander led a subdued Lilie past me,

shielding her so she didn't see me and burst into new fits. Guilt dragged at my bones. I wanted to hide. I wished he would glance up just once, to reassure me, and I wondered whether I would believe his reassurance if he gave it. He didn't. He was, quite rightly, far too engrossed in Lilie's concerns to spare a thought for mine.

"Sometimes this whole crowd is just a bunch of helpless kids," said Ariana.

After a long moment, during which we watched Kyriander and Lilie retreat into darkness, led by the yellow cone of his flashlight, I said, "You mean the artists? Aren't you one of them?"

Ariana looked at me in surprise, "*Moi?* An artist? Oh. I suppose I am. But I'm old, and I've long since outgrown my dramatic phase." She chuckled. "Besides, don't let any of them hear you calling me an artist, or you'll learn more than you want to know about the difference between art and crafts."

Now that Kyriander and Lilie were gone, the others threaded their way past us down the stairs, none of them paying the smallest attention to what Ariana said. "You're a craftsperson?" I asked her.

"Craftsman," she said. "I hate femlib personspeak." She seemed to think about it. "Actually I'm not sure craftsmen would claim me, either." She moved to look into the house, where a few people still bustled as though they had something to do. "Is everything taken care of here? Someone staying with Briande?"

"I can stay by myself," Briande said with injured dignity.

"Of course you can, lovey," said Ariana. "But it makes the grownups feel better if you let someone stay with you."

"Oh," he said. "Okay." From where I stood, I couldn't see him; but he sounded completely unaffected by events. "Will Charlotte fix dinner? Because I'll just go down to the Hall if she will." He moved into the doorway to talk to her, his round young face tilted so the light caught his expression, which was sweet and trusting and innocent.

"That's a good idea," said Ariana. "I expect she will. Why don't you ask a grownup to walk with you? I would, but I'm going to show Rose my work."

"Okay," he said agreeably, and turned away.

"That is," Ariana said, turning back to me with a questioning smile, "if you're interested?"

I was; but I'd been walking all afternoon, and I meant to do a bit more of it tonight when the Trouble might be out. The thought of a long trek now to another hillside cottage was daunting.

She smiled in sympathy. "We do get our exercise, don't we? But don't worry, my house isn't far. And it's not on a hillside. I live in the flats near the fountain."

"Salonian's fountain? I didn't know there were any houses near there."

"Mab's mittens," she said, "hasn't anyone given you a map of the valley?" She led me down the path into darkness, her flashlight picking out protruding roots for me to avoid. "Sometimes I wonder how they get their shoes on the right feet in the morning. Remind me when we get to the house, will you? I must have one around somewhere."

We went across the road and along it till we'd passed the Hall, in order, she said, to bypass Salonian's fountain. "I hate that thing," she said. "Especially at night. Talk about twisted genius! Poor man."

"Kyriander said that too," I said.

"Twisted genius?"

"Poor man. What's so poor about Salonian? He seems fine to me; and the fountain's gruesome, but that's part of the point, isn't it?"

"Yes," she said. "Be careful of this rock. You'd think they'd move it out of the path. Salonian's is a long story. I spoke without thinking. Here's where this path meets mine: we're almost there."

"In other words, you don't mean to tell me."

She laughed, not quite convincingly amused. "It really is a long, dull story, all about Faerie's aristocracy, and sacrifices for one's art. Would you accept the short version, for now? He had to choose between the thing he loved and the thing he needed."

She had left lights on. We turned a corner in the path and the forest opened into a small meadow with her house in the center of it, colored windows spilling light onto the bracken and sword's point ferns that grew like bushes around it. "Oh, it's beautiful," I said involuntarily. Like all the houses I had seen here, it was an airy structure of wood and glass that looked as much at home in the forest as the trees around it.

"Thank you," she said, leading me onto the broad, railed porch. "I like nestling down here among the redwoods instead of perching on the hillside like a goat. Come on in. Don't mind Tinker: he pretends he's dangerous, but once he gets to know you he's a pussycat."

Tinker, a fat ginger tom with yellow eyes and a torn ear, was perched on a table next to the door, growling. He took a swipe at me as I passed him, but with his claws retracted, fortunately, since the blow connected rather solidly. More solidly, perhaps, than he expected: he retreated at once to the far side of the table and crouched there, tail lashing, to see how I would respond.

"Be good, Tinker," said Ariana. "Would you like tea?"

For a moment I thought the question was meant for the cat, and I went on looking around the room, which was a confusion of color: deep purple curtains, a flower-print couch, woven wall hangings in every color of the rainbow on the pale wood paneling, a big pink chair, throw rugs in amber and rust and sea green, Tiffany lamp shades, and shelves on every wall loaded with Depression glass dishes, cut-crystal figurines, china music boxes, glazed pottery vases, carved boxes made of exotic woods with metal inlay, jars of bright beads of every material sorted by size and color, spools of thread and balls of string. . . .

"Tea?" She sounded amused.

"Oh! Yeah, thanks," I said, embarrassed.

She went into the kitchen to make it, calling over her

shoulder, "I admit it's a trifle busy, but I like it. Sit, if you like. Or look around, if my trinkets interest you."

"Thanks." It was a wonderland of colors and shapes and shiny things to catch one's attention, a tidy magpie's nest or even a dragon's hoard of treasures. I found a gleaming necklace on one shelf: a circlet of gold with gemstone beads suspended from it in a rainbow of color. Near it lay a bracelet of woven gold studded with amber; and near that a confection of silver and amethyst whose purpose I couldn't guess.

"It's a tiara," said Ariana. I hadn't noticed her returning from the kitchen, but there she was, reaching past me to pick up the tiara with gentle hands. "Try it on. There's a mirror over here."

"It's beautiful," I said in awe. Feeling slightly foolish—my jeans and sweater weren't a fitting costume to go with something so exquisite—I let her set it on my hair and guide me to the mirror.

"It suits you," she said.

I stared at my reflection in the mirror. It did suit me. It would have suited anyone. It was a wisp of cloud and sky, a drift of rainbow, a splash of moonlight, a lovely thing that made me look lovely under it. "My God," I said.

"Mab's grace might be more appropriate."

"It is magic, then?"

"Of a sort," she said, looking a little sheepish.

I stared at her in the mirror. "This is yours, isn't it? This is what you do?"

"It's one of the things I do." Very carefully she lifted it off my head and replaced it on its shelf, handling it with the tenderness of a mother. "Everything you see here that isn't antique is a thing I do."

The teakettle whistled and she returned to the kitchen to make the tea while I turned slowly, examining the room again. The curtains were handwoven, a light, textured fabric that lifted in the smallest breeze through the open windows, but were opaque enough to block light and view entirely.

The flower-print couch held a tumble of exquisitely

embroidered throw pillows depicting flowers, forest scenes, abstract patterns. The woven wall hangings were all different, all handsome, in earth tones and pastels. The big pink chair had an afghan on it crocheted of bisque thread as delicate-looking as a spiderweb. The throw rugs, the Tiffany lamp shades, the cut-crystal figurines, china music boxes, wind chimes, beaded bags, jewelry, all this lovely cacophony of color, one woman's work?

"But I only sell the jewelry," she said, returning from the kitchen with teapot and cups on a rosewood tray. "I'd offer you cookies, but I think we'll be going over to dinner soon?"

"Yes, I ought to, anyway. You do *all* of this?" I couldn't quite take it in.

"Well, I'd forgotten there are some of Lorielle's vases on my shelves. Beautiful, aren't they? I've never learned to throw pots, and I regret it. Perhaps I'll convince her to teach me. But yes, I did the rest. Here, sit down and stop looking so awestricken. Don't forget I'm a good deal older than you, so I've had a bit of time to learn and practice my various crafts. And really, whatever you may think, none of it is fit to sell except the jewelry."

"It all looks fit to sell, to me." I sat in the pink chair, facing her across a low antique coffee table, and touched the pink afghan with cautious fingers.

"Don't be afraid of it," she said. "Tinker has just about kneaded it to shreds: you can't hurt it."

"You let your cat *knead* it?" I said in horror. It was softer even than it looked, a joy to touch.

She chuckled. "I'm sorry," she said. "That's made of Faerie thread. No mortal could resist it."

I tucked it across my lap and ran my fingers across its silky folds. "With all this, the others still don't think of you as an artist?"

"Well, no more should they," she said. "I'm only a craftsman. Skilled, even talented. But not an artist." She put a cup of tea before me.

"But that's no reason for the others not to like you, is it?" I asked.

"Of course not. They don't dislike me, dear. They only, very naturally, want to establish their artistic superiority." She smiled. "It doesn't bother me. I've made a point of it only to save you possible embarrassment when you're talking with the others. I'm an artist of a sort, certainly; but theirs is fine art and mine is commercial. Now, let me show you the works I'm most vain about."

I had to take her word for it that what she showed me was not fine art.

11

All was subdued at the Hall when we arrived. The bright lights seemed dazzling after the dimness of the forest. There was a child crying in Rosetta Fulmer's lap on the far side of the room.

"Here you are at last," said Finandiel, dipping his head in the most miniscule of bows in our direction. "Well met, well met indeed, for we've evidence of the Trouble, don't you know."

"What evidence?" Ariana asked sharply.

"Young Leaf has seen it," said Finandiel, nodding meaningfully toward the couch where the child in Rosetta's arms, taking in our appearance, nestled closer against her mother and sniffled juicily.

I went to them and knelt beside the child. "Can you tell me what you saw, honey?" I asked.

"Bigfoot," she said with pride.

"Now, are you sure, lovey?" asked Rosetta. "Bigfoot would be hairy all over, and tall, not that everybody wouldn't look pretty tall to you, but even taller if everything one reads is to be believed, though I don't know whether it is, necessarily, since for all we know nobody ever *has* really seen it—"

"Mama." Leaf sniffled again, enthusiastically. "I was *telling*."

"Of course you were, lovey," said Rosetta, chastened.

Leaf turned her wide brown gaze to me. "It was big," she said, gesturing toward the ceiling. "I was just going outside with Peaceable."

"That's the dog," said Rosetta.

"Because I'm hungry," said Leaf, "and Charlotte

wouldn't give me dinner." She glared toward the kitchen, where I could hear Charlotte stirring something. "So I was going to play, only there was this big man there."

I glanced around at the company. All the men present, even Finandiel, were huge compared with Leaf. "Not somebody you know?" I asked.

"We were all inside," said Finandiel.

"Besides, if they hadn't been, they'd have come in to apologize when they found out they'd frightened her," said Rosetta. "Since nobody here would want to frighten a child, which all of us know perfectly well, so it can't have been."

"Not," said Leaf. "Everybody I know would have said hello; but Bigfoot doesn't speak English, does it?"

"Nobody knows," said Rosetta.

"Well, it didn't," said Leaf.

"Dinner," said Charlotte, coming to the kitchen door. "You first, Leaf."

"Yay," said Leaf, scrambling off her mother's lap to run to Charlotte. "Is that because I saw Bigfoot, is that why I get to eat first? Because I'm really hungry."

"Yes," Charlotte said ambiguously, taking her hand. "We'll fix you a plate while the others wait."

"Well," said Ariana.

"Well?" said Finandiel, seating himself comfortably at the table while Cuthbern moved toward the kitchen to serve him.

"At least we know it isn't Lilie," said Ariana.

"Or Kyriander," I said. "Unless they doubled back instead of going to the hospital: but that we can check. Why, did you suspect Lilie?"

"Always suspect teenagers." She smiled at me and sat opposite Finandiel. "But seriously? No, I didn't suspect her or Kyriander, or any of the other residents."

"What makes you so sure?"

"Well, we wouldn't, would we? Nobody here would deliberately frighten children."

"Nobody likes to think that somebody they know would do something unpleasant," I said.

"You are mistaken," said Finandiel. "It pleases me to know that all my friends will be as unpleasant as they wish, just as will I."

"Thus speaks a Trueblood," I said. "You're right, Finandiel. Thanks. I do tend to think in human terms. But still, you wouldn't frighten children, would you?"

"Of course not."

"No elf would deliberately frighten a child," Ariana said firmly.

I studied her. "What aren't you telling me?"

"Many things, but none pertinent to this. Why do you ask?"

"Many reasons. For one, you're not concerned about the Trouble, even when it frightens a child."

"That's because I'm sure that whatever it is, it's not a danger." She watched as Leaf returned from the kitchen bearing a loaded plate. "It only makes sense: if it were a danger, it surely would have hurt someone by now."

Across the room, Ritchie Morita made a rude sound. "Oh, right. Nothing bad has happened, so nothing will. Don't be stupid."

"Stuff it, Ritchie," she said mildly. "May we serve ourselves now, Charlotte?" Charlotte agreed to it, and there was a small rush on the kitchen. Ariana stayed where she was. Catching my look, she made a wry face and said, "I'll wait till the crowd thins."

Food had taken everyone's mind off us. "You do know something, don't you?"

"I know any number of things," she said, and smiled at my look. "But seriously, I can't help you solve the puzzle of our Infestation."

That was obviously the best I was going to get from her. I went outside to look for clues. Peaceable followed me as far as the stairs and sprawled at the top of them, watching me lugubriously. I swept the area with a borrowed flashlight and found nothing useful; but just as I gave up and flipped off the light to return to the Hall, I heard Gary's dirt bike approaching. I'm not sure why I waited for him. The sound of the motorcycle grew rapidly to a painful pitch as it approached and, with a devastating roar and clash of gears, swept into the parking lot.

Its headlight swept over me, but I don't think Gary saw me; he wouldn't have expected anyone to be standing in the dark. He revved the engine and skidded the bike to a halt right next to the front porch. The ear-ringing silence when he killed the engine was promptly filled with bellows of pain and rage as the residents inside came to doors and windows to curse the noise.

Gary sat for a moment, smiling unpleasantly to himself. The elves were loudest in their wrath. It says much for the successful mesh of elf and human society in the valley that not one of them responded with the instinctive magical wardings one might expect elsewhere. The bike, if not Gary himself, would almost certainly have suffered in any society of elves less influenced by humans. I think he knew that. I think he took advantage of the restraints under which Fey Valley's elves lived: as rebellious teenagers will, he was deliberately testing the limits without any regard to who got hurt.

I wondered just how much longer he would get away with this calculated little cruelty. Elf-baiting, even in a well-integrated society like this one, is not a healthy practice. Sooner or later they will snap. The artificial restraints placed on them by humankind will give way. Elven honor does not require generosity toward mortals at all, much less toward mortals who deliberately cause them pain.

Gary kicked the bike up on its stand and stepped off it. The disturbance inside the Hall was settling down again. "Did your parents neglect your education, or do you like living dangerously?" I said, stepping into the light.

He started nervously. "What? Oh, it's you." He smiled again, rather nastily. "What do you mean?"

"Somebody should tell you some fairy stories."

He shrugged. "I've heard them."

"And yet you torment the elves?"

"I'm not afraid of them."

"Perhaps you ought to be."

He made a rude sound and turned away from me. "Bugger off, bitch. What're you doing sneaking around in the dark, anyway? Snooping on somebody?"

"You might say that. Where've you been?"

"None of your business."

Since there hadn't been time for him to frighten Leaf, run off somewhere to get his motorcycle, and return so noisily from as far away as I'd first heard him, he was probably right. I shrugged. "Fair enough. But you know, you really should get a muffler for that thing."

"Stuff it." He clumped up the stairs away from me; and I let him go, because I couldn't think of any way to get the message through to him. So far, the elves still saw him as a child. Maybe he would learn sense before he lost that protection.

Peaceable moved aside for him. He stepped into the light and closed the door behind him. I stood a moment longer, till the singing insects started up around me, but there was nothing more to do here. Whatever had frightened Leaf was long gone, and had left no trace. I followed Gary into the Hall, with Peaceable trailing anxiously behind.

Kyriander and Lilie returned from the hospital while we were still at dinner. Kyriander looked worried and exhausted, Lilie sullen and resentful. The two of them disappeared into the kitchen and returned a moment later with loaded plates. Lilie took hers to a far corner of the lounge area and sat sideways in a big overstuffed chair so her back was to the dining table. Apparently her appetite was healthy tonight; her plate was easily as full as Kyri's.

He sat at the table opposite me with his back to his sister and applied himself to his dinner without a word. Briande, several chairs down from Kyriander, looked from one to the other of them and then went back to his own meal, his expression troubled.

Several conversations that had broken off at their arrival started up again now: Chance Winter and Galinda were talking photography at the far end of the table;

near them, Rosetta Fulmer was talking over Leaf's head to a man I recognized as George Jenks, a well-known painter; and at the near end of the table a tall, thin, sun-wrinkled woman I hadn't met was talking animatedly with Ritchie Morita, who responded civilly. Curious, I tuned out the others enough to hear Ritchie saying, "Have you tried Schultz's Instant? One of the Scotland Yard people put me onto it, and it's the best all-round fertilizer I've used. My dracaena must have doubled in size the first month I tried it."

The woman looked dubious. "Pot roses are so delicate," she said. "I need something that won't burn the roots."

"Schultz's is a concentrate," said Ritchie. "You can mix it up as weak as you like. I can mix up a weak solution for you, if you like, so you could try it before you buy any."

"Good heavens, he raises houseplants?" I blurted.

Kyriander glanced at me. "Who?"

"Your angry young man," I said.

"Oh, Ritchie?" said Kyriander.

"What?" said Ritchie.

Kyriander looked at him. "Nothing. Rosie was surprised you keep houseplants."

"There's nothing to be ashamed of in a fondness for plants," the woman with Ritchie said firmly. "Hello, Miss Lavine. I'm Mildred Potter, Fey Valley's postmistress and folk artist."

"By that," said Ritchie, "she means she has no talent."

"As to that," said Mildred, "there are those who say you've no talent either, Ritchie Morita."

"And by that she means she doesn't like my books," he said comfortably. "Damned woman reads *romance*." He made it sound in very poor taste.

"Ritchie thinks only stupid people read romance," said Mildred.

"No, no, no: only stupid women."

"Of course," she said. "Sorry."

"What's the good of insulting someone if she can't even understand the nuances?" he said.

"You're right," she said.

Lilie Stone had rushed through her meal and carried her plate to the kitchen. Now she headed for the front door with a muttered, "I'm going home."

Kyriander said, "No," without looking.

Lilie stopped, glaring at him. "I want to," she said.

"I don't want you out alone," he said.

"I saw Bigfoot," Leaf said proudly. "Right outside."

Lilie lifted her chin to look down her nose at Leaf. "I don't believe in Bigfoot."

Leaf's face crumpled. "But you said," she said.

"Don't be a baby," said Lilie.

Leaf mustered her dignity. "Well, I saw it," she said.

"Sit down," Kyriander told Lilie.

"No. I want to go home," said Lilie.

"Soon," said Kyriander.

"Now," said Lilie.

Before Kyriander could respond, Gary Cameron came to Lilie's aid. "I'll take her home," he said almost politely, "if that's okay?" He ruined it by adding sullenly, "She shouldn't have to stay if she doesn't want to."

Kyriander hesitated. "You'll go on foot," he said. "No motorcycle."

Lilie looked down her nose at him. "Don't be stupid. He couldn't get the bike up our path anyway."

"Lilie," Kyriander said.

"Well, he couldn't," she said.

"We'll walk," said Gary, wheedling. "She'll be all right with me."

After a moment's hesitation Kyriander said reluctantly, "Yes, all right. But be careful. Lock the door when you get there, Lilie," and the children departed in a cloud of triumphant self-righteousness.

It had been a long, fruitless day, and it was a long, fruitless evening. After dinner I stayed at the Hall chatting with the residents till most of them had gone home. The only new information this turned up was that

George Jenks was Leaf's father, Ariana made more money with her crafts than any of the others made with fine art, and Charlotte planned to make tacos for lunch tomorrow. Finally I said good night to the remaining residents, borrowed a flashlight, and set out for my cottage and bed.

I took my time on the way, watching for intruders or clues, but the only signs of life I saw were what I thought was a barn owl, and a startled deer that bounded crashing away into the darkness when I came upon it eating from one of Scotland Yard's tidy flower beds.

Salonian's fountain seemed to glow in moonlight. I paused to watch shadows play over it. Someone had said he called it "Mab's Grace": there were so many possible meanings in that, I hadn't even tried to sort them out. But it occurred to me as I looked at it that it's very hard to tell a human skull from an elf's. Ariana said he'd been obliged to choose between what he loved and what he needed. Obliged by whom or what? And what were the things he loved and needed?

I turned away from the fountain, climbed the steps beside the blackberries that led up to my cottage, let myself in, and closed the door on all the tangled questions until morning.

12

Blue jays woke me, screaming outside my bedroom window. I opened my eyes to swimming shadows and could not at first remember where I was. The light was dim and the room unfamiliar. It was the noise of the jays that reminded me finally, when I rolled over to stare at the moisture-beaded window that gave, from that angle, a view of the lowering sky. It had been raining in the night, and from the look of the sky I thought it would rain again today.

It was while I was contemplating what a long, cold way it was to the bathroom that I remembered, with a shock, the purchases I had made in Moraga yesterday and then left in the car when I went wandering off in search of clues. They included ground coffee. Good God, what if the cabin wasn't stocked with coffee? The mere thought of making the long, shivering trek to the car before my morning coffee made me burrow deeper under the covers. No, it was too horrible. There must be coffee in the kitchen.

I should have known by then that Charlotte would have overlooked nothing as important as that. When I finally climbed out from the warm nest of my bed and into my robe to scurry barefoot and shivering to the kitchen, I found a tin of coffee in the cupboard, with fake cream and little packets of sugar to go with it. The coffeemaker was a percolator, which wouldn't have been my first choice; but it was fine for camping out. With care it would produce something hot and strong and caffeinated.

While I waited for it to perk I eyed the Franklin stove

in the living room, complete with piled logs and kindling to start a fire; but it seemed more trouble than it was worth. Instead, I returned to the bedroom, found clean, warm clothes in my suitcase, and carried them to the bathroom, where I had a steaming shower that chased the last of the morning chill from my bones.

The coffee was ready when I went back to the kitchen. Bundled in jeans, warm socks, and a heavy sweater, I felt much better prepared to face the day. I still didn't know what I was going to do next, though. So far I'd found no physical clues to the Trouble's nature or even its existence: I'd taken everybody's statement who'd seen it, and couldn't find anything useful in them: and my own experience with it had told me as little.

There were residents I hadn't talked to. The next step was probably to canvass the entire valley, which sounded even less attractive on a cold, dreary day like this than it might have if the weather were more pleasant. At least it wasn't yet raining.

The front window of my cottage looked straight out on misty clouds of glowing acacia, mounds of dusty eucalyptus, and dark spires of redwood: a landscape of treetops rolling smoothly across the valley to the hanging forests on the other side that spilled down through hidden ravines in rivulets of foliage between dark outcroppings of rock. I could just make out a curl or two of the road as it wound its way down the far valley wall. It looked like a satin ribbon threaded among the trees.

At the foot of the valley wall there was a place where the forest canopy opened into meadow for perhaps a quarter of a mile and the road lay exposed, a dark swath cutting through plush green velvet. As I watched, a shining blue pebble rolled swiftly through the velvet to disappear at the bottom where the road tunneled into the forest again: a car coming into Fey Valley from the west, from Oakland or Berkeley. Shannon? Her car was blue. But I hardly noticed it. I was thinking of Killer and the island singsong of his voice.

That had surprised me, the first time I'd heard it. We'd been backstage at a Cold Iron concert, in the interval after the warm-up band. I'd bumped into him in the darkness and struggled when he gripped my shoulders to steady me. He held me at arm's length, dodged my knees and feet easily, and grinned down at me from behind the permanent half mask of ebony curls that hung in his face. "Hey," he said. "Hey." His voice was sweet and shy, completely at odds with his fierce appearance.

I subsided, blushing, and told him I'd mistaken him for someone else.

His amiable grin widened. "Glad I ain't." There was friendly amusement in his tone. "What did he do to deserve all that?" He released me watchfully, as though he thought I might attack again the moment I was free. I had not seen him at such close range before. His face was partially visible through the mass of curls, and it was as sweet and uncomplicated as his voice.

But life is seldom uncomplicated. If we didn't know that before, we learned it at Maunalani before he went on tour. I had learned things about myself, on tour with Cold Iron, that I didn't want to know. Alone with him afterward, I could not let those things go. I could not learn to trust him. I could not accept what he had to offer: there was no room in my life for love.

I drank my coffee, put the empty cup in the kitchen, unplugged the coffeemaker, made sure all the lights were off, and went out into the chill gray morning.

There were fewer residents in the Hall for breakfast today, probably because my presence was less of a novelty and they were getting back to their normal schedules. Charlotte had prepared a feast for those of us who wanted it, though. Salonian was there, and Chance Winter, both breakfasting largely. Benjamin Barski, a sculptor I'd met but hadn't really talked to, was sitting with Mildred Potter. She was drinking coffee and looking very professional and distracted, like an important businesswoman on a break.

I piled my plate with bacon, sausage, eggs, and potatoes and carried them, with a steaming cup of coffee, to the big oval table to eat.

The front door was closed today against the morning chill. Someone had started a fire in the Franklin stove by the stairs. I chose the seat at the table nearest that. Peaceable was sprawled on the other side of the stove, in the warm circle of its radiance but for once out of the main traffic pattern. He lifted his head briefly and put it down again with a heavy sigh, watching me with rolled eyes and pricked ears.

"Good morning, Peaceable," I said.

He slapped his tail against the floor once and kept watching me, nose twitching. When I declined to share my breakfast bounty, however, eventually he sighed pathetically again and closed his eyes.

Finandiel, who was seated at the other end of the table eating waffles with evident enjoyment, asked brightly, "How fares your investigation?" Cuthbern hovered behind him, ready to refill his coffee cup or pour more syrup. I wondered when he would get to eat. Or did he rise early to eat before his master?

"Okay," I said noncommittally. "It's early days yet. And how are you enjoying our world?"

He seemed pleased that I'd asked him. "It matches not such expectations as I had been led to hold."

"So it's a disappointment?"

"In no way." He speared a piece of waffle with his fork and eyed it appreciatively. "It is in all ways more wondrous than I dared hope."

Peaceable rose abruptly and paced to the door, toenails clicking on the wooden floor. Just as he reached it, I heard a car pull off the main road onto the crunchy gravel of the parking lot. A car door slammed and Peaceable made a sound low in his throat. "It would seem we have a visitor," said Finandiel. "Were you expecting anyone?"

"Not really," I said; but I remembered the blue pebble that might have been Shannon's pale blue BMW. She would have been delayed, stopping at the first house visible from the road to ask directions, since I hadn't told her how to find either the Hall or my cottage.

"Be at peace, Peaceable," said Finandiel. Peaceable retreated obediently to the stove and flopped down again, head on forepaws, to watch Shannon open the door.

She is perhaps the most beautiful woman I have ever met. She compounds this offense by being unaware of it. She moves with invariable, unself-conscious grace, is charming and outgoing, a good conversationalist, with a wry and self-deprecating sense of humor. I believe if she weren't my best friend I would hate her.

Naturally I watched the men as she came in. Salonian didn't seem to notice her just at first. Finandiel had met her before, and comported himself admirably. Chance Winter stared rather slyly, pretending to keep eating but missing his mouth with his fork; and Benjamin Barski completely forgot poor Mildred Potter's existence.

Shannon, blissfully unaware of anything out of the ordinary, stepped inside, closed the door behind her, and smiled. Chance Winter dropped his fork. "Rosie," said Shannon, and even Salonian looked up at the sound of her voice. "I'm glad I found you. From the directions I got at the last house, I thought I'd have to traipse through acres of forest, not to mention bogs and the odd cliff or two."

"You were going to traipse through cliffs?"

"You know what I mean," she said. "Gosh, a stove, that's wonderful; it's positively freezing out. And that coffee smells wonderful."

Charlotte, who had come to the kitchen door to see who was arriving, went to get her a cup without being asked. Women are not immune to her charm. I introduced her all around while she huddled over the Franklin stove, dancing with the cold and greeting everyone like a long-lost friend.

Charlotte brought her coffee. Chance hung up her coat for her. Salonian pulled a chair nearer the stove for her. Mildred Potter asked whether there was anything else she needed. Benjamin Barski hovered, but couldn't find anything to offer. Finandiel watched the entire process with the air of an anthropologist observing native rituals.

Shannon beamed at him and thanked all the others with grace and sincerity. As far as she knew they behaved that way whenever anyone entered the room. "Thanks, yes," she said, "I really would like some breakfast." She didn't have to go get it; she told people what she wanted and they brought it as though their natural role in life were to wait on her.

I relaxed and ate my breakfast.

Afterward she helped me carry my groceries from car to cabin. "Acres of forest," she said. "I knew it."

"At least there's no bog, and not more than one or two sheer cliffs to scale."

"You're joking," she said, horrified. She was even more citified than I.

"Well, there are stairs," I said.

"Up sheer cliffs?"

"Up a hill, anyway."

She laughed. "I believed you, you know."

"If you didn't, you wouldn't be any fun to pick on." We threaded our way between mounds of dull green bracken and sword fern. There were no golden patches of sunlight spilled through the trees today; the glimpses of sky that I could see through the leaves were uniformly gray and threatening. The occasional oxalis, with its crisp green leaves and cheery purple blossoms, wore the brightest colors in the whole gloomy landscape.

"This is really grim, isn't it?" said Shannon.

"It's actually rather pretty on sunny days," I said.

"Oh, yeah, big consolation that must be, considering how the sunlight must simply stream down through the solid roof of trees."

"It does, rather," I said.

She turned to stare at me. "You like it here." Her tone was accusing.

"I didn't at first. You get used to it."

"I don't *think* so," she said.

"Give it a break. You're seeing it at its very worst."

"Show me the mall and I'll give it a break," she said. "Good God, what's *that*?" We'd just come in sight of Salonian's fountain. She paused, then moved forward again cautiously, rather like a cat confronted with a change in its environment.

"It's a fountain."

"It's a sprite," she said. "No, an elf. But what is it— Eeeuuuw, it's watering skulls! *Human* skulls."

I laughed at her. "It's a work of art."

"It's gross."

"That, too," I admitted. We paused in the clearing, staring at it. The oxalis at its feet bloomed bright yellow, almost like splashes of sunlight. The trillium was white fading to rose: together they seemed to light the fountain from below.

"I mean it's really gross," said Shannon. "Is it meant to be depressing?" She shook her head. "Well, I guess it must be. You don't decorate something with skulls to cheer people up."

"I'm not sure depressing is the word: I find it scary. Creepy."

She shook her head slowly. "No," she said certainly. "Sad. Awfully sad. Why do they have it here? God, it's like somebody died." She shuddered and turned deliberately away from it. "Which way? Let's go on."

"This way." I showed her the way between young Scotch broom to the narrow path of rich green moss and Corsican mint that led to the bridge over the stream.

She was silent till we came to the flagstones that paved it near the stream. "This is nice, anyway," she said then. "But don't you feel isolated? I feel like we've been walking away from civilization for hours."

"I kind of like it," I said.

"You like being all alone out here?"

"Yeah," I said diffidently.

She laughed. "Jeez. Better you than me. Is that a stream I hear?" We came in sight of it just then, and she paused again. "Nice bridge. Is it a year-round stream?"

"I think so."

She shook her head. "No wonder they don't want to give up this valley. It's really something, isn't it? If you like this sort of thing? And a year-round stream—they won't find another easily. Is that maidenhair fern on the far bank? God. If they just had a mall, you know, this could be okay."

It started raining as we crossed the bridge. Despite our burdens we ran the rest of the way, up the stairs and onto the porch, and burst into the cottage in such a welter of giggles that it didn't register at first that someone had broken in while I was gone.

13

"I'd swear I locked the door when I left," I said, kicking off my damp shoes on the way to the kitchen. I stopped when I saw the upside-down sugar canister on the floor in a mound of sugar. "Oh. Damn."

"What?" Shannon was shedding bags and jacket by the doorway. "God, it's just so typical that it would rain as soon as I get here. I mean, has it been raining before? The weather's been fine in town, and I naturally assumed— That's weird. What's this?" She picked something up off the upholstered chair nearest the door.

I backed up and started to put my bags down on the couch; but that was where the flour canister had been dumped. I put them on a clear section of floor near the wall instead. "I don't know," I said without looking. "What is it?" A bottle of cooking oil had been poured artistically over the sugar and coffee on the kitchen floor. Mustard and butter were spread thoughtfully on the counter and cupboard doors. Ketchup, horrifyingly blood red, sprayed the refrigerator and the wall behind the sink.

"It seems to've been frozen peas, at one time," said Shannon. "God, Rosie, you're a lousy housekeeper."

"Yeah, right." I kicked an empty bottle of maple syrup aside. It rolled, dripping thinly, to a stop against the stove. "*Damn* it."

"Your Trouble?"

"I don't know. I guess so." But I hadn't heard of it doing anything of this sort before. I thought of it as a nuisance that only frightened the children, and that very possibly without intending to.

"Well," she said heartily. "Housecleaning is a nice indoor activity for a rainy day."

"Not my favorite."

"No." She shed the rest of her bags and rolled up her sleeves. "Any identifying marks? A signature, maybe, or at least some nice fingerprints?"

"No such luck that I can see." Of course I couldn't see fingerprints without dusting; but I could see there was very little that would take a print. Anyway, she was joking. If we did find prints, and print all the valley residents, and find a match, that would only show that person had been in the cabin. Since they all owned it, they all had a right to've been there at one time or another.

And if we found nonresident prints, we still wouldn't have anything useful. They wouldn't help us track the perpetrator. The only possible use they'd have would be if I filed a police report of the incident and they found not only the perpetrator but also enough additional evidence to make a case. I didn't feel inclined to run to the police over a spot of vandalism, particularly if it had been done by the Trouble I was hired to stop.

"I suppose that would be too much to ask. Who has a key, besides you?"

"I didn't know anyone had. Maybe Charlotte."

"We'll ask her." She surveyed the chaos, hands on hips. "What do you think, this proves it's a human? Or it's an elf and that's what he wants us to think?"

"It's certainly not an elvish sort of destruction."

"No. But anybody who's been among us even a short time might figure out it is a human one."

"Which means it tells us nothing but that the Trouble—or somebody—hopes I'm easily scared off."

"And are you?"

"Nope."

"Then I guess we have to clean this up."

We did. It took the whole morning and wasn't any fun. Wandering around outdoors in the rain and mud would have been pleasanter. I hate cleaning. It's so domesticated.

Most of the damage was confined to the living room

and kitchen, and I was relieved to find my handgun unmolested on a high shelf in the bedroom closet. I'd have
been happier still if the rest of the cottage had been
equally unmolested. There is something very creepy
about knowing a hostile stranger has had access to one's
personal possessions. The damage was negligible really,
but I felt as though I had been violated.

By the time we were finished the rain had stopped.
"If we're lucky, we can still get tacos for lunch down at
the Hall," I said, surveying the results of our labors. The
place looked cleaner than it had when I moved in.

"That's one thing," said Shannon. "It can't have been
anyone who was down there this morning when you
were."

"No. For all the good that does us."

"Who's left?"

"Only about a hundred residents, counting kids. Who
should by all means be counted: this was a very kid sort
of thing."

"Okay, who're the kids?"

"Of an age to do this? The only ones I've met are
Kyriander's siblings and Charlotte's boy, Gary. He
drives a motorcycle. A dirt bike."

She laughed at me. "That proves it. Must be Gary.
What's he like besides the dirt bike?"

"Sullen, unpleasant, rude, and unpleasant. Oh, and did
I mention he's unpleasant?"

"No, but I was able to piece it together from what
you did say. Prime suspect?"

"There's nothing to point to him except that it's just
the sort of thing he would do. And he doesn't like me,
because Lilie doesn't like me. He might hope to scare
me off. Loathsome creature."

"What's he done to you? Or is this just your general
fondness for children?"

"Gary's worse than most. But he hasn't done anything: it's really just the motorcycle, I suppose. He's so
arrogant about it. Doesn't give a damn that he's hurting
every nearby elf with the damn thing—hell, it's so loud
it hurts *my* ears."

"If it's that loud, it's a wonder he doesn't get a ticket."

"Fey Valley's private property. And if he drives it outside the valley at all, it's probably only to school in Moraga. Maybe he just hasn't yet encountered a cop."

"Oh, well. And the grownups you've met who weren't at breakfast?"

I counted them off for her, pausing at Ariana. "She knows something she doesn't want me to find out," I said, "but I don't know whether it's about the Trouble or something else."

"Interesting," she said. "She's the craftsperson?"

"Craftsman."

"Right." She thought about it. "I'm hungry. Let's go get lunch." I agreed to it. She opened the door and paused. "Oops. What's this?" She bent to retrieve something shiny, and held it out for me to see.

"It's one of the prickly bits from Gary's motorcycle costume," I said. "So he was here."

"Or someone wants us to think he was."

The sky was still gray and the forest dripped as steadily as if it were still raining. The air seemed luminous, and the forest a sea of shadows below us, gloriously scented of rain and light and leaf mold. The stairs down from the cottage were slippery with wet and mud and moss. A thin mist was rising among the blackberry tangles beside the path, a smudge among the leaves so faint it was barely more than a blurring of the air.

Shannon paused on the landing to survey the drenched and dripping valley. " 'I am sister to the rain,' " she pronounced, stretching out her arms and inhaling deeply. " 'Fey and sudden and unholy.' "

"I'll buy the 'unholy' part. What's that from?"

"Dorothy Parker."

"Is she an elf?"

"With a name like that? Of course she wasn't, you literary ignoramus."

Soggy drifts of dead leaves were strewn at the feet of bracken and sword fern on both sides of the path and clung to shoes and pants that brushed them. I saw motion in the corner of my eye and turned my head in time to see a coastal deer slipping through the trees. Tendrils of mist writhed up from the warm soil to curl around his legs and brush his belly as he paused, looking back at us, ears flicking. Then he slid quietly out of sight among the trees and, a moment later, I heard the plash of his hooves in the rushing water.

When we came to Salonian's fountain Shannon paused, tilting her head to study it while the forest dripped placidly around us. Here too, a thin mist was rising from the warm ground into the cold air, smudging the base of the fountain. "Tell me again about the artist who did this?"

"You met him," I said. "Salonian. The tall, gaunt fellow with battered hands."

"I think I know the one you mean." She reached to touch one glistening skull, thought better of it, and tucked her hand into her pocket.

"Did you say he's an aristocrat? If so, there seems a plethora of it here."

"I didn't say, but I think he is. Who else, besides Finandiel?"

"If Lorielle isn't an aristocrat, I am."

"Lorielle? Where did you meet her?"

"When I stopped to ask for directions, at the house just at the bottom of the hill. She's FOOF, and I'd swear she's somebody important in Faerie."

"Pooh. Why would she come here, then?"

"To do something artistic? I don't know. Why'd Finandiel?"

"I don't know: I haven't asked."

"What's she do? For that matter, what's he do?"

"I don't think anyone's said. About either of them. I can't even remember whether I've met Lorielle, or only been told about her. What's she like?"

"Gorgeous."

"That's it? That's your whole description?"

She glanced at me. "If you'd met her, you'd know it's adequate."

"I hate her already."

She grinned at me. "Me too."

And then we were at the Hall, and so distracted by the luscious scent of Charlotte's cooking that we forgot all about Lorielle. Few residents had braved the rain for lunch, and they had gone already.

"I'm going to offer tacos again for dinner," said Charlotte. "Everything will keep, and otherwise it'll just go to waste."

"We'll be back for dinner, then," said Shannon. "This is delicious. Do you have spare keys to the cottages?"

"Thank you," said Charlotte, much pleased. "Keys? Yes, I have most of them. Why?"

"Where do you keep them?"

She looked mystified. "I have a rack for them in my kitchen," she said. Which meant Gary had easy access to them. "I used to keep it here, but we decided that was too public; anybody could get at them. So I took it home. Is something the matter?"

"No, not really. What's Lorielle do for a living?"

"Lorielle? She throws pots, why?"

"Throws pots?" Shannon asked in surprise. "Why would she do that? Who'd pay for it?"

"It means she makes them," I said.

"You've been boning up on this stuff." She glared at me accusingly.

"No, I used to know a potter."

"Lorielle's pretty good," Charlotte said grudgingly.

I wondered whether pottery was a craft instead of art. "Now I remember: Ariana has some of her work, hasn't she?"

"I wouldn't know," said Charlotte, in the tone of one discussing prostitution.

Shannon looked at Charlotte in surprise and lifted a querying eyebrow at me. I didn't feel that was just the moment to enlighten her, so I shook my head and said, "Lorielle's new here, right?"

Charlotte, diverted from frowning thoughts of Ariana, said yes, Lorielle was new here.

"Since the Trouble started, or before?"

"Just before," she said rather grimly. "Hasn't anyone

told you which of them came right before the Trouble started?"

"Well, I knew Finandiel and Cuthbern," I said. "Finandiel said there were others, but he didn't say who."

"Let me get a cup of coffee," she said, and bustled toward the kitchen.

"Doesn't get out much, does she?" Shannon said in an undertone.

"Actually I think she does," I said, remembering her trips to Moraga. "But she's lonely anyway."

Charlotte returned before we could say more. She sat at the table with her coffee cup cradled between her hands and said, rather portentously, "There was no Trouble in Fey Valley before the newest elves moved in."

She waited for one of us to respond to that. Shannon said finally, patiently, "And who were they?"

"All elves," she repeated meaningfully, looking fiercely at Shannon as though expecting a challenge. "Belalin. Jeran. Lorielle. Cuthbern. Lord Finandiel." She tolled the names slowly, dragging every last hint of drama from the recitation.

"You think one of them is the Trouble?" asked Shannon.

Charlotte sipped her coffee, smiling to herself, taking the same sly pleasure in this as a child would in telling on a pesky sibling. "I couldn't say that," she said judiciously. "But it's quite a coincidence."

Shannon looked at me. "Have you met all these people?"

"Not Belalin or Jeran," I said. "Nobody's even mentioned them before."

"They don't come down to meals," said Charlotte. "Some people are too high-and-mighty to eat with the rest of us."

"Why? Are they aristocracy too? Doesn't Finandiel eat here?"

Her expression softened. "Lord Finandiel is a good man, for an elf," she said. "Even if he is a lord. No, it's their art that makes Belalin and Jeran snobs: haven't you heard of them?" She looked pleased at the notion.

"I don't think so," said Shannon.

"They're painters," she said, to nudge our memories, and watched sharply to see whether it worked.

"I'm afraid I don't keep up much with the art world," said Shannon.

Charlotte looked triumphant. "And who can blame you, with movements like theirs getting so much attention. The *Fauxnaifs,* they call themselves. At least they got that right. Bunch of spoiled brats is what they are, pretending they aren't pretending to be better than their betters."

That remarkable accusation stopped even Shannon for a moment. I saw her mentally parsing it, and came to her rescue, since I'd read about the *Fauxnaifs* and had at least a vague idea what it was they stood for. "They're the ones who came out of the *Fauve* revival?"

Charlotte nodded. "Right, the *Faux Fauves,* and then the *Fauxnaifs*."

"Do you think one of them is responsible for the Trouble?"

Her expression closed. "As to that, I can't say. I only know there was no Trouble before they moved in."

"They, or Lorielle, Cuthbern, and Finandiel, I think you said?" said Shannon.

"Well yes," she admitted, "but of course it isn't Lord Finandiel or Cuthbern. Anyone can see that. And I don't suppose Lorielle would do anything so mean-spirited. She's a nice enough elf, if she is just a potter."

"Some of the things that have happened seem like they might be a child's pranks," said Shannon.

Charlotte scowled at her. "Nonsense. None of the children in Fey Valley would do such a thing."

"What thing do you mean?"

"Any of it. They wouldn't pull such pranks." She stood abruptly, coffee cup gripped angrily in both hands. "People always want to blame children. Whenever anything goes wrong they always accuse the children. Well, it isn't, that's all. They just wouldn't."

"Are they all in school today?" I asked.

She looked surprised, then suspicious. "Of course not. It's Saturday. Why?"

As though to underline the point, Gary chose that moment to roar into the parking lot outside on his deafening dirt bike. Even Charlotte grimaced at the noise. Shannon looked pained; and upstairs, an elf's voice bellowed for silence.

Gary, of course, didn't hear that. I looked out the window to see why he was sitting with the motor running. Lilie was just getting off the passenger seat, though I was pretty sure Kyriander had forbidden her to ride with him. She leaned over to kiss him and turned toward the Hall. Gary revved the motor and the elf upstairs bellowed again. I glanced around for Charlotte. She had retreated to the kitchen.

Well, if managing Gary wasn't her job, it sure wasn't mine. And while I wanted to talk to him about the wreck of my cottage, I would be at a strong disadvantage trying to bellow questions over the roar of the motorcycle.

"Let's go," said Shannon, rising abruptly and heading for the kitchen with her dishes.

"Where?" I asked, following her.

"I'll tell you on the way."

14

When we went out, Gary and Lilie were still in the parking lot, Gary on his bike and Lilie just leaving him on her way to the door. Both of them were drenched to the skin; it had started raining again while we were inside, and neither of them wore adequate protection. They didn't seem to mind. Lilie paused when she saw us, and turned back toward Gary, who ignored us. He turned off the motorcycle and put it up on its center stand. In the merciful silence, the creek seemed loud in its rain-swollen rush over its stony bed.

I paused beside him and pulled the prickly piece of silver from my pocket. "Is this yours?"

He took it from me with a nasty scowl. "Maybe. Why?"

"I found it at my cottage."

He handed it back, looking revolted. "Isn't mine, then. I haven't been to your stupid cottage." He smirked at Lilie, making sure she saw him defy me.

Lilie giggled. "It's just a piece of trash." She fingered her heavy bead necklace, which was far too fancy to wear with blue jeans and a tee shirt; it made her look like a little girl playing dress-up.

"Yes, perhaps it is," I said, and followed Shannon.

"You were right," she said. "That dirt bike is illegally loud. And the boy that comes with it is no prize. Who was the girl wearing her mother's baubles?" She started the BMW and turned on the heater.

"That's Kyri's little sister Lilie. She seems nicely recovered from cutting her wrists last night."

Shannon stared. "You mean attempted suicide?"

"That seems to be what we're meant to think."

Shannon was studying me, puzzled by my tone. "You don't think she really meant to succeed?"

I looked out the window. "People who want to die, die. It's shockingly easy, really."

"She's a child," said Shannon.

"Well, a very young woman."

"As were you, once." The BMW purred through the tunnel of the trees, splashing briskly through puddles, windshield wipers whisking back and forth relentlessly.

"Yes, damn it." I stared through the streaming windshield at the swirling mist full of soaked-forest colors. "Okay. It was a cry for help. I don't know how to help her."

"Not your job," Shannon said comfortably.

"No man is an island."

"You're not in charge."

She was right. That didn't make it any easier to accept. "I miss Killer," I said abruptly.

"I know," she said.

The diffused light was remarkable: it was as though the forest itself were luminous. Each radiant green frond of bracken or sword fern, bent to the soaked ground under the weight of the rain, shone like emeralds. Tree trunks were rough-cast in bronze and copper, their bold limbs traced in gold. There were no shadows. The light came from everywhere and nowhere, turning the entire forest into a numinous wonderland of clear, pure colors and shapes.

Here and there a tiny waterfall poured down a bank onto the road, to pool in muddy sheets that the BMW skated through without a check. "Okay," said Shannon, guiding the car effortlessly through a broad, shallow puddle. She glanced at me again, sighed, and said, "Let's talk about the case."

"Let's talk about where we're going."

"Right. Swilhurst Associates has a branch office in Moraga. I made us an appointment with them. We're interested in investing in the Valley Nuevo project." She looked smug. "That's what they call the Fey Valley take-over. There are brochures in the glove compartment. They're going to build a gated, luxury community—if they can get Fey Valley. Their investors are pretty impressive: Fey Valley is in a really good location for a project like this. Spiff up the road and utilities, build a golf course and some luxury residences—there are some architects' sketches for those in one of the brochures, I think—add some very select commercial enterprises, and viola! A classy rich folks' zone."

"The viola is a musical instrument," I said. "The word you want is *voilà*."

"I don't know what you have against violas," she said. "They'll probably destroy most of the forest, and dam the stream, and tear out all the existing cottages."

"The violas will?"

"The Valley Nuevo project will. And Salonian's fountain: I don't think they'd want to keep that."

"I don't think he'd leave it," I said. "If he had to move, he'd take it with him. Unless they paid extra for it, which why would they if they're going to tear it out?"

"Right, whatever. So the point is, you have a classy project here, and some investors who are more than usually committed to it: it's not just money, it's the principle of the thing. They want to live here. And they don't take kindly to a bunch of scraggly artists saying they can't."

"Those 'scraggly artists' include some of the best-known and highest-paid artists in the country."

"Oh, like that matters. They're still artists. They can be as rich as sin and it won't make them well-bred. High society doesn't let in just any old multimillionaires, you know."

"No, I suppose not."

"Artists are such riffraff. Not to mention elves and halflings."

"It sounds as though the Valley Nuevo project would please Moraga's residents a lot more than the Fey Valley Association does. So we're going to claim we want to invest in it? Surely they won't mistake us for members of the moneyed elite?"

"Well, not us, exactly. But you may be forgetting Konny's background." Konny was her boyfriend, Konrad Silverfinch. There was much about his name to spark amusement. Luckily he had a strong sense of humor.

"Silverfinches have an in? I knew he was rich, but I didn't know he was old money."

"That's because he doesn't care about it, so it doesn't show. Much. He's never had much to do with Society people, but if he says he's decided he wants in on something like this, they'll buy it in a New York minute."

"You know, I've always wondered: what's a New York minute?"

"I don't know," she said. "Just that it's fast. So anyway, we're investigating the Valley Nuevo project on Konny's behalf."

"Why didn't you tell me this before we left the cottage? I'm not exactly power-dressed." I looked ruefully at my grubby jeans, stained sweatshirt, and muddy running shoes.

Shannon shrugged ineffably. "Rich people don't have to power-dress."

"But we're not rich people. We're not even pretending to be rich people: only emissaries."

"Those don't have to power-dress either."

She was probably right. Anyway I hadn't brought any clothes to Fey Valley that I thought might pass for a rich person's. "I guess we'll see," I said.

The rain had slackened, but the sky had darkened, promising further downpour. Shadows began to form and thicken in the gloomy depths of the forest. Shannon stopped the car so suddenly that I was thrown forward against my seat belt. "What?" I said, staring at the empty road ahead.

"That." Shannon wasn't looking at the road: she was staring up at the steep shoulder of the hill next to it.

I leaned forward and twisted my head to see what had caught her attention. The windshield wipers whisk-thunked briskly, wiping the glass clean of mist. Beside the road, the shoulder of the hill thrust steeply upward like a slanted wall, its surface thickly carpeted with bracken and sword fern except where falling water had cut a path in the soil, loosening and scarring it till it formed a miniature ravine, rocky and naked, spilling mud and debris onto the road even as we watched.

"What?" I said. "That waterfall? What about it?"

"That waterfall," she said grimly, "is evidence that you're right about that boy and his dirt bike. He is arrogant and destructive and deserves to be shot."

I looked again and realized that falling water alone hadn't cut that gash in the hillside. Gary's dirt bike had made the initial incision down which the water, always seeking the easiest path, had tumbled so destructively today. And this would not be the last rain of the season; nor, unless the Scotland Yard workers were able to do miracles, would the foliage recover enough by next winter to hold the hillside together again. In one careless off-road joyride he had jeopardized the structure of that hillside forever.

"Shooting would be too kind." That particular hillside wasn't more important than a boy's life, of course. And I didn't really want to see him shot. But the boy who would destroy one hillside for pleasure might destroy anything for pleasure. "You see why I thought of him when I found the cottage wrecked."

"Yes." She put the car in gear and nudged it forward. "Why doesn't someone stop him? Maybe he's too young to know any better, but his parents aren't." We followed the road around the hill, through the gate, and into the last long curve before the straightaway. "He should be made to mend what he's ruined. Fey Valley is entirely landscaped, isn't it? He could work with the gardeners." She shook her head. "You know, it's a wonder one of the FOOFs hasn't killed him by now."

"I thought the same thing at first. But of course they haven't: they would never hurt a child."

"Not even a feral twit?" She shook her head. "No, you're right. Besides, even FOOFs know the rules are different here."

"I don't think it's okay to do away with just anyone who offends, even in Faerie."

"Perhaps not. But anybody who offends the land . . . "

She was right. Gary was lucky our rules were kinder than Faerie honor, and that the elves here willing to obey them.

The Swilhurst Associates branch office was just down the street from the grocery store I'd visited the day before. The building was old; all the buildings in Moraga were old. This one, like the Scotland Yard building, had been extensively renovated in an effort to achieve quaintness. Unlike the Scotland Yard building, it looked repellently cute, and quite out of place on a street of battered old buildings with authentic charm.

By the time we got there I had glanced through all the brochures Shannon brought and had a good idea what they meant to do with Fey Valley. They would remove all the existing structures. They would obliterate Scotland Yard's work and most of the forest to turn the entire floor of the valley into an open, grassy golf course. Then they would line the valley walls with stucco villas that might just as well be in Texas for all the view or value they'd get of one of California's loveliest valleys.

Every element of the design would be fine somewhere else. Not one was appropriate to the rocky woodland they would destroy for it. The only thing they wanted of Fey Valley was its location. I wondered whether the same company was industriously creating a woodsy California valley somewhere in the Plains States. "This is crazy," I said, indicating the sketch of the golf course on the front of one of the brochures.

"This is the way rich people do things," said Shannon. "Put that away and don't look so offended. With any luck at all they'll never get Fey Valley."

"Right. So they'll go ruin some other valley instead."

"Well, very likely you'll never know about it if they do." She led the way to the Swilhurst doorway.

The receptionist scowled down her nose at us, but she didn't seem to mean anything by it. She was middle-aged, ugly, and very well dressed, with jewels by Tiffany.

Maybe she couldn't afford Ariana's work. She greeted us with chilly civility to which Shannon responded with icy charm. The woman seemed impressed by that.

After the initial introductions I might just as well not have been there for all the notice either of them took of me. The receptionist seemed to have taken a fancy to Shannon, and became almost garrulous. After a few minutes' bored attention to the conversation, I began to look around the waiting area.

The furniture was expensive and uncomfortable. In place of paintings, the walls sported maps and aerial photographs of planned communities and shopping malls. Swilhurst Associates seemed to have many projects like Valley Nuevo. I took up a collection of brochures and pamphlets for communities, malls, and small cities, some proposed and some already under construction. I didn't find evidence of any already completed.

Swilhurst had ties to construction, lumber, tile, chemical, and other companies, some less clearly related to the building of planned communities. I found one reference to the space program, and wondered whether they had any brochures for planned communities on the moon.

I tucked the pamphlets and brochures in my purse, admired the maps, examined the model-under-glass of a community in Oregon that may have been meant to look Cretan, and was just starting through the brochures again when Shannon wrapped up her conversation with a profusion of insincere politeness and started for the door. I looked up to find the receptionist eyeing me with strong disfavor, so I smiled and followed Shannon out the door.

"Cheryl Baxter," she said when we got back to the car.

"Gesundheit." Cheryl Baxter was not among my favorite people. She was wealthy, elegant, smart, vindictive, and as egocentric as an elf. We'd met her in the course of an investigation a year ago, and she'd done her best to see us both killed, or at least maimed. When

she learned she'd mistaken us for someone else, she
didn't waste time apologizing; it just didn't occur to her.

Shannon backed the car onto the street. "Cheryl is a
pillar of the community."

"Yeah. The drug community."

"Now, now. She's involved in far more lucrative en-
deavors than just that."

"True. Why do you mention her?"

"She's one of the primary backers for Valley Nuevo."

That was interesting. Cheryl certainly wouldn't hesitate to hire people to frighten the valley residents into
selling. Hell, she'd hire people to kill them if she thought
it worth the bother. She might not be Fey Valley's Trouble, but she certainly was trouble. "You going to talk
to her?"

"Yup." She turned the car toward Fey Valley. The
lowering skies dropped a few fat drops of rain, heavy as
thrown pebbles, onto the roof of the car.

"I'll go with you," I said.

"Nonsense. I'll be fine. Besides, that's tomorrow. Tonight I have a plan."

15

It looked for a while as though the weather would prevent us from trying Shannon's plan that night. By the time we got back to Fey Valley, the rain was falling so hard the forest canopy afforded no protection. It seemed wetter under the trees. Most of the rain fell straight through; but some of it collected on leaves and branches till the weight of it bent them down enough to spill the whole in sudden drenching waterfalls.

We parked in the Hall's lot and waited for a break in the storm, while the windows fogged and rain thundered on the roof in deafening torrents. It was so loud that conversation was nearly impossible. There's something intoxicating about weather like that. We found ourselves giggling with excitement, bellowing comments over the roar of the rain, and seriously considering making a run for the cottage not so much because we were impatient as because we were reduced by the noise and motion to a childlike exaltation in which the possibility of a drenching seemed almost thrilling.

I understood Shannon's Dorothy Parker quote then. "Fey and sudden and unholy" described our mood. It was a benign and joyous madness. Mercifully, it stayed with us most of the way through the mad dash we made, at the first slackening of the rain, through the forest and up the hill to my cottage.

We arrived dripping and giggling, out of breath and shivering as much with excitement as with the cold. The door was properly locked this time, as I had left it. The cottage was unmolested. We burst inside in a welter of laughter and damp garments, shed our muddy shoes by the door, and moved as one to the Franklin stove to start a fire.

It was only after we'd begun to get warm and dry that we spoke again of the Trouble, and then only to complain of the weather and the fact that he, if it was he, had left no identifying clues when he invaded my cottage. "He's left no clues anywhere, has he?" asked Shannon.

"No, but as far as I know he hasn't been inside anywhere before. And I don't suppose he has been now. I think it was Gary. And I don't think Gary is the Trouble."

"Well, I suppose it was Gary; he has easy access to the keys, and dropped that silver bit besides. Unless someone else left that to frame him. But I don't know why you're so sure he isn't the Trouble. If he would trash this place, he would certainly do the other stuff the Trouble has done." She gave her hair one last rub with the towel and asked where my comb was.

"In the bedroom," I said. "I'll get it. But I have a sense that all the other stuff has been more playful than malicious. This was malicious."

"True. Maybe you made him cross."

"That's right, laugh at me. It's just what I'd expect when even the weather conspires against us."

But by evening the skies had cleared and the wind picked up, drying the air and shaking the rain down out of the trees. When we went down to the Hall for dinner, the ground was still soaked and muddy in spots, but it was enough drier that Charlotte had a fair turnout for her reheated tacos. They were delicious.

The men who had been present at breakfast were there, of course; they must have hoped for another glimpse of Shannon. Their faces lit when we entered. Finandiel very politely made me welcome while everyone else greeted Shannon. He even pulled out a chair for me. It was sweet of him, and surprisingly thoughtful for an elf.

"How goes the investigation?" he asked.

"Not too bad," I said. "We may have a lead: Shannon will be following it up in town."

"Indeed," he said. "I am much impressed."

I shrugged. "It may come to nothing."

"Still, that you have a notion of where to look bodes well. Will you have a drink? Cuthbern, a drink for our angel. What will you?"

I wondered whether, if I asked for ambrosia, Cuthbern would conjure it for me. But I didn't, for fear he would. "Just wine," I said, expecting him to pour me a glass from the bottle on the table.

He didn't. He conjured ambrosia from thin air, pouring it from an unseen bottle that he held with both hands while he used it and simply released as though it didn't exist when my glass was full. The wine was delicate, dry, and delicious. Finandiel smiled at my expression when I tasted it. He said complacently, "It is the wine of my house."

"It's wonderful," I said a trifle too intensely.

His smile remained decorous, but there was an impish twinkle in his eyes. "The head of my house will be grateful to learn of your approval," he said.

I eyed him suspiciously. "Who *is* the head of your house? Your brother, Lord Dyrimar?"

"My brother is head of the family," he said. "Daelinn is the head of my house."

One of the children on the other side of the room squealed in sudden anger, startling me and making an elf at the other end of the table spill her wine. She used a paper napkin to sop it up, scowling at the child's mother, and looking as arrogant about it as any elf would. They are as graceful as cats; and, like cats, they cover their rare missteps with a ferocious indifference that almost convinces one they really did mean to do whatever they've done, no matter how silly.

"Are you all right, Lorielle?" asked Charlotte. "Here, let me clean that up." Lorielle accepted her services without surprise or thanks.

Finandiel was looking at me expectantly, and it took

me a moment to remember what we'd been talking about. But even I had heard of Daelinn.

"The Duke of Daelinn?" I said. "I hadn't realized you were related to him." I knew very little about Faerie aristocracy, but I knew the Duke of Daelinn was the next thing to royalty.

"That is probably the best English translation of Kimendan's title," Finandiel said judiciously. "Yes, I am a minor cousin of his. It is a distant relationship only, but gives me access to the best of Daelinn wines." He smiled affably at me and sipped his wine, surveying the table over the rim of his glass with a bland and rather silly expression that made me instantly suspicious. An elf as powerful as he, who contrives to look that stupid, is even more dangerous than most elves; and that is very dangerous indeed. But I'd guessed that about him already.

When we'd finished eating, Shannon made noises about how late it was, and that she'd better be getting back to town. I followed her as far as the front porch, assured her I would call tomorrow to see what came of her meeting with Cheryl Baxter, went back inside for the umbrella she'd left by her chair, and finally waved good-bye as she pulled out onto the road and turned toward town. Night had slid in under the trees while we were at dinner. I regretted not having brought a flashlight with me from the cottage. Luckily Charlotte had a stock of them in the kitchen that people had left in the Hall. She gave me one, and told me how nice Shannon was and how lucky I was to have such a charming partner.

When I went back into the great room, Finandiel pressed another glass of Daelinn wine on me, and recited the elven equivalent of limericks till Salonian asked him, rather peevishly, to stop, then took advantage of the silence to tell me how charming my partner was.

Kyriander looked worried, which seemed to be his normal state these days. It made me want to swat Lilie: all her brother's creative energies were being spent worrying about her dramatics. As far as I could tell he hadn't written a word since I'd been in Fey Valley, and he used to be quite a prolific writer. He didn't mention Shannon, but Chance Winter told me at considerable length how lucky I was to have such a charming partner, and pestered me with personal questions about her.

I fled, finally, on a chorus of reluctant "good nights" from those who wished I had stayed to answer their questions about Shannon as well.

It had been at least forty-five minutes since she left. Ample time, I hoped. I had made much, while I was in the Hall, of the fact that I meant to take a nice, long evening walk. If the Trouble were any of the people now in the Hall, we had to allow time not just for Shannon to get in place, but for whoever it was to get out and ahead of me, or at least far enough from the Hall to seem not to be coming right from it; so I dawdled along the way.

The reported incidents had taken place all over the valley, but the highest concentration was near Salonian's fountain. Most had been on the path on the far side of it, so that was where Shannon would be in hiding and where we hoped the Trouble would find me. But there was nothing to say I wouldn't find it anywhere along any path, so I was on my guard from the time I left the Hall.

Once I thought I heard someone behind me; bushes rustling, and something that sounded like a foot scuffing in fallen leaves. But it was only some wild thing about its rightful business in the night. When I flashed my light toward it, I heard it bound away, startled, into the underbrush, to fall silent deep in some secret place among the trees.

Salonian's fountain was only a bulk of shadow beside the path. I kept my light from it, feeling very little inclined to admire a nymph nurturing death. Instead of turning toward my cottage, I continued on toward Ariana's and all the other dwellings between the road and the stream. Shannon should have parked in the pull-off above Ariana's house and made her way back down the crosspath to this one.

Unfortunately I'd begun to realize how very optimistic it was of us to have thought anything would necessarily come of this. The Trouble didn't manifest every night, or attempt to frighten everyone who took a walk alone on the Fey Valley pathways. Nor did it only manifest after dark. Shannon had just as good a chance of meeting it when she was getting into position during the last fading light of dusk as I had now in full darkness.

But what seemed by far the most likely was that neither of us would see it. There was no reason in the world for it to be out on a miserable, dripping, chilly night like this, just waiting for us to catch it.

As though to emphasize my point, a vagrant breeze through the leaves above my head shook down a miniature waterfall on my head. I cursed under my breath and shook my head hard to get the water out of my hair, while cold drops slid under my collar and down my back. Surely nothing and no one who didn't have to would be out on a night like this.

I found the place where Ariana's path crossed the main path, and slowed my pace; Shannon should be in hiding near here. The trickle of water down my back was slow to warm to my skin temperature. I shuddered. Next time maybe I would think to wear a warmer jacket.

The forest smelled fresh from the rain. The only sounds were the muffled scuff of my own feet in the thick layer of damp leaves, and the sporadic drip of rain from one leaf to another or the occasional brief torrent when the weight of the collected raindrops became too much for some slender branch. My shivering shook the flashlight, making shadows leap as the bright oval of its light danced across bushes and tree trunks.

One of the shadows kept moving when the light was still. I flicked off the light. Had it seen me? Was Shannon near enough to see what happened? I stood still, straining to hear. Our hasty plan suddenly seemed ridiculously makeshift. Shannon might be too far away. Or the movement I saw might even be Shannon. But I didn't think it was.

It glided toward me, a darker shape in the darkness. Sudden, primitive, gibbering instinct overtook me, and I had to resist a nearly overwhelming urge to turn and flee before it was too late. In a city I might have done better; but here, this approaching blackness might be any monster, any horror, anything. This was the stuff of nightmares.

It was still ten feet or more away from me when I could not endure the uncertainty any longer. The flashlight was a feeble enough weapon, but it was all I had. I jerked it upward and flicked the switch to pinion the unknown in its yellow cone of light.

16

Ariana blinked at me in surprise. "Who's that?"

So much for dramatic gestures. "It's me: Rose," I said. "What are you doing out in the dark?"

"Just taking a walk," said Ariana.

"In the *dark*?"

"Well, it's probably not as dark to me as it is to you," she said apologetically.

I'd forgotten that most halflings' night vision is almost as good as elves'. Even with the moon concealed by clouds, the forest must look very nearly daylit to her. "Oh, right. Well. Have you seen anybody else out tonight? Or any sign of the Trouble?"

"No sign of anything untoward," she said. "I had a lovely walk, though the path does get muddy a bit farther on. If you don't have a particular goal in mind, you might want to walk another way."

"Thanks," I said. "But first I need to find my partner." A certain crashing of underbrush gave us a hint as to where I might look for her. I grinned at Ariana's expression. "We're city folk," I said, shrugging. "We're doing our best, but it's an alien environment."

"Rose?" called Shannon. "Is that you?"

"Here," I said. "You okay?"

"I think so." She stumbled into the circle of light and scowled at her muddy shoes. "Thank goodness: I thought I might be wandering in the damn forest forever. I seem to've misplaced the path a little bit."

Ariana laughed. "My cottage is just along here," she said. "Would you two like to stop in for a cup of tea?"

"Thanks, yes," Shannon said gratefully. "Especially if

you have towels." She shook her dripping hair. "A bush rained on me." She had to raise her voice to make herself heard over the noise of Gary Cameron's motorcycle passing by on the road.

"Damn that boy," said Ariana, wincing and covering her ears.

We turned back toward the path to her house, walking three abreast since the main path was wide enough. "I thought at first he had no muffler," I said, "but now I wonder whether he hasn't installed one designed to enhance rather than muffle the sound."

"Is that possible?" asked Ariana, taking the turnoff to her house. We had to go single file on the narrower path.

"I believe so."

"Someone will kill him one day," she said, in much the tone one might use to say it could rain tomorrow. "Poor Charlotte. But he has been warned."

"You mean somebody's threatened him?" asked Shannon.

Ariana looked at her in surprise. "Threatened? Of course not. But more than one of us has taken him aside to explain the danger. I thought at first that he must not realize how he was hurting us, especially the Truebloods." She hesitated. "Indeed, I still think that. He's been told, but I don't think he quite believes it."

"He's been raised among elves. Why wouldn't he believe it?" asked Shannon.

"Because he's an egocentric toad," I said.

"That isn't *quite* the way I'd have put it," said Ariana, "but yes. Just so."

Shannon had to take off her shoes at Ariana's door since they were covered with mud. Ariana gave her a towel to dry her hair, and disappeared into the kitchen to make tea while we settled in the living room. The cat Tinker was deeply offended by our presence, and crouched on a table with his ears laid back, growling deep in his throat.

"What a handsome tom," said Shannon. He hissed and raked his claws through the air in her direction. "Friendly, too." Her gaze shifted from him to the Tiffany lamp behind him. "Oh." She turned slowly in place, taking in all the cheerful colors and shapes of the room. "Oh, how pretty."

"Isn't it?" I felt almost proprietary; after all, I'd seen Ariana's work first. "She made most of these beautiful things, you know."

"I'm impressed," she said, meaning it.

Ariana brought us tea and watched indulgently while we admired the shelves full of wonders. She told us a little about her crafts, and showed us a case of gorgeous jewelry I hadn't seen before, and offered us cookies.

It was some time before Shannon finally said, "It's getting late. We should go home."

"You're surely not going to drive back to town tonight?" asked Ariana.

"No, I meant Rosie's cottage," she said, yawning. "I'm too tired to drive anywhere."

We took our leave of Ariana and walked in flashlit silence back past Salonian's fountain and up the path to my cottage stairs. Shannon kicked off her wet shoes on the porch and left them there. "So," she said, flopping onto my couch. "What d'you think?"

"What shall I think it about?" I kicked off my shoes and wondered whether it was worth the effort to start a fire.

"Ariana, for starters," she said. "How did she look when you caught her?"

"Caught her?"

"In the forest."

"Jeez, I didn't catch her, I just ran into her."

She shrugged. "How did she look?"

"Fine. Surprised. I need a shower. I'm cold."

"Why not start a fire?" she asked in surprise.

"It's too much trouble," I said.

"No, it isn't." She built a fire in the stove, held a match to it, blew on it for a moment, and sat back down on the couch while tender little flames crackled joyously along the wood. "Did Ariana look guilty at all?"

"More like embarrassed, but I figured that was because I'd startled her. Do you suspect her?"

"Not necessarily; but if she isn't the Trouble, I think she's covering for it. She's certainly hiding something."

"If Leaf really saw the Trouble beside the Hall last night, Ariana can't be it; she was with me."

"Good point. But we don't know what Leaf saw."

"We don't, in fact, know what any of them saw. Or whether they saw anything. That's the problem."

"You saw something, the first night you were here."

"Felt," I said.

"And right before you met Ariana tonight," said Shannon, "I thought I heard somebody sneaking around in the forest. Maybe people speaking very softly. And then one of them hurrying away. And then you met Ariana."

"So you think she is the Trouble or was talking to it?" I asked. She shrugged. "But she could have been talking to anybody," I said. "Jeez, considering we heard him take off right afterward, she might have been talking to Gary."

"And that's another thing," said Shannon. "What was Gary doing out there at that time of night? Why did he drive away right then?"

"I really can't imagine him and Ariana in cahoots. You heard her talking about him getting killed for his noise. Did she sound like she was talking about her partner in crime?"

Shannon shrugged. "Who can tell, with a halfling? Maybe she inherited elven morality. Or maybe she's just been around them so much, she's adopted their code of honor."

"If it was Gary you heard with Ariana, I don't think he could have got back to the road in time to start the motorcycle and make that racket so soon after we met her."

"I don't know. This isn't getting us anywhere. Go to bed. Do you have any blankets for me? I'll sleep out here by the fire."

I found blankets for her in the bedroom closet and went to take a shower. When I came out again, the lights were off in the living room, but Shannon wasn't asleep yet: "I'm going to see if Ariana is connected with Swilhurst Associates in any way."

It only made sense. "Okay," I said. "Check the others while you're at it. It's as good a motive for any of them as for her."

I went to sleep to the sound of the fire crackling in the Franklin stove in the other room. It was a comforting, homey sound, soothing to some primitive part of me that doubtless believed a brisk campfire would ward off mastodons.

Sometime later, when the fire had died down and the night was otherwise utterly still, I woke to the haunting strains of Faerie music played somewhere deep in the forest.

Others were discussing the music the next morning at the Hall. Several of the residents had heard it, and no one admitted to making it. It seemed this was another, rather ghostly, manifestation of the Trouble.

"So now we have an intruder who pushes people into streams, frightens children, steals food and tools, vandalizes cottages, and plays music in the night, is that it?" Shannon said when the others had gone.

"That would seem to be the idea," I said. We were sitting over coffee after breakfast. Several people had eaten with us but promptly gone about their business afterward. Charlotte was still in the kitchen cleaning up, but otherwise we had only Peaceable for company.

"Seems an odd intruder, to me," Shannon said.

"Well, yes," I said. "Nobody said it wouldn't be odd."

"Or intruders, more likely," she said. "At least two: one for the vandalism and maybe the thefts, and one for the rest of it. Or maybe a third one for the music."

"What a busy valley."

"Isn't it?" she said brightly. "Let's go get my car so I can drive back to town and get to work."

It was another miserable, gray, ugly day. We drove in silence through the center of the valley and around the first hairpin turn toward town. The forest seemed more claustrophobic than ever to me after last night's fruitless excursions, and I found myself glancing skyward, looking for a break in the canopy, when I could take my attention off the road.

Which is why even though I was driving, it was Shannon who noticed the skid marks on the road, and the broken underbrush beside it. "Stop the car," she said.

I put on the brakes at once. "What? Why?" I was looking for some hazard to driving, and saw none.

"Find a place to pull over," she said. "I think there's been an accident." She pointed.

"Oh, damn." It was easy enough to see, once she drew my attention to it. The long skid and scrape marks where he had tried to regain control led straight off the road at the curve. "Can you see any sign of him down there?" I found a pull-off, not quite wide enough for my car, but I made do.

"I'm not sure," she said, opening her door. "Let me out before you cram the car up against those bushes."

"Oh, right." I waited while she got out, then parked and followed her.

She had stopped at the edge of the road; there was no need to go farther. It was Gary, and it was evident from here that he was beyond our help. The motorcycle, wedged against a madrone just down the slope from the road, looked only a little the worse for wear. Gary, lodged grotesquely in the broad fork of a live oak some distance farther down, had been less fortunate. "I guess one of us should stay here," said Shannon.

"Right. I'll go back down to the Hall."

She looked at me gratefully. "You sure?"

"Yeah." Staying with the body would be a lot less onerous than having to tell people what we'd found. But I'd known them longer, so that seemed to be my job. "I'll be back up as soon as I can."

"No hurry," she said. "Try not to bring the entire population back with you."

"I'll try." We both knew what chance I had of success. "There's a camera in my car. You better photograph whatever's crucial before anyone gets here."

"Right." She came back to the car with me to get it. "Good luck."

"Thanks."

I parked in front of the Hall and climbed out of my car, feeling old and useless. Peaceable lumbered to his feet to greet me with great joy and relief, as though I were one of his very favorite people and had been gone for hours, perhaps days. I patted him absently, wiped his slobbery kisses off my hands, and stepped into the Hall.

Charlotte was just wiping the table. She started to smile: it was hard to tell with her, but I thought she was genuinely pleased to see me. But she saw something in my face, and the smile died unborn. "What?" she said. "What's happened?"

She was bent over the table, one hand outstretched with the cloth in it to wipe away crumbs, her head lifted from the work, her face already shadowed with the tragedy she had not yet heard. I wanted to hug her, but I knew better: that fierce independence would not welcome or even tolerate sympathy. "Charlotte," I said helplessly, "I'm sorry."

She straightened slowly, her face very still. "What? Tim? Gary?"

"Gary," I said. "He's had an accident."

She carefully folded the cloth in her hands. "What kind of accident? Is he—?" Her voice was level and steady, but she couldn't finish the question. I think she knew the answer.

"A motorcycle accident," I said. "I need to call the police. I'm so sorry, Charlotte." For some reason I could not force myself to say it, any more than Charlotte could. We stared at each other in silence for a long moment before she finally sighed, doggedly finished wiping the table, and then sat down and closed her eyes.

Her movement released me from thrall. I moved across the room to the telephone, noticing for the first time that there were others present: Benjamin Barski and Salonian were discussing something in a corner of the great room, and Ritchie Morita was so busy typing that I don't think he had noticed my arrival at all. Mildred Potter sat near the two sculptors, studying a huge account book. And Chance Winter was fussing with a camera and several lenses at a table in a far corner of the room.

I went to the telephone, dialed 911, and waited. By the time the response came, everyone in the room was watching me. I made my report as clear and succinct as I could and agreed to meet the investigating officers at the site. Just as I hung up, the back door to the kitchen slammed and I glanced up to see Tim Cameron leaning against it, staring at me.

"What did you say?" he demanded.

17

"There's been an accident," I said. "Gary crashed his motorcycle coming down the last hairpin from town. I'm sorry, Mr. Cameron."

"I don't believe it," he said, shaking his head. "No. He was too good with that thing. It's not possible."

"Even a good driver could hit an oil slick," I said. "Or a rock, or something. Motorcycles are risky vehicles."

"Nonsense." He glared at me, then reached for Charlotte. "Come on, woman. We'll see about this." He sounded threatening.

Charlotte just stared at him. "If I told him once, I told him a hundred times," she said. "One day one of them would just snap. I warned him."

"One of what would snap?" I asked. "What are you talking about?"

"Never mind," said Tim. "Come along, Charlotte."

"One of the elves," she said impatiently. "They didn't like the noise, you know. It hurt them. And they don't think like we do."

I glanced at the elves in the great room. Salonian was the only Trueblood there. He looked at me for a moment, then leaned over to say something under his breath to Barski, who nodded and set aside the papers in his lap to get up.

"We'll go get him," said Tim.

"He has to be left for the police," I said.

"He should be brought home," said Tim. "He'll be more comfortable."

I stared at him in exasperation. "Mr. Cameron, you can't help him."

"Yes." He nodded and opened the door, reaching for Charlotte to come with him. "We'll just see about this."

"Mr. Cameron, your boy is *dead*."

The back door closed gently behind him and Charlotte, who had moved after him in a daze. Several of the people in the great room were trooping toward the front door. I realized abruptly that Shannon might need help preserving the scene till the police got there.

I managed to be first out of the parking lot, and I parked in the same spot on the hill, leaving no good place for any of the other cars. No one seemed to mind. They parked wherever they happened to stop. Fortunately most of them seemed willing to stare from the road, but Tim Cameron headed straight across the verge toward his son.

Shannon stepped in front of him before he'd got off the pavement. "Mr. Cameron," she said. "You'll destroy evidence of what happened."

"I don't need evidence," he said, shoving her aside.

She stepped in front of him again. "The police do," she said.

He put out his hand to push her aside again, but by then I was there beside her, blocking his way. "Stop it," I said. "Mr. Cameron, stop it. Stay on the road. The police will be here soon. Leave things as they are till then."

He nearly knocked me down. If Ritchie Morita hadn't decided to play tough guy, Tim might have walked right through us to his son's body. As it was, Ritchie provided just enough additional barrier: and he offered fisticuffs in defense of me and Shannon, which was diverting.

"Mind your own business," said Tim, towering over Ritchie. But the very notion of being attacked by this feisty little tough guy had distracted him enough that I thought the crisis was past. Tim had been drinking, but he wasn't stupid yet. He knew he didn't really want to hit anybody.

"This is my business," said Ritchie. "It's all our business."

Tim looked surprised. "You didn't even like my boy."

His voice caught in his throat as he realized he'd used the past tense.

"I like murder less," Ritchie said portentously.

"We don't know it was murder," I said.

"I warned him," said Charlotte. She stood helplessly at the edge of the road, alone, her shoulders squared and her face grim, tears dripping unnoticed from her chin. "I told him elves don't think like we do. They're sociopaths. They can't help themselves."

"I think the proper term is affective personality disorder," Ritchie said pedantically.

"No it isn't," she said certainly. "It's not a disorder with them. It's the way they are. They don't know any better, and they can't learn. If I told him once, I told him a hundred times, you just don't *do* something that hurts elves like that. You just *don't.*"

"Charlotte," Ritchie said patiently, "there's nothing to say that an elf was responsible for this accident."

"I know what I know," Charlotte said belligerently. Tears were dripping onto the front of her shirt. She seemed unaware of them.

"Charlotte," said Tim.

"And that's another thing," she said, turning on me and Shannon. "If this is the goddammed Trouble," she said, "and not some elf killing Gary just because he made a little noise with his motorcycle, then I think it's just gotten out of hand, and I think it's about damn time you start earning your goddammed keep, because you sure as hell haven't done us any good so far."

Another car had pulled up while she was talking. I glanced around, hoping for the police, but no such luck: it was Rosetta Fulmer, with Lilie for a passenger.

" . . . So I'd bring her," Rosetta said as she got out of the car. She was talking to us, not to Lilie, though none of us had been able to hear the beginning of the sentence. "Since I didn't want her wandering the forest in that state, but I can't think it's wise." She paused at the side of the road with the rest of us. "Oh, dear," she said, genuinely distressed. "Charlotte, I am so sorry. Are you all right? Tim, oh dear. You should both sit down.

Would you like to sit down? We could get something for you to sit on. You could sit in my car. Did you bring a car? I don't think you ought to be standing here, and of course none of us can go down there yet, not that it's going to be any better when we can, because anyone can see it's not going to be better, but I wish I could *do* something," she finished vaguely, expressing the helplessness I think we all felt.

I was distracted by her chatter and forgot all about Lilie. I didn't see the child coming till she collided with me, hitting and kicking and biting me furiously, like a trapped animal, in desperate and deadly silence. She caught me so much by surprise that I nearly killed her without thinking.

Fortunately Shannon saw what was happening. "Rose!" she said sharply. "No! It's only Lilie."

It was sheer luck she spoke in time. I didn't quite comprehend the words; if it had been anyone else than Shannon, I would have acted first and figured them out afterward. As it was, I froze. Shannon wouldn't risk my life by speaking when I needed to protect myself.

It took a moment to figure out that while I shouldn't kill her I could defend myself. By then Shannon was pulling Lilie off me, but not before she got in a few good kicks, slaps, and yanks on my hair. I nearly broke her arm for that.

"Don't, Rosie," said Shannon. "Lilie, cut it out. Stop that. You're acting like a child. The only reason you can hurt her is that she's letting you, can't you see that? Stop it!"

Lilie, as seemed usual by now, was hysterical and incoherent. I didn't even try to make sense of her words, but turned instead to greet Ariana as she came bustling up onto the road from the forest path just below the hairpin.

We were pretty much all there by then: everyone who had been at the Hall had come along just after us, and word seemed to have spread, so half the valley's residents had come along since.

Kyriander came down the path from the other side of

the road to take Lilie from Shannon's grasp. Benjamin Barski and Salonian had taken over the job of keeping Tim Cameron from going to his dead son. Mildred Potter and Chance Winter were with Charlotte, trying to comfort her. She stood grim and resolute and solitary between them, staring down through the underbrush at her son's body with a bleak, angry look, as though by dying in this way he had at last offended her past bearing.

Salonian seemed to be the only Trueblood here. I began to think if we waited long enough, every halfling and human in the valley would show up; but Truebloods, for whom death is rare and, barring accidents or malice, unlikely, seem in general surprisingly indifferent to it. Not so Salonian, who sculpted it.

The police arrived at last, we told them what had happened, and they began to investigate and interview. After a time the coroner arrived. Gary's body was removed. Kyriander took Lilie away on the path through the woods toward their cottage. Ariana, watching the others disperse, glanced at me and said, "Charlotte will be fixing a meal at the Hall if you two are interested."

"Good God, why?" asked Shannon. "That was her *son*!"

Ariana looked at her. "She is aware of that," she said expressionlessly. Then, relenting: "She's an artist. Cooking is her art. She can submerge herself in it, and it will soothe her, as our other arts soothe the rest of us." With a wry smile she added, "But don't tell that to the Fine Artists among us." The capital letters were audible. "Cooking is even less esteemed than crafts."

"I see," said Shannon. Ariana nodded and strode away into the forest, looking in her flowing skirts and shawls so like the plump matron (and possible witch) in a fairy tale that I stared till Shannon said, "Earth to Rosie. Hello."

"Oh, right. Sorry." I looked at her. "Well. Shall we go down to the Hall for lunch?"

"Yes, please." Her car was within walking distance, so we separated at mine.

Everyone who had driven up to the scene of the accident seemed now to be parked in the Hall's parking lot; those who had driven to the accident had, most of them, driven back, even if they ordinarily walked to the Hall from their homes. And I was very likely not the only one who paused among all the cars, absently listening for the shattering roar of Gary's motorcycle, before remembering he wouldn't be by that way again.

As Ariana had predicted, Charlotte was immersed in her cooking and seemed oblivious to everything else. Tim was in the great room, absorbing a bottle of gin. Kyriander had not brought Lilie here, for which I was grateful. That child seemed to believe quite sincerely that I was at the root of every difficulty in her life, and I was getting just a trifle sick of it.

Among all those present, interestingly enough, few seemed to be talking about the accident. I heard discussions of the weather, of Scotland Yard's gardening, of the general condition of the main road through Fey Valley, of the school, of Charlotte's cooking, of Tim's drinking, of art, and even one mention of the Trouble, but not a word about Gary until Finandiel and Cuthbern, who had not been at the scene of the accident, arrived at the Hall for lunch.

Then it was as though floodgates opened. Everyone gathered around the newcomers to report. It was as though they had all been awaiting an excuse, or perhaps permission; as though they had believed they ought not to discuss it casually, but the new arrivals gave them an excuse.

Cuthbern stayed in the background, listening with a grave expression. Finandiel responded in his usual silly, twittering way. "You don't say," he said. "But how unspeakable. And Charlotte? Tim? Is there nothing we can do for them?" Finandiel's face actually paled as he thought of it. "Their *child*," he repeated, in the reverent tone of one naming incalculable treasure. "Their child. It is unthinkable." He sat abruptly at the table, his narrow aristocratic face somehow even more frail-looking and vulnerable than usual. "A drink, Cuthbern," he said in genuine distress. It made him seem petulant and unexpectedly old. "I want a drink."

"Yes, my lord." Cuthbern didn't ask what drink his master wanted. He produced one by magic and helped Finandiel's shaking fingers wrap themselves around the gleaming Faerie-gold goblet in which it arrived.

"Tim and Charlotte are human," Galinda reminded him. "They don't feel it as we would."

"Oh, right," said Chance Winter. "Absolutely. Humans have no real emotions, not like elves, who have to make do with a complicated system of honor because they have none at all."

"They have emotions," said Ariana. "As have humans. And you know it. Come on, people. Don't be petty. We have to pull together to get through difficult times."

"Is this difficult for you?" asked Galinda, glaring like a belligerent child. "In what way?"

Ariana glared back, childish too. They all looked childish to me in that moment. They were squabbling over nonsense, over nothing, just so they wouldn't have to look at an ugliness that none of them wanted to see. This bratty fractiousness was their best defense against simple reality.

The notion seemed odd at first, since each of them dealt in art with the knottiest problems and grimmest aspects of reality; but of course that was art. That was, perhaps, what made their work most powerful: that they didn't even know how to look at life except through the filters of their artistic vision.

The writer saw everything in terms of words; the painters in terms (perhaps) of hues and values; the sculptors in terms of shapes and form; the photographer in terms of light. Each of them would know exactly, instinctively, how to express Gary's death and all the attendant emotions in the medium of his art, but none of them knew what to do with it in ordinary conversation.

"I don't like it," said Marc Starr, looking petulant. "It's not what I'm used to." I half expected him to tell us to make it go away; but before he could say more,

Charlotte emerged from the kitchen to announce the meal. She stood to one side of the kitchen doorway, stirring something in a deep bowl, while people filed through to fill their plates with lunch.

We were eating when the police finally came down the hill to tell us they had concluded their investigation. Gary had been driving too fast, lost control, and skidded off the road, they said. It happened all the time to teenage boys with motorcycles too powerful for their limited skills.

Gary had not been wearing a helmet at the time of the accident. The police were aware that he deliberately made his motorcycle illegally loud. Their conclusion, that he was in other ways that most common of careless drivers, a teenager more interested in thrill and power than safety, was a logical one.

According to Charlotte, it was also wrong. She had come out of the kitchen to listen to the police report. She stirred her bowl of whatever-it-was throughout the tall, apologetic policeman's little speech. Near the end of it she began shaking her head; and when he was done, she said, "No. You're wrong. He was a very good driver. He would never have lost control like that without help."

The policeman, red-haired and becoming red-faced, but still frightfully polite, said carefully, "Ma'am, I understand how you feel. But the boy was on a motorcycle. They're dangerous vehicles. Even the best motorcyclists can lose control in difficult circumstances. Your boy was going too fast, ma'am, and he encountered an oil slick. No matter how good he was, there was nothing he could do to save himself."

She shook her head stubbornly. "They've made it look like that. But he wouldn't have lost control."

"By 'they,' ma'am," he said, "who do you mean?"

"The elves, of course. If I told him once I told him a hundred times, if he didn't make that machine quieter they would kill him. Elves don't think like we do, you know. He was hurting them. They would kill him. Anyone knows that."

The policeman looked helplessly at the roomful of impassive elves and halflings. "Ma'am, do you have any evidence of this?"

"I don't need it," she said, still stirring implacably. "I know what I know."

18

After lunch Shannon and I went back to the scene of the accident. We parked where we had before, and walked back to the edge of the road where everyone had milled around earlier, obliterating any footprints the perpetrator might have left.

We were pretty sure the police were wrong: it hadn't been an accident. Or at least, not an unassisted accident. But that didn't mean Charlotte was right about the elves. Gary was just an annoyance really, and usually even elves don't kill in annoyance. More important, he was still a child. Elves do not kill children.

Which was also a defense for the Trouble, if the Trouble was an elf. "But," said Shannon, "he was getting old for them to call him a child. It's perfectly possible somebody from outside would think he was adult." She stared for a moment at the skid marks on the asphalt, glanced uphill to make sure no traffic was coming, then walked downhill a little distance past the place where Gary had gone off the road.

"What are you doing?" I asked.

She turned around and walked back up the hill to where the skid marks started. "Right here," she said. "Look on the sides of the road."

"What am I looking for?" But I saw it before she answered: a pale, fresh scrape mark circling a madrone trunk on a level with my knees. "Oh."

"You found it?" She moved to the opposite side of the road, looking for a tree on a level with mine, found it, and bent to peer at the trunk. "Me too." She bent to touch it. "The wire's still attached."

"At this end too." I pushed aside shrubbery to get at the thin, fine brass wire that had been fastened securely around the madrone. It took a moment to untangle it from the bushes, but I did it, and dragged it out into the road. Shannon was doing the same on her side, but hers was the shorter piece.

"It broke on the high side," she said, "instead of where he hit it. Do you suppose it left a mark on his tire?"

"If it had, wouldn't the police have found it?" But we were both moving toward the wreckage, leaving the wire behind.

"They weren't looking for it," she said.

But we didn't find it either, even though we knew what to look for. Eventually we went back up to the road and I picked up the end of the wire again. "I've seen this sort of thing somewhere," I said.

"Wire is fairly common, worldwide," she said.

"I meant here," I said. "In the valley. In somebody's home, I think."

"Well, how many homes have you been in, here?"

"Mine, Kyri's, and Ariana's," I said.

"Right." She was silent for a moment. "The police know about the Trouble, right?"

"They were called in on it before I was," I said.

"That doesn't mean they know about it, exactly."

"No. I get the strong impression they don't really believe it exists. Or at least, not outside certain artistic, overexcited imaginations."

"Let's get back in the car," she said, hugging herself. "It's chilly."

"So it is." We returned to the cars and got into hers. The morning fog had burned away. Great, angled pillars of sunlight stood among the trees and leaned their long shadows across the hillside.

"The music-maker was out last night," she said abruptly. "That might be who I heard with Ariana just before we met her. But even if you assume the Trouble is one entity, music-maker and vandal and thief, it's done nothing seriously harmful before except push you when frightened. It was a nuisance, nothing more. Why would it kill Gary?"

"No telling," I said. "And there's no telling it did."

"You don't think Gary's death was an accident."

"No, of course not. That wire wasn't an accident. And it hasn't been there long; it's not even tarnished, and the scrapes it made on the trees are still seeping."

"So that leaves plain old ordinary murder, right?"

"A nasty thought, but so much more likely than things that go bump in the night."

She shook her head. "But we already *have* things that go bump in the night. In this case, you're complicating things if you add a separate murderer."

"Hey, I didn't add a separate murderer. If there is one, he added himself."

We were silent for a moment. "Do you suppose," she said suddenly, "that if the Trouble isn't the murderer, it—the music-making part, anyway, since it was out last night—saw the murder?"

"You mean the wreck itself, or somebody tying the wire to the trees?" I said. "Either way, I s'pose it could have. You think that's a help?"

"Could be, if we catch the Trouble."

"True. Got any ideas on that?"

"We know some people it can't be."

"For parts of it, yeah. Everybody who was at breakfast the other morning is cleared of the vandalism of my cottage. That's Finandiel, Cuthbern, Charlotte, Mildred Potter, Chance Winter, Salonian, and Benjamin Barski." I ticked them off on my fingers and thought about it. "I can't remember whether Ritchie was there.

"Ariana is cleared of being what Leaf saw outside the Hall. Ritchie *probably* didn't push me into the creek, but I couldn't swear to it; there might have been time for him to get back to the Hall before I did." I thought about it. "Did I mention that Kyriander thinks magic is involved, but said we couldn't rule out halflings on that account?"

"You mentioned. I'm not sure that helps any. I'm not

yet willing to rule out humans: I'm not convinced magic is involved. Are you?"

"Not convinced, exactly," I said. "Willing to believe, I guess. Everything I've seen could've been done without it just as easily . . . except the concealment. If it's not using magic, why can't the elves catch it? Unless they're in on it."

"For that matter, if it *is* using magic, why can't they catch it? So anyway. Who was *in* the Hall when Leaf was frightened?"

"Rosetta, Charlotte, Finandiel, Cuthbern, Ritchie Morita, Chance Winter, Galinda, Mildred Potter, and I know there were other elves there, but I can't remember who. Salonian, maybe. Both Lilie and Kyriander were outside the valley that night, since Lilie had just cut her wrists, and they were still at the hospital. Oh, and Gary arrived so soon afterward, I was pretty sure it couldn't have been him."

"Okay," she said. "Duplicates: Finandiel, Cuthbern, Charlotte, Mildred Potter, Chance Winter, and maybe Salonian and Ritchie Morita." She had written the lists down, and she waved her little notebook in the air to illustrate the point. "For whatever that proves. Do we have a list of likely candidates?"

"Everybody," I said. "There's nothing to go by. Except that wire, if I could remember where I've seen it."

"That's if the Trouble killed Gary, which we don't know." She tapped her pencil against her teeth. "There must be somebody who had opportunity every time. Somebody with motive. Somebody who maybe showed up suspiciously soon after, or seemed to know too much."

I shrugged. "What motive? Either everybody has one, or nobody has. And my guess is half the people here know too much."

"Yeah," she said. It wouldn't be the first time we were hired more for show than to get results. If some members of the group wanted to show the rest they had nothing to hide, how better than to hire private investigators they thought couldn't catch them?

Obviously the elves in Fey Valley had something to hide. There was no way they could not know who or what the Trouble was. So the real question was, why were they in collusion with the Trouble, even if only by their silence?

"Are we going to look into Gary's murder?" I said.

"It's not our job," she said. "But . . . yeah."

I sighed. "This is a mess. I hate the country. Did I mention I hate the country?"

"You do not," she said. "You like it. You don't even miss shopping malls."

"Okay, I hate elves, then."

She started the car. "Get out. Go to work. I'm going back to town."

"Lucky you." I got out. "I'm going to take the day off, and sleep a lot."

She nodded seriously. "Good idea," she said, as though I'd suggested some strong, positive course of action.

"You're making fun of me," I said. "Go away."

"Okay. Call if there's news."

I walked back to my car as she pulled away. In moments she was around the next bend in the road. I could still hear the BMW engine purring, but the sound seemed muffled by the stillness that lay over the forest like a blanket. Leaves rubbed against each other, whispering. A raven yelled hoarsely from somewhere far away. The sound of the car engine receded. Silence descended. I paused by my car, listening to nothing, remembering music.

The scream of a jay overhead made me jump. Leaves shifted, and sunlight blinded me. The quiet that had seemed soothing seemed suddenly ominous. I got in the car, slammed the door, and started the engine. My hands were shaking. I kept thinking of Gary's body smashed against a tree on this hillside last night while just below, in the valley, someone or something played haunting Faerie music through the long, still hours until dawn.

I was being ridiculous. "Get a grip," I said, and hauled the car around in a U-turn, bumping over the edges of the road on both sides. Fortunately, since I hadn't bothered to look, there was no traffic. There was never traffic. Only Gary's motorcycle had routinely shattered the solitude on this road, and now even that disruption was stilled.

19

When I got back to the Hall it was nearly deserted: only Ritchie Morita was still there, inevitably clattering away at the typewriter. He interrupted himself to tell me, when I asked, that Tim Cameron had got drunk and Charlotte had taken him home. "Which deprived the others of their entertainment," said Ritchie, "so they've all gone home too."

If it were a personality contest, Ritchie would have won the prime-suspect category long since. He was, really, everything a person could want in a handsome and charismatic bad guy: arrogant, loud, foul-tempered, sharp-tongued, and completely unhuman in his apparent lack of empathy. I sometimes wondered, not seriously, but amazed at how possible it seemed, whether he was an elf in disguise.

"Will Charlotte be okay?" I asked. "She shouldn't have to tend to a drunk at a time like this."

"You'd make a lousy psychologist," he said. "Taking care of Tim will keep her busy. It's good for her: she needs to take care of people. Why the hell do you think she married Tim in the first place?"

"Not because he was a drunk!"

"Maybe not. Frankly, I don't know whether he did drink then. But you can bet he was needy. Sleazy crumbs like that are always needy. And passive-aggressive women like Charlotte are always attracted to them."

I sat in an easy chair near his typing table and looked past him out the window at redwood branches dappled with shifting sun. "Maybe. I still think it's a hell of a time for her to have to tend to his self-indulgence. She must be devastated."

He shrugged. "I guess. She's better off without that obnoxious brat making her life hell, but she probably doesn't see it that way."

"Somebody always cares for obnoxious brats," I said. "Don't you have people who care for you?"

"Yes," he said, "I have," and grinned appreciatively at me. "You're sharper than you look."

"Don't overwhelm me with praise. I'm not sure I can bear up under the shock of it. You didn't like Gary?"

"Who did, besides Charlotte?"

"Lilie," I said, remembering that narrow, gamine face twisted with the cold savagery of grief and rage.

He smiled faintly, almost fondly. "Oh, right, Little Miss Drama Queen." He had been tapping away at the keys between comments, his occasional glances at me supercilious and bored. Now his hands went still and he turned to study me, his expression openly curious. "Frankly, it looked to me as though Lilie was pretty damn lucky this morning."

"What do you mean?"

"I mean if your partner hadn't seen what was happening in time, when Lilie attacked you, she could have ended up badly hurt—or dead. Am I right?"

I felt myself blushing. I wanted to face him down, but I couldn't do it. "I didn't hurt her," I said, looking away.

"I wasn't criticizing. *Au contraire*. I'm glad to know we've hired someone who can cope with adversity."

"Good God," I said, staring. "Cope with adversity? You do have an interesting way with words."

"Thank you," he said, much pleased.

"It wasn't a compliment."

"I know." He smiled at me, quite amiable for once. "You'll forgive me if I take it that way."

"I can't stop you." I nodded toward the stack of paper beside the typewriter. "What are you working on there?"

He looked at the paper in surprise, and then back at me, his expression unreadable. "You might actually be interested; it's not one of my meatier works," he said in a tone meant to irritate. "As you may know, publishing being what it is, I'm forced to turn out the occasional potboiler, to keep up the mortgage payments, between my esteemed but not lucrative literary masterpieces."

I couldn't tell quite how I was meant to take that, but I rather thought he meant exactly what he said, with no overtone of self-mockery at all. "I didn't know," I said noncommittally.

He ignored that. "This one is a retelling of *Romeo and Juliet*," he said. "It takes place largely in Faerie. The protagonists are elves, a boy and girl from, how shall I say it, families unsympathetic to each other. How much do you know of Faerie aristocracy?"

"Not much at all." Peaceable, at his usual guardpost blocking the front door, shifted to let Lorielle come in, and I lifted a hand in greeting. She looked at me nervously and then pretended she hadn't seen me.

Ritchie shrugged. "It's not important: let's just say they're remarkably human in some ways." He nodded in greeting at Lorielle with no change in expression, and looked irritated when she smiled tentatively in response.

"Know you the whereabouts of Mildred?" she asked.

"No," said Ritchie.

"No, sorry," I said; and to Ritchie, "I take it you know quite a bit about it?"

"Enough. I've made a study of it. They're like us in many ways: families at war, that sort of thing. This boy and girl are from such families. A series of accidents brought the children together, and they're modern elves: they love each other. But it's a tragedy. Their families naturally oppose the match."

"So they kill themselves?" I asked him.

"They flee Faerie," he said.

"Oh."

Lorielle had gone into the kitchen, stumbling over the corner of a rug on the way. I had noticed before that she seemed surprisingly clumsy and self-conscious; it was she who spilled her wine the other night at dinner. I'd never before seen a clumsy elf.

"Singularly graceless, isn't she?" said Ritchie, quite as though she wouldn't be able to hear him.

"I think she's just shy," I said uncomfortably.

"A shy elf?" said Ritchie. "Good God, save me from bleeding-heart liberals. There's no such thing as a shy elf. You're anthropomorphizing."

"Maybe, but what do bleeding-heart liberals have to do with anything?"

Lorielle returned from the kitchen with a steaming cup of tea and looked uncertainly at us.

"Just sit down somewhere," he told her impatiently, as though she'd asked. "I'm sure Mildred will show up with the mail soon."

"She brings it here?" I asked.

"The boxes are here," he said, nodding toward a door I'd never paid any attention to, beside the front door. It had always been closed when I was there. "She sorts the mail at home and brings it here to stuff the boxes. Stupid arrangement. She should have it delivered here, so she could stuff the boxes as she goes; but try to tell her that."

"I don't suppose I will," I said. "It's none of my business how she does her job."

"No," he said, "it isn't. How refreshing of you to realize that."

I stared. "But you just said," I said.

"That I knew better than she how she should do her job? Yes. My natural superiority is such that it hardly matters that it's none of my business, does it?" he said amiably.

Whether he meant it or not, it was a funny line, so I laughed. He didn't seem offended. He just kept up his intermittent typing and ignored me.

"Is it not past time for the mail?" asked Lorielle.

Ritchie looked at her. "Who would write to you?"

She stared at him. "You are impudent," she said conversationally.

"Yes," he said. He typed a few lines before continuing: a practice I was beginning to find irritating. It seemed excessively arrogant, even for him. "Why do you mention it? Do I annoy you?"

"No." She sipped her tea, watching him.

He typed another line or two. "Good for you." To me he added, again as though she couldn't hear him, "She's young, and FOOF. It's an unfortunate combination." This time he didn't even pause in his typing. I began to wonder whether he was just doing typing exercises to impress us.

"Unfortunate for whom?" I asked him.

But Mildred Potter entered just then, so he didn't answer me.

She was dragging trays of sorted mail on a wheeled cart, and had to shove Peaceable aside to get up the last step and through the door.

When she had accomplished that, she looked up and smiled at us. "Waiting for the mail? I'll have it put away in just a few minutes now." She maneuvered the cart with some difficulty through the door Ritchie had pointed out, which indeed did lead to a mail room: the walls were lined with cubbyholes in varying sizes, with little paper labels to show whose was which.

"Let me help you," Lorielle said eagerly.

Mildred smiled kindly. "No, thank you, dear. I can manage." She reached into the topmost of the trays on the cart and pulled out a long, cream-colored envelope of the finest-quality paper. "Here, I've kept yours separate. I thought you'd be waiting for it."

Try as I might, I got only the merest glimpse of some sort of crest in the printed return address before Lorielle tucked it gratefully into the pocket of her skirt. "Oh, *thank* you!" she said with quite unelven enthusiasm. "If you only knew—"

Mildred nodded fondly. "I thought it must be important," she said, and disappeared into the mail room.

"Love letter?" Ritchie inquired knowingly.

Lorielle didn't bother to answer him. Apparently transported with joy, she gave him only a quick, blank look before she floated out the front door, all her clumsiness forgotten.

Curious, I went to the door of the mail room. "Who was that from?" I asked.

"What, Lorielle's letter?" Mildred looked up from her cubbyhole stuffing to shake her head at me. "I can't tell you that."

"You mean you didn't notice? But there was some sort of crest on it. Surely that caught your eye."

"I'm not meant to tell tales out of school."

"But these aren't locked. Anyone could have taken it out of her cubbyhole to see who it was from."

"Perhaps. If she'd left it in her box. But she didn't, did she?" She returned to her work, politely ignoring me.

"Mildred, you hired me to investigate the Trouble. You won't help me do my job by keeping secrets."

"Lorielle's mail has nothing to do with the Trouble."

"You don't know that. Anything that happens here could be to do with the Trouble."

She shrugged. "I'm a postal employee," she said. "I won't break federal law to solve a local problem."

"You're telling me it's against federal law for you to tell me what was on the outside of someone's mail where anyone could see it?"

"Look, I'm busy now," she said. "Do you mind?"

I did mind, but it wasn't going to do me any good, so I left the mail room. Ritchie was typing again, ceaselessly now that there were no interruptions. Apparently he was able to churn out his potboilers just about as fast as he could type. I stepped past Peaceable onto the front porch and stood there beside him, inhaling the sweet scent of redwood and leaf mold, and wondering what to do next.

Very probably neither Ritchie's Romeo and Juliet nor Lorielle's love letter had any more to do with the Trouble than Gary's death had. I should stick to what I had been hired to do. Which meant interviewing more residents, since I'd run out of any other leads.

I spent the next several hours on fruitless interviews. Rosetta Fulmer was very forthcoming but spent a good half hour saying nothing but that she was frightfully sorry that nasty Cameron boy had died. Her live-in lover

George Jenks was as quiet as she was talkative, and while apparently eager to assist in any way he could, had nothing to contribute. He didn't even mention regret over Gary's death.

Marc Starr and Melanie McGraw were voluble in their outrage over the Trouble, and quiet about Gary. "He was Charlotte's son," Melanie said. "You had to care about him for her sake. But it's a mercy, just the same."

"It's an annoyance," said Marc Starr. "People shouldn't pay so much attention to it. I told the police that. We should all just forget it. I know I mean to. What do you think of these colors? I'm painting Melanie as a vestal virgin, and I need to find just the right mauve for the shadows. Nothing too pink and babyish, you understand: I want a sophisticated color. I realize you may think that inappropriate to a vestal virgin, but I mean to portray her as a *modern* virgin. Do you think this one?" He held up a daub of color to the light. "My soul craves the shadows," he said, wandering away, muttering abstractedly.

Chance Winter showed me his photographs. On the subject of the Trouble he expressed weary indifference and had nothing useful to offer. He showed me more photographs. It was too bad Gary had to die in that horrid way, but the fact was he hadn't been at all a pleasant boy, had he? Wouldn't I like to see more photographs?

Salonian said almost nothing at all. He was working on a massive chunk of solid granite, chiseling bits of it away by hand with a rawhide mallet and cold chisel, and didn't want to talk about it. No, he didn't really want to talk about the fountain either. No, he didn't know a thing about the Trouble. No, he didn't know anything about Gary's death. No, as a matter of fact, he wasn't sorry about it: why did I ask?

Benjamin Barski was more talkative than Salonian, but not more help. He didn't seem to be working on anything at the moment, or at least there was no evidence of it in his home if he was. He told me with innocent, childlike arrogance that while he was of course the best *human* sculptor who had ever lived, Salonian was by far the better of the two of them and deserved more recognition.

He told me nothing useful at all about the Trouble, and ignored queries about Gary's death. By the time I left his cottage I was exhausted and discouraged and full of tea (it seemed by far the most popular drink in the valley), so I went home to use the bathroom. All was as I had left it, with no sign of further invaders. Of course I hadn't seriously expected there would be; but I would probably never leave the cottage again without wondering what I'd find on my return.

The one subject that had seemed to crop up at least peripherally in every interview that afternoon was Faerie aristocracy, which several people mentioned but nobody seemed willing to try to explain. Maybe it was time I found someone who would. Finandiel, being a member of it, seemed the best candidate for that.

His cottage was actually not far from mine as the raven flies. But trackless forest and at least one steep ravine lay between us, so I thought it the wiser course to go the long way around by the path past Salonian's fountain, around the Hall, and back across the creek by the path where the Trouble assaulted me on my first night in Fey Valley.

I locked the cottage, looked longingly at the comfortable lawn chairs basking without me in the golden afternoon sun, and set off down the mossy path toward the fountain.

20

Faerie aristocracy, as Finandiel described it, seemed rather like British aristocracy. He assured me that there were differences, but he wasn't altogether successful in acquainting me with them, perhaps because I wasn't much more familiar with the British class system than with Faerie's.

Both systems started with a queen at the top, and worked down from there. Both systems had nobles of various sorts, called dukes and earls and marquises and whatnot. Both were hereditary class systems. In Faerie a position passed from its holder to his or her eldest offspring without regard to sex, which I gathered was different from the British way, where some if not all of the titles could be held only by males.

Since elves lived practically forever, barring illness or accident, nothing got passed from one to another very often; and since they tended to produce their few children rather early in their careers, that meant that ownership of a title or a property frequently skipped a generation or two.

Those who would be passed over—once they had reproduced to ensure the line—were those who most commonly moved to the world of iron. The queen, it seemed, forbade not only the highest nobility but any titled person's sole heir from leaving Faerie. "Death is so much more common here, don't you see," said Finandiel. "We're so much more vulnerable to accident or illness, here where our magic is blunted and our senses dulled."

"Your queen seems awfully autocratic to me," I said.

He tried not to smile. "That is perhaps not surprising since she is an autocrat."

"There's that," I said. "Doesn't it annoy you to have somebody boss everybody around like that?"

"No."

That seemed clear enough. We moved on to the head-of-household thing, but that was beyond me. In America the head of one's household was a member of the immediate family: someone who dwelt in the household. In Faerie aristocracy, the head of the household was the highest-ranking noble in a line. But when I tried to pin him down closer than that things got complicated. I didn't understand, I suppose, what was meant by a "line." I got a vague impression that it might be "all those descended from the holder of a given title," but that wasn't clear.

Strictly speaking, the queen would seem to be the head of everyone's household, since I understood all the Faerie nobility to be related to her. Finandiel assured me that in one sense and for some purposes that was exactly true. But taking his line for example, the Duke of Daelinn was the head of every household under his—which included Finandiel's—rather than the queen, and he couldn't make me understand why. Perhaps she was just too busy to attend to so many households. She did seem to have rather a lot to do.

However, the duke did answer to the queen, and I was interested to note that Finandiel seemed just a trifle reticent on that point, as though he were embarrassed. I couldn't tell why, or about what, and he certainly wasn't inclined to tell me. I wondered whether the duke had maybe done something the queen didn't like or approve of. But at that point Finandiel very firmly changed the subject and it was all I could do to drag him back to discussing Faerie's aristocracy at all.

We came back to it by way of Salonian. I hadn't realized he was an aristocrat too; I'd just despaired of getting Finandiel back on track and decided I might as well ask about the other problem that had been bothering me. What was it about Salonian that made people, whenever his name was mentioned, go into raptures of sympathy they would then refuse to explain?

"Well, it is a long story," said Finandiel.

"Yes, that's what everyone says," I said. "Abridge it. Ariana said he had to choose between what he loved and what he needed: what did she mean by that?"

"Just what she said," he said, and sighed. "Very well. As you know, Salonian is a great artist. Like all great artists, he needs to work. With him it is no real choice; nor with many of the other residents here. Their art drives them. No more can they give it up than they can give up breathing."

"That's poetic license, surely? They wouldn't just collapse and die if they stopped whatever art they do."

"To be sure, not as directly as were they to cease breathing. But with the elves at least it truly is a matter of life and breath. To cease one's art is to cease one's life. The . . ." He hesitated, frowning. "I know not by what name you call it. The heart? The soul? The *essence* of a person; that which defines him." He smiled without amusement. "What separates men from beasts?" He didn't wait for me to answer. "That, by any name: *that* dies in the absence of one's art.

"Perhaps you mortals can live on in such a case. No elf could . . . or would." He shuddered at the thought and looked for a moment into a distance only he could see, before he remembered me and smiled crookedly. "So you see it was a choice that was no choice. There was naught he could do but that he did."

"So his art was what he needed? What was it he loved, that he couldn't have if he had his art?"

He looked, oddly, embarrassed. "The Princess Tintiminiel."

"He was in love with a princess?"

"Was and is," said Finandiel with a small shudder. "Cuthbern, bring me wine."

Cuthbern promptly produced a filled goblet and placed it at his master's hand. I never noticed him lurking in wait, yet whenever Finandiel wanted something, he was there.

"Will you have some, my lady?" he asked me kindly.

"Thanks, no. But do you have coffee?"

"But of course, my lady. One moment." He bowed and disappeared in the direction of their kitchen. Coffee, apparently, was not conjured from the air as wine was.

"If he's in love with this princess, why did he have to choose between her and his art?" I asked.

Finandiel stared at me over his wine as though I'd asked whether the sun would rise in the morning. "I must have failed to explain: she is a *princess*. She cannot leave Faerie." Something darkened his eyes and he looked away from me, his expression abruptly cold and distant. "It is not done. The queen commands: none of the highest aristocracy may enter the land of iron. None, not even when they have produced an heir."

That raised a number of questions in itself, but I dealt with the obvious first: "Then why did he?"

"Why did he what?" He sipped his wine and put down the goblet carefully, as though it were fragile, though it appeared to be made of Faerie gold. If so, it would withstand nuclear attack as long as he wanted it, though it would crumble to dust the moment he was through with it.

"Why did he leave Faerie, if she couldn't, and he loved her?"

"But I've told you," he said, mildly puzzled. "For his art."

"He couldn't sculpt things in Faerie?"

His face cleared. "Ah, I perceive the difficulty," he said. "What of his work have you seen?"

"Only the fountain. What's that to do with anything?"

"It is the very crux of the matter," he said, twirling his goblet between his fingers. "But how to explain? You are not, I think, an artist?"

"Nope."

"Nor yet a connoisseur of the arts?"

"Nor yet," I admitted.

He nodded soberly. "The tale is longer than I'd means of knowing," he said. "Much of its pathos depends upon a clear understanding of Salonian's relationships with his queen, the princess, and the land; none of these, I think, is accessible to you, however long we might dwell upon them. It is why none has bothered to try, I think."

"But the art?"

"Yes, the art," he said. "That matter, just possibly, I can clarify." But he did not seem inclined to begin at once. He sat staring into his wine and twirling the goblet while I waited.

Cuthbern returned with a steaming mug of coffee and put it before me with the air of one bearing great treasure. "Will you take cream or sugar, my lady?" he asked.

"No, black's fine," I said. "Thanks."

Cuthbern disappeared again. Finandiel stared at his wine. I waited, sipping excellent coffee. After a long while Finandiel shifted, sighed, and seemed to notice me. "Yes, very well," he said, as though I had been nagging. "You understand, I think, that all art that has vitality must have its basis in love."

It took me a moment to absorb that: it was not at all the sort of thing I had expected to hear an elf say. "I can see why someone would say that," I said finally. "I'm not sure I know it's true."

He gave me a look of such startled arrogance I nearly smiled. "Have I not said it is true?"

"Strictly speaking, no, you haven't," I said. "Besides, what makes you think I'll just believe whatever you say, without question? I won't, you know."

The haughty look melted into a smile of genuine amusement. "Silly me," he said. "I was forgetting where I am and with whom I'm speaking. Blessings upon you, my child, for it's wisdom you speak, and I think you *are* the angel of our salvation."

"Right, like you really needed salvation. Whatever the Trouble is, it's no threat to anyone that I can see."

He lifted one eyebrow. "Think you— That is, don't you think it killed Gary?"

"The police called that an accident."

"The police are irrelevant."

I shrugged. "And incorrect, in my opinion. But whoever killed Gary, I don't think it was the Trouble."

"Do you not, then? Interesting." He sipped his wine. "To return to the question of art, let us remember to differentiate between what is merely pretty and what is art. Thus for example the goblet you see before you is pretty, but is it art?"

I shrugged. "It looks like art to me. It's gorgeous. Like the best of art nouveau. I like art nouveau."

"A Faerie movement, at base," he said, nodding. "Yes, the goblet is art. Indeed, it is art nouveau, and rather old and precious to me." He turned it between his hands and let one long, graceful finger trace the curve of a vine, the shape of a leaf. "This craftsman loved," he said. "There is within this goblet a love of art, of nature, and of the gold itself. Remove any one of those and you will remove beauty with it."

"Okay, if you say so."

"I do say so." He admired the goblet. "Come now: surely you can see that for yourself?"

"It's prettier than mass-produced stuff. Sure. I can see that."

"It is a beginning. Very well, we have that much. Now. Can you see any difference between this work and Salonian's fountain?"

"The fountain's bigger," I said promptly.

He looked pained. "You are facile," he said.

"Okay, okay." I thought about it. "No," I said. "I can't. Except that the fountain gives me the shudders, and I like the goblet."

"There lies your clue," he said.

"My clue?"

"To the essential difference," he said. "Look at your words, child. The fountain gives you the shudders, but you only like the goblet. The strength of the one image does not equate with that of the other. You react powerfully to the fountain and only mildly to goblet."

I thought about it. "But that's their subjects, not their quality."

"The nature of your reaction is based on their subjects. The strength of your reaction is based in their quality."

"So you're saying the goblet isn't as good as the fountain: if it were, what? It'd give me raptures of joy, or something?"

"It would at the least delight you," he said complacently. "Just as the quality of the fountain delights you, even as its subject repels you."

"Okay. Maybe you're right." I thought about it. "So? One of them is better than the other. And?"

He nodded gravely. "And why is one of them better than the other?"

I didn't hesitate: I was out of my depth and I knew it. "Okay, I give up. Why is one better than the other?"

"Think, child," he said.

"I have thought," I said impatiently. "I'm not an artist. I don't know a thing about art. I don't necessarily even know what I like. Say it in plain words, Finandiel, or it's of no use to me."

He studied me for a moment, then studied the goblet again. "See the shapes, the flow of the vines, the grace of the leaves," he said. "This artist loved his subject. We are agreed?"

"I'll accept that, certainly."

"But the vine is trapped in eternity," he said. "It is perfection itself. There is no flaw. There is no *time*. Do you understand?"

"It's flawless, right. And, um, it's timeless? That isn't good?"

His lips quirked in just the hint of a smile. "Semantics," he said. "Here lies a difficulty. 'Timeless' is not the same as 'without time.' "

"Okay," I said doubtfully.

"I am no teacher," he said heavily, and drank the wine.

Cuthbern refilled the goblet for him. "If I may, my lord?" he said deferentially. "I wonder if I might not have a useful thought on this?"

Finandiel waved an arm expansively. "By all means."

Cuthbern straightened, holding the wine bottle protectively against his body. "It is an intangible," he said. "It is not always present in the subject or itself visible in the art. Yet mortality—an awareness of it, a portrayal of it, a knowledge of it—is the essence of my master's point. Do you understand, the vine in life is more beautiful than any portrayal of it: and the beauty is based, in part, in its impermanence. We love it the more because we know it will die.

"The artist who would portray it truly, must convey to us somehow that tragic sense of mortality. I do not say that when we look at a great work that it will make us think consciously of death. That would be . . . unpleasant."

"As is Salonian's fountain," said Finandiel.

"Yes, my lord," said Cuthbern, unperturbed. "If it is the artist's intent, of course we will think consciously of death, and we will find the work unpleasant in that regard. What I wish to convey now is that the death is there, in a great work, whether we think of it or not. It is that hidden tragedy that makes the work great."

"That, of many things," said Finandiel.

"Of course, my lord. It cannot be the only attribute."

"You're saying truly great art can be done only by mortals?" I asked.

Finandiel looked startled. "By no means. Only observe the many elven talents. No, what I say is that the immediacy of mortality is in many cases what . . . provokes, I think. What provokes the greatest of his skill from the artist: what provokes the greatest artists to their work."

"I don't know how to know whether that's true," I said. "It doesn't feel exactly right, but I don't know." I looked at him. "If it's true, would that mean there's no great art in Faerie?"

Finandiel sighed and looked away. "If it is not *the* explanation," he said, not quite answering me, "it is *an* explanation. For Salonian, it is the only explanation that matters. He could not do his greatest work in Faerie. He can do it here."

"Well, why didn't you just say that?" I said. "Jeez,

that's clear enough. Never mind *why* it's so. If it is so, it explains why he had to make that choice."

"As you say," said Finandiel.

"But how awful," I said. "Did he really love her very much? How could he choose his art over her if he did?"

"I cannot understand love," said Finandiel. "To me the question is not how he could, but how could he not? Had he stayed in Faerie, how could he live? Even if he loves the Princess Tintiminiel, still he *needs* his work."

21

He smiled at me. "But comfort yourself: there is no surety the queen would have permitted the marriage anyway, had he stayed at home in Faerie."

"You mean she might not have liked Salonian for a son-in-law?"

"Not so: the Princess Tintiminiel's husband could not well be called a relative to the queen at all," he said in surprise. "Tintiminiel is princess of a minor principality far to the west where few venture who have no specific business with her or her subjects.

"It was by coincidence that she and Salonian ever met: the queen had brought Tintiminiel to Court for another matter that has no bearing on this tale. Salonian was there on a visit from this world. When Tintiminiel's business was concluded, he followed her home. Even that was, I suspect, against the queen's wishes, but as she had not said so there was nothing wrong in it."

"But why was it any of her business? Is Salonian her son, or something? But he can't be, or she'd be against his coming here. But if neither Salonian nor Tintiminiel is closely related to her, why is it any of her business who either of them sees or marries?"

"But my child, all that any of us does is the queen's business. How not?"

"You mean she's kinda like God?"

He smiled irrepressibly. "I do rather believe you mortals might think her so," he said.

"She sure seems to stick her nose in everything."

That shocked him, mildly. "I would not say just that to her," he said, and hesitated. "But yes, I suppose I

can see why you say it. To us it seems the most natural
of arrangements that our queen should involve herself
in every aspect of our lives: but to a mortal, accustomed
as you are to oddly impersonal and disinterested forms
of government, I can see that it might seem . . . stifling."

"Well," I said generously, "there are human govern-
ments that are stifling too."

"The cases are quite different," said Finandiel, "but
perhaps the similarities give you an understanding of the
choice Salonian faced."

"I'm not sure why he couldn't have both," I said.
"The way between worlds doesn't seem exactly difficult
for the average elf. Why couldn't he marry his princess
and commute to work here? That's probably what a
human would have done."

Finandiel looked shocked. "We may say this stands as
proof to us that Salonian is not human," he said, "were
we in doubt."

He seemed inclined to change the subject, but I
wasn't. "So an elf just wouldn't do it that way, and
that's that?"

He sighed, studying me. "I believe you do not mean
to be offensive," he said. "But I must say your peculiar
obstinacy on this point is puzzling."

"People keep saying Salonian's story is tragic," I said.
"But it doesn't seem tragic if there's an obvious solution
and no clear reason he didn't take it."

He nodded slowly. "Yes, I see that. I had known, of
course, that humans are singularly without honor, but it
seems I had not guessed the full extent of it."

I stared. "What does honor have to do with this?"

"But, my good woman," he said. "If one's queen commands that one make a choice, where is the honor in
finding a way around it?"

"Do you mean she *wanted* him to be unhappy?"

"Of course not."

"Well, then?"

It was his turn to stare. "I fear I am out of my depth,"
he said at last. "I cannot see the difficulty, you understand. You tell me that if your queen commanded a

thing, and you could find a way around it, you would take it?"

"I don't have a queen," I said.

He nodded.

"But if I had," I said, thinking about it, "I'd say in a way you're right. I would see nothing wrong in finding a way around the uncomfortable part of a situation like that, if she hadn't said I mustn't.

"Say I was Salonian. I love Tintiminiel, and I need my work. Tintiminiel isn't allowed to go where I need to be to do my work, but I can go there and return to her easily. Of course I would do it, yes. Unless I thought my queen *meant* me to be unhappy. Maybe even then; what obedience would I owe a queen who decided for no reason to make me unhappy?"

"You see nothing wrong in interpreting her orders to suit yourself?" He said it dubiously and cautiously, as though asking whether I really meant to say I approved of rape.

"You'd have to, wouldn't you? I mean jeez, even in an ordinary situation, you have to interpret what she says. What you hear might not be exactly what she meant to say. You have to figure that out. If you want to obey her exactly, you still have to interpret what you hear."

"Certainly not. One does not interpret: one obeys."

"But it's 'interpretation' just to figure out what the words mean."

"Very well, I grant that," he said. "One interprets to that extent, yes. And one obeys the precise, literal meaning of the words."

"That's the honorable way?"

"Of course. How else?"

"What if you know your queen meant to please you, but what she's commanded will make you miserable instead? What then?"

"One would, in honor, obey her," he said in the tone of one explaining that rain is wet.

"I see. And thank her, perhaps. How very odd you people are."

He smiled unexpectedly. "My thought exactly." He reached impulsively across the table to touch my hand. "Forgive me, Rosalynd: I have been inclined to judge you by my standards, but that cannot be right." He withdrew his hand, looking self-conscious, and sipped his wine. "For one of us to try to second-guess our queen—what you call interpreting her words—would be such arrogance one might call it madness. But for you, it would seem that such a course is as natural as breath itself." He shook his head. "This is a thought on which I must ponder," he said. "I had not realized how *alien* you mortals are."

"Jeez," I said. "I thought I understood a little something about elves. God knows I learned a lot while I was with Cold Iron. But this! You're saying you have to do what your queen says, to the letter, no matter what you think she really meant?"

"Of course," he said.

"Okay, new subject," I said. "What happens if you don't? What if you disobey?" I half expected him to tell me no one would. I think I would have believed it.

Instead his eyes turned cold and distant, his expression unhumanly bland. "That would depend upon the circumstance," he said.

This was interesting. "Would it? Which circumstances? What are the options?"

He looked away from me, but not before I saw the unexpected shadows in his eyes. "They are far too many and the question too complex for me to explain to you in an afternoon's sitting," he said coldly.

It was a new view of Finandiel. I had not, at the outset, thought much of him: he was handsome, and his tailoring exquisite, but his manner was arrogant and his eyes were cold, and unpleasantly cynical. Even his smile had seemed at first contemptuous, curling his lips, but leaving his eyes hard and glittering like stone.

Then we had arrived in Fey Valley where his friends were, and he had relaxed. I had rather liked him then. He had played the fool and smiled with real amusement that not only warmed his eyes, but transformed him in-

stantly from an aristocrat of haughty composure to an
easy-mannered fellow with a strong sense of the ridiculous, and considerable charm. That the transformation
was in large part deliberate, and the charm very carefully
cultivated, had not diminished the result.

Now I was facing the contemptuous aristocrat again,
but with a difference: this time I knew it masked discomfort. That didn't make it any easier to talk to him, and
I was glad when Cuthbern interrupted us on some frail
pretext. Since it was clear I would get no more useful
information here, I very politely took my leave of them.
I had plenty to think about already.

I really had thought I knew pretty much what elves
were about, after my time with Cold Iron. Elfrock play-
ers tend by their nature to be out of control, of course,
and can't by any stretch be thought representative. But
there's something to be said for learning a race by close
study of its outcasts. Who doesn't fit into a society can
be as telling as who does.

But this question of honor had never come up, with
Cold Iron. Indeed, now I thought of it, we'd never mentioned honor in any way that I could recall. That in itself
was an interesting omission, considering how frightfully
important honor was to elves. The fact that I hadn't
noticed it at the time was unremarkable: I'd been as
much out of control as the band members. Only, unlike
them, I hadn't known it.

Someone had turned on the water to Salonian's fountain. The nymph's vase spilled a thin thread of glistening
water over the skulls, where it was joined by trickles
from hidden sources that wove their rushing way
through the bones, meeting and separating again, gathering in volume till they made quite a cheerful splash in
the pool below. Sunlight flashed on streams and droplets,
and a tiny rainbow was cast up where the water from
the vase first touched the skulls. The delicate plash of
the tiny falls meeting the pool blended intimately with
the rustle of wind in the redwoods high overhead, creating a whispery symphony as beautiful to the ear as the
sculpture was to the eye.

Salonian was right: without water it had been only impressive. With it, it was stunning. And with what Finandiel had told me, I could see far more in it than just the shuddery paean to death I had taken it to be. Looked at this way, the nymph became the beauty of Faerie linked by all the fury of love and need to the terrible price that came with growth and change: mortality.

Looking at her, I thought unexpectedly of Killer, who was far away, and precious to me, and mortal. I wanted to hit something. I turned abruptly and stalked back toward the Hall, with no particular purpose in mind but to avoid going home alone.

If Salonian, a Trueblood, could feel the deep, conflicting emotion that fountain communicated, what did that say about popular wisdom? What if elves, for all their absent empathy, felt everything else as deeply as we? Was it possible? *Could* one, for instance, love, without empathy?

Stupid question: I knew very well they could love, and did. Either love didn't require empathy, or elves weren't as lacking in it as I'd always been given to understand. The Faerie researcher Evans-Wentz said elves had "every charm but conscience," which was supposed to be the reason they needed such a rigid code of honor. Their society would have fallen into chaos without rigid honor to substitute.

I'd always taken that to mean they had no empathy either, since surely the two went hand in hand. Yet would honor even work as a substitute if they *really* had neither empathy nor conscience?

I had never thought to wonder before what made elves adhere to their code of honor. If not conscience, what? Logic? Just the knowledge that each of them must, or their society collapse? But wouldn't a sociopath, unable to recognize the reality, the humanity (or in this case the elvenness) of his fellows, imagine that he of them all could freely flout the rules? It was what human sociopaths did.

Yet sociopaths were seldom careless. Indeed, it

seemed that without a capacity to tell right from wrong in the moral/ethical sense, they were somehow better able to see the big picture, untroubled by pesky moral quandaries along the way. It was probably why they were so successful in business and politics.

As were elves, when they felt so inclined, which perhaps fortunately wasn't often.

22

Unless there were others silent in the rooms upstairs, Ritchie was alone at the Hall. He was busily typing, and didn't even look up when I came in. Peaceable was absent from the doorway. It hadn't occurred to me before to wonder whose dog he was. He'd just always been there. So had Charlotte: maybe he was hers.

I went into the kitchen for coffee and took it to the table in the great room. Ritchie ignored me. Good. I ignored him. Late-afternoon sunlight cast a bright oblong from the doorway across the worn old wooden floor. I sat alone at the table and stared out into the parking lot at fallen leaves limned with gold between the long shadows.

So far I hadn't learned anything useful about Fey Valley's Trouble. I hadn't yet met all the newest elves, so that was the logical next step for tomorrow. Meantime, what had Romeo and Juliet to do with the problem? Ritchie's novel and Finandiel's story about Salonian and Tintiminiel were too similar to dismiss. Beware of coincidences, for they may not be.

The only children in Fey Valley the right age for Romeo and Juliet were Lilie and Gary, and their families weren't warring. If the story was being repeated in life, though, there was no reason it mightn't happen to adult elves; it seemed pretty clear that the Faerie queen wouldn't hesitate to stand in the way of any romance to which she happened to take a dislike.

But what would that have to do with the Trouble? Why would either of the participants bother to haunt Fey Valley, wreck my cottage, frighten children, and otherwise make a nuisance of him- or herself? Just elven high spirits?

That wasn't impossible, of course. If one of them were disobeying the Faerie queen by coming here, wouldn't that be such a major wrongdoing that a little dishonorable mischief would seem negligible by comparison?

Gary's death hadn't been exactly what I'd term "mischief." Until now, the Trouble had seemed essentially harmless: but not if it killed Gary. Hard to believe an elf would do that, though. Of course it was always hard for a human to believe what elves would do. It was only very rarely that one had a glimpse past their charisma to the eerie indifference that underlay it. And their charm was such that, even then, one was always reluctant to believe the worst of them.

It was still possible that, instead of a Fey Valley elf behind the Trouble, there was some ordinary human cause that Shannon would uncover in her investigation of Swilhurst Associates and its investors. But that seemed even less likely than any of the other possibilities. And the Hall seemed very empty without Charlotte in the kitchen. I finished my coffee, carried the cup to the kitchen, washed it, and fled.

Dinner at a nice mom-and-pop restaurant in Moraga was comforting. A good night's sleep afterward (even though it was interrupted in the wee hours by distant, haunting music I felt sure was made by the Trouble) restored me to a somewhat more sensible state. I wasn't even enraged when I'd hiked all the long way back into the depths of Fey Valley to "the mansion" to visit Maerian, only to learn that she wouldn't let me near.

There was no fence around the mansion, but Maerian was an elf who did not want visitors. It took all my concentration just to get to the front yard; from the moment I came in sight of the mansion I had to fight against a strong tendency to turn around and go the other way. Indeed, my first realization that Maerian was refusing visitors was when I found myself walking back toward the Hall with no clear recollection of having turned around.

I turned back toward the mansion and stood still, looking it over. It was no more than fifty yards from me; trees, not distance, had blocked it from my view till now. Unlike all the other valley residences I'd seen, this one was an old three-story Victorian clapboard house complete with complicated gingerbread trim. There was a wraparound porch on the ground floor, and several second- and third-story balconies. The entire structure was painted palest yellow with gleaming white trim. The tall windows glittered like crystal in the morning sunlight. Mounds of lilac bushes lined the front porch, their heavy purple blossoms sweetly scenting the entire clearing. In the front yard, a stone sundial was surrounded by tumbled peonies in every color.

Immediately around the house some sort of miniature daisies dotted the emerald carpet of the lawn, clustering as they got farther from the house. By the time they met the forest they were of normal height and tangled with morning glories and mustard in a riotous jumble of color. The nearest blossoms were actually in the shade of the forest: it was interesting to see how abruptly they stopped, like a wall around the clearing. On this side, and all the way back to the Hall, it was an ordinary California valley forest, with bracken and . . .

And I was walking the wrong way again. "*Damn* it!" I stopped abruptly and turned around. In that brief time I had walked far enough back into the forest that the mansion was hidden by trees again. Scowling, I trudged back toward it, determined this time not to be sidetracked by magic.

I made it all the way to the sundial, but I think it was only because there was now a man on his knees by the peonies with a trowel in his hand and several potted blossoms by his feet. I concentrated on reaching him. He was wearing coveralls with a white square on the back on which "Scotland Yard" was printed in what I thought was meant to be an Olde English script, heavy with curlicues and ornamentations.

He didn't give any sign that he noticed me staring till I was nearly upon him. Then he sat back on his heels and looked up at me, expressionless: an ordinary gardener interrupted at his work. He was young and handsome with red hair and freckles, and dirt under his fingernails, and his ears were pointed. "Morning," he said, his voice as expressionless as his face.

"Good morning. Where did you come from?"

He shrugged ineffably. "Trying to visit the mansion, are you?"

I restrained my first impulse, which was rude. "Yes."

He shook his head and turned back to his plantings. "Can't be done," he said. "You've done well, but you won't do better. Might as well give it up."

"Why?"

"Herself don't like visitors."

"Herself?"

"The Lady Maerian."

I hadn't known she was aristocracy. Fey Valley was beginning to seem rather thick with it. "I have business with her."

He shrugged again. It was a very human shrug, and looked odd on someone with those ears. "Wear yourself out," he said. It was a warning, not a suggestion.

"How do people get in to see her?"

"They don't."

"Have you seen her?"

He gestured vaguely toward the back of his coveralls. "I work here."

"But have you seen her?"

"Not to speak to."

"Does anyone see her?"

"Dunno." He had dug a neat hole for a new peony. Now he tipped it out of its pot and slipped it gently into the hole. "None of my business."

"How long have you worked here?"

He looked up, startled. "Here? In this flower bed?"

"In Fey Valley."

"Oh. Since Scotland Yard got the contract."

"You've been with them all that time?"

He nodded. "Name's MacLeod." That was Scotland Yard's founding family. Presumably he'd been with them all his life. If I couldn't get to see Maerian, this fellow might be almost as useful.

"I'm Rosalynd Lavine. The Fey Valley Association hired to me look into what they call the Trouble. Do you know anything about that?"

"I know what's said." He moved to a new spot and gently separated the peonies, pulled out a withered one, and used the trowel to make room for a fresh one.

"And what's that?"

He tipped another peony from its pot, slipped it into the hole he'd prepared, and tapped the soil firmly in around its root ball. "Just stories," he said. "Things that go bump in the night. Nothing worth hearing. Private eye, are you?"

"Investigator," I corrected absently. "Have you ever seen any sign of it?"

"What sorta sign?" He found another wilted peony and uprooted it.

"I don't know." I sat down on the grass near him, staring at the mansion. "Anything out of place in the forest. Footprints of anything strange, or where you wouldn't expect anybody to have been. Cars parked at night where they shouldn't be. Anything."

"Nope." He turned his back to me as he said it. Ostensibly, he was only reaching for another potted peony; but when he had it in hand he remained turned just slightly away from me, and it struck me that the shoulder nearest me seemed oddly defensive.

Interesting. "Have you seen anybody you didn't recognize, then?"

"Nope." He sounded almost relieved at that.

Curiouser and curiouser. "Okay, anybody you recognized, who shouldn't be here?"

He dug another hole and put a peony in it.

"Mr. MacLeod?" I said, reminding him of my existence.

"Willie," he said.

"Excuse me?"

"Willie. It's my name. William MacLeod." He looked at me, then, dusting his hands and sitting back on his heels, his face as expressionless as before. "Sounds odd to be called mister. That's my dad."

"Oh, I see. Okay, Willie. Have you seen anybody in Fey Valley who doesn't live here?"

That didn't faze him. "Nope."

But he had seen someone or something he didn't want to tell me about. I just had to find exactly the right way to ask. "Would you tell me, if you had?"

That shrug again. "Why not?"

"I don't know," I said. "I just had the impression you might not." I looked directly at him, trying to meet his gaze. He looked away. "It's one thing to help hide a mischief maker who means nobody any real harm," I said, "but this is maybe a murder case now."

That caught his attention. "Not. You mean the motor-cycle brat? Police said it was an accident."

"I don't think it was."

"You know better'n the cops?"

"Maybe."

He met my gaze. "So what d'you think happened, if you know so much?"

"I think somebody tied a thin, strong wire across the road just before the curve. When his front tire hit it, the wire broke; but the damage was done already. He lost control and went off the road at speed."

He stared. "But that would be murder."

"Yes."

"But why would anybody do that?"

"I can think of half a dozen reasons. Especially if the anybody was an elf."

He turned away abruptly to plant another peony. I waited, watching the house. Nothing happened, not even the twitch of a curtain: the place might have been deserted. Only there were curtains, neatly hung and brightly clean. There were wicker chairs on the porch, with a table between them and a vase of cut flowers on the table. Also what looked from here like a book, left open and facedown, breaking the spine. Signs of occupancy, but no signs that the occupants were at home just now.

"Even if he was murdered," Willie said abruptly, "why would you think it's anything to do with the Trouble? There's been nothing like that before."

"Wouldn't it be quite a coincidence to go along for years with no criminals here, and then suddenly acquire two separate ones at the same time?"

"Maybe. Coincidences happen. Besides, what makes you think the Trouble's a criminal? Maybe it's Bigfoot."

"I don't think so."

"Still isn't necessarily a criminal, is it?"

"Vandalism is a crime."

He looked up again. "What vandalism?" I described what had happened to my cottage. He was shaking his head before I was halfway through. "Nope, nope, nope. No reason to think that was the Trouble. It's not like what else the Trouble has done, any more than murder is." He began to gather up his tools. "Nope, I'd say you got two problems here: a criminal, who messed up your cottage and killed the motorcycle brat; and the Trouble, who just scares people once in a while and plays pretty music at night."

"And you know who the Trouble is, don't you?"

He picked up his toolbox and the empty peony pots and rose, looking into the forest. "Gotta go," he said, and glanced down at me with a brief, empty smile. "See you around."

I scrambled to my feet to go after him, but I wasn't really surprised when I found myself a short while later on the path back to the Hall, with neither Willie Mac-Leod nor the mansion in sight. I didn't bother to turn around and try for the mansion again. Without a little magic to counter the guard spell around it, I could try all day and I'd never get any closer than that sundial. I might not even get that close again.

23

Things seemed to have returned to normal when I got back to the Hall. Peaceable was back in position across the doorway, and thumped his tail at me in greeting. Charlotte was in the kitchen preparing lunch. Mildred Potter was in the mail room distributing the mail, with Benjamin Barski standing in the doorway to keep her company. Ariana Malloy and Chance Winter were at the table chatting over coffee. Rosetta Fulmer was on a couch in the great room, tittering over something Galinda said to her. And Ritchie Morita was typing, as always.

I got a cup of coffee and said hello to Charlotte, who looked at me with no evidence of recognition, said hello in a ragged voice, and returned to her cooking. Her eyes were swollen from crying and her nose red and raw from blowing, but although she seemed even grimmer than usual and mildly befuddled, there was no sign of further tears.

I took my coffee to the table. Ariana smiled and said, "So, what have you been up to?"

"I tried to go see Maerian," I said, grimacing.

"Someone should have warned you," said Chance. "All that long walk for nothing. How tedious."

"Well, it wasn't entirely wasted," I said. "I've been wanting to talk to a Scotland Yard worker, and I met Willie MacLeod while I was there."

They both stared. "You did?" said Chance. "I wonder why?"

It sounded odd, but I knew what he meant: I would never have met Willie if he hadn't decided to permit it.

"I don't know," I said. "Did everyone here know that the mansion is spell-protected? Why *didn't* someone warn me?"

"I don't suppose anyone thought of it," said Ariana. "I know I didn't. I'm sorry."

"Why is Maerian so reclusive? Is there something wrong with her?"

"No, no, it's nothing like that," Chance said promptly, then looked startled and turned to Ariana. "*Is* it?"

"You mean you haven't met her?" I asked.

"Nobody's met her except Ritchie and Ariana," said Chance.

"And I don't know about Ritchie, but I know I only met her once, when she first was here," said Ariana.

"I think Ritchie only met her the once too," said Chance. "Before she had selected the mansion." He looked at Ariana again. "But you deliver her mail. Do you mean to say you never see her then?"

"That's right," said Ariana. "I put it on the porch table for her."

"Isn't it a little odd for her to be so secretive?" I asked. "What does she do, anyway?"

"I don't see anything odd in it," said Ariana. "She's a painter. I don't know how she manages her business. By mail, I suppose: that's how she bought into Fey Valley and arranged for mail delivery to the mansion." She looked thoughtful. "I don't pay much attention to what I'm bringing her, but it seems to me I've seen the name of an artists' agent now and again, so I expect that's how she does it."

"What about selling her work?"

"Now that, I do know," said Chance. "Someone delivers her work here, packaged for shipping, and the gallery sends a truck for it. A few of the other painters use the same gallery and ship their work the same way."

Ariana nodded. "The van comes by once a week," she said. "Borderlands Gallery. Tim Cameron deals with them too."

"Charlotte does, you mean," said Chance.

"Well, she does the business end of it," said Ariana. "But it's Tim's paintings she's shipping."

"There's enough work for them to come by that often?" I asked, surprised. "I had the impression it took months to do some of these paintings."

"Oh, it does," said Chance. "So slow, not at all like photography."

"But with several artists working through the same gallery," said Ariana, "there's usually something ready for shipment each week."

"So none of them actually deals directly with the gallery? Go in, I mean, and talk to the owners, and whatnot?"

"Oh, most of them do, I think," said Ariana. "Just not every time they send in a painting."

"But Maerian never does?"

"Not to my knowledge."

"And you don't find that odd."

"No." She smiled at me. "You'll find that most fine artists have quirks of one sort or another. Reclusiveness is hardly a startling one."

"Wait a minute," said Chance, striving to look offended. "I think of myself as a Fine Artist, and I've no quirks to speak of." He seemed not in the least offended when Ariana burst into peals of laughter at that. He just smiled sweetly at her and sipped his coffee.

"What's so funny?" I asked.

"Ariana would say I'm neither a Fine Artist nor without quirks," he said complacently. "She takes a biased view of these matters, she being only a craftsperson." He prissed his lips and shifted his shoulders in a childish "I win" gesture that sent Ariana into new gales of laughter.

Much as it seemed to gratify its other participants, this conversation was getting me nowhere. Before I could decide what to try next, however, people began to arrive for lunch. I don't know how they knew Charlotte would be there to prepare it for them instead of home mourning the loss of her son. Perhaps it simply didn't occur to them that her needs might take precedence over theirs.

At George Jenks's request, Peaceable moved heavily out of the doorway, groaning and whuffling to let him know what an enormous imposition it was. Leaf Fulmer-Jenks, coming in with George, paused to comfort the dog. Kyriander stepped in past her and smiled with real pleasure when he saw me. The smile lasted just as long as it took Lilie to follow him in.

"You!" she said feelingly, staring at me as though I had developed a strongly offensive odor. "Kyri, make her go away."

"Don't be stupid," he said shortly.

She burst into loud, wailing tears and groped faintly for support. "How can you be so cruel?" No one came to her aid, so she stumbled forward till she could grip the back of a chair, eyeing me venomously through her tears. When Kyriander ignored her, she forgot her frailty and stamped her foot quite solidly on the wooden floor. Pointing a trembling finger at me, she said, "Murderer!" in tragic accents.

Chance Winter applauded. "Very pretty, my dear," he said graciously. "You really ought to try out for the school play this year."

She stared at him in furious shock.

"Tell us, who did Rosie murder?" he asked.

She said in failing tones, "My father. She killed my father."

Kyriander, returning from the kitchen, said placidly, "Just so. And had she not, we would the both of us be dead. Cease and desist, brat. Your fits weary me."

She snarled, "I'm not a *child*," at him and turned again to me. "See? You turn my own brother against me. Why don't you get out, bitch? Go away. Leave us alone. We don't need your kind here."

"Actually, we do," said Ritchie Morita, startling me as much as he did Lilie. I hadn't noticed that he had stopped typing, much less that he had abandoned his usual place at the typing table to approach us. "Do try to be calm, Lilie," he said. "We've hired Rose to do a job, and it would be foolish to send her away before it's done."

"She's had long enough," said Lilie. "She can't do it." She looked at me. "You can't, can you? Why don't you admit it and go away?"

"Because no one wants her to, Lilie," said Ritchie. "Let it go, infant. Come sit down."

To my amazement she released her grip on the dining chair and followed him almost docilely. "Good heavens," I said involuntarily. "And he even called her 'infant.' I'd have thought she'd take that for adequate incitement to riot."

"Not from Ritchie," said Chance. "There's not much he could say that she wouldn't take."

"Mab's mittens," said Ariana. "Are you saying she's transferred her affections to that popinjay?"

Chance had turned to follow Lilie's progress into the great room, but he turned back at that with an expression of delight. "Popinjay? My, I don't believe I've ever heard anyone called that in life," he said. "One sees it in books, of course."

Ariana waved that aside and looked at me. "You poor child," she said. "Pay her no mind: she's overwrought."

Chance giggled. "Overwrought? Ariana, you have such a way with words."

"Leave off, oaf," said Ariana.

"Lunch," Charlotte said from the kitchen door.

Several people promptly rose to crowd into the kitchen. Charlotte stepped out of their way and watched with a proprietary air. "Are you all right, dear?" Ariana asked her.

She looked surprised. "Yes, thank you. I'm fine."

"How's Tim?" asked Chance.

"Drunk," Charlotte said shortly. "What do you suppose?"

"Just that," said Chance. "But is he all right?"

She shook her head and turned away. "He'll be fine." She did not sound convinced of it.

"If you can get him to work," Chance began, but she interrupted him.

"I know it," she said harshly. "I've lived with the man

for thirty years. Do you think I don't know that much about him? Give me some credit."

"Speaking of popinjays," said Ariana.

"Don't rub it in," Chance said, and turned to me. "So. Your investigation is going well?"

I didn't have to answer him: Kyriander returned just then, with two plates of food. "I hope you like chicken and rice," he said, putting one of them in front of me.

"Oh, thank you," I said. "Yes, I do."

"I couldn't carry a drink without spilling," he said, sitting next to me. "You'll have to get that yourself."

"I have coffee, thanks."

After a moment's hesitation he said, "Rose, I'm sorry about the way Lilie behaves toward you."

I shrugged. "I'm tough," I said. "I can take it. Worry about her, not me."

"I do," he said, and sighed heavily. "What can I do? I know her health is not good, but she refuses all aid."

"She's had a hard time," I said. "And it's a difficult age in the best of circumstances. Give her a break. She'll settle down when her hormones do."

"I hope you're right," he said, unconvinced.

I looked past him at Lilie and Ritchie in earnest conversation on a couch by a window. Lilie was leaning toward Ritchie and smiling demurely. Reflected sunlight glinted on her golden curls and limned her face with light. She looked so young and innocent of guile, I could almost believe it.

24

The daylight faded while we were eating, so it came as no great surprise, when I went outside afterward, to find that a luminous midday fog had settled over the valley. It was so thick I couldn't see the trees at the far side of the parking lot, yet enough of the midday sunlight was refracted in it that the overall effect was far from gloomy. The nearer forest was a Chinese watercolor of mist and leaves and ambiguous distances. The only sound was the occasional plop of condensation dropping from one leaf to the next.

When I sat on the edge of the porch to think, Peaceable shuffled over next to me and nosed my hand for attention. I put my arm across his shoulders and he subsided, sighing. Kyriander joined us, sitting on Peaceable's other side and rubbing the base of his ears.

After a long, silent moment, I said, "How's your work? You haven't mentioned it since I've been here."

I thought for a moment he wouldn't answer. He sat rubbing Peaceable's ears for a long moment before he said, "That is because I've done no work since you've been here. I cannot. How can I, when I am so concerned for Lilie?"

That was unanswerable, so I didn't try. "How is she now?"

"Ritchie has her in hand," he said heavily. "Rose, I am sorry about what she said. I think she must know in truth you were forced to it, lest he kill us."

"I know," I said. "It only bothers me because there should have been a better way."

"Perhaps there should have been," he said agreeably. "But there was not."

I shrugged, and we sat in silence again. Inside, someone put a CD in the stereo: Ravi Shankar's eerie sitar music, sweet and mysterious and excitable, oddly suited to the ambiance of the fog. The only thing more suited might have been the wild Faerie music of the night.

"I had thought her health might be improving," he said. "She seems less often nauseated, and is perhaps gaining weight. Think you not?"

"Yeah, maybe she is filling out a little. Hard to tell; I've only been here a few days, you know."

He nodded soberly. "And in any case her emotional stability shows little improvement, as we saw," he said, rubbing the top of Peaceable's head. Peaceable groaned in pleasure. "These fits of hers unnerve me. And the suicide was terrifying."

"D'you think she meant it?"

He looked up in sudden hope. "Might she not?"

It really hadn't occurred to him that a troubled teen-ager afflicted with a taste for drama might do a thing like that for the attention it provoked. "She might not," I said. "She wouldn't have thought of it if she weren't feeling pretty desperate about something, but it needn't be suicidal. Any distress might do it. A suicide attempt might just have been the strongest action she could think of." I hesitated. "Or she might have meant it, in a way. Your father . . . what your father did to her . . . "

"He molested her," he said bitterly. "I think the foul son of a human may have raped her."

I smiled absently, my reasoning sidetracked. "You should choose your curses more carefully: you're the son of a human yourself." At his impatient gesture, I said, "Sorry. What I was going to say is, she was small when that started. She won't have known exactly what was happening: only that it was frightening, and maybe painful, and that she had no defense. The mind is a weird place, Kyri. If she thought she couldn't survive, her subconscious may have decided she *didn't* survive."

He frowned at me. "You are saying she thinks she is dead?"

"Not that, exactly. But . . . some people with her experiences . . . discover that they've spent the rest of their life unconsciously thinking they *should* be dead."

"You mean they want to be," he said, frowning.

"No, not that, either. It's difficult to explain. But if her childish mind thought she was being killed, and her subconscious mind thinks she was killed—the subconscious isn't exactly rational, you know—she could easily try to kill herself in an effort to set things right. To make the perceived reality match the real reality. Oh, hell. I'm not saying this very clearly. And I don't actually know enough to be saying it at all. I meant it for comfort, Kyri. To say that she might easily try to kill herself without wanting to be dead. But I've made a botch of it."

"No, I begin to see, I think. But in that case ought she not to have trained help? I'm far from competent to cope with such as that."

"I understand it responds well to treatment," I said. "You should think about it. But don't forget, we don't even know whether that's how she feels. I've . . . I've heard about cases like that, is all."

He looked at me for a long moment, but all he said was, "Thank you, Rose."

The subject of our conversation came outside just then, dancing past us off the porch and into the mist. She was wearing a tight sweater the color of moonlight and a flowing skirt patterned like rain. The beaded necklace went better with this costume. And suddenly I knew where I had seen rolls of fine brass wire: in Ariana's cottage. It was beading wire.

Lilie pirouetted before us, laughing wildly, her golden curls flashing with light even in the mist. "What beautiful weather!" she cried. "Oh, glorious!" Laughing again, entirely for effect and without amusement, she whirled to a halt before us and spread her arms to encompass the sky. "Isn't this *wonderful* weather?"

"It's just fog, Lilie," said Kyriander.

"Just fog. *Just* fog!" She whirled again, arms outstretched, her shrill laughter skittering across the quick, tumbling sitar progressions. "Oh, Kyriander, you are so *mundane*."

"Yes," he said, apparently embarrassed by this failing in himself. "I suppose I am."

"Just *look*!" she commanded, gesturing gracefully if somewhat wildly toward forest and sky. "Just look at it! The mist, the leaves, the light. How can you not see it?"

"I'm not sure," he said humbly. "I do perceive the mist, you know. And the leaves, and even the light. But perhaps I am yet missing some crucial point?"

"It is transcendent," she announced, and giggled with genuine amusement. It transformed her in an instant from perilous sprite to ordinary, overstimulated teen-ager. "Oh, Kyri, it really is awfully nice out. I just love this weather. Gary says—" She caught herself. "Oh."

"Honey," said Kyriander, half-rising to go to her.

She backed away. "No," she said, shaking her head and staring. "No. Don't. I don't want you. I hate you. Leave me alone!" With that she whirled again, skirts flying, and fled into the forest.

Kyriander straightened, looking after her. "I know not what best to do," he said almost frantically.

"I don't know either, Kyri," I said. "I'd say let her go. But you know her better than I."

In the end he decided to let her go, but it wasn't easy. He sat for a long time looking after her, while we listened to Ravi Shankar and the slow drip of the fog, before he sighed finally and said, "So. You believe with Lilie that Gary was killed. By the Trouble, do you think? I had taken it to be more or less benign."

"I don't know," I said. "I thought that too. But his death wasn't an accident. Anyway, it's my job to find the Trouble. If it isn't responsible, it still may have seen something that would help. It seems to spend more time loose in these woods at night than anyone else."

"Then you must find it," he said. "How can I help?"

"I don't know that, either. I was just trying to figure out what to do next. Besides Maerian, there are still two new elves I haven't talked to: I suppose that would be the next step. Belalin and Jeran."

"Our *Fauxnaifs*," he said, nodding. "But I would not have thought it of either of them."

"Would you have thought it of anyone here?"

"No. Have you eliminated the rest of us?"

"No. But in the absence of leads, all I can do is interview more possibilities. Or possible witnesses."

"Then you must interview the *Fauxnaifs*. You know where to find them?" I admitted I didn't, so he told me. The lunch crowd was beginning to leave now, and his directions were interrupted several times for polite leave-takings.

I was surprised to see Ritchie Morita among the departures. "I thought you lived here," I told him in surprise. "In the Hall, I mean."

"You were wrong." He was cheerful and brisk about it. "You shouldn't leap to conclusions: it's a bad habit for a private investigator. I have a cottage across the road. Sometimes I just find it more comfortable to work down here."

I was surprised he bothered to explain himself. "Isn't it quieter at your cottage?"

"Yes," he said. "Too quiet. I like some activity around me. But." He shifted, glanced at the Hall and at the forest and anywhere but at my face, and shrugged expansively. "Sometimes it gets to be too much." A nervous smile pulled at his lips, but he turned it into an arrogant scowl. "Shouldn't you be working?"

"I am," I said.

"Oh," he said. "Well, then." He looked at me finally, his expression unreadable, then turned abruptly and walked away.

"You vex him," said Kyriander. "He knows not what to think of one who accords him no awe."

"He's sure got something on his mind," I said.

"His novel, belike," said Kyriander. "Even the potboilers mean much to him. Perhaps he has encountered a difficulty in the writing."

"Perhaps." Like Ariana, Ritchie gave hints that he

knew more about the Trouble than he was saying: but that might be self-importance only. He wouldn't like a mystery he wasn't in on.

"Or," said Kyriander, "perhaps he thinks I will not like his attentions to my sister. He has been flirting with her much of late." He frowned after Ritchie. "I know not whether it is wise; but it takes her mind from her troubles."

A sudden ringing inside the Hall startled me: I had forgotten there was a telephone. Kyriander ignored it. So, apparently, did everyone else. It kept ringing. "Shouldn't someone answer that?" I said.

Kyriander shrugged. "Doubtless someone will."

It rang a few more times. "Well, hell." I stood up. "I'll get it."

Kyriander looked up at me. "You see?"

I made a face at him and went inside to find the phone. It turned out no one had answered it because no one was there. Even Charlotte had washed the dishes and gone.

The phone call was for me, anyway. It was Shannon, calling to say the Swilhurst Associates lead hadn't panned out. "They want Fey Valley, all right," she said. "And Cheryl is pretty miffed that they can't get it. But there's another plot a little north of there that'll do them just as well. I found out this morning they've put in a bid on it. And I happen to know they can't handle both right now. So I'd say they're out of the picture."

"That leaves Fey Valley residents, I guess," I said.

"I've been through all their public records," she said. "There's nothing there. Not that I really thought there would be. But you never know. What have you got?"

"Not much. You coming out here, then?"

"Be there this afternoon."

"Good. We'll talk then. I'm on my way now to interview the *Fauxnaifs*. That's the last of the new residents besides Maerian, and I haven't figured out a way to get in to see her yet. You can help."

"Why can't you just go knock on her door?"

"Because she's spell-protected it," I said. "You know,

that hateful kind of spell where you're trying to go somewhere and you don't notice you're being redirected? I
got close, once I realized what was happening, but I
couldn't get through."

"Interesting. What does she have to hide?"

"Maybe she's just a recluse."

"You think so?"

"That's sure what everyone says."

"Everyone including Ariana, who knows more than
she's telling?"

"Just so."

"And you believe her?"

"No. Or at least, I'm not sure." I stared out the window at the fog. "I'll tell you about it when you get
here."

25

It was another long hike through the woods, since both *Fauxnaifs* lived almost as far from the Hall as Maerian did. What's more, now the woods were dripping with fog, and the drips had a nasty affinity for the back of my neck. I was not having a good time. The one lucky thing, as far as I could see, was that Belalin and Jeran lived next door to each other, rather than miles apart in opposite directions.

Of course "next door" in Fey Valley didn't mean quite what it did in town. They weren't in shouting distance of each other. In fact, from Belalin's porch I couldn't even see Jeran's house. Belalin answered the door before I had time to get depressed about it.

He was one of those shockingly handsome elves who turn most human women's knees to jelly. Long, silver-blond hair; blue eyes the rich, deep hue of a brilliant summer sky; perfect Cupid's-bow lips; strong jaw; straight nose; the works. And that was just his face.

He was dressed rather piratically in hip-hugging bell-bottoms, ragged at the hem and tied with rope at the top. No shirt, no shoes. Just naked elf skin, sleek silver-gold not much darker than his hair, rippling with powerful, well-defined muscles.

"Good God," I said involuntarily.

"No, just me," he said, smiling. And that was a surprise too: it was a friendly, open, really rather human smile, quite without the unconscious arrogance one expected of elves. "How can I help you?"

"You're not FOOF," I blurted. The intrepid detective, alert to the most insignificant nuance.

His smile broadened. "Nope," he said. "Had you wanted one? I understand there are enough of them down in the valley."

With that coloring he could not possibly be a halfling; but I had never in my life heard a Trueblood speak such casual English. "No," I said. "You're Belalin?"

"Bela," he said, nodding. "And you?"

"Rose Lavine." I tried not to stare, but God he was gorgeous. I began to understand what men went through when confronted with my partner. It was very difficult to think when all my hormones were demanding an opportunity to produce this man's child. "I'm a private investigator. The Association hired me to look into the Trouble."

He was nodding again. "Yes, sure," he said. "I've been expecting you. I must be one of the prime suspects, right? Since the Trouble didn't start till after I'd bought into the valley."

"Well," I said coherently.

He opened the door wider and stepped back to let me past him. The room beyond him was a bewildering jumble of color and light. "Come in," he said. "You've had a long walk in the cold. Let me get you something to drink. Coffee? Tea? Wine?"

"Coffee would be great. Thanks." I stepped past him and paused, trying to make sense of too much visual input. Broad windows and a skylight overhead let in so much daylight the room was as bright as outdoors. The walls were lined with stacks of paintings, their brilliant colors competing violently for attention. The furniture looked as though it came from Faerie: beautiful, glowing woods hand-carved in vaguely art nouveau patterns of leaves and vines and flowers, with very few straight lines anywhere.

The tables and floor were littered with paint supplies, old rags, empty cracker boxes, junk mail, magazines, books, and sketch pads. It seemed to be clean litter—there was no dust, no dirty dishes, no food spills or accumulated drink tins or overflowing waste baskets—but it was certainly litter.

He cleared a beautiful cherrywood chair of stacked books and magazines, brushed the petit-point cushion to clear it of any lingering obstruction, and gestured for me to sit. "Make yourself comfortable," he said, putting the books and magazines from the chair onto a precarious stack of similar materials on a nearby table. "The coffee will only take a minute; I just made a fresh pot."

"Thanks." I sat. The chair was definitely from Faerie, or at least impregnated with magic. I couldn't feel the wood shifting to accommodate me, but I knew it must have. I tensed, waiting to feel the subtle mood alteration that usually went with comfort magic; but nothing tried to ease my tension or soothe my worries. Either that wasn't included, or this chair was so good it could tell how much I disliked that sort of thing.

Bela returned from the kitchen bearing two ordinary, chipped mugs of steaming coffee, and grinned disarmingly at me. "I hope you take it black. I'm out of milk and sugar."

"Black is fine," I said. "This is a good chair."

"Thank you." He shoved sketch pads aside and sat on the couch facing me.

I sipped my coffee. "Are those your paintings?"

He looked around at them as though surprised to find them there, and nodded. "Yes."

"Why aren't they at a gallery? I mean, I was just talking to people about how the painters get their work to the galleries, and I got the impression they send them away as soon as they're done."

"I'm too prolific," he said apologetically. "My agent thinks it would be bad for my career to turn them in as rapidly as I paint them. And that is the sort of thing I employ him to know."

"But what will you do with them?" I'd had time to really look at a few of them by now. The top one on the stack nearest me, for example, was a study of a rocky bank next to a road, with bracken and madrone and a few oxalis blossoms. It could not have been a more mundane subject: yet somehow, in the way the light fell through the leaves and sprayed across the broken rock, and the way the edge of the road curved and the trees bent down toward it, and the glimpse of distance seen through the topmost branches, it recalled the ineffable sense of potential adventure I felt sometimes on the valley road, as though around the next curve or beyond the next rise I might find *any*thing—a gate to Faerie, a window into another time, a unicorn, anything.

"I suppose I'll sell them eventually," said Bela. "Or give them away, or carry them back into Faerie. I don't know."

I looked at him. "You don't sound as though you care."

"I don't suppose I do," he said, apologetic again. "For me, the pleasure is in the painting. I know it's supposed to be communication, and I'm supposed to want people to see them." He shrugged, muscles rippling under the silken skin. "But to me . . . I suppose it's like singing in the forest. You don't need an audience: the pleasure is in the act."

"Do you sing in the forest?"

"Sometimes," he said. "When I'm working." He smiled shyly, and I realized with a start that he didn't even know how gorgeous he was. Or, if he did, he didn't care about it any more than he cared whether people saw his paintings.

Unfortunately I couldn't achieve such comfortable indifference. I had a sudden, debilitating vision of that magnificent body, barefoot in the sunlight, standing at his easel in the forest, singing while he worked.

"Are you all right?" he asked.

I swallowed coffee and looked away from the bottomless blue of his eyes. "I'm fine," I said. "You have a fine, um, voice."

"Thank you."

"Um," I said, gathering my wits. "What I came here to ask, though, was about the Trouble. Have you seen or heard anything that might help me find it?"

"I hear music at night," he said. "I suppose that's why I thought of singing for no audience. The Trouble doesn't care who hears it or doesn't."

"How do you know? Maybe it means for us to hear it."

He shook his head. "No, it's almost always solitary music. Maybe you haven't heard it clearly enough to tell. Or if you're not familiar with elven music, I guess you wouldn't know. We're a musical lot, at home, you know, in Faerie. Music for every occasion. What I hear the Trouble play is songs meant for solitude. And love songs, but the sort you sing or play when your lover isn't with you, and you're alone."

"So the Trouble is lonely?"

"Not necessarily. Unlike so many mortals, most elves enjoy solitude."

"You think it's an elf?"

He shrugged. "I don't know. It sounds like an elf. It's elven music. But maybe a mortal could sound like that." He seemed dubious.

"You said almost always."

"What?"

"The music. You said it's almost always solitary music. What is it when it's not solitary?"

"Love songs," he said promptly.

"Not the sort for when your lover isn't with you?"

"Not," he said, looking mildly interested. "I hadn't thought of that. Sometimes—not often, but once in a while—it's songs you sing or play *for* your lover."

"When your lover is with you."

"Exactly."

"So if it's an elf, sometimes it's not a solitary elf."

He shrugged. "Or it defies convention."

"Oh," I said, deflated. Elves were so routinely conventional, I tended to forget they *could* defy convention.

"If it's any comfort," he said, "I doubt that." At my questioning look he added reluctantly, "I don't know why, exactly. It's something about the music. It sounds, when it's meant to be heard, as though it's *being* heard. I don't know how to express it."

"No, but I think I know what you mean. Have you heard someone actually sing, or only an instrument?"

He thought about it. "Yes, actually, I have heard him sing."

"Him?"

"Yes," he said. "Now I think of it, it was a male voice."

"Well, that's something, anyway."

He grinned irrepressibly. "Assuming you believe me."

"Yes," I said. "Assuming." I had no reason to believe him, and every reason to wonder whether he was himself the Trouble. But I did believe him. "We'll assume that for now, shall we?"

"Fine by me," he said.

"So that makes the Trouble male, probably an elf, and . . . in love? I thought elves didn't do that."

"Love?" he said, smiling again. "So we would have you believe. It's not what you'd call socially approved."

"So why do you have music for lovers?"

"Why do you have music for drug abusers and teen gang members and marriage breakers and the like?"

"Point taken." I thought about it. "And you're saying sometimes the Trouble's lover is with him?"

"Yes, I think so," he said dubiously. "It's not a lot of evidence to go on, though, is it? Just how I feel about music I've heard when I was half-asleep?"

"No, but it's good enough to go on with," I said. "A hypothesis. You never go down to the Hall, do you?" He shook his head. "How well do you know the other valley residents?"

"Not well," he said. "Except Jeran, of course: my fellow *Fauxnaif*. You know we came here about the same time?"

"I was told that. You knew each other before?"

"We've known each other for decades." He smiled as he saw the word register with me: I'd been thinking of him as about my age. But he was an elf. He might be three hundred, and I wouldn't know it from looking. "We share interests and opinions, we've studied together, we've worked and played together. In all but blood, we're brothers."

"So you'd say he isn't the Trouble, right?"

"Right."

"I take it he isn't FOOF, either?"

"Nope, he's not. We've both been in and out of the ironworld for nearly as long as we've known each other. Why?"

"I just have the feeling the Trouble might be FOOF. I don't know why."

He smiled again, and for the first time I saw the cold elven arrogance beneath the boyish charm. "Then that's double assurance it's neither of us."

"If I'm right. And if you're not lying." I put my coffee down and rose, aware I was being dismissed. "Did you know Gary Cameron?"

He rose too, trying to guide me toward the door. "The boy who died? No."

I stood my ground. "Could you hear his motorcycle from up here?"

"Quite painfully," he said.

"Did you kill him?"

He looked at me in what appeared to be genuine surprise. "I thought he died of a motorcycle accident."

"Yes," I said, taking a last look around at the paintings. "He did." The rocky roadside bank caught my attention again: it was smaller than most of the others, but the colors were vivid and the image was oddly familiar and quite compelling. I wanted to step into that world: things would be simpler there, and safer, and more beautiful. I resisted the impulse to ask its price. It would be far beyond my means. "Thank you for your help," I said. "And for letting me see your paintings. They're gorgeous."

"You seem particularly drawn to that one," he said, nodding toward the one I wanted. "Take it. It's yours."

26

Shannon hadn't arrived yet when I got home to the cottage, bearing my prize. I ought, of course, to have refused it; and I had politely tried to. Bela was adamant. It isn't really sensible to argue for long with an adamant elf. Besides, when he picked up the painting and thrust it into my hands, it seemed farcical to keep trying to give it back to him. I suppose I could have just put it down and gone, but I didn't. He was right. I wanted it very much indeed.

He wrapped it for me in butcher's paper and string to protect it from the fog. It was just a comfortable size to carry under my arm, so I continued on my way to Jerian's house with it; but either he wasn't home or he wasn't answering the door. By then I thought Shannon might be arriving, so I was just as happy to put off my visit to him.

I unwrapped the package as soon as I got home, and took down a framed print to make room for it on the cottage wall opposite the couch, where I could sit and stare to my heart's content. The golden wood of the paneling was a good background for it.

The light was beginning to fail when Shannon finally got there. I was just thinking I would have to get up and do something about the painting when I heard her on the stairs. "You home?" she called. Something heavy bumped onto the porch.

"I'm here." I went to the door to help her. Knowing Shannon, I figured she would have brought her entire wardrobe in case of need, but it turned out to be just two good-sized suitcases. They were both the roller kind,

or I don't think she could have got them so far by herself. I collected one and left her to manage the other.
"You're late," I said. "Trouble deciding what to pack?"

"Don't start," she said.

"I probably should have got a two-bedroom cottage.
I don't know whether we'll have room for your clothes."

"I probably should have got a cottage of my own, so
I wouldn't have to put up with you." She deposited her
bag by the door and flopped onto the couch with a sigh.
"I don't think I can get used to all this hiking."

"You'd walk twice as far in a mall just to compare
prices."

"That's in a mall. That's different." She was looking
at my new painting. "That's a *Fauxnaif* work," she said
in tones of strong accusation. "Where did you get that?"

"From a *Fauxnaif*," I said smugly, sitting beside her
to admire it some more.

"It's on loan, right? You couldn't afford to buy it.
Good God, did he *give* it to you? Do you know what
that's *worth*?" She glanced around the room. "Don't you
have a safe you could put it in, or something? What the
hell are you doing, accepting a gift like that? You can't
do that. At least tell me the artist isn't a suspect. He's
not, right? Right?" She stared at the painting. "Oh,
shit."

I panicked. "What? What's wrong with it? What happened?" I was out of my seat, going to inspect it more
closely, before she could reassure me.

"No, relax, it's okay," she said. "Only the artist is a
suspect, isn't he? Who is it?"

"Belalin," I said. "One of the new elves. Only he's
not FOOF, just new to Fey Valley."

"Damn," she said.

"What?"

"Look at it," she said.

I looked. It was gorgeous, flawless, evocative, wonderful. "What? What?"

"It's that same bank," she said. "The one Gary ruined
with his dirt bike. The one on the way to Moraga. Don't

you remember? Hell. This is a painting of something he killed."

I sat back, looking at it. "Oh. So, like, you're saying he killed Gary for ruining something he'd painted?"

"No, only that he had a motive: Gary ruined something he found beautiful."

"He may not even know Gary's ruined it."

"True." She sounded relieved. "All right, I suppose it's a reach. But it's a dumb little bank beside a road, not something a painter would usually choose out to make a painting of. Usually nobody would even notice it, especially."

"A painter might. As far as we know, this painter did. Unless you think he found it damaged, painted it the way it had been, and then went off and killed Gary over it."

She made an impatient gesture. "Okay, okay. No. It sounds feeble when you put it that way. Hell, he's an elf. Who knows? It's just that . . . Look, if one of the humans had painted something that evocative, of an unlikely little roadside spot you wouldn't even expect him to notice in the ordinary way of things, that had been ruined by somebody who's since been murdered, it wouldn't very likely be a coincidence."

It took me a moment to unravel that. "Okay, right, I understand. And maybe it is significant. I don't mean to say it isn't. Only Bela isn't human. And I asked him whether he'd killed Gary."

"Right, and he said no, and you believed him."

"Actually he said he'd thought Gary died of a motorcycle accident. And I believed him."

"The way elves think, he could have caused the crash and still innocently express surprise if someone called it murder."

"True. The way they think, he could have stabbed the kid to death with his dinner fork and still innocently express surprise if someone called it murder. Just the same, I don't think he did it. I think he really thought the motorcycle crash was an accident."

"He still might be the Trouble."

"I don't think he's that, either." I repeated the gist of my conversation with Bela. "Of course he could have made up all that about the music."

"But you don't think he did. Okay, your instincts are usually good. So now the Trouble is one of the men— an elf, considering the nature of the music—and one of the women is in on it with him. Okay, so why are they haunting the woods at night when they could be comfortable in one of the cottages together?"

"Well . . . Because elves like the outdoors?"

She hooted in derision. "They like their creature comforts more than we do. I can't imagine them going camping for the fun of it, when there are perfectly good empty cottages they could be in."

"They don't even need to find an empty one; they must both live somewhere. Why not just go home?"

"Maybe they both live with somebody else?"

"Maybe. So what does that give us? Adulterous elves?"

"Or kids who live with their parents."

"There aren't any Trueblood children the right age here. They're all way too young."

"Halflings, then."

"They wouldn't have learned Faerie music, would they?"

"I don't know. Are there even any halfling children here, besides Kyriander's siblings? They'd hardly be out in the woods singing to each other. Who else has kids?"

"I don't know. But would anybody's kids be out in the woods singing to each other? It's not the way children usually entertain themselves."

"Romeo and Juliet were children," she said.

"And Lilie's the right age for Juliet. But who'd be Romeo? Gary? Nothing kept them apart." I told her about Ritchie's story, and what Finandiel had told me about Salonian. "Hell, maybe it's Salonian himself, and his girlfriend comes to visit him."

"Salonian has a house here somewhere, hasn't he?" she said. "Why would he be out in the woods in the dead of night when he could be comfortably at home?

And if his girlfriend comes to visit, all the more reason to get indoors where it's comfy."

"You're going to say that about anybody we think of."

"Only because it's true. I don't see how the Trouble can be any of the residents: it doesn't make sense for them to be out in the middle of a wet, cold forest when they could be at home by a warm fire."

She was right: even elves weren't that silly, though the popular misconception was strong. The storekeeper in Orinda thought it perfectly possible that elves of an artistic bent would tend to wander the woods at night, singing. People who believe that don't know elves. "The only way it makes sense is if it's somebody who doesn't live anyplace. Where does that leave us? We have a wandering minstrel, homeless, subject to fits of looking like Bigfoot, and well versed in elvish musical traditions. Does that sum it up?"

"And fond of occasional vandalism," she said. "Don't forget the vandalism."

"How could I? I'm still finding dried beans in the corners. But more likely Gary did that." I thought about it. "Should we add his murder to the mix?"

"No, I don't think the Trouble did that, either," she said. "It just doesn't fit."

"So now we're up to three perpetrators? The Trouble, a vandal, and a murderer?"

"The Trouble might come in two parts: music-maker and mischief-maker. And I think the vandal and the murderer could easily be the same person," she said judiciously.

"So, between two and four perps, depending. We haven't a clue," I said, suddenly depressed. "I've been here for days, and I haven't learned one thing we couldn't have learned by asking Finandiel more questions when he hired us."

"Right, and it's all your fault that Gary's dead and we haven't achieved world peace."

"I'm not sure I can accept the blame for the world-peace part." I grinned at her reluctantly. "Okay, I'm overreacting to the lack of information. But jeez, you'd think I'd have accomplished *some*thing in the time."

"Yeah, I naturally assumed that by now you'd have revealed the Trouble, caught the murderer, and maybe learned how to throw pots in your spare time."

"I already know how to throw pots," I said. "If you're not careful, I'll throw one at you."

She ignored me. "We should update our lists. Can you eliminate anyone for the murder?"

"No, not really. Everybody was home asleep. But I did remember where I saw that fine brass wire."

"We'll finish the list first: who's eliminated for the vandalism?"

"You already wrote them down." I counted them off on my fingers: "Salonian, Chance Winter, Mildred Potter, Charlotte, Benjamin Barski, Finandiel, and Cuthbern."

"Good, okay," said Shannon. "And the Trouble: is there anybody you know it couldn't have been, the night you ran into it? Or anything about it that gave you a clue who it could be?"

"No, and no," I said impatiently. "The only person whose location I even maybe knew was Ritchie Morita, and there's nothing to say he didn't do it anyway."

"And you found no clues?"

"I could tell it was probably not Bigfoot—not enough hair—and that it was probably around my height. I couldn't see a thing, I didn't smell anything but forest, and I didn't hear anything unexpected. When I went back the next day, I couldn't even find footprints."

She nodded. "Okay, who was inside the night Leaf saw it outside the Hall?"

"Where's the list we made before?"

"I want to make a new one, and compare the two."

I sighed. "Okay, okay. I'm not sure, since I didn't get there till afterward. I think Rosetta Fulmer. She's Leaf's mother. Finandiel and Cuthbern were there when I got there, and Finandiel said they'd been inside at the time. By the way, if it makes any differences, Leaf called it a 'big old man.' But all the men are big to her, and anybody over sixteen is probably old."

"That's the trouble with child witnesses. Go on. Who else was there."

"Charlotte, of course; she was fixing dinner. Ariana was with me. Lilie and Kyriander were gone: we can check with the hospital to make sure they were there at the relevant time, but I think it's a safe assumption for now. Ritchie Morita was there. Gary wasn't: he came along later, and hurt the elves' ears with his racket."

"Which means there were elves there. Which ones?"

"Galinda: she was talking with Chance Winter. Um. George Jenks was there, but he's not an elf. He's Leaf's father. I think Salonian was there. Finandiel and Cuthbern were there, but I don't think either of them would have bellowed at Gary. But I do remember elves bellowing."

"Fat lot of good that does, if you don't know which ones. Okay: where did you see the brass wire?"

"Ariana's cottage. It's beading wire."

"Damn." She put aside the paper and pen and scowled at me. "What do you have here to eat?"

27

Neither of us wanted to believe Ariana had killed Gary. There was nothing we could do about it just then anyway, so we ignored the problem and spent the rest of the evening like girls at a slumber party, eating and giggling and nonstop talking.

The next morning we went over the lists again.

"Ariana was with you when Leaf saw whatever she saw," she said. "But I'm not sure we should count the people cleared then. From Leaf's description, that could have been a passing stranger. Or nobody. She might have imagined the whole thing."

"That could be said of just about any of the sightings," I said. "What makes hers different?"

"She's young, impressionable, wanted attention, and had Peaceable with her. He didn't bark."

"All the more reason to think it was someone he knew. Only he doesn't bark, necessarily. At least, didn't when he first saw you. Or me."

"Good point. Okay, what does that show us?"

"That we haven't a clue, which I could have told you last night. In fact I believe I did. Let's go down to the Hall for breakfast."

"Did we eat everything you have here?"

"No, but I don't want to cook anything. Do you?"

"No. Does Charlotte cook every meal, every day? Doesn't she ever take time off?"

"She skipped a meal right after Gary was killed."

"And that's it? She's cooked every other meal since you've been here? Wow." She put her coffee on the table and stretched luxuriously. "What's her husband like?"

"I haven't seen much of him. I gather he's an alcoholic, or the next thing to it. But he's also a brilliant painter."

She nodded. "I'm familiar with his work. Is he pretty supportive of hers?"

"You mean of her cooking for everybody? I'm not sure he particularly notices, as long as she keeps his house tended and meals on his table." I pulled a blanket loose from the welter of them she had slept in the night before and added it to those wrapped around my shoulders.

She had insisted last night that the couch was even better than the bed since it was nearer the stove. She had added that she certainly couldn't be bothered to keep the stove going all night, so she would need all the spare blankets we could find. They didn't leave much room on the couch for sitting, but since we hadn't started a fire this morning and the room was icy-cold, that didn't seem to be a problem; we both just dug nests.

"She cooks separate meals for him?" she said. "That's outrageous."

"Why, if she doesn't mind? If he wants meals at home, and she wants to cook for the whole valley, seems like either they have to live at the Hall or she has to cook in two places."

"Then they should live at the Hall."

"Apparently they don't want to. I wouldn't."

"You wouldn't cook for the whole valley."

"No. But if I did."

"How can you know what you'd want if you also wanted to do something you wouldn't ever want to do?"

"It's too early in the morning to sort out a sentence like that," I said. "So are we going down to the Hall for breakfast, or what? Because I'm hungry, and drinking coffee is not an adequate solution."

"But we'll have to get dressed," she said.

"It was bound to happen sometime," I said, making no move to get out from under the covers.

"You should have started a fire while you were making the coffee," she said.

"What I should have done," I said, "is turned on the oven and left it open. That's lots easier than starting a fire."

"But not as picturesque."

"Actually I think it has a certain charm."

"Heat would be charming enough by itself," she said, and sighed. "All right. I'm hungry too. Is there at least hot water? I could get up more easily if I thought I'd get a hot shower out of it."

"There's plenty of hot water."

"Okay." She fished her slippers out from under the couch and put them on, so her bare feet never had to touch the cold wooden floor, reluctantly pushed the covers aside, and headed for the bathroom.

While she showered, I contemplated the lists. Nothing came of it. Why would Ariana have killed Gary? She'd been out that night, and we'd met her coming from the general direction of what would be the murder scene. But why would she have done it? He hurt her ears. Was she elf enough to kill over that? I just didn't know.

When we finally ventured out, freshly showered and bundled in warm sweaters, I was afraid we'd delayed so long that there wouldn't be any breakfast left at the Hall. But Charlotte had made French toast and sausage, and had not yet cleaned the pans. She had sausage and batter left over and expressed herself eager to cook them for us.

The Hall was surprisingly crowded, considering how late it was. There were a dozen or more people lingering over coffee. Finandiel was among them, with Cuthbern hovering unobtrusively at his back. Both seemed pleased to see us, though Cuthbern expressed it only by the most dignified look of approval.

Kyriander and Lilie were in the great room. I wondered how Briande was coping with his sister's freedom from school, granted only for what he would very possibly see as childish fits. It spoke well of him—or perhaps of the Fey Valley school—that he hadn't imitated her to get the same benefits. Lilie was deep in conversation with Kyriander and hadn't seen us yet, for which I was grateful.

Finandiel invited us to sit with him. So did nearly all the males present, since Shannon was with me; but Finandiel was nearest, and had empty chairs beside him, so we took them. I thought he might want to ask us about the investigation, but he was more interested in the breakfast he had just eaten. "A remarkable dish," he said. "We've nothing of the sort in Faerie. It is robust; a workers' meal; yet with a delicacy of flavors worthy of a prince's table. Have you had it before?"

We assured him we'd had French toast before, and liked it. He kept up a steady flow of light conversation while we ate. I paid little attention to him, being more interested in keeping an eye on the next room. To my profound relief, when Lilie finally noticed our presence, she satisfied herself with a venomous sneer at me; I had rather thought she might feel obliged to throw another fit. Kyriander, following her gaze, smiled a helpless apology for her look, but I knew he was as aware as I that it was the best of bad possibilities.

"A lovers' song," Finandiel was saying. "And the voice most sweet. Heard you nothing of it?"

"Nothing," Shannon said. "I slept like a log. About what time was it, do you think?"

"In the hour before dawn," said Finandiel. "I regret you heard it not. The singer was quite skilled."

"Could you tell whether it was male or female?"

"Masculine," he said decisively. "Though as I understand it, the distinction might have been less clear to a human auditor."

"Masculine," said Shannon. "Interesting."

"Had you thought the Trouble female?"

She shook her head. "There's not enough information yet."

"I rather thought," he said slowly, "that the sound

last night originated somewhere at the end of the valley. Near the mansion, perhaps."

"You know I tried to go to the mansion yesterday?" I asked.

"Yes," he said. "Will you try again?"

"Maybe," I said, at the same time as Shannon said, "Yes." We looked at each other. I shrugged. "Okay, yeah," I said. "We'll try again."

He dug with one finger in a tiny vest pocket, and withdrew a battered sprig of lavender. "Carry this," he said. "With it in your possession you should find Maerian's barrier less imposing."

I took it from him. "A sprig of lavender? Are you serious?"

"Nearly always." He shrugged ineffably. "Look not to me for reasons. I know the ways of magic, not the whys of it."

"Okay," I said dubiously, and put the lavender in my pocket. "Thanks. Will any lavender do, or is there something special about this bit?"

"Any should help," he said, "but in truth I have enhanced that I gave you with a spell of my own. Keep it with you, and others' magic will have less power against you."

"Thanks," I said. "That could come in useful." We didn't try it on Maerian's mansion that morning, though. Shannon wanted first to go back to the scene of Gary's murder. "We've been over that," I said.

"We'll go over it again," she said, in an infuriatingly superior tone. I hated when she did that. "Your car, or mine?"

"Yours," I said, moving toward it. "It's your wild-goose chase. We'll use your gas for it. You're just trying to put off the long walk to the mansion, aren't you?"

"Well, that and make sure we didn't miss anything."

"Gary's murder isn't even our problem."

"If it isn't ours, it's nobody's. The police disregard it, and everyone here seems to have forgotten it already. Even the most vile of noisy boys deserves better than that."

"I don't think Charlotte has forgotten."

"I don't suppose she will," said Shannon. "I meant the others, of course."

The Scotland Yard people hadn't yet been by to mend the broken shrubbery and tend to the bruised tree. The scene looked much as it had when we were there before.

"Oh, well," she said. "Will there be a funeral?"

"I expect so. No one has mentioned it, though."

"We should go, if there is," she said.

"Of course."

"I meant for clues, not for politeness. Though I guess it would be polite, wouldn't it? That's good: then it won't look odd."

"What clues do you expect to find at a funeral? I suppose you mean to watch everyone and see who looks guilty?"

"Something like that," she said. "Do you have that map of the valley with you?"

"Always, why?" I pulled it out of my pocket.

"Because I think we're nearer the mansion here than we were at the Hall. Maybe there's a path from here to there."

28

There was a path, but we had to walk back up to the road to find the starting point, and the map was not at all clear on whether it would actually take us all the way to the mansion, or only about halfway there. It looked to me as though it led directly to one cottage that wasn't on the main path, and stopped there. "I don't even know who might live there," I said.

"I don't either," Shannon said cheerfully. "We'll ask." She was leading the way, looking remarkably jaunty and self-confident for a city girl in the wilderness. I followed with less enthusiasm.

Even here, on a path that must be rarely used, Scotland Yard kept the underbrush at bay and designed the plantings to surprise the hiker with enchanting vistas and sudden vivid splashes of color. Yet their work was unobtrusive enough that it was easy to imagine this perfection was the natural state of the forest. There was nothing obviously artificial about it. We might have been walking through uncharted wilderness hundreds of miles from the nearest gardener or even the nearest residence.

"It's sobering, isn't it?" said Shannon.

"What is?"

"Being out here so far from anything. Do you realize this is the way it was for our ancestors? Imagine hundreds of miles of this in every direction," she said in awe, "and not one shopping mall!"

"You're right," I said. "That is sobering."

She looked around suspiciously. "You're laughing at me."

"No, just at what you said."

"Oh, that makes all the difference."

"I knew it would."

We rounded a turn and the forest opened onto another delightful vista so lovely even Mall-Girl paused to stare in pleasure. It was a parklike meadow bordered with overgrown rosebushes heavy with sweetly scented blossoms. "I guess there were compensations," she said.

I had lost the thread. "Compensations?"

"For the lack of malls. It is pretty, in a primitive sort of way. Look, some of them are longish-stemmed. We could cut a bouquet."

The notion was charming and romantic and ridiculous. I had a fleeting vision of us in Victorian dresses and broad-brimmed hats with baskets of roses over our arms. "What would we do with them?" I asked quellingly.

"Oh," she said.

We walked through the meadow, past the rosebushes, and the forest closed in on the path again. Bracken and sword fern brushed our running shoes. "You know, I've just thought," I said. "We're walking downhill."

"True," she said. "Is that a problem?" ·

"Not till we start back."

She stopped short. "Good God." She looked back the way we'd come, though we were past the turn that revealed the meadow, and there was nothing to see but trees and bracken. "That's a disconcerting notion."

"I thought so."

After a moment she shrugged and faced forward. "Well, there's nothing for it. Maybe if this path does connect with the main path at the bottom, we could walk back to the Hall and get your car, and drive back up to mine."

"If this path connects at the bottom."

"I'm pretty sure it will," she said, not sounding sure at all. "Besides, we're young and healthy. A little exercise will do us good."

I decided not to dignify that with a response, so we walked in silence for a while.

"D'you s'pose this is really what Faerie is like?" she asked as we reached another carefully planned vista, this one of a smooth emerald slope down to a tiny brook bubbling over colorful stones, the whole artfully framed by a cascade of blooming Scotch broom. "I mean in its natural state, without gardeners working day and night behind the scenes the way they do here?"

"I don't suppose they work at night," I said, diverted.

"You know what I mean," she said.

"Yes," I said. "And I don't know the answer. It is what people keep saying, that Scotland Yard is turning Fey Valley into an imitation of Faerie. So I suppose it is, but how would I know?"

"Or that's what they want to think." She moved on down the path. "You know, how we always remember a place we liked as more beautiful than it really was?"

"Do we?"

"I do," she said, surprised. "Don't you?"

"I don't know. I hadn't thought about it. What's this, a fork in the path?"

It was indeed a fork in the path, and nothing to choose between the branches. "Damn," she said.

"We're young," I said. "A little exercise will be good for us."

"Shut up," she said.

"Oh," I said.

"Hell, one of them could go for *miles* before it ends up at somebody's house instead of at the other path."

"One of them could go for miles before it ends up at the other path. Neither of them might lead to the other path. Which way shall we go, Fearless Leader?"

"Who put me in charge?"

"Hey, you're walking in front of me. I must be following you."

"Nonsense. I'm following you."

"Okay, we'll try that way." I pointed.

"I think that one goes a little more uphill than this one does," she said doubtfully.

"Okay, then this way," I said, pointing the other way.

"But I think that one curves the wrong way just past that big green bush up there."

"Which green bush? They're all green. No, never

mind: how about we just turn around and get the car, drive back to the Hall, and hike in by the real path?"

"This path is real."

"Yes, but which one?"

"They're both real," she said.

"Shannon," I said.

She grinned at me. "Okay, okay. Look, let's just try this one for a little way: if it's really going uphill, we'll know it soon enough, and we can turn around and try the other."

I shrugged. "Fine by me. Exercise is—"

"Don't say it," she said.

"Right."

She cast a last glance at the fork we weren't taking and started up the one she had selected. It seemed to me that it was indeed going uphill, which almost certainly meant it would lead to a dwelling instead of down to the main path on the valley floor; but Shannon didn't slacken her pace. I decided if it led to a dwelling, we could just interview the residents to make the trip worthwhile.

But there were no residents. The path followed the side of a ravine under a tunnel of tangled branches till, after about a quarter of a mile, it opened out suddenly onto a broad flagstone patio beside a large cottage that had been concealed by acacia on one side and a bank of blooming azalea on the other.

The windows glittered emptily in the light. There was an ineffable sense of desertion about the place, though naturally there were no weeds overgrowing the flagstone and no shrubs in need of a trim. Scotland Yard had been here, as everywhere.

After an initial pause to stare, we both moved forward, and neither of us thought to call out in case we were mistaken about the tenantless state of the place. We just walked up to the nearest window and looked in. The room off the patio was large and wood-paneled, and devoid of any furnishings but a Franklin stove against one wall. "How odd," I said. "Usually they're all furnished, I thought."

Shannon moved to another window, and then on around the cottage to a window that looked on a different room. "Not this one," she said. I followed her. The next room was the kitchen, but it held only built-in cupboards and sink. The places for stove and refrigerator were empty.

I would probably have gone right around the house looking in windows; but Shannon, bolder than I, tried the kitchen door. It opened readily. Neither of us hesitated to walk in, since it was clear nobody lived here. For the same reason, there was no particular reason to go in; but the lure of an empty house is powerful.

There was a loft above the front room, which we hadn't been able to see from outside because of the angle of the light. None of the downstairs rooms—kitchen, living room, bedroom, and bath—held anything of interest. It was a pretty house, clean and in good repair, and I have enough nesting instinct that I automatically considered where I would put my things if it were mine; but we weren't house-hunting, and there were no clues to the Trouble there.

I paused in the front room to look out onto the patio at all the flowering bushes and trees. It was a very different view from that I'd seen in other Fey Valley residences. Looking out this window you'd hardly know we were halfway up the canyon wall. It was a closer, more intimate view, and I liked it more. It seemed homier.

While I was admiring it, Shannon climbed the ladder to look into the loft. "Eureka," she said happily, and scrambled up the last few steps to disappear from view.

"What?" I turned from the window to follow her up the ladder. "What did you find?"

"Someone's been here," she said. "Someone was living here."

"Well, of course: it's a house. That's what it's for."

"No, I mean recently," she said impatiently.

"Well, it was a house then, too," I said. I reached the top step and peered through the gloom at her. She was in the far corner, bending over something. "What is it?"

"Camping out," she said. "Someone was camping out

here. Look. A burnt candle stub, dead matches on the floor, and dripped wax."

"Maybe the last residents were messy."

"And nobody's cleaned it up since? Everything else in this place is dusted and waxed and polished to perfection, and they didn't bother to scrape up spilled wax and throw away dead matches? I don't think so."

"It's not much of a clue."

She sat back on her heels and looked around the loft. "Maybe not, but it's the first concrete evidence I've seen that the Trouble even exists."

"You're jumping to conclusions: somebody may've camped out here, but we don't know it was the Trouble."

"Who else would?"

"I don't know. Kids, maybe. The door wasn't locked. It'd be a good place for teenagers to do a little private necking—or more—by romantic candlelight."

She accepted that, grudgingly. "But I think it was the Trouble," she said, walking around the room peering at the floor as though she expected another clue to materialize.

"If it was, I don't know what that tells us."

"That it isn't a resident," she said. "I didn't think it would be, but this is the first evidence we've seen of an outsider."

"If it isn't a resident," I said, "then all your list-making was for nothing. We're back to square one, with nothing to go on."

"Except a burnt candle, matches, and spilled wax," she reminded me.

"Fat lot of good those do us."

"And another thing," she said. "This house is relatively close to the road. I'll bet the sound of Gary's motorcycle was a real trial from here. If whoever was staying here was an elf . . ."

"That's a lot of ifs. If it was an elf, if it was the Trouble, if Gary's noise wasn't muffled by trees, then maybe the Trouble killed Gary. Which we already knew was a possibility in the first place."

"But it didn't seem likely before."

"And it doesn't seem likely to me now," I said. "If whoever was staying here was an elf, and the noise bothered him, why wouldn't he just move? That's if somebody was staying here, which we don't know."

"Where would he move?"

"To another empty cottage. The valley must be littered with them. I think somebody said there was enough housing here for half again as many people."

"Okay, this doesn't prove anything. Okay." She followed me back down the ladder and looked around the lower rooms again, hoping to find further evidence of invasion. "There's soap in the bathroom," she said.

"Is it wet?"

"No. But like the candle, it has to've been left after the cleaners were here, or they'd have thrown it away."

"Okay, that's more evidence somebody may've stayed here."

"But there's nothing to say who, or when. I know, I know." She sighed. "It must be lunchtime by now. Let's go back down to the Hall to eat."

29

After lunch we sat down with Charlotte to go over my map, marking in all the empty dwellings and the smaller paths. "But I haven't been to some of these cottages in months," she said. "I don't keep after them, you know; we hire a service in Moraga to clean them when someone moves out, and again when someone wants to move in. Betweentimes, I depend on Scotland Yard to keep an eye on them, and let me know if anything big goes wrong. Which there's no telling whether they really bother to do, of course. They're a careless bunch, most of them too young to understand responsibility. But it's just the best I can do. I can't be everywhere."

"No, of course not," said Shannon. "I don't understand how you're able to do as much as you do. How did you get stuck with so much work, anyway?"

Charlotte bridled at that. "Well, nobody *else* would do it," she said in tones of extreme superiority. "*Some* people are too *good* for mundane, day-to-day matters like cleanliness and nutrition." She glared sourly around the empty dining area as though daring a resident to materialize to refute her claims.

"It must be a burden to you," Shannon said.

Charlotte's face relaxed into her usual expression of dissatisfaction. "I don't mind it so much," she said. "It gives me something to do."

"You like cooking," Shannon suggested.

"It's not so much that I like it," she said. "But I'm good at it. I'm not talented like all these other people. I don't have any skills. I can't make beautiful things like they do. But I can make good, plain meals, and they're glad enough to eat them."

"Your meals are delicious," said Shannon. "That's an art, isn't it? A good chef isn't easy to come by."

"Oh, I don't know how to do what a *chef* would," she said quickly. "I don't have the training, and I probably couldn't do it if I did. I can't cook gourmet food, you know. I just know how to put things together so they taste good, that's all. Anybody could do what I do. It's no big deal."

"I can't boil water without burning it," said Shannon.

"You could if you had to," said Charlotte. She was determined not to accept praise of any sort, or favorable comparisons. It was important to her not to be admired, though she wouldn't have put it that way and would have been offended if someone else had.

Doubtless she imagined she was only being realistic about herself. But her bitter outlook, while it might have protected her from failure by keeping her from trying any but the tasks she knew she could manage, and disclaiming skill at those, also protected her from any real success. She could move forward only in the smallest increments, never reaching for what was beyond her grasp, never stretching, and thus never achieving anything new.

She must fear failure very much indeed, to devote her life to it. I've always known that some people are happiest when they are unhappy, but when I meet them I'm still amazed and a little incredulous. I want to tell them not to be silly. I wanted to bully Charlotte into some minor risk, to show her she might succeed and, if she didn't, that failure isn't fatal in most pursuits. Luckily I restrained myself.

Shannon guided her gently back to the subject of empty cottages, and learned that the last time she had been to the one we visited that morning was months ago, well before the Trouble started. Yes, she had been through the entire place at that time, to make sure the cleaners had done a good job. Yes, she had examined the loft, too. She remembered, because she'd found the windows there quite streaked, and had to do them again herself, which was particularly annoying because she hadn't brought her long-handled cleaning sponge and squeegee. She had to improvise with an ordinary sponge tied to a stick, and it hadn't worked nearly as well.

"I had a word with the cleaning people after that," she said. "Some people will skimp wherever they think they can get away with it." She sniffed disdainfully. "They told me if we didn't have anyone moving in there right away, it wouldn't matter how well the windows had been done, because they'd just have to be done again when somebody did move in. I set them straight about that, let me tell you. There's no sense doing a job at all if you're not going to do it right."

"No, that was very sloppy of them," said Shannon. "Do you use the same cleaning company for all the houses?"

"Yes, just once a year for the empty ones, and when someone moves in or out," she said, and looked at me. "Except when there's no warning," she added disapprovingly. "I didn't have time to have your cottage cleaned again, and I'm sure there was dust at the least, and probably worse."

"It was fine," I said.

"Well, it's just lucky that it hadn't been long since someone moved out," she said. "Spiders get in, and sometimes mice, and you never know what all. If you'd given me even a day's warning I could have had them in to clean it."

"It wasn't necessary. Really," I said.

"And this is the same cleaning company you've been using for some time?" asked Shannon.

"Yes, always," said Charlotte. "In general they're pretty good. Probably as good as one could hope for. There's always some little thing, but you just can't expect hired help to do a perfect job."

"No, people are very careless," Shannon agreed gravely. "What company is it you use? I think I'd like to talk to them, if I could."

Charlotte told her. "But I doubt if they can tell you anything useful," she said repressively.

"I don't suppose they will," said Shannon, "but we have to cover all the bases, if only to give you a better impression of hired help than some people have done."

Charlotte looked shocked. "You're not hired help," she said, alarmed. "I didn't mean you, for goodness sake. You're professionals, not . . . not domestics."

I wanted to tell her the so-called domestics probably thought of themselves as professional housecleaners, but I didn't. Instead I said, because I suddenly realized what was missing from the Hall, "Where's Ritchie?" He wasn't in the great room typing.

"I don't know," said Charlotte. "I'm not his keeper. Nasty, foul-tempered bully, anyway. I don't truck with his sort, I don't care how many awards his books win. Have you read any of them? They're just as nasty as he is. Tiresome and cranky too. If a person can't bother to be polite about things, he might just as well go live in a cave for all I care."

The image of Ritchie living in a cave was diverting. "He'd have to have it wired for electricity," I said, "for his typewriter."

"He could get a laptop computer," Shannon said reasonably, and turned back to Charlotte. "We found a candle, you know, in that cottage this morning. Burnt nearly down, and with matches and spilled wax around it."

Charlotte stared. "Those weren't there when I went through," she said. "Someone has Been There." The capital letters were audible.

"Well, yes, we think so," Shannon said. "We were wondering whether you knew anything about it."

"Certainly not." Her peevish expression deepened as she thought about it. "Who would do such a thing? That is so inconsiderate! Now I'll have to go all that way up there to inspect it, and have the cleaners out again. Some people behave just like animals. They have no consideration at all."

"We thought," Shannon said diffidently, "that it might have been the Trouble."

"The Trouble? Staying in an empty cottage? With a *candle*?" She said it as though the possession of a candle were the worst of the Trouble's offenses. "But why?"

"Well, if it hadn't anywhere else to stay?"

"No, I mean the candle. The electricity should be on up there. I do flip the main breaker when I know a cottage is going to be deserted for a time, but anybody who wanted to stay there would just have to flip it on again."

"Maybe he thought a candle would be less noticeable," said Shannon.

"Or maybe he doesn't know about breakers," I said.

Charlotte wasn't interested in reasons. "This is just so typical," she said. "Artists. You can bet it was one of them. Or those brats they raise. You'd think they could exercise some control over their children, but no." We were both struck speechless by that, Gary having been by far the most obnoxious child in Fey Valley. "I'll call the cleaners right away. If this sort of thing is going on, we'll have to start locking the cottages. What a shame. Some people just have to ruin things for everybody."

"Well," said Shannon, "if it was the Trouble . . ."

"Even so," Charlotte said crossly. "I can't be having the Trouble staying in empty cottages either, can I? Oh, God, how can people be so *thought*less? And to do it now, after everything else. It's just too much." Tears spilled unexpectedly down her cheeks. She seemed unaware of them. Her sour, lined face was suddenly old and helpless. "I just don't know how I'll go on, if it's going to be like this." She looked from one to the other of us as though for advice or reassurance.

"We'll find out who it was," Shannon said gently. "We'll put a stop to it."

Charlotte looked at her gratefully. "Thank you," she said. She became aware of the tears then, and brushed them away with the heels of her hands, blushing unbecomingly. "Oh, I'm so embarrassed. It's been like this ever since . . . since Gary . . . I just cry sometimes," she said helplessly. "I don't mean to."

"No, of course not," said Shannon. "And that's something I wanted to ask you, Charlotte. Will there be a memorial service? We'd like to attend, if that would be all right with you."

"Of course," she said. "Thank you. Tim wanted one." She cleared her throat and looked past us out the front door, her expression hardening again. "I don't hold with them myself. Superstitious claptrap. But it's what Tim wants." Her chin trembled. "He doesn't ask for anything very often, so when he does, I try to give it to him."

"And he asked for a memorial service?"

"He says it's important," she said, not quite ridiculing the notion, but clearly wanting to. It was becoming clear that as far as she was concerned there were only two ways of doing anything: her way, and wrong. "I didn't want to say anything when I could see it meant so much to him."

"It's a help to some people," said Shannon.

"I don't see any point to it," said Charlotte.

"Perhaps it's a sort of closure for them," Shannon said diffidently. "Sometimes people need closure."

"I wouldn't know anything about that," said Charlotte, repudiating the entire concept of closure. "That's some of your intellectual prattle, I suppose, but I'm no intellectual. I'm a plain woman, and I don't need any intellectual, psychological, religious mumbo jumbo to tell me my son is dead."

30

"Okay," said Shannon. "We have music in the night, small thefts, vandalism, murder done with what might be Ariana's beading wire, someone camping out in an empty cottage, let's see. One of the new elves you didn't interview—Jeran? And you didn't get in to see Maerian. What else?"

She was sitting on the porch, yelling through the door at me. We had returned to my cottage to regroup after our chat with Charlotte, and I was making coffee. I didn't answer her till it was finished and I could bring it onto the porch, which for a wonder had dried in the wind and what little sun there was, and was a bearable temperature for people wearing heavy sweaters and jeans, which we were.

"Are we making yet another list?" I said, putting the coffee on the small porch table. The view from there was stunning, which was why we were sitting in the wind instead of inside by the Franklin stove. The sky showed patches of blue through the high fog. The air was soft and luminous, the forest vivid emerald splashed here and there with glowing yellow clouds of acacia.

"Lists," said Shannon, sipping her coffee. She ticked them off on her fingers: "Evidence of the Trouble. Other incidents that might or not be related. And leads we haven't followed."

"The evidence of the Trouble is still what it was: people frightened, music at night, little things stolen."

"That's something," she said. "What sort of little things? I think you told me once, but I've forgotten."

"Laundry from clotheslines," I said. "Small tools. A

dog dish. Boards. Brushes. Shoes. A rake. Just about anything anybody might leave outside, I guess. I couldn't see a pattern to it."

"What kind of small tools?"

"Whatever," I said. "A hammer, I think. A drill bit. A screwdriver. A tape measure. I don't remember what else."

"Hmm. What kind of clothes? Men's? Women's?"

"And children's," I said. "The shoes were kids' shoes too. If it's the Trouble that's stealing stuff, I don't think it's to wear them or use them. I think it just takes whatever comes to hand."

"Has anybody ever found any of the missing stuff later? You know, a cache of it? Or maybe it was just misplaced after all?"

"Nope, neither. At least, not that anyone admits."

"Okay, that's no help." She looked at the pad of paper on her lap. "Music. Finandiel and Belalin both say it's a male singer, and the songs are love songs."

"Some of them," I said. "Bela said some of them are just what you sing when you're alone and feel like singing. And Galinda said the song she heard was a lullaby."

"And it was a male singer?"

"Yeah."

"You figure Belalin's right?"

"I figure he knows more about it than I do."

"Or he's the Trouble, laying a false trail."

"I really don't think one of the *Fauxnaifs* is going to turn out to be the Trouble. Good God. They're rich as sin, successful, rich. And did I mention rich? Why would they want to do anything like that?"

She shrugged. "Everybody here is rich, successful, and rich."

"Good point."

"But you thought Belalin was telling the truth?"

"Yeah, I did."

"Okay. What sort of person *is* a likely candidate for the Trouble?"

"I don't know. Maybe kids. I liked Gary for it, except for the music. He'd have enjoyed frightening kids and making a nuisance of himself. But he couldn't hide what he did with magic."

"No. That takes an elf or a halfling." She thought about it. "Gary and Lilie together?"

I sipped my coffee and stared across the valley. "We'll just have to wait and see whether the nuisance part stops now that he's dead, I guess. But who killed him? And who makes the music?"

She cradled her coffee in her hands. "Ariana really may have done the murder. But anyone might have done the murder: that sort of wire isn't exactly rare, and I doubt if she keeps hers under lock and key." She sighed. "The musician is an elf. That seems to be the consensus, right?"

"It's elven music," I said. "And apparently an elf's voice, though I can't say for sure I've heard that."

"A male elf," she said.

"According to Belalin."

"Who is, we should mention, a male elf."

"And one who moved here right before the Trouble began."

"Right. But you don't think he's it. Okay. So we should find out whether there've been any incidents since Gary died, we should interview Jeran and Maerian, we should look through other empty cottages for evidence of camping out, and maybe we should talk to the police about the wire."

"I have an idea they'll say there's no way to prove it caused the accident."

"And rightly so, damn them," she said. "I wonder whether one of the elves could tell?"

"With magic? I don't know. Maybe. Don't the police have forensic elves for that sort of thing?"

"I'm not sure they have, in Moraga. It's a very small town."

"Point taken." I put my feet up. "This is good. What a beautiful day."

"See if you think so when we start hiking around in the underbrush. You know, Lilie throws a lot of fits. In fact," she said, looking thoughtful, "she exactly fits my notion of what kind of person would want to do the mischief part of the Trouble."

"You think she did it without Gary's help? Okay, yeah, she's a good candidate. I s'pose she's even a good candidate for vandalizing my cottage, come to that. She hates me quite cordially enough, and she could easily have got the key from Gary. Would she have planted evidence meant to lead us to him, though? I thought she loved him."

"I don't know. Who can say what a romantic brat with delusions of importance might do?"

"Speaking of people with delusions of importance, I want to know where Ritchie Morita was today while we were talking to Charlotte."

"Why?"

"Because he's always at the Hall."

"I expect he goes home once in a while," she said, smiling. "In fact, I think you mentioned him doing it once."

"Yeah, okay, okay. But he flirts with Lilie."

"And?"

"And considering how oddly he behaved in front of Kyri the other evening, I really wonder whether he does more than flirt. He seemed almost embarrassed. I guess you haven't been around to notice, but he goes all puckish in Lilie's presence and makes more of an ass of himself than usual. I think it's part of the angry young man thing: an angry young man should be able to fix the interest of a beautiful young woman, right?"

"What's he got to be angry about?"

"The world doesn't suit him."

"Ah." She nodded sagely.

"You haven't read his books?"

"No, should I?"

"You wouldn't like them."

"Then I won't. But his love life is surely none of our business. Do you have a reason to want to know where he was, or are you just feeling snoopy?"

"He used to yell at Gary as loud as the elves did," I

said. A sense of fairness made me add, "But so, proba- bly, did anybody whose house is too close to the road."

"Why wouldn't they just move farther from the road?"

"Move because a snotty teenager has no consider- ation? I know a lot of people who'd sooner kill him."

"You know a low class of people," she said

"Granted." A hawk soared placidly into a patch of blue sky and hovered majestically. "I guess I was just being snoopy. I really think the murderer was more likely an elf. Or a pretty sick human, which none of these seem to be. They're strange enough, some of them; but not evil, and murder is an evil act for a human."

"Let's get back to Romeo and Juliet," she said. "If Lilie is Juliet, was Gary Romeo?"

"I don't think Lilie is Juliet," I said. "Some of them told me the Romeo and Juliet story after Gary died. I'd think death would rule him out, and there aren't any other humans or halflings to be her Romeo."

"Well, what about elves? There might be one around young enough for her."

"I don't think so. She's too young: even a young elf would think of her as a mere child. Unless he's as young as she, in which case he'd be less mature than she, and not yet interested in girls."

"Okay, then say Romeo and Juliet are some whole different pair. Who? Salonian and his princess?"

"I haven't met any young female elves here besides Galinda and Lorielle," I said.

"And no young male elves to go with either of them, unless you've forgotten to tell me about someone," she said. "But we haven't yet met Maerian. Maybe she's the best candidate for Juliet, since she's so reclusive."

"Since she's so reclusive, our Romeo could just move in with her and nobody'd know it."

"Well, but why wouldn't he just move in with any of them? Even if somebody would know it? What's the point of hiding?"

"I don't know," I said. "I wish we knew more about Faerie aristocracy. Maybe that would tell us why Romeo would hide instead of moving in with his Juliet." I thought about it. "Let's say Romeo is aristocracy. He's not supposed to come to the ironworld at all. Queen's rules for higher aristocracy, I gather."

"Okay, why don't he and Juliet stay in Faerie?"

"Say he loves Juliet, but there's something against them marrying. Their families don't like it, or the queen doesn't, or somebody. So they come here—if they're not too aristocratic, nobody would mind, except the family they're running away from. Which, if you're running away, is part of the point, I should think."

"Right," said Shannon. "They have a pact: they'll meet here. They can't be together in Faerie, so they'll come where they can be together. Only elves are about as thick on the ground here as they are in Faerie, so they find out they can't be openly together here, either, for fear word will get back to the queen. Or whoever."

"Probably better make it the queen," I said. "It's gotta be somebody who has the power to make them go back to Faerie if they're discovered."

"Okay, the queen. They're hiding from the queen. But they came here to be together, and that's what they want. So one of them buys into Fey Valley. Why doesn't he or she choose one of the most isolated cabins and move the other one in?"

I thought about it. "Everybody knows one of them came here. Let's say it's Salonian. Maybe he wasn't especially supposed to come here, but nobody minds if they don't know Tintiminiel followed him. Wouldn't they notice if she did, though?"

"You'd think they'd at least notice she'd gone missing."

"Maybe they did. Maybe as soon as she went missing, they started watching Salonian."

"Good," said Shannon. "So they're watching him, and they'd be way suspicious if he took an isolated cottage and nobody ever saw him; but as long as he's fairly visible and known to be living alone, they won't bother him."

"So Tintiminiel can't live with him, but they can meet

in the woods at night. Only the music-maker is a man, and according to Belalin, he sometimes sings solitary songs. Why would Salonian be wandering around singing when he's not with Tintiminiel, and he could be comfortably at home?"

"Well, maybe it's not Salonian and Tintiminiel," said Shannon. "Maybe it's Lorielle and somebody. Remember the love letters?"

"We don't know they're love letters."

"Her Romeo could have arranged to have letters come from Faerie," she said, "so no one would know he's here."

I looked at her. "And to while away the daylight hours, Romeo steals screwdrivers and children's shoes?"

She shook her head. "No, no, that's the mischief-maker. Romeo's the music-maker."

"Or I suppose," I said, thinking about it, "he really might. Elves are easily amused by odd bits of mischief at humans' expense. Plus it scares us out of the woods, so they can meet at night with less fear of exposure."

"Maybe, but wouldn't he have noticed he's scaring the children? I can see that happening by accident, but no elf would keep it up once he knew it was scaring kids."

"Maybe he doesn't know. Maybe nobody told him."

"Lorielle/Juliet would, surely?" she said.

"You'd think so. And where does the murder tie in with all this? Did Romeo have do it, because he was staying in that cottage so near the road, and the noise hurt him? An elf that FOOF, with none of the standard orientation information, might not think twice about murdering a nuisance human."

"A child?"

"Maybe he didn't know Gary was a child? Maybe Gary was old enough not to qualify as a child?"

"Finandiel spoke of him as a child."

"Finandiel was looking at it from Charlotte's point of view."

She nodded. "True. Okay. But how awful, if that's it. Romeo the wilderness singer is quite a romantic figure. Romeo the remorseless killer is not."

"We did know that about elves."

"That doesn't mean we have to like it," she said.

"No. That's why there's so much fiction in which elves feature as austere but noble folk who come to humans' rescue in a pinch."

"Well, sometimes they're like that."

"When they come to humans' rescue, it's because they see some benefit to themselves. None of them would take a step out of his way for us except for selfish reasons."

"You could argue that's true of humans, too."

"Yes, if it were. But mostly it's not. And it's normal for them. It's not for us."

"I think it must be different," she said. "They do manage not to slaughter each other or us, most days."

"So does the average sociopath. They don't go around slaughtering everybody in sight. They behave quite well, as a rule. And many of them are dangerously charming. Just like elves."

"Well, what's your point?"

"Just that Romeo might very well be a remorseless killer. It's his nature: elves *are* remorseless."

31

"This is getting us nowhere," said Shannon. "I fear it's time to get off our duffs and do some intrepid hiking through the underbrush."

We didn't have to: there were clear paths everywhere we wanted to go, often with stairs on the steeper inclines, and bridges when we needed to cross the creek. We went to Jeran's house first, but he wasn't home: there was a note stuck to his door that said he was out painting.

"I wish these people used telephones," said Shannon. "We wouldn't have had to hike all this way if we could have called first."

"It was a nice walk," I said.

"It was a long, miserable hike," she said. "And not one pretzels-and-espresso stand on the way."

"Yeah," I said. "Nice, huh?"

"I don't choose to dignify that with a response," she said. "Maerian's mansion is how far in the other direction?"

"Only three quarters of a mile or so," I said.

"Only!" She sighed heavily and started down the stairs toward the valley floor. "Let's get it over with."

Despite her complaints she seemed to enjoy the walk, but we were both getting tired by the time we approached Maerian's mansion. I didn't realize we were near it till Shannon paused to admire a trillium and then started back the way we had come. "Where are you going?" I asked in amazement.

She paused and looked around. "Oh. I guess I got turned around." She started on with me, but very soon

paused to admire something else and, afterward, started
to go the wrong way again.

"I think we're running into Maerian's barrier spell,"
I said, stopping her. "You keep going the wrong way."

"Oh." She looked at me. "Why doesn't it affect you?"

"I have that sprig of magicked lavender Finandiel
gave me." I dug it out of my pocket and looked at it.
"You s'pose it'd still be good if I broke it in half? Then
we could each carry half, and maybe get through: otherwise we'll have to hold hands, I think."

"Let's try that first," she said. "No sense breaking the
lavender if we don't have to."

It didn't work: she still tried to go the wrong way.
When I pulled her along with me, she began to get dis-
oriented and uncomfortable. After only a few yards of
slow, increasingly irritable progress we stopped again
and I broke the sprig of lavender in half.

As soon as she had it in her hand her expression
cleared and she stared around her in surprise, as though
waking from sleep to find herself elsewhere than she'd
expected. "Jeez, that's some spell," she said.

"Which? Maerian's or Finandiel's?"

She looked at the lavender. "Both, I guess." She
stuffed it in her pocket and started forward again, heading the right way this time. "Well, let's get on with it. I
don't think I'm going to like this woman."

We didn't get to find out that afternoon. The lavender
got us all the way to the porch, but no one answered
the door when we knocked, and there was no sign of
life anywhere about the place. "Maybe she's out painting, too," I said.

"Then she should have left us a note," said Shannon.

"She didn't know we were coming," I said.

"Neither did Jeran, but *he* left a note," said Shannon.
"Well, now what?"

"Now let's look around some more, as long as we're
here," I said. We searched the grounds and found nothing out of the ordinary. Nor did Maerian return from
wherever she'd gone. It was getting late and we were

getting hungry when we finally gave up and turned back toward the Hall. "What a wasted day," said Shannon.

"I don't know. We've learned some stuff. We have a whole raft of empty cottages to investigate."

"We ought to rest up," said Shannon. "I've been thinking. You keep hearing that music late at night, right? We should try to track it down."

I'd been thinking that too, but I'd hoped we'd learn something to prevent the necessity. I wasn't excited about traipsing around in the woods after midnight, presumably by moonlight, since carrying flashlights would give the Trouble every opportunity to see us before we saw it. Still, she was right: it was the next step.

Ritchie was at the Hall for dinner. He said he'd been at home that afternooon, working. When I expressed surprise, since he'd been working in the Hall ever since I'd come to the valley, he said, "Yes," with elaborate patience. "As I've told you, I usually enjoy the distractions; but I'm coming up on a deadline and I can't afford to be delayed. What is this, twenty questions, or do you suspect me of being the Trouble?" His tone was challenging and his expression one of veiled mockery.

"Neither," I said, and walked away. I'd been unfailingly polite to him before, and he'd been unfailingly rude. I was tired of it.

Kyriander, Lilie, and Briande came in just then. Kyriander headed straight for the kitchen, smiling at me on his way past. Lilie went directly to Ritchie and settled beside him with innocent certainty of her welcome. Briande went past her to a corner where Leaf Fulmer-Jenks was settled with a huge box of crayons and a thick coloring book.

Lilie noticed me after she was seated, and scowled at me, but Ritchie said something to distract her and she didn't bother to throw a fit. That was a relief.

Kyriander returned from the kitchen with a plate full of food and took a chair at the table next to me. "You have already eaten?" he asked.

Since the evidence was before me, in the form of a

dirtied plate I hadn't yet carried back to the kitchen, I admitted it.

"Found you a candle in one of the cottages today?" he said between mouthfuls.

Several people around the table looked up at that, waiting to hear my answer. "Yes," I said. "Where'd you hear about it?"

"From Charlotte," he said. "She is much in a pelter over the shoddy habits of the cleaning crew." He looked at me. "Was it left from the last dwellers?"

"I doubt it," I said. "It looked as though someone had been camping out."

He nodded. "The Trouble, then," he said.

"Maybe," I said.

"What else?" asked Chance Winter. "Has to be the Trouble if it wasn't the last tenants, doesn't it?"

"It could have been kids," I said.

"Our kids?" asked Marc Starr, a painter whose arrogance very nearly equaled Ritchie's and whose personality was far less pleasant. He was usually rendered tolerable company only by the absurdity of his completely self-centered outlook. Now he sounded ready to take deep offense at the notion that any Fey Valley children would have left a candle in an unoccupied cottage.

"D'you think someone else's kids come into Fey Valley much?" I asked, looking at him.

Melanie McGraw, sitting next to him, put a restraining hand on his elbow and said gently, "Dorina is too young. The older children might, Marc. We've always known one or more of them might be behind the Trouble."

"I don't believe it," he said belligerently. "It's asinine to suggest that they would. Send these people away, Melanie. The very thought of their base accusations must offend. It does offend. It intrudes its grossness on my sensibilities; it blights my vision of the light. I must have peace, do you understand me? Send them away."

"Marc, I can't," she said. "We're not at home."

He looked around in some amazement. "What are we doing here? This is not where I want to be. I don't like it."

"You wanted one of Charlotte's meals," she said.

"Oh. All right. But tell them Dorina didn't light any candles."

"Well, we don't really suspect Dorina," said Shannon. "If it was kids, it would probably be older ones, looking for a place to make out." She shrugged apologetically. "We have to consider all the possibilities."

Melanie nodded earnestly and patted Marc's arm. "There, see?"

Marc irritably twitched his arm away from her. "I see how it is," he said, glaring at her. "You want to shift the blame to someone else's children so yours won't be suspected. It won't do, you know. The Trouble will not be a child: that would be unpleasant. I don't like unpleasantness."

She shrugged ineffably. "Fine by me," she said. "I certainly don't think it's a child." She rose abruptly, plate in hand, and asked, "Shall I get you anything from the kitchen?"

"No," he said disagreeably. "Unless there's more of this green stuff. What is it? The color pleases my eye: subdued, yet very rich and complex. See how the light touches it? I want more of this. Get it for me. What is it?"

"It's spinach," she said. "I'll get another helping."

"Hurry up," he said impatiently. "I want it."

Rosetta Fulmer watched her go by and then scowled at Marc so ferociously I was amazed that he was able to return her look with complete indifference. When she noticed me watching her she looked briefly flustered and then said, very kindly, by way of explanation, "He was rude, you see."

"Yes, I did see," I said, with a side glance at Marc to see how he would react. He didn't.

"He often is. He has the manners of a spoiled child. He's very famous, you know. I often think," she added ruminatively, "that fame has a sort of a bad effect on some people. Have you ever noticed that?"

I choked. Shannon came to my rescue, pounding my

back while she told Rosetta, "You know, I've noticed that myself. It's like it goes to their heads."

Rosetta studied her. "You're making fun," she said. "But it's perfectly true. I've seen any number of artists pass through here who might have been nice people if they hadn't been famous. I don't say they lose their perspective, because the plain fact is they wouldn't be famous if they did lose their perspective, at least the ones whose work is representational, because without perspective it would go all the wrong sizes and wouldn't be representational after all, and I wouldn't say they lose their sense of proportion either." She paused, which was a relief as I'd begun to wonder when she would breathe.

After a moment's consideration she said, "I know, we've all seen paintings by artists who have no sense of proportion: they enjoy fads, and sometimes they're even quite good, but I think we all recognize that's not Marc's trouble. Not that he isn't quite good, because he is, and we've all seen that too, though I must say I don't care much, myself, for the direction he's been taking lately, because I think he's using too much phthalo green and that's all there is to it. It's too acid for what he intends."

"You're right!" he said, thrusting his spinach at her. "This is what I've wanted. I didn't realize it before. This subtlety, this earthiness, this richness. It is exactly why I wanted to come to dinner here. Charlotte's cooking is food for the soul." He subsided, pensively consuming his spinach.

Rosetta shook her head. "You see? Exactly like a half-wetted child, which I'm sure I've always wondered why they don't just dry off if they're so wet, and in any case we know he's quite smart when he isn't immediately involved in a painting, which seems to suck the intelligence right out of him. But it's none of my business, and I know that, so I'm just saying it's rude not to say thank you when someone offers a kindness, especially when it's the mother of his only child." She looked at Marc fiercely, as though daring him to challenge this apparently deeply felt opinion.

He stared at her, apparently considering her point of

view. After a long moment he shifted his gaze to the kitchen door and bellowed, "Melanie! Get me some coffee. And come take my plate away. I don't want it." He pushed the offending object away.

"Do you still want your spinach?" called Melanie.

"No, no, I've seen enough," he said impatiently.

Rosetta shook her head. "That's exactly what I mean," she said, and rose to carry her own plate to the kitchen. "Can I get anyone coffee while I'm up?"

Mildred Potter, who was sitting beside Benjamin Barski, both of them eating quietly and neither taking any apparent interest in Rosetta's speech, suddenly turned to examine Marc as though he were an object she found inexplicably out of place. After a long moment she turned back to her food. Marc snickered. Mildred said quietly, to Benjamin, "He's always rude to me, you know. I thought it was because I'm not a proper artist."

Marc sneered at her. "You're not any kind of artist. If Benj hasn't noticed that, he's as big a fool as you are. Go away. You irk me."

"Here, now," said Benjamin, looking confused. "Mildred don't claim she's an artist—do you, love?—so there's no call for you to be telling her she ain't one," he said with less than perfect clarity, putting one arm protectively around Mildred's shoulders and glaring at Marc.

"Oh, Benjamin," said Melanie, arriving from the kitchen at that moment with Marc's coffee. "That's so sweet. I didn't know you two were seeing each other."

"How not, when they eat their meals here?" asked Finandiel in perfect innocence.

"It's a euphemism," said Shannon.

"It is? For what?" asked Finandiel, looking pleased.

"It means they're going together, dating, you know."

"Sleeping together," Marc said, nodding.

If Shannon and I were going to haunt the woods tonight, it was time we left the residents to their bickering and got some rest. I was about to say so when Lilie rose abruptly from Ritchie's side and announced across the room, glaring at me, "I want to talk to you."

32

"Oh, Lord," I said. Shannon gave me a look. "Yes, all right," I said; and, to Lilie, "Yes?"

"Privately," she said firmly.

There was less drama in her tone than usual, and her expression was merely determined. I still wasn't thrilled. But I noticed Kyriander trying to look as though he weren't paying any attention, and I modified the tone I'd been tempted to use. "Okay," I said. "Upstairs, or outside?"

"Let's go outside," she said, sounding almost friendly.

The light of sunset was still in the western sky. Twilight lay under the trees in deep and secret shadows. I watched Lilie as she led the way down off the porch and around the corner toward the path to Finandiel and Cuthbern's cottage. I tended to think of her as a child, but this was a lovely young woman, her slender body moving through the soft light with the calm grace and assurance of maturity. Bemused, I followed her in silence.

She knew the paths better than I did. She found a side path not far from the Hall that led away from the stream, to a tiny clearing carpeted in violets and bounded by lavender shrubs. There was a bench just where the path opened out, so one could sit and admire the flowers, and inhale their rich, pungent odor.

We sat for several minutes in silence. The purple of the lavender and violets seemed to mingle with shadows in the air over the clearing, deceiving the eye. I kept thinking I saw large moving shapes in the shadows, but they dissipated when I stared at them. I finally realized it wasn't large shapes, but hundreds of tiny moths come to taste the flowers.

"It's beautiful, isn't it?" said Lilie. "I like to come here in the evening, just to sit."

"It's a lovely place," I said. "Thank you for showing me it."

I wasn't looking, but I felt her shrug beside me. "No biggie," she said. "Rosie, I wanted to say I'm sorry if I've been a twit. I know I have. I just—I'm sorry."

I stared. "What brought that on?"

She ducked her head, girlish again, as shy and sweet as the violets at our feet. "I don't know," she said. "I've been thinking about . . . things. Mostly about, you know."

I thought I did know. "About your father?"

"Yes." She was silent for a long moment. "I hated him, you know," she said in a matter-of-fact tone. "I wanted to kill him. I would have, if I could." She turned to me impulsively, her expression troubled. "I was glad when you did."

"I know."

"How can you?" she asked in surprise.

I sighed, wondering where to start . . . and just how much to say. "I should have talked to you about it then," I said helplessly, "but I couldn't. I didn't know what to say, what to think . . . I just felt so guilty I wanted to go away and forget it ever happened."

"You felt guilty? But you saved our lives."

"Yes," I said. "By killing him. There should always be a better way."

"But Rose! He would've shot us. There wasn't time for you to do anything else."

She was right. "I know. That doesn't make it right."

"Would it have been right to let him kill us?"

"No, of course not. Of course I don't mean that." I wished I knew what was going on behind those wide, shadowed eyes. "But there was all the time before that moment, when I could have talked to him, or maybe turned him in to the police, or something. I don't know. There must have been a better solution than waiting till

I had to kill him to save you." I stared into the purple darkness, breathing the strong, sweet scent of the flowers, trying not to think.

"Yes," she said. She turned away from me, her voice subdued. "That's what I wanted to tell you. It's my fault." The thought was dramatic, but she sounded uncharacteristically sincere. "I could have called the police that morning," she said, her voice rising, but still tightly controlled. "I knew he had the gun. I could have warned you. I could have warned Kyriander. Oh, God, there were so many things I could have done, and I didn't care. I *hoped* you'd have to kill him." Her tone steadied. She said grimly, finally, "I let it happen."

"Good heavens," I said, "you couldn't have known it would turn out like that."

"But I knew he had the gun," she said.

"Yes, and I expect he'd had it for quite some time, hadn't he? So how were you to know he'd use it that day? Was there anything to tell you?"

"I *should* have known." She sounded determined, but just a little uncertain.

"Perhaps. And I should have found a better way than to kill him."

"*I* killed him," said Lilie, beginning to sound dramatic again. "It's my fault, because I didn't tell anyone about the gun."

"I guess we're both to blame, then, aren't we?" I said, feeling my way. "We handled that pretty badly. If we were half-competent we'd have seen into the future and prepared for it. What a pair of bunglers we are."

After a shocked moment she snickered. "You shouldn't joke about something so serious."

"I should have joked about it sooner," I said. "Why not? It's better than wallowing in guilt and self-pity."

"Self-pity?"

"Oh, poor me, I killed my father. Isn't that what you've been thinking?"

"Oh," she said, startled. "Yeah. Sort of."

"Which is silly on the face of it."

"I guess it is," she said slowly. "But . . . I can't help it, I still think I should have done better."

"I disagree. I think you behaved quite sensibly, and it was I who should have done better. Shall we argue about it?"

She studied me for a moment, though I don't suppose she could see me very clearly in the growing dark, even with halfling night vision. I could just make out those large, haunted eyes, like dark shadows in the indistinct oval of her face. "You're joking again," she said uncertainly.

"Yes," I said.

"You mean we couldn't have done better?"

"Oh, I don't know. I expect maybe we could have. But we did our best, and it's done now. We can't change it. Feeling guilty about it isn't helping anyone."

"Oh." She was silent for several minutes. I wondered again what was going on behind the haunted eyes that darted sideways glances at me in the silence. We inhaled lavender and violet, and watched moths flit among the shadows. "I called you a murderer," she said finally, in a stifled voice.

"Yup," I said, in what I hoped was a cheerful tone.

"I'm sorry," she said.

I looked at her. The dusk had deepened: she was a darker shape among darknesses. It seemed appropriate. For all her sweet airs, she was still Lilie, and her apology was reluctant at best. "Are you?" I said.

"I think so." Poor, battered imp. Maybe she was trying to be honest. "You're supposed to say something," she said.

I smiled, confident she couldn't see it. "Am I? What should I say?"

"Why are you *do*ing this to me?" she demanded, all high drama again in an instant, and ready to go into hysterics at the drop of an opportunity.

"I'm not sure," I said placidly. "Maybe if you could describe what it is I'm doing to you?"

"You're, you're being rude," she said, flustered by her failure to impress me.

"Am I? I'm sorry: I don't mean to be."

She shook her head, looking away from me, fighting for control. I wondered why. "No, it isn't that, anyway," she said. "It's just, you don't do what I expect."

"No," I said. "I try not to."

She looked at me. I could feel her sharp gaze even in the darkness. "You do?"

"Sorry, yes. It's a bad habit. Occupational hazard."

"Oh!" She was silent for a moment. "You do it on purpose, to suspects," she said, "to keep them off-balance? To get them to say things they don't mean to?"

"Exactly," I said.

"Does it work?"

"Sometimes."

"But now it won't work with me," she said, "because you told me. Should you have told me? Don't you consider me a suspect?"

"Should I?"

"Of course not."

"Well, that's settled, then."

"No, but seriously, who do you suspect?" She was all child again now, sweet and innocent and careless.

"Of being the Trouble? I'm not sure yet."

"Do you think it's an elf?"

"I don't know. Really."

"Do you think . . ." She hesitated, and her voice tightened. "Do you think the Trouble killed Gary?"

"I don't know."

"The police said it was an accident. Do you think it was an accident?"

I hesitated. "No."

"Everybody says he was such a good driver, but even good drivers have accidents on motorcycles. I mean, they're dangerous, you know?" She sounded small and pathetic. I thought it rather mean of me to feel suspicious of her: but I wondered what this meeting was really about.

"Yes," I said. "Even good drivers have accidents."

"You don't think he did. Who do you think did it? The Trouble?"

"Lilie, I just don't know yet."

"You wouldn't tell me, anyway. Would you?" she said petulantly.

"I don't know that, either. It would depend on who I thought did it, I guess."

She didn't seem to have heard me. I felt her watching me, her gaze speculative. "You think I'm just a child. But I'm not. You'll see."

"Of course I will."

She rose abruptly. "God, I hate when grownups do that." She mimicked me: " 'Of course I will.' *God!* You might just as well pat me on the head and tell me it's bedtime. I should have expected this. It's just typical."

I sat there for a long time after she'd gone. If she really felt guilty about her father, it could explain the way she behaved toward me. But I was pretty sure she hadn't needed or wanted any words of wisdom from me about her father's death. She might well feel guilty about it, but she wouldn't turn to me for answers.

Whether or not she felt guilt over that death, I certainly did. And it was all very well to say what's done is done and can't be fixed; but if what's done is someone killed, that's just not good enough. Nothing would be. And I wasn't doing anyone any good, sitting in the dark, regretting the past. Sighing, I rose and followed Lilie back to the Hall.

Lilie wasn't there, but Kyriander met me on the porch, ready to apologize if she'd misbehaved. "No, no, she was just fine," I said. "Don't worry about it."

"I do, and I must," he said. "Rose, I am sorry: when I made the suggestion to hire you to investigate our Trouble, I had no idea Lilie would take such offense at you. She was always jealous, but never as she has been these last days."

"I know," I said. "It's okay."

"I had hoped, when you came here, when we saw each other again . . ." He paused, apparently uncertain how to go on. He wasn't talking about Lilie anymore.

"I know," I said. "Me too. Maybe that's partly what bothers her."

Colored light from the stained-glass windows illuminated his wry smile. "I did not hope we could take up where we left off," he said.

"No," I said.

He seemed not to hear me. "But I had rather thought . . . I hoped . . ." He turned away abruptly. "Mab's grace," he said, "I could not know it would be this difficult."

"Kyri," I said gently, "it's all right."

"That it is not," he said, and turned back to me. "Are you content, Rose? Is all well with you?"

I wanted to say yes, and end the matter, but I couldn't lie to him. "No. But there's nothing to do. I don't even know what I'd want us to do if Lilie weren't in our way. I don't know what I want."

"You have your elfrock star, I know," he said.

"Nobody has an elfrock star." I laughed shortly. "Nobody sane would want one."

"Do you love him not?" He sounded surprised, and maybe hopeful: I couldn't tell.

"I don't *know*. Oh, God." I took a deep breath, held it, and let it out again while he waited. "That's not the problem with us," I said.

"No: Lilie is the problem with us," he said. "More, it is the problem with me. I am well aware." He turned his head, and the light through a blue pane of glass turned his cheek sick white and threw his eyes in shadow. "It is with us as it is with my work, with my life. I am not fit to father a child. I know not the ways of it. How can I? Through most of her life I was away, about my own pursuits, and—" He hesitated. "And fleeing my father. I left her to that. It is only meet that I must cope with the consequences."

"Good Lord, it's not your fault she's the way she is, Kyri," I said.

"Perhaps. I gave her no support when she needed it."

"You were a child."

"I was her brother."

I couldn't answer that, so I shifted the subject back to what I knew. "Anyway, it's not just that, with you and

me. It's not even mostly that. If I hadn't had to— If
I hadn't . . ."

"If you had not killed my father. Yes, that is between
us still, is it not?" he said. "You wish to say things might
have been different. Quite so: my siblings and I would
be dead."

"No, I mean if it hadn't come up, Kyriander. If things
had been different."

"Things were not different," he said implacably.

"Rosie, are you out here?" Shannon came through
the door, blinking as her eyes adjusted. "Who's here?"

"Just me and Kyriander," I said.

"I must go," said Kyriander. "Grace be with you."

"Good night, Kyri," I told him, and turned to Shannon. "Just me, then."

"Did I interrupt something?"

"We needed an interruption," I said. "You know, I
didn't remember him being so damn elvish, before."

"Well, I don't think he was," she said. "It's living with
them that does it, I expect. Listen, if we're going out
later tonight, we better get some rest now."

33

The moon was well up in a cloudless sky when we went out again, but it was a waning moon, so we went as much by feel as by vision much of the way.

We had agreed beforehand to go toward the back of the valley, past Maerian's mansion, since that was the direction I thought I heard the night music from, and to go the whole way without flashlights if at all possible. It was possible, but not easy. If we hadn't taken that same path earlier in the day on our way to the mansion, we couldn't have done it at all. As it was, everything seemed completely different in the dark, and I wasn't half sure from one turning to the next whether we were really still on the path, or had wandered off it into some unusually clear area of forest in which we would get hopelessly lost till morning.

There was plenty of time to think while we felt our way inch by inch between live oak and bracken. If the Trouble really was the lovelorn Romeo we'd dreamed up, what was he running from? I could see elven parents rampaging into our world to take back a rebellious child, though I thought more usually they'd tend just to keep an eye on him as best they could from Faerie. But if he and Juliet were adults, who were they afraid of? Who was going to come after them?

Well, we'd covered that by making him an aristocrat, of high enough rank that it was against his queen's decree for him to come here. But even if he were someone really important, would she bother to come (or, perhaps more likely, to send someone) after him? How important would he have to be to get such personal attention from the queen of all Faerie?

If he were all that important, it very likely meant he'd be powerful as well, not just politically but magically. That fit with the Fey Valley elves' opinion that he was using magic to conceal himself from them, I supposed.

But in that case what in the world did we think we were going to do with him if we caught him? We'd surely be powerless to hold him. Was he afraid we'd find a way to betray him to his queen? What would she do to him if she caught him? Would she chase him down? I'd never heard of such a thing; but even if it happened every day, there was no reason to think I would hear of it. If the Faerie Queen bothered to chase after truant subjects here, she might go to a little trouble to conceal the fact, just for the sake of appearances.

Come to think of it, one didn't ever encounter many aristocratic elves. I'd met more during my stay in Fey Valley than during my entire life before this. Assuming my experience to be representative, that would seem to mean that in general they did obey her and stay in Faerie. I wondered what that meant. It might mean they preferred to stay in Faerie, or that they honored their queen and chose to obey her decrees, or that they feared her and/or believed her too powerful to defy.

Certainly all the old fairy stories gave the impression that last was the correct guess. She was supposed to be incredibly powerful, and completely indifferent to others' needs and feelings. Not an attractive combination. I wondered whether, if Romeo were running away from her and she just hadn't yet made a push to find him, she would object to our finding him first? Jeez, what if she were keeping an eye on him and took offense at our interference?

I pushed the thought away. Either she wanted him back or she didn't. And either she was powerful enough to find him or she wasn't. If she wanted him and could find him, why wait?

We were making very slow progress in the darkness. It really seemed pointless even to continue: if we found the Trouble at all, it would be entirely by accident. The protective arm I was holding before me on a level with my chest encountered another live oak branch and I stopped short. Cursing. "This is stupid," I said.

"Shush," said Shannon, a little distance ahead of me and, to judge by the sound, engaged in her own close encounter with the shrubbery.

"Why?" I said. "We're blundering around like a pair of cows. Anybody out here for miles has heard us by now. There's no way we're going to sneak up on the Trouble unless it's deaf."

She stopped thrashing the offending underbrush and thought about that. "You may have a point." At just that moment, the nightly serenade began. Shannon hadn't heard it before. She stood transfixed—or so I guessed from the dead silence in her direction—for a long moment before she said, "*Damn!*" and blundered forward again, in a hurry now.

"Shannon, stop," I said. "You'll hurt yourself."

There was a crash, a muttered oath, and silence, except for the distant, haunting melody. "You're right," she said.

"Are you okay?"

"Yeah, I think so." I heard her pick herself up and dust off her clothes. "Did you bring a flashlight?"

"Yeah. Did you?"

"Well, yes. But not the enormous police-sized one I think would be appropriate to the situation." She switched on a penlight and laughed shortly. "Quite the reverse," she said. "But it'll keep me from running into any more trees. Is yours more powerful?"

"Nope." I had nearly come away with no light at all; but at the last moment some glimmer of intelligence had prompted me to stuff a penlight in my pocket. Its feeble gleam exactly matched Shannon's.

"Well, at least maybe they'll be a little harder to see at a distance than real flashlights would be," she said.

"I wouldn't count on that," I said.

"No." She looked toward the sound of the music. "Shall we?"

"After you."

Our progress was a bit quieter after that; which, if it achieved nothing else, at least left us able to listen to the music. I'd never before been fully awake when I heard it. It was a male elf's voice, singing a cappella, hauntingly sweet and clear. It was pure magic, of the powerful involuntary sort any true musician used. We were too far from him to hear the words, which were probably elven anyway. But the words didn't matter.

If we hadn't been searching for him we'd still have gone instinctively toward that sound. It called to every inner longing, every romantic instinct, every dream. It was compelling, caressing, irresistible. We went without thinking. Our penlights gave us just enough light to stay on the path, but effectively blinded us to anything that was not caught in their tiny cones of yellow light. It didn't matter. As long as we could move toward that sound, we were content.

We had gone a good half mile, and the music had changed from voice to woodwind, when we knew we weren't ever going to find it. "It's no closer," said Shannon. "He knows we're here. He's playing with us." She stopped and looked around. "Look, we've gone in a circle. Here's that root I stumbled over ten minutes ago."

It was indeed the same root. Our Trouble was running a barrier spell, and the charmed sprig of lavender that had got us through Maerian's spell hadn't the least effect on it. "Damn," I said. "You brought your lavender with you?"

"It's in my pocket," she said, and got it out to be sure. Like mine, it looked the worse for wear, but it was still mostly intact and should have worked.

"His magic is more powerful than Finandiel's?" I said.

"At least more powerful than what Finandiel used on this," she said, stuffing it back in her pocket. "What a waste of time." We stood for a moment, listening to the distant, haunting strains. "Well, at least we got to listen to him. That's worth something."

"Doesn't get us much forwarder, however."

"No." Her penlight flickered, and she shook it.

"What's more, my batteries are going dead." She sighed and looked toward the sound of the music. "Well. D'you want to go on, or shall we give up?"

"Give up," I said. "We'll never break the spell."

"No," she said. "Okay. Which way?"

It took us a few minutes to figure out which way was home, but not long after that to reach Salonian's fountain and, from there, my cottage. The music stopped just as we reached the porch. The night seemed empty without it.

We slept nearly till lunchtime the next morning, and I still woke feeling grumpy and slow and ugly. Shannon, on the other hand, was cheerful and beautiful and full of energy. It was enough to make a person hate her, and I didn't hesitate to tell her so.

"You'll feel better after a shower and coffee," she said sympathetically.

I threw a pillow at her and locked myself in the bathroom. When I emerged ten minutes later, cleaner and more awake but still not sprightly, she had coffee ready and was frying bacon. Usually she's no more enthusiastic a cook than I, but she has moods; and she's far better at it than I, when the whim does strike. I accepted coffee and, at her suggestion, carried it onto the porch to drink.

The day was warm and sunny, and the air fresh. The forest spread out before me, vivid in every shade of green, with splashes of acacia or broom, and in the distance the dark ribbon of road cutting back and forth down the valley wall. I leaned against the porch rail admiring the view till Shannon brought bacon and eggs to the table.

"Do you want orange juice?" she asked.

"No, thanks," I said. "How far d'you think we walked last night?"

"You mean how far did we walk or how far did we get?"

"We walked miles," I said. "How far d'you think we got?"

"Not far enough," she said.

"I knew that already." I ate my breakfast, looking through the railing at the forest canopy. The whole eccentric colony and its Trouble might have been on another planet, or at least in another valley, for all I could tell from there. It was very peaceful.

"What's the plan for today?" Shannon brought her breakfast to the table and sat down beside me, ignoring the view in favor of bacon and eggs.

"Talk to people, I guess," I said unenthusiastically.

"I know: if anyone had told you how much talking to people would be involved, you'd never have become a private investigator."

I ignored that. "Don't you have a list of things we're supposed to do?"

"Right here somewhere," she said, gesturing vaguely toward the pile of her belongings beside the couch where she'd slept. "I remember a few things. Search empty cottages. Interview Jeran and Maerian. Look for clues."

"Oh, that's a good one: look for clues. Did you write that down? It's important that we don't forget that one."

She ignored me. "I think we should talk to Ariana and Ritchie Morita again. Considering the wire, especially Ariana."

"Yes."

"And maybe Finandiel." She sipped coffee, eyeing her eggs with disapproval. "Too much cheese. They all know something they're not telling."

"Just the right amount of cheese," I said, referring to the eggs. "And I know they're concealing something but I don't understand it. If they know who or what the Trouble is, why did they hire us? If they don't know, what is it they're keeping from us?"

"That's why we need to interview them again," she said patiently. "Have some more bacon. You'll feel better."

"I feel fine." But I ate more bacon anyway.

We spent the rest of the week in fruitless interviews, searches of both the forest and the empty cottages, investigating the site of Gary's death again, and talking to the police, who listened very politely to everything we'd surmised or discovered, examined the wire, and told us there was nothing to show it had been put there to kill Gary. "Motorcycles," they said, "are dangerous." We hadn't really expected better, but it was frustrating just the same.

34

The memorial service for Gary was held on Saturday in Fey Valley's chapel. I hadn't seen the chapel before. It was hidden in the woods just past the school, with its grassy lawn sloping down to the creek and its shingled roof shaded by towering redwoods. The valley children, with the help of Scotland Yard, had decorated it with vases and wreaths and tubs of flowers beside and behind the altar, in the apse, in the aisles, along the walls, and everywhere, many of them arranged with willow and reeds for mourning. The air was dizzying with their mingled fragrances. They lent the chapel a wild, Faerie quality, as though the forest had begun to creep unchallenged through its heavy, intricately carved oak doors.

Tim Cameron arrived sober, but with a bottle in his pocket from which he took fortifying swigs frequently enough to assure the state wouldn't last long. In the pew beside him, Charlotte sat still and grim and silent, dressed in sober black. Her eyes were raw and red, her face stark white, her lips compressed in habitual disapproval. She nodded blindly at anyone who spoke to her, but I thought she wasn't really aware of her surroundings. She was too deeply involved with grief to attend to anything outside it.

All the adult residents I had met so far attended, and many I had never seen before. Kyriander, attending alone, having left his siblings at home, stood at the back of the room with Shannon and me and quietly identified people as they came in. I didn't know how he'd convinced Lilie not to come, but I was glad of it. Her histrionics wouldn't have done anyone any good.

The elusive Jeran was as handsome as his friend Belalin. They came in together, and I felt absurdly pleased with myself just for managing not to drool. It seemed highly improbable they could be unaware of the effect they had on women, but they behaved with charming modesty. That in itself was attractive in this lot of arrogant artists.

The service was secular and mercifully brief. No one waxed lyrical over Gary's virtues, he having had few enough of those. There were no pretentious lies, no glowing eulogies, no insincere regrets. The focus of what was said was more on the living, and meant as a comfort to Charlotte and Tim more than anything else.

To my amazement, the ceremony ended with an announcement that refreshments awaited us at the Hall. I wondered whether Charlotte had spent the morning preparing food before getting dressed up to attend the service. Very likely she did. She probably didn't even think there was anything odd in that.

We all trooped back to the Hall by way of a creekside path that ended in the Hall parking lot. The day was misty, the air cool and still, the diffused light casting no shadows even in the deepest wood. Most of us were silent, and those who spoke did so quietly. Our footfalls were muffled in the soft carpet of redwood needles. The music began so softly and subtly I could not afterward decide just when it started, but only when I became aware of it. Of course the elves heard it before I did. I knew they were hearing something, and I listened more carefully, and paused when I heard it too.

It was the Trouble; the night music; the sweet, unearthly woodwind that haunted Fey Valley's deep forest midnights. But clearly it meant no trouble now. It was playing a slow, clear, eerie melody I recognized: a Faerie dirge.

No one said a word. We paused, and listened, and started on again with the sweet strains still in our ears. I found myself thinking of Gary. Not of the noisy ruffian who cared not at all who might be hurt by his actions, but of Charlotte's son. I could almost see her counting the infant's toes, kissing away his tears, cosseting and loving him with all her heart. As a toddler he must have laughed and cried and hugged his mother the way any toddler would.

At what point had the change come? When had the normally bewitching infant, the delightful toddler, the perhaps gawky and endearing youth, transformed himself into the unpleasant young man I had known? Where along the line had he ceased to care what others thought of him, or perhaps even to know that others had thoughts and feelings? Did he think of himself as human and the rest of us more or less furniture, as his behavior implied? Why? What made him that way? And the most painful question of all: could he have grown up human? Could he, had he lived, have been redeemed?

Of course he could have. I remembered the way he had looked at Lilie, and how he had leapt to her defense when he thought it needful. In his guarded way he had loved her. Very likely nothing would ever have come of that—they were young, and the young transfer their affections freely—but the boy who can love even one other person is not lost.

A glance at the others told me I wasn't the only one thinking along those lines. There in the misted light of the forest whose peace he had so thoughtlessly disturbed, we heard him sung softly into the past. The music didn't judge him. It didn't seek to cover his flaws. It couldn't hide what he'd been and done. It only mourned the boy he might have been, and the man he could have become.

None of us went inside till the music ended. When it faded on a long, low note of sorrow and regret, we stood for a moment longer in the stillness before Charlotte straightened, wiped her eyes, and broke the spell. "Come eat," she said.

The meal she had prepared was simple but plentiful: trays of little sandwiches, cut vegetables, crackers, cheese, pickles, and olives were quickly transferred from refrigerator to table and as quickly fallen upon by the ravening horde. I interviewed Jeran between sandwiches, and learned nothing to move the case forward. Shannon spent some time talking to Ariana and Ritchie. I tried to corner anyone I hadn't talked to before, and did get a couple of new reports of Trouble—a missing jar of paintbrushes, and a late-night encounter with someone who shoved and fled—but nothing useful.

Tim Cameron drank quietly and steadily till he had to be carried upstairs to sleep it off. Charlotte oversaw his disposal as she oversaw the food service, with grim civility. She accepted formal declarations of sympathy graciously, but with a mildly puzzled expression, as though uncertain they were really meant for her.

Inevitably, the gathering turned into a party of sorts by late afternoon, with artists talking shop and getting drunk and vying with each other for attention. I was afraid Charlotte would be offended by their forgetfulness, but she seemed pleased. Perhaps she was glad to be out of the spotlight: unlike the artists, she never sought attention, and didn't seem comfortable with it when she had it.

Or perhaps she was just innocently pleased to see them enjoy themselves. She admired them, more than some of them deserved, and I knew she felt honored to be a part of their lives. It would not have surprised me to find that she was worried that her tragedy might disturb their pleasures.

If it did, it didn't disturb them for long. George Jenks and Chance Winter engaged in an amiable but noisy disagreement as to the relative merits of painting and photography. Mildred Potter, seated at the table in Benjamin Barski's lap, gestured broadly with her wineglass and giggled girlishly when the wine spilled. Marc Starr argued volubly with Rosetta Fulmer about obscure painting techniques, her speech thick with malapropisms and his with didactic pronouncements. Galinda, glass in hand, danced gracefully by herself in the center of the great room. People I hadn't met before clustered here and there, chatting and arguing and occasionally yelling.

And Charlotte went among them with trays of refreshments, humbly encouraging the festivities. "It pleases her," said Kyriander. I hadn't noticed him approaching. The noise level by that time was such that he had to raise his voice to be heard, even when he was right next to me.

"Who, Charlotte? So it would seem," I said. "Fine way they mourn her only son."

"Yes, is it not?" he said, missing or ignoring my sarcasm. Perhaps he was right. If Charlotte was content with the state of affairs, it certainly wasn't my place to criticize. "Your partner seems quite taken with Ritchie," he added, gesturing toward the great room, where Shannon was hunched beside Ritchie at his typing desk, talking earnestly, with much waving of hands.

She looked cheerful and animated and as though she were enjoying herself very much. I wondered how much of that was an act to disarm him, and how much she really had fallen for his rather brittle charm. Very possibly more of the latter than she would admit: he didn't seem as impressed with her beauty as most men were. That would please her. "I s'pose she is," I said. "Where are Lilie and Briande?"

"They are, I hope, at home," he said. "Lilie desired to attend the service, but I thought it perhaps not best."

"I think you were right."

"Unfortunately she did not agree." He looked pained. "Of late, we come to words on every matter."

"How long has she been like this?"

"I am uncertain," he said. "For some time we have been at odds on many issues; I am given to understand that is expectable in the raising of a child. But her mood swings increase of late. I know not what to do."

"Maybe you should make her see a doctor whether she likes it or not."

He gestured helplessly. "She is wild, Rose. Child that she is, yet she knows well how to counter my wishes. Manage her I cannot. Will she not confide in me, I am at a stand, for I know not how to bend her to my will."

"This is untenable," said Marc Starr. "I will not have

it. Look at this." I turned involuntarily to look at the wineglass he held aloft. "Burgundy. Faugh. Throw it away: the color is an offense to the sensibilities." He made to dump it on the floor, but Rosetta stopped him.

"Now, Marc," she said. "Waste not, want not: there are people here whose sensibilities are less delicate. Give it to me."

He handed it to her, obedient as a child, and wandered past Kyri and me toward the front door. "Verdure," he said. "I must have verdure. I am filled with a vast discontent, for my soul craves verdure."

Rosetta put down the glass he had given her and followed him to the door. "I hope no one left the keys in their car," she said worriedly. "There's no telling what he might not do." But he seemed content with the view of verdure from the porch: he sat down on the edge of it and stared in apparent rapture. "Oh, good," said Rosetta. "That's fine, then." She wandered back into the room, smiling absently at us on her way past. "He's very negligible," she confided. "Truly great artists often are."

35

The party broke up in the late afternoon, as people in various stages of drunkenness began to wander away for their homes. Shannon and I returned to my cottage and brought coffee onto the porch to watch the misty daylight fade into evening. "At least we know none of those at the party is the music-making part of the Trouble," she said.

"Unless that was a recording," I said sourly.

"If it was, somebody's got a sound system to die for."

"Not impossible," I said. "Any of them could afford it."

"I'm not sure there is a sound system that good, even for the very rich," she said. "Let's just say it was live, okay? I think it was. The Trouble has never made music in daylight before, has it?"

"Not that I know of."

"And he played a dirge. He knew what he was doing."

"You mean he knew about Gary. But that doesn't mean he killed Gary."

"Well, no. I don't think he did. But don't you see, the fact that he knew about Gary—and not only that, but knew when we were having the service—means he's not isolated from the community. He knows what's going on. He's talking to somebody."

"That doesn't necessarily follow. He could have got that information by careful observation."

She thought about it. "Okay, yeah, I guess. So we'll say *probably* he's talking to someone, okay?"

"Okay. So the Trouble isn't anybody we know, but he's in cahoots with somebody we know. As I believe

I've said, though perhaps not so eloquently, before: fat lot of good that does us."

"Well, but it does," she said. "Well, sort of. Naturally a signed confession would be more conclusive. But failing that, I really think we can make something of the information we have. For instance, when the music played this morning, did you notice that Ritchie looked pleased, as though a pet had accomplished a trick? And Ariana looked indulgent?"

"Oh, jeez, Shannon. No. But we've had this talk before: you can't read minds. Really. Expressions are great clues, but they don't *mean* anything. You just can't count on having read them right."

"Well, I talked to both of them afterward, and I think I did," she said. "They wouldn't tell me anything, of course. But they both know something."

"We knew that already," I said. "So does Finandiel know something. But none of them is telling, and I don't know how we're going to get it out of them. Hell, if what they know is about the Trouble, and they hired us anyway, you can bet they don't mean to tell us and don't expect us to find out. They hired us for show, to impress the others with their supposed desire to learn what they already know."

"Patience and persistence will pay off," she said.

"If any of them actually knows the Trouble, I wonder whether they ever go visit him?" I said. "We can't get to him, but maybe we should stake out the paths toward the back of the valley where we've heard him, and see whether anyone else goes there?"

"You s'pose we could get through, if we were following somebody the Trouble lets in?"

"I don't know. Even if we couldn't, at least we'd know that person did get through. We could question whoever it was afterward. Maybe they'd be more forthcoming if they knew we know they've been to see him."

"Your pronouns are becoming confused," she said, laughing at me.

"Yours would be confused too, if they had to describe

so many unknowns. Tell me what you learned from Ritchie."

"Nothing," she said.

"Nothing?"

"Well, almost nothing. He's totally not going to talk about the Trouble if he can help it," she said. "But he likes to brag, and to sound important, so I was able to get him to make broad hints about how much he knows. For whatever good that'll do. He's very smart, you know, and he's gotten accustomed to thinking that everybody he knows isn't. So he does let something drop now and then."

"Like what?"

"Like that Lorielle is a princess of some lesser kingdom or principality or some such."

"A princess? She can't be: Finandiel says the highest aristocracy isn't permitted here. And she's not hiding or anything."

"That's because it's complicated," said Shannon. "The stricture against highest aristocracy coming here seems to apply only to those in a direct line with the queen of all Faerie. Ritchie says the queen's name is Tytonia, by the way, but I don't know how much he knows about it."

"The Faerie Queen? Shakespeare said Titania."

"Yes, and some people say Mab, but everybody knows Mab's only queen of the little ones we never see."

"We never see them because there's no such thing," I said. "Jeez, don't tell me you believe in pixies and fairy tales."

She looked at me. "But the elves all swear by Mab's grace," she said. "You've heard them."

"Right, and some people swear by heaven or hell, but that doesn't prove those places exist."

"Well, no," she said, surprised. "I hadn't thought of that."

"So the point," I said, "is that Lorielle is some sort of royalty, but not important enough for the queen to worry about?"

"Or anyway, not among those the queen doesn't want coming here," she said.

"Do we care whether she's royalty?"

"I thought she might be Juliet."

"Because she's a princess?"

"Well, the whole thing is a fantasy," she said. "We don't really even know the Trouble is Romeo. But say he is. And say there's a Juliet. The whole thing hinges on their being important enough for the queen to care what they do, and that means royalty of some sort, doesn't it?"

"That's certainly what Ariana, and maybe Finandiel, want us to think," I said. "At least, I suppose that's why they're always on about it, and trying to explain the intricacies. I wish I had thought to ask one of them what exactly it is that the Faerie Queen is going to do to somebody who disobeys her."

"I rather think no one does disobey her," said Shannon.

"But our whole conjecture is that someone did," I said.

"Well, yes," she said, "I guess it is. What *do* you suppose she'd do? Maybe nothing worse than whisk them back to Faerie; but in that case, what's all the fuss about?"

"If they don't want to go back to Faerie, and she has the power to take them back, I suppose that would be worth fussing over. Especially if Romeo and Juliet are real: once she'd whisked them back to Faerie she'd doubtless separate them as well."

"Yes, and they wouldn't like that. But if she's so powerful, would she take such a personal interest in the doings of her subjects?"

"She might, if they're such important subjects," I said. "Royalty, and all."

"There must be a lot of royalty, though, and you'd think she'd have something better to do than be whisking them this way and that for no particular reason. What *is* her reason for wanting them not to come here, anyway? Do you know?"

"That's another thing we should have asked," I said. "I don't know. I can't imagine."

"Maybe it's in case, once here, they'd marry humans and produce half-royal halflings," she said.

"Would that be so bad?"

"I don't know. I shouldn't think so; but I'm not an elf queen. You know how elves feel about halflings." They felt the way white humans had once felt about mixed-race children, but that didn't prevent the occurrence. It just made things tougher for everyone involved. "Maybe it'd be sacrilege, or something, to have halflings who were half-royal."

"Maybe it'd serve them right," I said crossly.

Shannon smiled. "Well, maybe it would, but I don't suppose that would make them any more resigned to it."

"But you know, that can't apply to Romeo and Juliet; they aren't going to be making halflings when they're in love with each other. Anyway, if Lorielle is a princess, and the queen doesn't want princesses coming here, and she takes such a personal interest that she whisks them back if they disobey, then why hasn't she whisked Lorielle?"

"Well, I already said: she's a princess, but not important enough to be whisked. That's my guess. I think it's okay for some of the aristocracy to come here—I mean hey, Finandiel doesn't seem to be hiding, and didn't you say Salonian is an aristocrat too? So Lorielle is in the category of okay to come here. The only thing is, if she's Juliet, she's in love with Romeo, and he isn't in that category. He's supposed to stay in Faerie."

"Okay, that's where it falls apart," I said. "Lorielle isn't hiding. Only Romeo is. But they, you know, the queen or whoever, knows she and Romeo are an item. So when he goes missing, wouldn't the queen just look wherever Lorielle is?"

"If she's smart, she would."

"One thing I think it's safe to assume about the Faerie Queen," I said, "is that she's smart. Which means if our Romeo and Juliet theory is right, they aren't so smart, or they'd have known she could find them quick as a wink."

"Yes, but she hasn't."

"So maybe the whole theory is a crock."

"Or maybe the queen has some reason for not whisking them back to Faerie?"

"Sure, okay. What reason? I can't think of anything. Can you?"

"No, but I'm not the Faerie Queen. She could have reasons we wouldn't think of."

"Oh, elves," I said. "They might do anything. But it doesn't make sense that she'd make a rule, and see somebody break it, and not bother to do anything about it until and unless the whim struck her."

"One thing I've really noticed about elves is that their notions of what to do don't always make sense to us. *And* that they're governed by whims as often as not."

"Good point," I said. "Okay. So we should stake out Lorielle as well as Ariana and Finandiel. We might be stretching ourselves a little thin."

"We won't stake out any of them," she said. "We'll stake out the main path to the back of the valley. Romeo holes up somewhere back behind Maerian's mansion. We know that, because that's where the music always comes from, right?" In a city, of course, one couldn't have heard it over such distances. But as Finandiel had said when he hired us, in the still valley air, a penetrating sound like that clear Faerie music would carry for miles. "So if we stake out the path that goes there, we'll catch anybody who goes to meet him."

"Or, presumably, anybody who goes to visit Maerian."

"She's a recluse. Nobody does."

"Except Ariana, with the mail."

"I was thinking of nighttime stakeouts," she said patiently. "I don't think they'll visit Romeo during the day. And I don't think Ariana delivers the mail at night.

"You know," she said abruptly, "I wish you wouldn't get us involved in cases like this. It's so much easier to investigate industrial espionage, and insurance fraud, and finding lost people, and whatnot. All this business with elves and FOOFs and all is just too vague. There are no records to check."

"Hey, you were the one who wanted to take the case."

"Well, sure," she said, "but I thought it was just going

to be finding out who wanted to buy the valley that the residents wouldn't sell to."

"So, like, we should only take simple cases, is that what you're saying?"

"Maybe not simple ones, so much as just ones we know how to cope with," she said. "This wandering around the wilderness in the dead of night, and chasing Bigfoot, and trying to figure out who's sending letters to FOOFs—because, you know, I just remembered that Lorielle's been getting love letters, and how can it be Romeo if he's here?—just isn't my sort of thing."

"No, nor mine either. I don't suppose you know anybody in the post office?"

"There's always Mildred Potter."

"I asked her about Lorielle's letter, already. The one I saw. She wouldn't tell me who it was from."

"You think she knew?"

"There was a crest by the return address. I'd be willing to bet she noticed it, and knew whose it was."

"Because the trouble with another postal person, even if I knew one who might have handled the Fey Valley mail, is that, you know, how likely is it he'd have noticed Lorielle's letter in particular? Not very, I'd guess."

"No, I suppose not. But you wanted to check something more in the ordinary way of things."

"Yes, and I would, if it made any sense: but to anybody outside Fey Valley it would have been just one letter in millions. Okay, it's something to think about. But meantime we'd better have a plan, because I don't see what we can do with that."

"Stakeouts are good," I said. "Only I wish we didn't have to do it in the forest. It's nice enough here in the daytime, especially from a comfortable porch with a beautiful view of the valley; and I even like it down among the trees during the day. I'm getting used to it. It's pretty. But at night is a whole 'nother matter."

"Well, it's not exactly my fave either," she said. "There are spiders and things. Mud. Let's not talk about it." She went back inside for a fresh cup of coffee and said, when she returned, "I noticed you and Kyriander talking. Things going okay with you two?"

"Not the way you mean," I said. "We can't seem to get any time alone together. If Lilie doesn't interfere in person, his worry about her does."

"What seems to be the problem?"

"She's a teenager," I said.

"That usually isn't terminal. Is she involved in all this, do you think?"

"I tend to think she's just having a difficult adolescence. How could she be involved? I'm pretty sure she's not the Trouble, because she's too small. I doubt she's Juliet, since Juliet is probably an elf. And she'd hardly have killed Gary; she fancied herself in love with him."

"Well, usually people are murdered by their friends or family," she said. "Why kill a stranger?"

"If the stranger were Gary? I should think most people who encountered him even briefly could think of at least one reason to kill him. Maybe two or three."

"Well, Lilie has the same alibi for the night of his death as most of the residents: she was home in bed. That's not an alibi. I'd be willing to bet she routinely sneaked out to meet him. It wouldn't be any harder to sneak out to kill him."

36

One of the empty cottages we had investigated was at the back of the valley, not far from Maerian's mansion. We'd been particularly hopeful about that one, considering its location; but there was nothing to indicate that anyone had been there since the cleaners. It was a charming little two-bedroom home completely buried in the forest, and would have made a good place for Romeo to camp out since lights in its windows couldn't be seen from any distance at all. But either Romeo hadn't been there, or he'd learned to be more careful to leave no traces behind.

After a night of fruitless stakeout, Shannon decided we should move in there. "We'd still have to go out in the middle of the night and get all cold and muddy," she said, "but at least we wouldn't be so far from nice warm showers and laundry facilities."

"We'd be miles from meals at the Hall," I said.

"Not even one mile," she said. "And if we take along your groceries, we'll have enough food for a siege. We wouldn't have to go down to the Hall unless we felt like it."

"We'll feel like it," I said. "Unless you're going to take up cooking."

"Well, most of your groceries don't require a whole lot of cooking," she said. "I think I could manage to boil water for instant soup, or nuke the occasional frozen burrito."

"God, I hate moving." But the plan made sense, so we did it. It took us three trips to get all our accumulated belongings moved. "This shows the level of our desperation," I said, sprawling on a lawn chair beside the sweet broom that bordered the flagstone deck, having deposited the last of our groceries in the new kitchen. "If we had any hope of solving this case by any means but brute force and ignorance, we'd never have gone to all this trouble."

"You call it brute force to move nearer the source of the problem?" she said.

"You know what I mean. There's no way we're going to figure this one out, sitting comfortably in front of a fire somewhere. It doesn't lend itself to figuring. We're going to have to catch somebody at something. Hell, we don't even know who to catch. We just hope somebody will happen by. Brute force and ignorance. That's us."

"I'll be ignorance," she said. "You be brute force."

"No. It's too much work. Besides, I'm so good at ignorance."

"Okay," she said, "I can't argue with that. You win."

I was too tired to throw anything at her, so I settled for demanding lunch. "You said you'd cook."

"I did not," she said. "Let's go down to the Hall. I want to talk to some people anyway. Maybe I can get Mildred Potter to tell me about that letter of Lorielle's. And if Ritchie's there, I want to have another go at him; I *know* he's concealing something."

"So's Ariana," I said. "And maybe Finandiel."

"Yes, but of those three, which would you expect to slip up in conversation?"

"Ritchie," I said. "Especially in conversation with you. Finandiel's impervious, and Ariana's a woman."

"Don't start," she said, because she did not believe me when I told her what a strong effect she had on men. She thought they were that way all the time: simple and easily flustered.

The weather was sunny again after days of fog and rain. Unfortunately the sunlight couldn't penetrate to the forest floor to dry it, so we still had to slog through damp leaves and occasionally dripping branches. The walk to the Hall wasn't a full mile, but it seemed twice that when we'd gone most of the way and back so many times already today.

The trip seemed well worth it, though, when we sat down at last to another of Charlotte's excellent meals. Ariana and Ritchie were both there. After the meal Shannon took Ritchie aside and I brought Ariana a second cup of coffee to encourage her to stay and chat. She was visibly amused. She thanked me for the coffee and responded amiably to my conversational gambits, but she very expertly diverted every attempt to get any real information from her.

I made a show of giving up and letting the conversation take its natural course. That didn't fool her for a second. I hoped Shannon was having better luck with Ritchie, but from the sound of it they were talking about his work, not ours, and I didn't really suppose anything useful would come of it. Nor did it: when we left the Hall at last to go searching the woods for clues again, she said so.

"You know," she said, "since it's Ariana, Finandiel, and Ritchie who know something about the Trouble, and refuse to tell us, I'm sure it's something harmless that they think will solve itself."

"Unless Ariana is the murderer."

"Do you think she is?"

I had to admit I didn't. "But that's a gut feeling. The plain fact is it was probably her wire."

"And probably anybody could get hold of it," she said. "Maybe she doesn't lock her door. Or, if she does, the spare key is hanging somewhere public in Charlotte's place, and she doesn't lock her door. And what I figure is, probably we're right about Romeo and Juliet, and those three don't want us to interfere."

"Then why did they hire us?"

She dismissed that with airy unconcern. "Well, probably the others insisted on it, and they were afraid to be too forcefully against it."

"So you're saying they hope we don't do what we were hired to do. Tough. If they didn't want the job done, they should have hired somebody incompetent."

She grinned. "I wonder whether they didn't think that was what they were doing? Ours isn't the biggest ad in the yellow pages."

And our office was in one of the oldest and most ramshackle buildings in downtown Berkeley. And they might know Kyriander hadn't been exactly rolling in money when he hired us last summer. "If that's what they thought, screw 'em," I said.

"Well, we'll just have to prove them wrong, won't we?"

A noble sentiment, but unfortunately I'd begun to wonder whether we could. Nor did the afternoon's fruitless interviews and investigations encourage me. We were, in fact, at a standstill, with plenty of guesses but no evidence and no sign of getting any anytime soon. Except for a visit to Maerian, which we hadn't yet achieved, we had followed our few leads as far as they would take us, and got nothing for our trouble but tired.

The only thing we really had going for us was the wire we'd found at the site of Gary's accident; and since we hadn't been hired to look into his death, and hadn't even that much of a clue in the case we had been hired to solve, that wasn't much comfort. We were somewhat subdued when we went down to dinner that night.

Kyriander didn't bring his family to dinner every night, but they were there that night. Briande was playing with toy dinosaurs with Leaf Fulmer-Jenks, and cheerfully ignored us as he did everyone else. Lilie was on a couch by a stained-glass window with a book forgotten in her lap. She glanced up and smiled politely at us, but I had the feeling she didn't really even notice who we were. The book in her lap was one of Ritchie's. I wondered whether she had really been reading the thing or had it only for show, to flatter him. If the latter, she'd chosen the wrong night for it; he wasn't there. But maybe I was being unfair. Many people liked his work, and she was just at an age to be impressed by his earnestness.

Mildred Potter hadn't been there at lunch, so as soon as Shannon saw her this evening she cornered her with questions about Lorielle's mail. It looked to me as though Mildred was going to be as stubborn with Shannon as she had been with me; she was shaking her head regretfully, and looking a trifle stern.

Finandiel smiled at me. "Is your partner trying to convince Mildred to break your law?" he asked.

"I think she may be," I said. "How did you guess?"

"Mildred has that look about her, as of one caught between duty and diplomacy. What is it you want her to do?"

"Only tell us the return address on a letter she handled."

"Good grace, but she handles many! How is it that she might recall this one?"

"It had a crest," I said. "I'm sure she noticed it."

"Ah. Would it, by any chance, be one of Lorielle's letters?"

"Yes. How did you know?"

"The crest, don't you see," he said. "I fear it will be of little use to you: as it happens, I know the contents of those, er, missives."

"Plural? She's had more than one?"

"Ah, yes," he said, nodding complacently. "You see, one of my young relatives has formed an, er, affection for Lorielle; but as he is of a higher rank than I, he may not enter this world. They correspond by way of your postal service. Most convenient, that: I quite believe we should adopt something of the sort. Courier service is so much less reliable, and of course the cost is prohibitive for many."

Well, we hadn't seriously hoped that Lorielle's letters would give us a clue. What was worse, though, was that if she was in such delights to receive letters from some relative of Finandiel's still in Faerie, she could hardly be the Juliet for whom our conjectured Romeo had come to this world. I let him chat amiably about the mail service till Charlotte announced dinner, and then settled with Kyriander to eat it.

He flirted with me so outrageously that I soon forgot my frustration with the case and began to consider the benefits of having moved to a two-bedroom house. When we started home after dinner it seemed perfectly natural that he should walk beside us.

It was a beautiful, clear night, with stars so thick they filled the night with their spangled light. It was bright enough that Kyriander didn't need a flashlight, though Shannon and I did. Every break in the canopy gave us a glorious view of shimmering sky. Kyriander reached for my hand. Shannon ranged ahead of us till all we could see of her was the flicker of her flashlight among the leaves.

Neither of us spoke. The night was very still, our muffled footsteps the only sound. An owl hooted almost directly overhead, startling us both. We grinned at each other in the darkness and went on. Something crashed in the bushes somewhere far ahead of us, but it might have been a branch falling or a deer leaping. Neither of us paid much attention till we heard more scuffling in the underbrush, and a muted cry.

I called Shannon's name and ran forward. There was a muffled yell in response, but I couldn't tell whether it was her voice. I sprinted toward the sound, the light from my flashlight bouncing wildly across bushes and trees and path in a dance of panic. Kyriander loped silently past me, his longer legs and better night vision giving him a strong advantage.

Ahead of us, there were sounds of struggle, a single yelp that sounded like Shannon's voice, and just as I arrived on Kyriander's heels at the fountain clearing, silence. Not another sound. No movement, no voices, no footfalls. Nothing. "*Damn* it!" said Kyriander.

"What? What?" I crowded into the clearing behind him, waving my flashlight imprudently. I'm sure I would have behaved much more sensibly in a city street. Unfamiliar territory made me clumsy and stupid.

"Magic," said Kyriander, making it sound like a curse. At just that moment the beam of my flashlight caught on the crumpled shape of my partner's body sprawled against the base of Salonian's fountain, her legs bent under her, one arm flung limply out across bloodstained leaves, and her still face turned toward the stone.

37

She was alive. Barely, but she was alive. She had been so viciously battered there was blood splattered all over the clearing. She seemed to have put up a good fight, but her attacker had a weapon and she didn't; her flashlight was too small to be any use as a bludgeon, and too large for stabbing. Apparently the attack had been so sudden and unexpected that she hadn't time to find anything else, though she knew as well as I did how to make a lethal weapon of even so common an item as a pencil. He must have hit her from cover, so she never really had a chance.

I didn't care about any of that at the time. Kyriander assured me she could safely be carried. Together, somehow, we got her back to the Hall. Someone called for an ambulance. I argued that I could drive her more quickly, but they pointed out that the ambulance would come equipped with paramedics, and the elves assured me that their magic would keep her stable till the ambulance arrived. I subsided, not gracefully, but at least somewhat reassured.

The Hall seemed crowded and very brightly lighted. Most of the people who had been at dinner were there still, and everyone seemed to be speaking at once. I sat down on the floor next to the couch where Kyriander had put Shannon, and tried to wipe the dirt and blood from her face.

"One of you sneaked out, didn't you?" demanded Charlotte. "Didn't you? One of you killed my son, and tried to kill Shannon. I know it. Filthy elves. You're not fit to live."

"Charlotte, they're helping," I said, but she didn't hear me.

"Psychopaths, that's what you are, all of you. You don't think twice about snuffing a human's life if the fancy strikes you," she said.

"No, no," said Rosetta, "it can't have been an elf. At least, not one of the ones here in the Hall; we've been with them all evening."

"It could be one of the others, who weren't here," said Charlotte. "Or these could sneak out and use their filthy magic to hide it."

"No, it's the Trouble," said Rosetta. "Poor girl: we hired her to find the Trouble, and it knows it, and decided to stop her." She shook her head. "We should have hired big, muscle-bound men to find it, if only we'd known it would turn out to be dangerous. Which, you may remember, I said it would, didn't I, George? When it chased me that night, and all of you laughed at me, I told you it was dangerous, but you wouldn't listen, and now look."

"I'm sure this wasn't a manifestation of the Trouble," Ariana said soothingly. "It was probably somebody from outside the valley. Gang members, perhaps; we've talked about that possibility before."

Rosetta pressed her lips together with a disapproving frown. Charlotte said, "Of course *you'd* say so," and glared at the elves. I looked up at Ariana.

"What makes you so sure it wasn't the Trouble?" I asked. "Is there some evidence I'm missing?"

Ariana shook her head impatiently. "No, but he—" She broke off, flustered. "I mean I'm sure, from the other things the Trouble has done . . . This isn't his—its pattern."

"Yes, it is," said Charlotte, "when you think that one of the other things it's done is kill my Gary. You all know what a good motorcyclist he was. I don't care what the police say, they're wrong: it wasn't an accident. He wouldn't misjudge a curve and lose control like that. Not on a road he'd been driving over and over again every day of his life."

"Yes, well, all the more reason," Rosetta said firmly. "I don't care: this is the last reed. This proves the Trouble is dangerous, and I won't raise my child in a dangerous locution. We're moving. George, you can come with us if you like," she added kindly.

"That's as may be," George said, "but, my dear, moving?"

"And that's another thing," said Charlotte.

"You've said enough things, haven't you?" Ariana said mildly.

"I've only just begun," said Charlotte.

"Surely we might behave more constructively than this?" Kyriander said in apparent surprise.

Everyone stared at him. "Like what?" demanded Charlotte.

"It might do no harm to investigate the scene," he said. "Using magic." He glanced around at the elves. "I felt magic there. Her attacker used it at least to escape us, if not also against her. Someone skilled in it might yet track that."

"Let us try whether we might," said Finandiel, in the tone of one inviting friends to a card game. Several elves trooped out the door with him, waiting only long enough to ascertain from Kyriander exactly where the attack had taken place.

Charlotte watched their exit with an expression of exaggerated amazement. "Well!" she said finally. "Some people!"

No one seemed quite sure what this utterance signified, but as the approaching whine of an ambulance siren became audible just then, it was largely ignored. Kyriander went outside to direct the ambulance into the parking lot. Tim Cameron emerged from the kitchen looking sheepish, saw Shannon's bloodied form on the couch, and stood wavering in the doorway staring at her.

Charlotte, noticing him, forgot all about the elves, and spoke his name in such a fierce tone that he stumbled backward a step when he looked at her. "Huh?" he said. "What?"

"You've been drinking," she said.

He shook his head dizzily. "No," he said. "I was, um, I just wanted, I'm going to fix myself a snack."

"You just had dinner," she said.

"Oh. Yeah." He seemed surprised. "Well, I'm hungry again."

The ambulance pulled up outside and the paramedics trooped in, led by Kyriander and trailed by Lilie. She looked pleased and excited, and threw a look at me I couldn't interpret. I ignored it, concentrating on the paramedics. I was relieved to see that one of them was an elf. They went straight to Shannon, and in seconds had her on a gurney ready for transport. "Will she be all right?" I demanded.

"We have her stabilized," one of them told me, gently pushing me aside.

"Let them go, Rose," said Kyriander. "They'll take care of her."

"I'm going too." I left, and followed Shannon's ambulance to Orinda.

It occurred to me that we should have called the police, and I wondered whether anyone would think to do it; and whether it would be worth the trouble. If there had been magic involved, it was extremely unlikely they could do more than the Fey Valley elves could.

Except, of course, that nobody suspected the police of being involved. Had we sent the perpetrator out to look for clues to his own act? But no, surely not; none of the people at the Hall when we arrived with Shannon could have been her attacker. He might have been able to get back to the Hall before us, but he would surely have been out of breath and, more important, badly bloodstained. None of them had been.

Of course I hadn't been paying very close attention. Anyone could have slipped in after we got there and I wouldn't have noticed. And the perpetrator had used magic. He could easily have had enough of it to keep his clothes unstained.

Tim Cameron could have come in the back door and through the kitchen, feigning drunkenness so we

wouldn't suspect him. But he had no magic. It had to
be an elf or a halfling. And I had been too upset to pay
close attention to who was where, or whether any of
them came in after we did.

"Rosie Lavine, intrepid detective," I said aloud. "Always alert. Hell."

The hospital in Orinda was as depressing as hospitals
are everywhere. I made sure Shannon's paperwork was
in order, and spent the next couple of hours waiting to
hear how she was. When nothing came of waiting, I tried
asking questions, and then bullying, and finally making
a scene. That got me a weary doctor who threatened to
sedate me or call the police. When I explained what I
wanted, she told me Shannon had been treated and
moved to a private room, and gave me directions to
find her.

She looked better. They had cleaned off the worst of
the blood, and stitched the cuts, and the bruises weren't
yet as colorful as they would be. One eye was swollen
shut and her lips split, but the doctor had assured me
there was no permanent damage to her appearance.

She was concussed, which was why they were keeping
her, and the doctor had been very slippery in talking
about that because brain injuries are pretty unpredictable; but they expected her to be fine. She had a broken
arm, two broken ribs, and a lot of really bad bruises,
but she'd been lucky. Her attacker had clearly meant to
kill her.

And I'd been right there. I'd heard the attack, and
been close enough that with any luck I could have
caught the attacker. But I hadn't. I hadn't even seen
him. All I knew about him was that he must be an elf
or a halfling; and since that described well over half of
Fey Valley's population, it wasn't much help.

I wished Killer were there. Not that he could have
done anything about the case; but he could have comforted me. Killer had a way of making me see, when I
was depressed, that things weren't as bad as I thought.
He would put his arms around me, and say, "Hey," in

his sweet, soft, island accent, and everything would seem less daunting somehow.

But he wasn't there, and he wouldn't be. I'd told him I didn't have room in my life for him, and I'd walked away. Things had gone badly at Maunalani, and I'd taken the coward's way out of a rocky relationship. I hadn't been willing to work on it. I said I didn't have time or energy to devote to just getting along with a bedmate. There were plenty of guys where he came from.

The plain fact was I'd been scared. We were developing a good, strong friendship, and my experience with being friends with one's lovers was not large. I figured it was better to get out of it by my own choice before something went wrong. In order to keep him from dumping me, I dumped him.

Of course I didn't think of it that way at the time. I didn't think very rationally at all. My whole life had just been turned upside down. I had to confront each experience afterward as though I'd never done anything like it before. Or so I thought. But I brought with me all the suspicion, fear, and distrust I could carry.

That's a quick way to ruin a lot of things. It was a wonder Killer and I lasted as well as we did. But his desire to make it work balanced my wary reluctance to some extent, at least until I panicked and fled. In retrospect I could see that what I'd done was to deliberately destroy something precious because I feared someone else would. If I didn't do it first, I'd have lost control.

It had seemed sensible at the time. I loved Killer. Everyone I had ever loved betrayed me. It would be foolish not to learn from that. And the lesson is: if you love someone, you must leave him.

I left him. I'd been regretting it ever since. But what else could I have done?

The hospital provided surprisingly comfortable chairs for visitors. I settled into the one in Shannon's room, closed my eyes on all the weary second guesses and self-recriminations, and slept.

38

When I returned to Fey Valley in the morning, Finandiel was waiting for me at the Hall. It was another gloriously sunlit day. The interior of the Hall was splashed with brilliant color where the sunlight shone through stained-glass windows. Finandiel greeted me with the offer of Daelinn wine, served by Cuthbern in a graceful golden goblet. The goblet was a beautiful thing, heavy and very art nouveau, the base a cluster of perfectly detailed leaves and the stem a vine that tangled gracefully around the bowl. I accepted it and sat across from Finandiel at the table to drink the wine.

"How fares your wounded partner?" he asked.

"She'll live," I said. "What did you find last night when you went looking for clues?"

"Nothing of any importance: the weapon only, which reveals nothing useful. It was a branch taken from the forest. Anyone might have found and used it."

"I wonder why I'm not surprised that's all you found?"

"You think us to be concealing the truth?"

I sipped my wine. "Aren't you?" When he didn't answer straightaway, I put down my goblet and said bitterly, "What happened? Did one of you panic when you found out we're not as incompetent as expected? It wasn't necessary, you know. We were at a standstill. We might even have given up." I looked at him. "I won't give up now, you know."

"No, I should think not," he said with apparent sympathy. "Be assured I very much regret last night's incident."

"Attempted murder," I said.

"Yes," he said. "Attempted murder. Which is why I know I can assure you it was not the, er, Trouble."

"You know who Romeo is, don't you?"

He stared. "Romeo?"

"The Trouble," I said impatiently.

"Ah." He thought about it. "I see. Yes. Shakespeare. How apt."

I ignored that. "Is he staying with Maerian? Is that why she won't let us near her?"

"Actually it is not," he said. "She values her privacy, don't you know."

"I'm sure she does. How do I get in?"

"I thought you would ask," he said. "Indeed, it is why I have awaited you here."

"You're too kind."

"You are angry."

"How perceptive of you to notice."

He nodded. "I believe in your place I might feel much the same. One has one's pride." I didn't ask what pride had to do with it. For an elf whose partner had been assaulted, perhaps injured pride would be the dominant emotion. "Your anger is to be expected, though I hope when you know the whole you will understand we are not to blame. Cuthbern? Have you the key?"

"I have, my lord." Cuthbern reached one finger into a tiny pocket in his vest, emerging with a large gold skeleton key, which he presented to me with a graceful bow.

"What's this?" I said.

"The key to Maerian's spell," said Finandiel.

"Oh, right. Like the lavender spike."

"Lavender for mistrust," he said. "That took you to her door, did it not?" He gestured toward the key in my hand. "This will let you in. Talk to those you meet there. I put the future of my house in your hands, Rose Lavine. I believe you mean us no harm. Tread carefully." With that he rose and left the Hall, with Cuthbern a dutiful half dozen paces behind him.

I finished my wine in a gulp, and was startled when

the goblet didn't crumble to dust. I had assumed it was
Faerie gold, useless once the Faerie wine was gone. That
it had been Faerie wine was beyond question. Not only
was it more delicious than any ironworld wine ever
made, but it left me feeling as refreshed as if I had slept
in my own bed last night and had a fine, wholesome
breakfast this morning.

Doubtless Finandiel meant to pick up the goblet later;
but since it wasn't Faerie gold it must be worth a fortune. I didn't like to leave it in the unlocked Hall. No
resident was likely to steal it, but there was nothing to
stop a stranger from wandering in.

Neither did I particularly want to lug it with me all
the way up to Maerian's mansion and back, but I
couldn't think what else to do with it. I rinsed and dried
it in the kitchen and stuffed it into my jacket pocket,
where it made a heavy and extremely unwieldy lump but
wasn't likely to fall out, and set out on yet another hike
to the back of the valley.

I don't know whether it was the key or the sprig of
lavender that got me through the barrier spell and onto
Maerian's sunny front porch. I'd been that far before,
and wasn't in a mood to be impressed. There was an
ornate brass knocker on the door. I used it, as I had
before. This time the hollow echo had barely faded when
the door opened.

Maerian was the sort of elf one reads about in the old
fairy tales: ethereal, otherworldly, wholly unhuman. She
wasn't even attractive by human standards. The features
of her long, pointed face were too sharp and arrogant,
almost menacing. Everything about her seemed too long
and narrow, as though she had been painfully stretched
somehow, like an Arthur Rackham fairy lacking only its
wings. The one thing that saved her from looking utterly
grotesque was the consummate grace of her movements,
like a vine in the wind, by its nature incapable of
awkwardness.

She wore a flowing gown that seemed to be made of
leaves and vine, with matching vine and flowers tangled
in her hair. Her feet and arms were bare. Her long fin-

gers sparkled with gems. I had never felt so uncouth and frumpy in my life.

When she held out her hand for the key, I knew what she wanted, and gave her it. "Who sent you?" she asked. Her voice was as ethereal as everything about her, but at least it was unquestionably beautiful. It sounded like summer sunlight, and birdsong, and wind in trees, and the water in small streams burbling over polished stone. I could have listened to it forever. "Who sent you, child?" she said.

"Oh," I said. "Um. Finandiel."

"Meddling again," she said. "I might have known. Come in, then. Since you brought the key, I can't stop you." She stepped aside and gestured gracefully for me to pass her.

I did, and even managed not to stumble over the threshold. "I've come about Romeo," I said. "I mean, the Trouble. That is—"

"Hush, child, I know why you're here," she said. "Come: we'll sit where we can be comfortable."

My eyes hadn't yet adjusted to the dimness of the corridor when she led me, half-blind and wholly over-awed, into a sunlit conservatory that was a positive jungle of thick vines, flowering bushes, dwarf fruit trees, and orchids everywhere. The air was moist and warm and heavy with the rich, sweet scents of flowers and fruits. In the center of the jungle was a little clearing where she had her easel set up with a huge white canvas on it. She hadn't yet begun the actual painting; there were only a few charcoal lines on the gessoed whiteness.

Beside the easel were two small, ordinary canvas folding chairs. She took one, managing somehow to look regal and elegant even while lowering herself into a shaky little beach chair, and gestured me into the other. "Be welcome," she said. "May I offer you refreshment?"

That surprised me, I don't know why. "Um, sure," I said. Some bizarre whimsy made me pull Finandiel's goblet from my pocket. "I even brought my own glass."

She went very still, looking at the goblet. "How came you by such a vessel?" she asked sharply.

"It's Finandiel's," I said, looking at it in surprise. "He gave me wine in it."

"He gave you more than wine," she said, and studied me with fresh interest. "I am surprised. But perhaps Finandiel knows what he is about."

"I don't understand."

She ignored that. "More wine, perhaps?"

"Sure, that would be fine. Maerian—"

Her slender, heavily bejeweled hand waved away whatever I would say. "Has Finandiel told you who I am?"

I shook my head. "Only your name." I nearly spilled the goblet; it was heavy in my hand, full again. The sweet, tart scent of Faerie wine told me what was in it.

Maerian nodded. "And you know not what that name signifies?"

"Um, no." I sipped the wine. If it wasn't as good as Finandiel's Daelinn wine, I couldn't tell.

"I am sister to the queen, Tytonia."

I stared. "Then what are you doing here? I mean—"

"I know what you mean, child. You've been told the queen forbids us—the aristocracy—entry to the world of iron, and that is true. I do not always obey authority." Her cold smile in that sharp face was almost feral. The teeth it exposed were needle-sharp and deadly. "The queen my sister has commanded the best of us to stay in Faerie, to keep our power untainted and our land secure. She is right in this. Because she is, and because her power is great even among the Daoine Sidhe, our people obey her.

"Yes, I see your surprise. In all that Finandiel and Ariana told you of our ways, I suppose neither of them thought to tell you what you most need to know to understand this: we are not governed, as you mortals are, by base, ephemeral emotions. And this applies to all things, including our obedience to our queen.

"We do not love Tytonia, as you appear to love your rulers. The Daoine Sidhe do not love at all. And few of us feel any particular loyalty toward my sister the queen. She is powerful. Therefore, she is queen. Should someone more powerful set her aside, that one will take her place. Meantime honor—and perhaps fear, where honor fails—compels the Daoine Sidhe to obey her. Thus it has been throughout time."

She reached with one hand toward the low table at her side. There was nothing on it when she began the gesture; but when her long fingers cupped the air above the table, a goblet materialized to fill the curve of her hand. She lifted it and sipped the contents, her eyes focused on the blank canvas before her.

"But things and peoples change," she said, putting down the goblet and turning to look at me again, her strange, pale eyes shuttered. "I said the Daoine Sidhe do not love. So has it always been. So is it still, in the eyes of my sister the queen. And so should it be: it is our nature. We are not animals." She shuddered delicately, sipped her wine, and after a long moment added, almost to herself, "But nor are we trapped in time. Things and peoples change; we must change our thinking with them, or we die."

She regarded me contemplatively for a moment. "We have long been at war with . . . forces of whom you know nothing," she said finally. "It was not always thus; but for the past thousand years we have been locked in battle, and a whole generation has grown to maturity with no experience of peace. I know not whether it was that, or some other force at work against us; but that generation is changed. Oh, of course, not all of them, no. But some. Perhaps many."

When she fell silent and stayed that way for several minutes, I said, "Changed in what way?" though I had begun to think I knew. The elves had finally noticed that they weren't all as indifferent to mortals—or to each other!—as they liked to believe. Some of them, Daoine Sidhe or not, knew how to love.

I had never before realized what a departure from their comfortable expectations that would be. I knew, of course, that they frowned on romantic liaisons with mortals, and considered halflings distasteful at best and abominations at worst. We would very likely feel the same way about it if men were cross-fertile with sheep. But I hadn't taken it the logical step further: even if we approved of (or at least accepted) relations with sheep, could we really think well of the man who could *love* one? Maerian didn't use the word bestiality, but I could tell it crossed her mind.

But that was only part of the problem. Apparently the younger elves were showing unseemly affection for each other, as well. I wanted to ask incredulously whether all their reproduction in past had been conducted entirely without affection—if so, they surely hadn't much room to criticize anybody else's practices—but fortunately reason prevailed. This was not a creature one should anger without good reason.

"I do realize that the way these children behave seems perfectly normal to you," she said, smiling slightly. "But recall that we are not like you, nor wish to be."

I said I did recall that. She explained that when the queen first became aware of the problem, she thought it merely an aberration. Where possible, she separated such lovers, thinking they would get over their freakish notions in time. But with the ordinary day-to-day maintenance of her Faerie Court, plus the additional demands of the war, she simply didn't have the resources to keep track of all her subjects' love lives as well.

Maerian didn't put it in quite that way, of course; but I got the drift. "So you're saying she doesn't always separate them anymore?" I said.

"Not invariably, no," said Maerian. "But among the higher aristocracy, yes, I fear her policy is yet to keep them apart where possible. The task is overwhelming, and it may have been hopeless from the start; but the matter cannot be lightly dismissed. Surely even you can see that."

"Even I," I said. And the thing was, I thought I almost could. "But I just don't see how the queen even hoped to keep track of every one of her subjects. Good Lord, there must be thousands, maybe millions of them."

"Oh, yes," said Maerian, smiling kindly at my amazement. "What you may have forgotten is that her power is not merely political."

"Oh. Yes, I suppose I was forgetting that. So she spies on them by magic?"

That was careless. I knew it the moment the words were out of my mouth, when it was too late to recall them. She stared at me in shock and growing anger for a long, tense moment before, unexpectedly, a flicker of humor collapsed the rage into laughter. "Yes," she said, "I suppose you would see it in that quite unfavorable light. We do not."

"Yet you seem to disagree with her."

"No, why do you say it?"

"You're sheltering one of the lovers, aren't you?"

She studied me for another long moment before she nodded slowly and said, "I thought you knew. I am in honor bound: I shelter the Duke of Daelinn."

"Finandiel's cousin?" I asked in surprise.

"The same."

"Does Finandiel know about this?"

"I believe it will be the reason he has come to the world of iron."

"And the duke? Did he come for Lorielle?"

"Her parents forbade the marriage," she said. "They knew the revolting nature of their child's interest."

"You mean they knew she loved him."

Her nostrils quivered, as at an unpleasant odor. "Just so," she said. "They could not approve such a . . . such a *mortal* liaison."

"So then what happened? She ran away here, and he followed her? But surely if your queen is as powerful as you say, she could find them almost instantly. Why hasn't she? Are you hiding them from her? Can you do that? I'd thought you were only hiding him from us."

She looked almost, but not quite, contemptuous. "He needs no assistance for that."

"Ah. Right. Mere mortals couldn't hope to track him down."

She smiled coldly. "Have you forgotten the key that let you through my spell? That was no mortal's work."

"Doesn't matter how I got here, does it? Point is, I am here, and I know he's here." But she didn't get it; she was so secure in her arrogance that she couldn't see anything that didn't support it.

She was right, of course, that no mortal could have got here without magical assistance. But one of the things we have that elves don't is teamwork. We're in the habit of working with others to get what we want. If Finandiel hadn't decided to help me for his own reasons, I'd have found a way to convince him or another elf to do it for mine.

"You would not know that much, had I not told you," said Maerian.

"Okay, right," I said. It was fine with me if she wanted to think herself infinitely superior to mortals. In many ways, of course, she was. "The main thing is, I'm here, and so's Finandiel's cousin. I'd like to see him."

"Never!" said a young male voice from somewhere among the jungled vines around us. And, being an elf, he suited word to deed: as soon as he spoke, I couldn't see anything at all.

39

Before I even had time to protest, Maerian said, rather mysteriously I thought, " 'Ware, Kimendan. You behold the goblet."

My vision returned instantly. I had been blinded only for a second or two, but it was quite enough to put the fear of Faerie into me. Not that I was going to let anyone know that. I stared wildly around, looking for the source of my discomfort. Absurdly, Maerian was scowling at a bush not far from us.

I looked at it more closely, expecting to see Finandiel's cousin concealed behind it. Instead, after a long moment, the bush itself began to metamorphose into a sulky young elf, all bones and angles and surliness like any other teenager. Only he very likely wasn't exactly a teenager: he might easily be a hundred years old and still look like that.

"Apologize," said Maerian.

"There's no need," I began, but they both ignored me.

"Sorry," said the boy, scowling at me.

Maerian nodded her approval and said, "This is the mortal Rose Lavine. Rose, the Duke of Daelinn reveals himself: Kimendan, cousin to Lord Finandiel, and author of your valley's Trouble."

Doubtless I was meant to rise and curtsy or something. Instead I looked him over quite a lot more rudely than I would have done if he hadn't frightened me, and said coolly, "How tiresome you've been."

They both stared. "Perhaps you didn't understand," said Maerian, but Kimendan cut her off with the smallest of gestures and the flicker of a smile. "Have I?" he said with boyish pleasure. "I did mean to be, you know. Mortals are so easy to alarm."

That remark made it easy to keep my tone unfriendly despite his ready charm. "Yes. Our children, especially. Do you know how much you've frightened them?"

To my surprise he blushed horribly, the way adolescent boys do, right to the roots of his golden hair. "A miscalculation," he muttered. "I meant it not."

I believed him, but I didn't feel obliged to say so. "If you knew it, and didn't mean it, why didn't you stop?"

"I dared not." He moved forward to rest one hip on the edge of a potting table next to the blank canvas, trying to look casual. He succeeded only in looking more chidishly awkward. "You must see that. Of course I have become more cautious, and tried to avoid the children; but the adults must not be allowed to discover my presence."

"Why? What could we do?"

He looked me up and down with profound contempt. "You, nothing," he said. "You and the halflings are no danger to me, of course; but should you carry tales, the Daoine Sidhe among you might inform my queen."

"Yes? And what would she do?"

"Mab's grace," he said, "have you not guessed? I should be herded back to Faerie like some, some misbehaving child, and made to spend my life alone."

"Oh, come. You can't mean she'd lock you in solitary confinement, or something."

"As near as makes no matter: she would set it upon me that I *could* not be with Lorielle." He made it sound like a gruesome death sentence.

After a brief hesitation I said, "Maybe, in time, you'd be glad of it."

"No." He didn't even bother to attack me for presuming to second-guess an elf. "Never. She is my life. Without her, I die."

That wasn't just histrionics. He believed it. And so, apparently, did Maerian. She said slowly, and quite bitterly, "He might, you know. It has been known to hap-

pen." She glared at me as though I were responsible.
"You mortals know not the strength of our convictions."

"Um, no, I don't suppose we do," I said, wondering
whether she regarded it as admirable that an elf depraved enough, in their terms, to love at all, might will
himself to death over it if thwarted.

"It is not that I would wish to die," said Kimendan,
quite as though he knew what I was thinking. "Though
indeed I suppose I might. She is my light. She is the
breath of my life."

"Yet elves in your situation have survived," I said.
"Salonian—"

"Salonian," said Maerian, interrupting me, "has his
work. He made his choice as the queen my sister knew
he would. Kimendan's case is quite different."

"In what way?"

"They were older," said Kimendan. "*She'd* say," this
with a contemptuous glance toward Maerian, "their aberration wasn't as grotesque as ours."

"You mean their love wasn't as great."

Maerian shuddered at the word, but Kimendan nodded solemnly. "Just so."

"Tintiminiel and Salonian were separated a century
and more ago," said Maerian. "She has since wed another, and lives content; and he, having made his choice,
has learned to live with it as you have seen. These children are a different matter entirely."

"Okay, maybe they are," I said. "But it's a pretty
open secret, isn't it? Who else knows about them? Finandiel and Ariana know, don't they?"

"My cousin may have guessed," Kimendan admitted.
"And the halfling Ariana has been of use to us."

"Ritchie Morita has been dropping hints."

"That one," Maerian said with revulsion.

I laughed. "I quite agree," I said. "But I do think he's
guessed, or been told." I looked at Kimendan. "Did you
or Lorielle tell him?"

"My lady took him into her confidence," he said reluctantly. "You understand she was alone, and knew not
the ways of your world. The mortal Ritchie Morita

helped her when she needed help. He has provided us with a meeting place and . . . and with much useful advice. Indeed, I may well consult him regarding you."

He said that part mostly, I think, to annoy; I ignored it. "Is there anyone who hasn't been taken into someone's confidence? Finandiel, Ritchie, Ariana, and now me. Who else knows?"

"None," Maerian said certainly.

"Possibly the postmistress," said Kimendan. "If she has given the matter thought, she must have guessed."

"The letters," I said. "I'd forgotten those. What's that all about, anyway?"

"A game, only," said Kimendan, looking mildly embarrassed.

Maerian lifted an eyebrow. "Was it not meant to fool your cousin Finandiel?" At his look, she nodded. "As I thought." She shook her head in disgust. "It is to be expected that you understand these mortals not, but how you came to so misjudge your own kind I cannot comprehend. I may yet wash my hands of you. Either you are more alien to me than I knew, or you suffer a paucity of sense. Either way, you are not what I thought you."

"Nor you, what I believed," he said heatedly. "This isolation from your own kind, this obsession with the mortals' fine art to the exclusion of wholesome crafts, and your tedious objections to good fun, are unseemly. And this conviction that mere mortals will comprehend what they cannot! You think yourself so consequential, but being sister to the queen is not so much, not when compared with how . . . how *mortal* you have become."

She lifted a haughty eyebrow at him. "Think you that I am like to die?" She meant did he mean to kill her.

"You know I didn't mean *that*," he said, only mildly flustered. "I meant you're like unto them. Too like."

"Oh, do stop bickering," I said, and was gratified when they both stared at me in revulsion. "Are there any besides those four, and me, who're likely to know you're here, Kimendan?"

"I think not," said Maerian.

"You haven't told anyone else?"

"No," said Kimendan.

"Were you involved in Gary's accident?"

"Gary?" he said.

"The motorcycle?" said Maerian. "Certainly not."

Kimendan looked from her to me. "You ask whether I killed a child?" he demanded, drawing himself up to scowl at me quite fiercely. "You *dare*?"

"Don't be stupid. Of course I dare. Are you saying you didn't do it?"

"By Mab's grace, of course I didn't do it!" he said.

"Did you see who did?"

"No. I would have killed him."

"And you didn't try to kill my partner last night?"

"Certainly not," said Maerian.

"Did someone try to kill your partner?" asked Kimendan, evidently pleased by this intelligence.

"Yes, and I'm pretty sure it must have been the same person who killed Gary, if only because it strains credibility to think there might be two different murderers loose in Fey Valley all of a sudden."

"It's not I," Kimendan said almost regretfully. I believed him.

"Have you a suspect?" asked Maerian. "One more likely than the Duke of Daelinn?"

I didn't ask what was unlikely about the Duke of Daelinn. "I'm not sure. Kimendan, is this the only place you've stayed since you've been here?" I was thinking of the candle in the empty cottage. If he hadn't left it there, my guess was teenagers making out: and I was afraid I knew which teenagers. Kimendan shook his head, mystified. Kyriander's concerns for Lilie's health suddenly made a lot more sense.

I believed Kimendan. And I believed, too, that he would die without Lorielle. At least, he clearly believed it, and I didn't want to take the chance. No job was worth that.

"Okay," I said. "If you'll stop making mischief in the valley, Kimendan, I'm willing to keep your secret." I would have to quit the job, return the advance, and leave the valley. But what else could I do?

Kimendan bowed rigidly. "I thank you," he said, very politely concealing how much it galled him to owe a mortal anything.

"But I do wonder whether it's going to do you any good to keep hiding out here," I said. "Four people know about it already, and you've been here how long?"

"A month," said Maerian.

"At that rate, the whole valley will know by the end of the year," I said. "Long before that, someone will report it to your queen. Or she'll figure it out for herself, if she keeps as close eye on things as you say."

"But we have no choice," said Kimendan.

"Is your queen really so cruel she'd sooner see you die than marry for love?"

"Not cruel," he said. "Not that. It is only that she believes us not."

"I've told you theirs is not our way," said Maerian. "The queen my sister cannot know how it is with them."

"Has anyone thought to tell her?"

"I said she believes us not," said Kimendan. "Think you she denied us what we had not asked?"

"Very likely," I said; and added, before he could voice his offense, "I think you probably told her you loved each other and wanted to marry. If she doesn't like that sort of thing, she would naturally say no. And even if there's a mechanism for arguing with her decisions, and telling her why they might be wrong, I don't suppose you made any effort to take advantage of it, did you?"

"There is no such mechanism," said Maerian, revolted.

"Right. She makes arbitrary decisions, then?"

"She receives information and requests. Based on the information given, she decides. It is for us to present the information adequately to begin."

"And she's not interested in hearing it if her decision doesn't reflect all the information, because you neglected to tell her something?"

"One does not question the queen's commands."

"Was it a command? Or was it just a decision that she'd have changed if she knew she was condemning these children to death? I was under the impression your people had strong respect for the lives of children."

"And so we do," Maerian said, scowling. "You know not whereof you speak." But she looked discomfited enough that I wondered whether her real irritation wasn't that I'd caught her in an oversight.

"I know what you've told me," I said, "and the pieces don't fit."

Kimendan stared at her in wild surmise. "Think you my lady the queen might hear us?" he said.

"I think it not," said Marianden. "Be not a mooncalf, Kimendan. The queen my sister has more to do than to hear a pair of brats complain of her decisions."

"Has she?" I asked. "From what you've told me of her, I'd have thought she'd want to hear them. She may not care about their discomfort, but does she really want them to die?"

Maerian rose abruptly, towering over me in a cold, controlled rage. "Leave us," she said. "Your welcome here is at an end. Go." She pointed toward the front door, and the next thing I knew I was standing outside it, Finandiel's goblet in my hand and the echo of Kimendan's startled amusement in my ears.

Shrugging, I stepped off the porch and started down the path away from there. Since I'd promised not to tell the residents about Kimendan, he wasn't my problem. Let him and Maerian resolve their difficulties together. I'd found one Trouble. My job now, before I had to leave the valley, was to track down Gary's murderer and Shannon's attacker; and the one thing I was pretty sure of, after that interview, was that neither Kimendan nor Maerian knew anything about it.

40

With the Trouble absolved of violence, I had to assume that Shannon's attacker was one of the residents we knew. Maybe we had frightened someone into thinking we would track Gary's murder to him. That would have been a better starting point if we'd had any good suspects for Gary's murder. As it was, we had too many clues that led nowhere.

The wire that killed Gary was probably Ariana's, but it might have been put there by anyone. Anyone could have known Gary would be on the road that night; he usually was, and anyway his murderer could have set up that trap for him several nights before catching him; it wouldn't have bothered a car. Because of the time of night when the crash happened, it was difficult to rule out anyone; everyone was thought to have been at home in bed, but except for people who actually slept together that wasn't much of an alibi. Anyone could slip out in the night and in again after the murder, and no one the wiser.

Last night, none of us had seen Shannon's attacker. Kyriander and the elves said there'd been magic used, but that only meant it had been an elf or a halfling. The weapon was just something anyone could have found in the woods. I'd thought at first that it must be a large person; but a heavy stick like that could do considerable damage in a child's hands. Everyone who was actually in the Hall at the time must be absolved; but that left too many possibilities. Most of the residents we knew had been there, but by no means all of them; and there were many we didn't know.

I would have to start from scratch, interviewing everybody Shannon had talked to in the last few days, beginning with those she'd interviewed yesterday. If that didn't turn up a good possibility, then I could widen the search. To begin with, she'd spent a lot of time with Ritchie Morita, and he wasn't at the Hall last night.

At first glance he seemed an unlikely suspect; he hadn't elvish ears to have been offended by Gary's motorcycle, and no other obvious motive to do him harm. But even without the ears, he had seemed as offended as anyone by Gary's noise. And he'd been flirting so enthusiastically with Lilie lately that he was a little embarrassed about it in Kyriander's company. Could he have killed Gary out of jealousy, and to clear the way for his own suit?

It seemed a silly notion on the face of it: elves and children might think the way to deal with a rival was to kill him, but Ritchie was neither. Then again, some interpretations of the "angry young man" role called for a volatility easily equal to murder. Might he have got that involved in the role without quite realizing it?

He wasn't at dinner last night. If he had killed Gary, and Shannon had mentioned the wire to him, would it have alarmed him enough to attack her? Would she have mentioned the wire? Surely if she did, she would also have said how unlikely it was we'd ever find who used it; but he might not have believed that part.

Maybe it was a long shot, but I didn't have anything better to try, so I decided to drop by his house instead of going straight back to the Hall. I tucked Finandiel's goblet back in my pocket and took a side path that led across the road, toward Ritchie's house.

I hadn't asked Kimendan about the vandalism of my cottage, but I was pretty sure he hadn't done it. His sense of humor was unpleasantly elven, which meant he wouldn't have balked at that just because it might frighten me—I was an adult mortal; I could take my chances as far as he was concerned—but I really doubted he would have gone to that much trouble to annoy or frighten a mortal he had never met. Not unless he would be there to see my reaction; and he wasn't.

It was just conceivable Ritchie might have thought I'd find it creepy enough to be scared away by it. But surely Ritchie, or any of the other adults, would have realized I must encounter worse than that in the course of my job. No. If it had been done to frighten me, it must have been done by one of the children. If he had accepted Lilie's estimation of my character, Gary might have done it simply out of dislike. Or Lilie could have done it, in the hope of getting me out of Kyriander's life. Dorina McGraw was too young. Briande and Leaf were both old enough, and capable of it, and could probably have got the key from Charlotte's house. But neither had any reason to do it that I knew of. Neither seemed likely to do that sort of thing just for a lark. And those were all the children I'd had anything to do with.

Of Gary and Lilie, I preferred Gary for a suspect. But either way, it didn't put me any closer to knowing who had killed him and attacked Shannon. Unless I accepted the police belief that it was an accident, Gary hadn't killed himself. He certainly hadn't attacked Shannon. And I couldn't see any reason for Lilie to do that. If I'd been the one attacked, I might have wondered whether she was perhaps not quite as frail as she'd given Kyriander to understand. But why would she attack Shannon? . . . Unless she was jealous of the time Shannon had been spending with Ritchie?

Or, worse, Shannon had mentioned the wire to Ritchie, and he'd mentioned it to Lilie. If it had been she who killed Gary, and she feared we were getting close to finding out. . . . But that was preposterous. She wouldn't have killed him. She was in the throes of adolescent infatuation with him. If my surmise about who had left candles in that deserted cottage was correct, she might be pregnant by him, and I thought I'd have heard of it if they had a major fight. Knowing them, everyone in the valley would have heard of it.

In any event, his murder was not an impulse killing, done in a fit of rage. Somebody had planned it carefully.

Lilie wouldn't have done that amount of preparation in anger over a fight, unless she was able to hang on to her anger a lot longer than the average person. Which, I realized with a grimace, she could.

I arrived at Ritchie's door completely confused. Ritchie had the better motive to kill Gary, but none to attack Shannon. Lilie had no motive to kill Gary, but a possible one to attack Shannon. The idea that both of them went violent in such a short space of time seemed improbable at best. I wanted one suspect for both acts. Neither Ritchie nor Lilie seemed to be it, but they were the best I had.

I hoped Ritchie would be down at the Hall as he usually was at this time of day, so I could search his cottage for clues. But he wasn't gone. When my knock wasn't answered, I tried the knob. It turned easily. I said, "Hello?" and pushed the door open, just as Ritchie reached it.

He smiled sardonically at me. "Come right in. Did I startle you?" he said with heavy sarcasm.

"Yes, rather," I said, accepting his offer. "I thought you'd be down at the Hall. Oh. Hi, Lilie."

She was sitting demurely on the couch, and smiled at me quite sweetly. "Hi, Rosie. How's Shannon?" she said.

"I haven't been to the hospital yet today," I said, "but she was getting along fine last night, in no real danger."

"Good," she said. "I like Shannon."

"Do you?" I studied her while Ritchie closed the door behind me and went to sit on the couch.

"Sit down," he said. "Make yourself at home."

I ignored him. "How are you today, Lilie? Are you feeling okay?" She was as innocent and vulnerable as she was fractious and unpredictable. The idea that she might be either pregnant or a murderer suddenly seemed silly.

"I'm fine," she said. "Thank you."

I watched her, trying to see her as a stranger might. Trying to see her as the adult I knew she really was.

"I'm glad to hear it," I said. "Kyriander worries about your health."

She shrugged, dismissing Kyriander's concerns. "That must have been scary last night, when Shannon was attacked," she said, with frank fascination at someone else's disaster.

"It was, rather," I said.

"I think I would have screamed," she said. "I am so impressed that she would just fight back, like a man, instead of screaming."

How do you know she didn't scream? Damn. I knew in that moment how many clues I had dismissed because I hadn't wanted to know where they led. She was wearing her complex beaded necklace again. Even that was a clue, had I but paid attention. "Some people just aren't screamers," I said, keeping my tone level. I took the chair Ritchie offered and tried to look relaxed.

Now what the hell was I going to do? I'd come here half expecting to find a murderer. But I'd thought it would be a grown man, and one I didn't much like, at that. I had not seriously considered Kyriander Stone's sister, whom I'd still thought of as a wild, sweet, innocent child.

She was wild. She was not sweet, she was not innocent, and she was not a child.

Still, there was nothing for it but to cope as best I could. At least she shouldn't be any real danger, as Ritchie might have been. I was about to make some innocuous comment when Ritchie, frowning, said in sudden surmise, "Lilie? How did you know Shannon didn't scream?"

She seemed as anxious as I was to get out of this without conflict. That wasn't like her, but I certainly had no objection; so when she smiled at him and said sweetly, "Oh, I just guessed," I didn't follow it up.

Unfortunately, he did. "Damn good guess, it looks to me like," he said, stunned. He saw my expression and said, "She's right, eh? Lilie, how the hell did you know?" He didn't want to know the truth any more than I did. I could see him switching mental gears with an effort, finding a way out that left her innocent. "Do you know something about this? Do you know who did it?"

"Of course I do," she said comfortably. "It was the Trouble."

He shook his head. "I don't think so. You've been smirking around here all morning like something out of a bad spy movie. What do you know about it, Lilie? Who was it?"

"What makes you so sure it wasn't the Trouble?" she asked, intrigued. "Do you know who the Trouble is?"

"Never mind about that," he said. "It's none of your affair. I want to know what you know about the attack on Shannon."

She pouted prettily. "Don't treat me like a child, Ritchie. I don't like it."

"Then don't act like a child," he said brutally. He was over the first shock of realization, but was getting back his balance. "I don't know what's got into you today." He looked at me, one adult to another. "She isn't usually so twitty," he said, and turned back to her, his gaze speculative. "But come to think of it, this kind of moodiness is just what I'd expect on a monthly basis if she were a little older. Is that it, Lilie? Are you saying you're all grown up, and having PMS or something? What a shame, if that's it. You were a charming little girl, but if this is the way you'll be every month, you won't be anybody's notion of the ideal woman."

The color rose in her cheeks. Her eyes narrowed menacingly, and I remembered with a little shock of fear that her halfling status was no guarantee she had no magic. But she managed to control her temper, and said in a very cold, clear voice that she did not have PMS. Unfortunately she then promptly ruined the affect by giggling nervously and adding, "That shows what you know. I'm not having my period, either, so there."

"I am relieved to hear it," he said quellingly. "And now—"

"And I wish you wouldn't speak to me that way," she said. "I thought you loved me."

He stared, taken completely by surprise. "Loved you?

Good God, child! Of course I don't love you." Realizing how that must sound, he hastened to add, "I like you, of course. I've enjoyed our little flirtation. But I think you'll agree it's time we—"

"Flirtation!" She sat up straight as a rod and stared at him in malevolent amazement. "Fliration! Is that what you were doing? You were—you were just *flirting* with me? Toying with me, like a— Oh! Oh, you horrid, loutish, disgusting—" She broke off, swallowing tears of rage.

"There now," he said, clearly uncertain whether to soothe the child, or give an icy setdown to the woman. "I naturally assumed, I mean . . . " He glanced nervously at me. "I'm not sure what to do," he admitted, looking harrassed.

"Serves you right," I said, wondering what we could salvage from this. "Did you really think she knew you were just playing at affection? If so, you're dumber than you look."

"But," he said, and stopped, for once at a loss for words.

"And then saying I'm having my period!" said Lilie, making it quite clear this was his crowning offense. "I don't act different when I'm having my period. It's rude to say a woman's emotions are just all hormones. I hate that. And besides," she added logically, "I can't have my period. I'm pregnant."

Ritchie stared. "Good God," he said in revulsion. "It certainly isn't mine." That to me, with considerable intensity. "I naturally assumed the child was a virgin. I haven't touched her."

"No," I said. "I don't suppose you have."

"Is that all you care about?" demanded Lilie. "You just want to make sure everybody knows it isn't yours? Oh, I'm glad I found this out before I married you."

"Married!" Ritchie was clearly out of his depth.

Lilie, however, was enjoying herself. Drama always pleased her. "Yes, married. I counted on you, Ritchie. I believed in you. And now look. I'm ruined. Oh, Mab's grace, of course *you're* not the father," she said with loathing, "so you can stop *telling* everybody, because they'd never think that in the first place. You probably *can't* father children. I *won*dered why you didn't want to. You probably can't even—"

"Lilie," I said, taking my life in my hands for the sake of propriety, or for Ritchie's feelings, or possibly just for the hell of it. If we didn't stop her now, she would work herself into a fit of hysteria we might not be able to handle.

"I don't care!" she wailed. "He *deceived* me. He deserves whatever happens. He's the worst. I hate him. He let me believe that if it weren't for Gary . . . Oh! And *now* look!"

"If it weren't for Gary?" I said gently. "So you got Gary out of the way?"

"Of course I did," she said reasonably. "He couldn't make a good living like Ritchie can. He was nobody. He was just a child, and besides, he didn't want my baby. He wanted me to get an abortion. I thought—I thought—" She glared at Ritchie. "Oh, I believed him, and now look. There's nobody to father my child. I'm all alone. Oh, I hate you, I hate everybody." Her voice rose with every word.

"Lilie," I said.

"Leave me alone," she sobbed. "I hate you!"

"I know, love, but—"

"You're the worst," she said. "Trying to catch me out." She laughed wildly, her face wet with tears. "Oh, you thought you were so smart, trying to find out where everybody was when, and looking for clues where Gary died, and even in the cottage where we made love—so *stupid* of Gary to leave the candle—and all the time you were smooching up to my brother in that *loathsome* way. You wanted to blame me for the Trouble, didn't you?"

"I guess you showed me, didn't you, throwing fits like a spoiled brat so he couldn't spend any time with me?" I said.

Ritchie stared in shock, but Lilie was delighted. "You knew that was why? Maybe you're not as stupid as I thought you were." Her eyes narrowed. "But you are pretty stupid. You believed me when I made up to you, to find out how much you knew And you think you've caught me now, don't you?"

"I think if you killed Gary, you ought to give yourself up," I said. "You can't get away with it."

"Killed Gary?" Ritchie was still trying not to believe it. "But . . . Lilie, it was an accident. Wasn't it?"

"Of course not," she said irritably. "I knew just where to put the wire." She looked at me, briefly puzzled. "I thought that would lead you to Ariana: it was her wire."

"Wire?" asked Ritchie, bewildered.

"Across the road," she said impatiently. "I told you I'm not a child." She looked at me again. "Why didn't you suspect Ariana, when you found the wire? Didn't you know it was beading wire?" She touched the necklace in what was becoming a habitual gesture.

"Yes, I knew that much," I said. "And that it must have come from Ariana. But we didn't know who actually used it, you see. Was she teaching you beading?"

"Yes. Do you like my necklace?"

"It's quite nice"

She grinned enchantingly. "You believed me, didn't you, when I pretended I was so upset about Gary?"

"Yes, I did," I said.

"I knew it," she said, well pleased. "You were fun to toy with. But you shouldn't have brought your partner here." Her expression darkened, and it wasn't difficult at all to see the murderer behind those cold, alien eyes. "She was too good. I had to stop her." At that moment she was more elf than human, and with an elf's morality. Which, from a human point of view, is next to none.

"And now I have to stop you," she said in a voice as light and amiable as if she were inviting us to dinner. "Good thing I decided to bring this along." She pulled my handgun out of her purse.

41

I never should have brought the damn thing with me to Fey Valley. And, having brought it, I sure as hell should have kept better track of it. I'd thought it was safe enough hidden on a top shelf in my bedroom closet, but I'd reckoned without the snoopy nature of our little halfling villain. I hadn't been aware she even knew we'd moved. Apparently she not only knew, but had investigated rather thoroughly.

It was difficult even now to accept the truth about her. She looked sweetly innocent again, now that she had the upper hand. I could not think of her cold-bloodedly tying up the wire that killed Gary, and then waiting— had she waited?—to watch the result. Even in her rages she had always seemed to me a child throwing tantrums, more danger to herself than to anyone else.

"Surprised you, didn't I?" she said, gloating. She was aiming my automatic at Ritchie, and I was relieved to see he showed no signs of being a hero. He might have thought it a requirement; and he might have got us killed, if she knew how to use an automatic. Which I was very much afraid she did, considering the way she handled it, and that she had the safety off.

"I see you've been in my new cottage," I said. "Was it you who vandalized the first one?"

"Of course," she said.

"And left a clue so we'd think it was Gary?"

She smirked. "It worked, didn't it?"

"I guess it did."

"I think I'll make it look like you killed each other," she said thoughtfully, like a child deciding which dolls to invite for tea. "I was going to do that with you and Shannon, but now that Ritchie's turned out to be useless, he'll do just as well. Then I can go visit Shannon in the hospital. There are so many things that can happen in a hospital." She smiled at me quite charmingly, as though she really thought I would be pleased with this arrangement.

"Lilie," said Ritchie, making a fending gesture at her. "You can't mean this. Come on, honey, you can't."

She turned on him, rage flickering in her expressive eyes. "I can't? Why not? Because you think I'm a child? I'm not a child, you old poop. I'm glad I don't have to marry you after all. You're so stupid. Though I would have liked to have your money."

"Good God," he said. "I'll give you money, if that's what you want. How much? I'll write you a check right here. You can watch. Just tell me how much you want."

"That's a good idea," she said approvingly. "I hadn't thought of that. You write a check first, and then I'll kill you."

That wasn't what he'd had in mind, of course. The shock of her ruthless acceptance of his suggestion as an addition to rather than a change in her plans left him stunned. "But, but, Lilie," he said.

"Oh, stop bleating at me and get your checkbook," she said. "Where is it?"

"It's in my desk over there," he said. "But—"

"Shut up." She looked at the desk, and looked at him again, then rose and backed toward a wall where she could keep an eye on both of us while he moved. "Go get it."

I felt surreptitiously in my jacket pockets for a weapon and found only Finandiel's Faerie goblet. Well, it was heavy enough to do as a bludgeon, if I got a chance to use it. Certainly it was better than nothing. I wrapped my hand around it and began to ease it out of my pocket.

Ritchie looked really old, for the first time since I'd known him. The angry young man was a frightened old man, his tidy assumptions shattered. People in real life didn't always respond as predictably as those he wrote. I think he had forgotten that could happen, since much of the time he probably could guess most of our moves. People are more predictable than most of us like to think. But every now and then they will, as he was learning, step out of what we have come to think of as their character, and do something wholly unexpected.

He climbed to his feet unsteadily, his face haggard. "Okay," he said, "I'll get it." He tried to look belligerent. "What if I won't write the check, though? There's no reason to, since you say you'll kill me anyway."

"There's no reason not to," she said reasonably, lowering the aim of the automatic to a point somewhere around his knees. "And, you know, if I'm not happy, then they might find that Rosie didn't aim very good when she went to kill you. Maybe she'll shatter your kneecap first." She made a play of sighting on his knees. "Or maybe she'll aim a little higher?" The barrel lifted fractionally.

If a man could walk with his legs crossed, Ritchie would have done it. "Jesus, I'll write it," he said. "I'll write two checks. Three. Whatever you want."

She smiled charmingly, an innocent little girl again. "Just onc big onc," she said with pleasure. "Really big."

"Whatever you say." He reached the desk, and glanced meaningfully at me as he bent over it. Shit. He was going to do something stupid, and I had no way of knowing what it would be, or how to back him.

Lilie was concentrating on him, so I pulled the goblet out of my pocket where she couldn't see it, and got ready to move fast if I had to. She noticed the movement and glanced my way, but she didn't really expect any trouble from me.

I saw Ritchie brace himself as he bent to put his hand in a drawer. I hoped what he meant to do was provide a distraction. Anyway I would have to behave as though that were it; there was nothing else I could do. So the instant he made his move, I made mine. I dived out of my chair and across the room in one swift movement.

Ritchie pulled a snub-nosed police revolver out of the drawer and fired it in Lilie's general direction.

The shot went wild, knocking plaster down from the ceiling, and so did Lilie's startled answering shot. I thought I heard something outside right about then, but the crash of the two handguns in that enclosed space had just about deafened me. I landed on Lilie just as she realized I was coming and tried to turn the automatic on me. She didn't move fast enough. I did.

Unfortunately I chickened out at the last second. Never mind that she had my automatic in her hand and had just established her willingness to use it; I could not get it out of my mind that she was only Kyriander's high-strung baby sister, and I simply could not bludgeon her with a heavy chunk of gold.

I dropped that and went for her bare-handed. She hadn't had time to swing the automatic around, but she pulled the trigger anyway, and sent another shower of plaster dust sifting down from the ceiling. I got a good grip on her forearm and used the weight of my body to keep her from turning it on me, and yelled at Ritchie to stay out of the way.

Lilie wasn't physically strong enough to resist me. What I had forgotten, when I discarded the goblet rather than use it to batter a child, was that she had at least some magic at her disposal. In fact it was probably her magic that made me keep thinking of her as a defenseless child. If she'd had as much of it as Maerian, the affair would have ended right there. Very likely neither Ritchie nor I would have walked away from it. But apparently the best she could manage in the heat of the moment was a little shape-shifting.

It was almost enough. She caught me completely by surprise. I found myself clinging fervently to a Lilie-sized, furry wildcat, and I nearly let go when it snarled and snapped at me and tried to gut me with its deadly hind claws. But that would have been fatal; girl or cat, she'd have killed me the instant she was free. And as a cat, she couldn't hold the automatic. Keeping my weight on her forearms, I twisted away from her back claws and managed to kick the handgun across the room.

She saw it go, snarled in rage, and redoubled her efforts to rake my body with razor claws, or rend me with her long, carnivore's teeth. I scrambled forward to get all my weight on her arms, with one forearm across her throat to keep her head back. She got in one healthy swipe down my leg with her back claws before the hold choked her, forcing her to revert to her true form, which she knew very well I couldn't fight as ruthlessly.

I meant to. I knew my life depended on remembering that whatever form she took was deadly. But blond ringlets and clear blue eyes nearly did me in where claws and fangs hadn't. I could not crush a young girl's throat in self-defense. My instinctive reaction was to jerk back, away from hurting her, as she knew it would be. She was almost out of my grip before I caught her again.

And then, just as I caught her again, something far stronger than she was picked me up bodily and thrust me away from her. I found myself standing halfway across the room from her in less time than it takes to say it. I tried to get back to her, but the movement was blocked.

Kimendan and Lorielle had arrived. "*Damn* it," I said. "Mind your own business. What the hell do you think you're doing?"

"You must not hurt a child," Kimendan said, very kindly explaining the situation to me.

The child in question cackled in triumph and dived for the discarded automatic. Luckily they weren't protecting her from Ritchie, so he was able to kick the gun out of the way and put out a foot to trip her. She went sprawling, and he was pushed back against the desk to prevent him from doing her further harm.

"That *child* will kill us," I said, "if you don't let us stop her."

"No." He smiled indulgently when she picked up the automatic. "I cannot allow that, either." It was clear from his way of speaking that he was accustomed to being obeyed. Lilie wasn't inclined to gratify him: she pointed the thing right at him. From his reaction—which seemed to be only to smile at her—I was afraid he didn't know what it was. But he did, and he stopped it as easily as he had stopped me. "No, Lilie," he said. "It is Lilie, is it not? I thought so. Ariana mentioned you."

She snarled at him, almost as though she were the cat illusion she'd created to fight me—which, incidentally, had been real enough to claw right through my blue jeans and leave bleeding parallel gashes on my thigh. But Kimendan didn't let her turn into a cat again. He merely looked at her, with surprising sternness, and she subsided at once into thwarted schoolgirl status and began to cry.

"Oh, no," said Lorielle. "Now look, the poor baby."

"That 'baby' tried to kill us," I said.

Lorielle looked at me in surprise. "Of course. She was angry," she said.

Ritchie exchanged a knowing look with me. "Elves," he said expressively, and shifted his look to Kimendan. "I'm surprised to see you here in the daytime, Kim."

"Yes. We came to discuss the detective with you," he said as though I weren't there. "But how fortunate for you that I did. How did you expect to cope with this little one on your own?"

Ritchie looked at Lilie with revulsion. "I didn't know it would be a problem," he said. "Little monster."

"I hate you, I hate you," sobbed Lilie.

"I wondered whether you'd be here," said Kyriander, at the door. We were becoming quite a little party. "Stop that," he told Lilie. "What have you done?"

"Only tried to murder the lot of us," I said. "Kyri, I'm so sorry—" But I wasn't allowed to finish. Something very odd happened to the air in the center of the room, like a sparkling galaxy materializing in glorious colors, and suddenly the most beautiful woman I had ever seen in my life was standing among us.

She was as oddly elongated and her features as pointy as Maerian's, which shouldn't have been any more attractive on her than on her sister. But perhaps Tytonia, the Queen of Faerie, commanded glamour even I could not see through.

She was turning slowly, laughing at us all. "Children, children," she said in a voice as compellingly, magnificently beautiful as Maerian's, and considerably more amused.

With Kimendan distracted and apparently in shock, Lilie saw her opportunity to scoop up the automatic. She was intelligent enough too, to try to get rid of Kimendan and Tytonia first. I suppose she figured when they were dead would be time enough to deal with unmagical mortals. I distinctly saw her finger tighten on the trigger, and heard the automatic fire; and then we were standing in a twilight wilderness green with deep forest shadows, not in Ritchie's cottage at all.

There were little voices twittering in the trees overhead, and tiny lights blinking like fireflies in the air around us. There were incredibly soft, emerald green mosses underfoot, sending up clouds of scent like newmown hay wherever our feet crushed them. Lush blossoms trailed from alien trees, smelling of vanilla and cinnamon and something like frangipani, deliciously, almost cloyingly sweet. Delicate vines like rich green lace covered with little scarlet berries tangled thornless among the underbrush.

Ritchie was staring around him with huge eyes, his posturing forgotten in sheer wonder. Lilie was scowling at a rose in her hand as big as a cabbage, heavy and red and harmless. That seemed to be what had become of my automatic. She dropped it in sudden revulsion and glared at me as though I were responsible. On my other side, Kimendan and Lorielle were clinging to each other like children in a storm, their narrow faces white, their bodies rigid with fear and determination.

Kyriander didn't seem to have come with us. I turned to face Tytonia, and found her studying me with apparent interest. I smiled awkwardly. She made no response.

I put out my hand for one of the fireflies. It lighted on the back of my wrist with a dazzle of diamond wings.

Of course it wasn't a firefly. It smiled at me puckishly, flicked its wings, and flittered away.

I said slowly, thinking of the *Wizard of Oz*, and wondering whether a tornado mightn't have been less dangerous than the queen of all Faerie, "Somehow I don't think we're in California anymore."

42

When Tytonia returned Ritchie and me to Fey Valley, neither of us was ready to talk in any detail about what had happened in Faerie. Ritchie was intent on writing it down, and I figured the others could read about it when he was finished. He headed straight for the typewriter, put his Romeo and Juliet manuscript aside, and started typing.

That left me to field the questions of the residents who were in the Hall when we arrived. Facing Kyriander was the hardest. I had to tell him his beloved baby sister wouldn't be coming back to him. I knew he must have guessed already, but that didn't make it any easier. I started with a quick recap of what had happened at Ritchie's cottage before Tytonia took us to Faerie. He hugged Briande and stared at the floor.

"She's more elf than human, Kyri," I said. "Nothing she did was wrong for an elf." I smiled, remembering Tytonia's reaction to Lilie's threats. "She'll be better off in Faerie. They think she's perfectly normal, you know. They couldn't imagine what I saw wrong in her behavior."

"I suppose she is normal, there," he said. "I must apologize, Rose: I thought from the beginning that she might be the Trouble." He sighed. "And I would have rather she had been, than what she was. I am not an elf. I cannot think . . . I cannot like—" He broke off, staring at Charlotte, at a loss for words.

"Never mind, Kyri," said Charlotte, surprising us both. "She didn't know any better."

"She was only a baby to me," he said helplessly.

"How could I guess she was pregnant? How could I ever imagine she would kill someone?"

Charlotte shook her head. "If I told Gary once, I told him a hundred times. You have to *think* about people. He knew her better than any of us. He must have known she could be dangerous."

Maybe he did. Maybe he thought he could handle her. Or maybe he thought she wouldn't turn on him. Anyway, it was too late now to second-guess either of them, and I said so. Then I looked at Kyri. "You recommended us because you hoped we couldn't do the job, didn't you, Kyri?"

He stared. "Um," he said.

"It's okay," I said. "You were right. I haven't been thinking too clearly for a long time now."

"I thought you might catch her, if she was the Trouble," he said. "But I thought if you did, you wouldn't hurt her."

I laughed out loud at that. "Jeez, with my record?"

"You forget, I was there when you killed my father," he said. "I knew full well you wouldn't have done it only to save yourself." He looked guilty. "And I knew how much it had troubled you to kill a man. I hoped, if it came to that with Lilie, that you would find another way."

"Well, you were right. I darn near let her kill me. If I'd faced her alone, who knows what I'd have done? As it is, I suspect we'd all have been in deep yogurt if Tytonia hadn't showed up just when she did." I really couldn't blame him for choosing us for our incompetence. Not only had he been right, but he'd been grasping at straws anyway. I knew a little something about grasping at straws. When things got to that point, one wasn't always thinking quite clearly.

I smiled at Briande. "Her Majesty sent a gift for the two of you," I said. "Especially for Briande." I put the tiny golden acorn into Briande's hand. "Don't lose it," I said. "It's an invitation. If ever you feel you'd be happier in Faerie than here, just crack that open, and you'll go."

"I doubt we'll need it," said Kyriander, "but it is a pretty trinket."

"Yeah, I don't think you'll need it, either," I said, winking at Briande. I had one just like it, on a chain around my neck, that I didn't expect to need. But you never know, especially where elves and halflings are involved. "But Her Majesty wanted you to have it. I think she liked Lilie so well, she's hoping the rest of the family might be just like her."

"Well, we're not," Briande said, revolted.

"No, of course not," I said. "But she could hope."

The other residents had been patient, but there was a limit to how long they'd wait to get their questions answered. Marc Starr had been scowling at Ritchie since he sat down to type. Now he said peevishly, "What is he doing? I don't like it."

"He's writing a novel, I think," I said. "About his experiences in Faerie." I knew he was: it was all he'd talked about. He thought it would be the capstone to his career. He might be right.

Marc emitted a scornful sound. "What good is that?" He turned to me, his expression eager. "Tell me what it looks like there," he said. "With particular reference to the colors, and the quality of light. I don't suppose you took a camera?"

"No," I said, trying not to laugh. "I didn't think."

He shook his head mournfully. "No, of course not. It would be too much to hope that you might think ahead. The opportunity lost! It blights the soul." He sighed. "Well, describe it, then."

"Marc, I don't want to," I said gently.

He stared. "Why not?"

I shrugged. "Just selfish, I guess."

"But I want to know."

"I'm sorry."

"You were in Faerie a *whole week*, and you're not going to tell us about it?"

That startled me. "A week?"

"Ah," said Rosetta Fulmer, pleased. "There *is* a time difference. I've always known there must be a sound basin for that belief. How long did you *think* you were gone?"

I found I didn't want to tell them even that much. I just wasn't ready to talk about it. "Not a week," I said. "Tell you what, why don't you wait and read about it in Ritchie's magnum opus? I'm sure he'll cover all the pertinent details."

"You aren't going to tell us *any*thing?" demanded Shannon.

"I'm glad to see you too," I said. "When did you get out of the hospital?"

"The day after you disappeared," she said. "Luckily Kyriander knew what had happened, more or less; so I knew to wait for you." Though she still sported some colorful bruises and a plaster cast on one arm, she seemed mostly recovered from Lilie's attack. "But, you're not going to tell us all about it?"

"Ritchie will tell it so much better," I said. "Everybody can read his book when it's finished."

"But what about—who were they? Lorielle and Kimensomething?"

"Kimendan," I said. "Tytonia reconsidered their case, and decided to let them marry despite their love for each other." Ritchie would probably devote several chapters to that, because it wasn't nearly so simple; but the thought of going into detail about it made me tired.

"That sounds so odd," said Shannon.

"What, that they can marry even though they love each other? I know, but it's the way elves think." I could tell by looking at them that most of the elves present thought it was, at best, in poor taste. Even Salonian didn't look entirely comfortable with the idea.

"Actually, I thought she might," said Finandiel. He waved away the elves' objections. "I know, I know. But times are changing. We must change with them if we will survive." He looked at me. "Will you tell us what brought her to that decision?"

"It was no big deal," I lied. "Just that no one had told her before what it was like for them. That they really would rather die than live apart." And indeed, when I had convinced her of that, she had thought the idea so repellent that I had, for a moment, feared for all our lives.

Fortunately she had a healthy sense of humor, and strong curiosity. Kimendan and Lorielle were to be a test case. They had been very solemn under the burden of their responsibility. I smiled, remembering their earnestness, but I wasn't inclined to talk about it.

Nor did I mention Tytonia's odd parting words to me: "You have the iron will that makes your realm inimical to me and mine. Yet I see in you also a touch of the fey. In thanks for your kindness to these my poor wayward children, I leave you what you already own, and I grant you the wit to know its value."

I knew it all right. I'd known most of it since the night I spent beside Shannon in the hospital. I could hardly wait to get back to town and put in a call to Killer: I had been a fool to leave him, and all the reasons I had made up were nonsense. I'd been frightened of change, just as these elves were frightened of change.

I'd found out what Maerian had meant by the cryptic remark she'd made when she saw me with Finandiel's goblet. She'd told me he'd given me more than I knew, and she was dead right. Only a member of the house of Daelinn could hold that cup and drink its wine. Finandiel had, in a sense, adopted me.

That was part of the reason Tytonia had accepted and listened to me; but she'd also warned me that he might not have meant more than to protect me from Kimendan by making me a member of his house. "He may regret it, an he knows I hold him to it," she said.

But I could tell, from the way he smiled at me when he saw me pull the goblet from my pocket now, that he did not regret it, even now that I knew what it meant. Apparently he'd taken a fancy to me for some reason.

"Some wine for you, niece?" he asked. Without waiting for my response, he gestured for Cuthbern to fill the goblet.

That was one thing about Faerie that I was really

going to miss: that Daelinn wine was *good*. "Thanks, uncle," I said, laughing at him. "You'll be sorry."

"I think not," he said comfortably.

Tytonia said he did it because he recognized the fey in me. I thought even if that were so, his main reason besides protecting me from Kimendan was to make mischief. And, looking around at the elves' reaction to our interplay, I figured he was getting just what he wanted. Elven ways were changing. Finandiel was no fool: he would be at the forefront of the revolution, whatever it turned out to be.

Which was much the attitude Tytonia had taken when she understood how it was with Kimendan and Lorielle. "I have not kept my rule by blinding myself to what I could not like," she said. "A thousand years ago I might have killed these children for their aberration. Today I know it may be, not an aberration, but the future. There are signs that it is." She shuddered delicately. "And, while I need not embrace it until the nature of change is made clear, for now I believe I must begin to tolerate it." She had smiled at me, a predator's smile, and added with unthinking arrogance, "Perhaps even if my people acquire this base trait from yours, we can turn it to better effect than you have done."

I wondered what she had in mind, but I didn't ask. I probably wouldn't have understood if she'd told me. Elves are alien, whatever else they are. I remembered that conversation now, seeing the Fey Valley elves' reluctant acceptance of me as an adopted member of Finandiel's family and, through him, of the house of Daelinn, and thought that they are also remarkably human in some ways. But I would not insult them by saying so.

I think Finandiel knew perfectly well what I was thinking, but he didn't say anything about it. He just mentioned, in his silly, twittering way, that the Association owed us the rest of our fee for resolving the Trouble for them.

I started to say no, that Kimendan and Lorielle had

paid us amply; but Shannon stopped me. "And expenses," she said firmly. "You can pay my hospital bill."

They did it, without argument. The check was ready for us when we came down from our cottage with the last load of our belongings, just as the lowering sky finally let loose its burden of rain in a drenching torrent that soaked us to the skin in seconds. Kyriander, holding the check for us, stared from the shelter of the porch when we began to caper in it with our faces turned joyously to the sky. I laughed when I saw him. "It's okay," I said. "We're just welcoming our relative."

"I am sister to the rain," said Shannon, by way of explanation. She wasn't, of course. She was as consummately human as it is possible to be.

But fun is fun. "Me too," I said.

I was going to miss Fey Valley in all its moods and weathers. I discovered, now we were leaving it, that I'd come to like the country very much indeed.

"Fey and sudden and unholy," said Kyriander, surprising us both. I had forgotten that part of the quote. It struck me that it fit Lilie better than any of us.

And maybe I was more like her than I wanted to know. I closed my eyes. Raindrops slid down my cheeks like tears.

"Here is your paycheck, wood nymphs," he said.

I pushed my burdens into the car and ran through the shining silver rain to his side. "Kyriander," I said, dripping messily onto the dry porch floorboards. But I didn't know what else to say.

"I know," he said, looking at me. His eyes were dark and wounded, but he produced a sincere smile just the same. I wondered how much he might accomplish, now that he was free of the burden of Lilie's care. "I regret that I entangled you again in my family's difficulties," he said earnestly.

I shrugged. "It is what I do for a living." But we both knew I didn't routinely catch my friends' family members attempting murder. Only his. Well, at least this time I hadn't had to kill anyone.

That was when I first began to realize just how much

Faerie had affected me. Few mortals were allowed in Faerie, and none ever returned unchanged. Here was proof I wouldn't be the first: I felt regret, but no debilitating guilt, at having killed Kyriander's father. It had been necessary. I'd done it. I never wanted to have to kill anyone again, so I would be more careful in future to find nonviolent solutions before things came to such a pass. But I could live with having failed before, and I knew I would live with it if I failed again. We can only do our best. It won't always be good enough. That's life. Which was something I'd said often enough before, but only now really understood and believed.

Shannon burst onto the porch with us, shaking off water like a puppy. "It's raining," she said impatiently. "Are you going to stand around in it all day?"

"We're not in it," I said, laughing.

"You know what I mean." She glanced through the door at the Fey Valley residents settling down to enjoy the rainy afternoon. "We're finished here, aren't we? Let's go."

"Yes, okay," I said, and moved impulsively to hug Kyriander. I had already said my good-byes to the others: now I said it to him. "And good luck, to both of you." Briande had come to the door to see what was keeping him. "You be good, Briande."

"I will," he said, putting an arm around his brother.

"Tell your rock star he doesn't know how lucky he is," said Kyriander.

"He knows," said Shannon. "It's Rose who doesn't recognize a good thing when she sees it."

"I do now," I said. "Good-bye, Kyriander. Good-bye, everybody!" We ran through the rain to our cars, shouting with laughter, and scrambled in to make the long drive back to Berkeley, a little wiser and, as Shannon said, a lot richer. She didn't know how much richer. Money isn't the only wealth there is.